# THE BROKEN CODE

# WARRIORS

## THE SILENT
## THAW

# WARRIORS

## THE BROKEN CODE

*Book One: Lost Stars*
*Book Two: The Silent Thaw*

THE BROKEN CODE

# WARRIORS

## THE SILENT THAW

# ERIN
# HUNTER

**HARPER**

*An Imprint of HarperCollinsPublishers*

*Special thanks to Kate Cary*

The Silent Thaw
Copyright © 2019 by Working Partners Limited
Series created by Working Partners Limited
Map art © 2019 by Dave Stevenson
Interior art © 2019 by Owen Richardson

Library of Congress Cataloging-in-Publication Data

Names: Hunter, Erin., author
Title: The silent thaw / Erin Hunter.
Description: New York, NY : HarperCollins, 2019. | Series: Warriors: the broken code ; [2] |
Summary: "ThunderClan's leader, Bramblestar, has been behaving erratically after losing one
of his nine lives, and suspicion is quickly spreading across Clan borders. And when a strange
apparition sparks unrest in SkyClan and ShadowClan, each warrior must decide where their
allegiances lie—with their Clan, or the warrior code itself"—Provided by publisher.
Identifiers: LCCN 2019021110| ISBN 978-0-06-282355-7 (hardback) |
  ISBN 978-0-06-282357-1 (library)
Subjects: | CYAC: Cats—Fiction. | Fantasy. | BISAC: JUVENILE FICTION / Animals /
Cats. | JUVENILE FICTION / Action & Adventure / General. | JUVENILE FICTION
/ Fantasy & Magic.
Classification: LCC PZ7.H916625 Sjm 2019 | DDC [Fic]—dc23 LC record available at
https://lccn.loc.gov/2019021110

Typography by Jessie Gang
20  21  22  23    PC/LSCH    10  9  8  7  6  5
❖
First Edition

# ALLEGIANCES

## THUNDERCLAN

**LEADER**  BRAMBLESTAR—dark brown tabby tom with amber eyes

**DEPUTY**  SQUIRRELFLIGHT—dark ginger she-cat with green eyes and one white paw

**MEDICINE CATS**  JAYFEATHER—gray tabby tom with blind blue eyes

ALDERHEART—dark ginger tom with amber eyes

**WARRIORS**  (toms and she-cats without kits)

THORNCLAW—golden-brown tabby tom

WHITEWING—white she-cat with green eyes

BIRCHFALL—light brown tabby tom

BERRYNOSE—cream-colored tom with a stump for a tail

MOUSEWHISKER—gray-and-white tom
APPRENTICE, BAYPAW (golden tabby tom)

POPPYFROST—pale tortoiseshell-and-white she-cat

LIONBLAZE—golden tabby tom with amber eyes

ROSEPETAL—dark cream she-cat

BRISTLEFROST—pale gray she-cat

STEMLEAF—white-and-orange tom

LILYHEART—small, dark tabby she-cat with white patches and blue eyes
APPRENTICE, FLAMEPAW (black tom)

**BUMBLESTRIPE**—very pale gray tom with black stripes

**CHERRYFALL**—ginger she-cat

**MOLEWHISKER**—brown-and-cream tom

**CINDERHEART**—gray tabby she-cat
**APPRENTICE, FINCHPAW** (tortoiseshell she-cat)

**BLOSSOMFALL**—tortoiseshell-and-white she-cat with petal-shaped white patches

**IVYPOOL**—silver-and-white tabby she-cat with dark blue eyes

**EAGLEWING**—ginger she-cat
**APPRENTICE, MYRTLEPAW** (pale brown she-cat)

**DEWNOSE**—gray-and-white tom

**THRIFTEAR**—dark gray she-cat

**STORMCLOUD**—gray tabby tom

**HOLLYTUFT**—black she-cat

**FLIPCLAW**—tabby tom

**FERNSONG**—yellow tabby tom

**HONEYFUR**—white she-cat with yellow splotches

**SPARKPELT**—orange tabby she-cat

**SORRELSTRIPE**—dark brown she-cat

**TWIGBRANCH**—gray she-cat with green eyes

**FINLEAP**—brown tom

**SHELLFUR**—tortoiseshell tom

**PLUMSTONE**—black-and-ginger she-cat

**LEAFSHADE**—tortoiseshell she-cat

**SPOTFUR**—spotted tabby she-cat

**FLYWHISKER**—striped gray tabby she-cat

**SNAPTOOTH**—golden tabby tom

QUEENS

(she-cats expecting or nursing kits)

**DAISY**—cream long-furred cat from the horseplace

ELDERS

(former warriors and queens, now retired)

**GRAYSTRIPE**—long-haired gray tom

**CLOUDTAIL**—long-haired white tom with blue eyes

**BRIGHTHEART**—white she-cat with ginger patches

**BRACKENFUR**—golden-brown tabby tom

# SHADOWCLAN

LEADER

**TIGERSTAR**—dark brown tabby tom

DEPUTY

**CLOVERFOOT**—gray tabby she-cat

MEDICINE CAT

**PUDDLESHINE**—brown tom with white splotches

**APPRENTICE, SHADOWPAW** (gray tabby tom)

WARRIORS

**TAWNYPELT**—tortoiseshell she-cat with green eyes

**DOVEWING**—pale gray she-cat with green eyes

**STRIKESTONE**—brown tabby tom

**STONEWING**—white tom

**SCORCHFUR**—dark gray tom with slashed ears

**FLAXFOOT**—brown tabby tom

**SPARROWTAIL**—large brown tabby tom

**SNOWBIRD**—pure white she-cat with green eyes

**YARROWLEAF**—ginger she-cat with yellow eyes

**BERRYHEART**—black-and-white she-cat

**GRASSHEART**—pale brown tabby she-cat

**WHORLPELT**—gray-and-white tom

**HOPWHISKER**—calico she-cat

**ANTFUR**—tom with a brown-and-black splotched pelt

**BLAZEFIRE**—white-and-ginger tom

**CINNAMONTAIL**—brown tabby she-cat with white paws

**FLOWERSTEM**—silver she-cat

**SNAKETOOTH**—honey-colored tabby she-cat

**SLATEFUR**—sleek gray tom

**POUNCESTEP**—gray tabby she-cat

**LIGHTLEAP**—brown tabby she-cat

**CONEFOOT**—white-and-gray tom

**FRONDWHISKER**—gray tabby she-cat

**GULLSWOOP**—white she-cat

**SPIRECLAW**—black-and-white tom

**HOLLOWSPRING**—black tom

**SUNBEAM**—brown-and-white tabby she-cat

## ELDERS

**OAKFUR**—small brown tom

# SKYCLAN

**LEADER**  **LEAFSTAR**—brown-and-cream tabby she-cat with amber eyes

**DEPUTY**  **HAWKWING**—dark gray tom with yellow eyes

**MEDICINE CATS**  **FRECKLEWISH**—mottled light brown tabby she-cat with spotted legs

**FIDGETFLAKE**—black-and-white tom

**MEDIATOR**  **TREE**—yellow tom with amber eyes

**WARRIORS**  **SPARROWPELT**—dark brown tabby tom

**MACGYVER**—black-and-white tom

**DEWSPRING**—sturdy gray tom
**APPRENTICE, ROOTPAW** (yellow tom)

**PLUMWILLOW**—dark gray she-cat

**SAGENOSE**—pale gray tom

**KITESCRATCH**—reddish-brown tom

**HARRYBROOK**—gray tom

**BLOSSOMHEART**—ginger-and-white she-cat

**TURTLECRAWL**—tortoiseshell she-cat

**SANDYNOSE**—stocky light brown tom with ginger legs

**RABBITLEAP**—brown tom
**APPRENTICE, WRENPAW** (golden tabby she-cat)

**REEDCLAW**—small pale tabby she-cat
**APPRENTICE, NEEDLEPAW** (black-and-white she-cat)

**MINTFUR**—gray tabby she-cat with blue eyes

**NETTLESPLASH**—pale brown tom

**TINYCLOUD**—small white she-cat

**PALESKY**—black-and-white she-cat

**VIOLETSHINE**—black-and-white she-cat with yellow eyes

**BELLALEAF**—pale orange she-cat with green eyes

**NECTARSONG**—brown she-cat

**QUAILFEATHER**—white tom with crow-black ears

**PIGEONFOOT**—gray-and-white she-cat

**FRINGEWHISKER**—white she-cat with brown splotches

**GRAVELNOSE**—tan tom

**SUNNYPELT**—ginger she-cat

ELDERS     **FALLOWFERN**—pale brown she-cat who has lost her hearing

# WINDCLAN

LEADER     **HARESTAR**—brown-and-white tom

DEPUTY     **CROWFEATHER**—dark gray tom

MEDICINE CAT     **KESTRELFLIGHT**—mottled gray tom with white splotches like kestrel feathers

WARRIORS     **NIGHTCLOUD**—black she-cat

**BRINDLEWING**—mottled brown she-cat
**APPRENTICE, APPLEPAW** (yellow tabby she-cat)

**LEAFTAIL**—dark tabby tom with amber eyes

**EMBERFOOT**—gray tom with two dark paws

**SMOKEHAZE**—gray she-cat
**APPRENTICE, WOODPAW** (brown she-cat)

**BREEZEPELT**—black tom with amber eyes

**HEATHERTAIL**—light brown tabby she-cat with blue eyes

**CROUCHFOOT**—ginger tom
**APPRENTICE, SONGPAW** (tortoiseshell she-cat)

**LARKWING**—pale brown tabby she-cat

**SEDGEWHISKER**—light brown tabby she-cat
**APPRENTICE, FLUTTERPAW** (brown-and-white tom)

**SLIGHTFOOT**—black tom with white flash on his chest

**OATCLAW**—pale brown tabby tom

**HOOTWHISKER**—dark gray tom
**APPRENTICE, WHISTLEPAW** (gray tabby she-cat)

**FERNSTRIPE**—gray tabby she-cat

**FEATHERPELT**—gray tabby she-cat

**ELDERS**

**WHISKERNOSE**—light brown tom

**GORSETAIL**—very pale gray-and-white she-cat with blue eyes

# RIVERCLAN

**LEADER**

**MISTYSTAR**—gray she-cat with blue eyes

**DEPUTY**

**REEDWHISKER**—black tom

**MEDICINE CATS**

**MOTHWING**—dappled golden she-cat

**WILLOWSHINE**—gray tabby she-cat

**WARRIORS**

**DUSKFUR**—brown tabby she-cat

**MINNOWTAIL**—dark gray-and-white she-cat

**MALLOWNOSE**—light brown tabby tom

**PODLIGHT**—gray-and-white tom

**SHIMMERPELT**—silver she-cat

**LIZARDTAIL**—light brown tom
**APPRENTICE, FOGPAW** (gray-and-white she-cat)

**SNEEZECLOUD**—gray-and-white tom

**BRACKENPELT**—tortoiseshell she-cat

**JAYCLAW**—gray tom

**OWLNOSE**—brown tabby tom

**ICEWING**—white she-cat with blue eyes

**SOFTPELT**—gray she-cat
**APPRENTICE, SPLASHPAW** (brown tabby tom)

**GORSECLAW**—white tom with gray ears

**NIGHTSKY**—dark gray she-cat with blue eyes

**HARELIGHT**—white tom

**BREEZEHEART**—brown-and-white she-cat

**DAPPLETUFT**—gray-and-white tom

**HAVENPELT**—black-and-white she-cat

**QUEENS**

**CURLFEATHER**—pale brown she-cat (mother to Frostkit, a she-kit; Mistkit, a she-kit; and Graykit, a tom)

**ELDERS**

**MOSSPELT**—tortoiseshell-and-white she-cat

# THE BROKEN CODE

# WARRIORS

## THE SILENT
## THAW

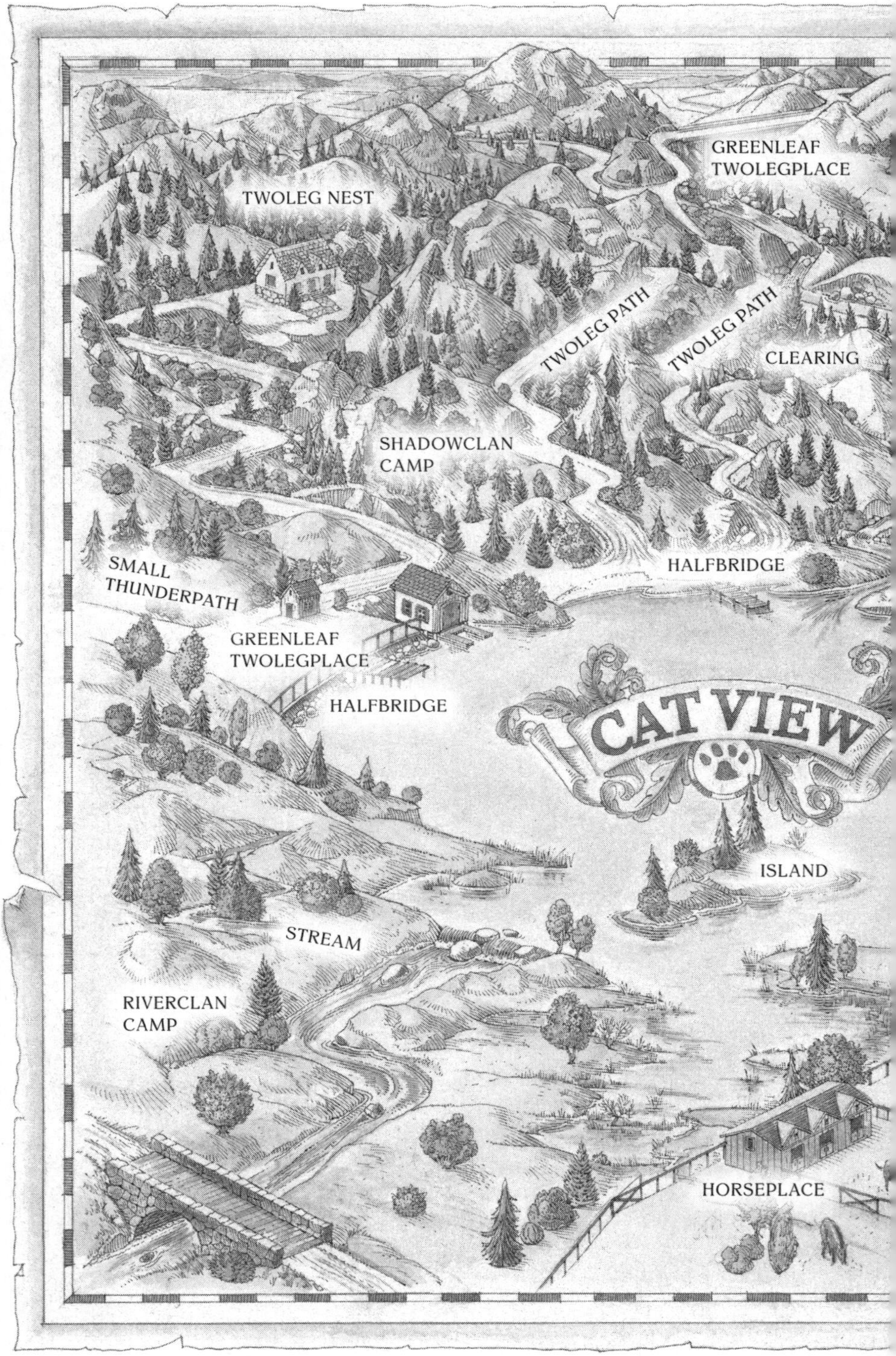
TWOLEG NEST
GREENLEAF
TWOLEGPLACE
TWOLEG PATH
TWOLEG PATH
CLEARING
SHADOWCLAN
CAMP
HALFBRIDGE
SMALL
THUNDERPATH
GREENLEAF
TWOLEGPLACE
HALFBRIDGE
CAT VIEW
ISLAND
STREAM
RIVERCLAN
CAMP
HORSEPLACE

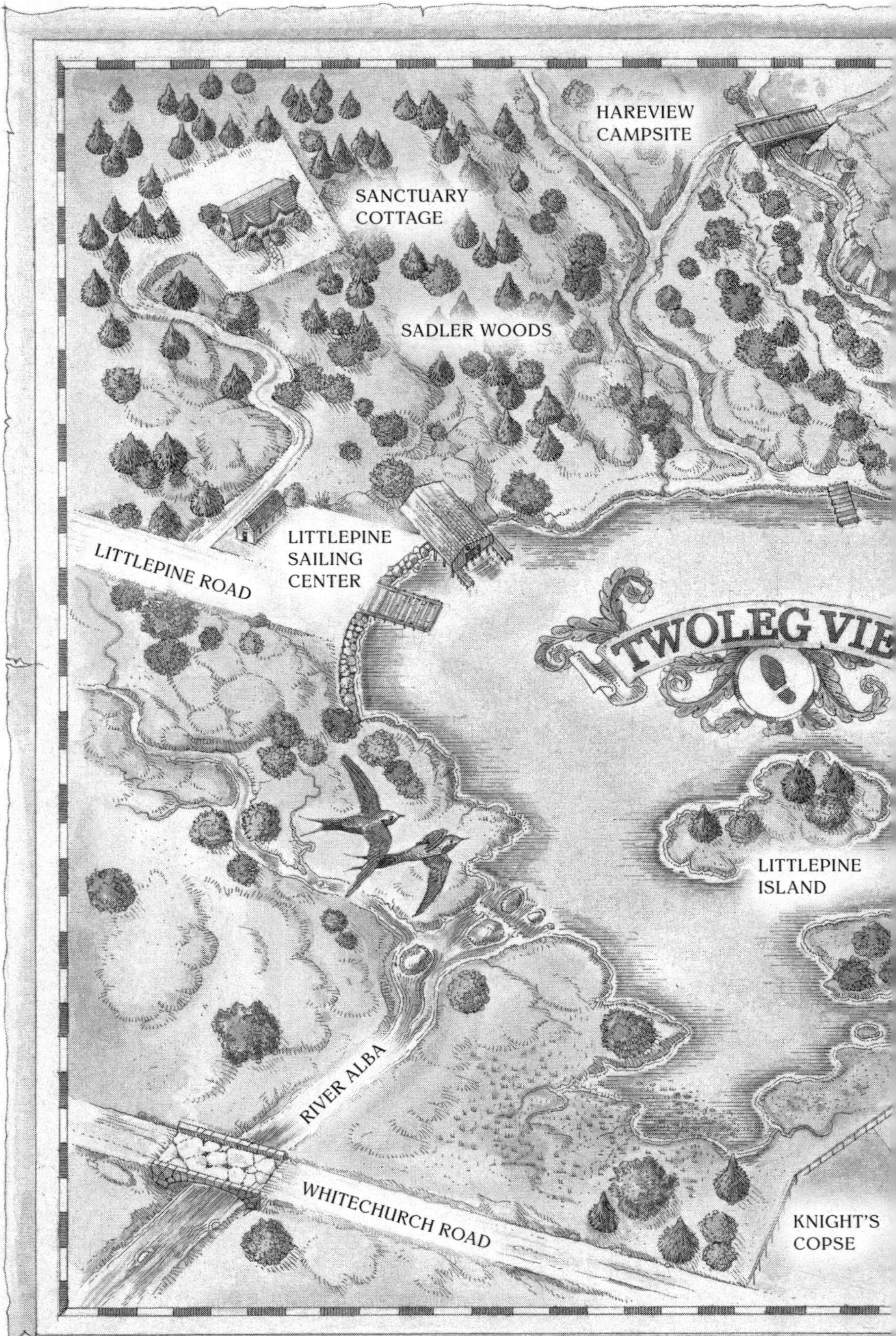

HAREVIEW CAMPSITE
SANCTUARY COTTAGE
SADLER WOODS
LITTLEPINE SAILING CENTER
LITTLEPINE ROAD
TWOLEG VIE
LITTLEPINE ISLAND
RIVER ALBA
WHITECHURCH ROAD
KNIGHT'S COPSE

# PROLOGUE

*Bramblestar shivered as wind whipped snow* from the frozen moor and stung his muzzle. He was as cold as the air around him, but he hardly noticed. His gaze was fixed on the body lying in the shelter of a cave carved from the snow. *That's me.* The thought seemed no more than a distant yowl. He was numb with shock. *I died.* The fever that had ravaged his body for days and days had finally claimed one of the nine lives he, as ThunderClan's leader, had been granted by StarClan.

Outside the cave, Jayfeather was glancing nervously at Puddleshine while Alderheart stared hollow-eyed at Bramblestar's body. *He saw me die.* Bramblestar watched his son tremble and wished he could comfort him. Shadowpaw and Tigerstar shifted anxiously beside Dovewing. *They're waiting for me to wake up.* Bramblestar glanced across the bleak, white moor, remembering vaguely that his Clanmates had brought him here while he'd still been alive in the hope that the bitter cold would cure his fever. How long would it take for him to begin his next life? He looked back expectantly at his body, then lifted his gaze to the sky, waiting for stars to pierce the snow-laden clouds. *Will StarClan welcome me soon? Will I share with them before I return to my body?*

The wind hardened as the moments passed. Bramblestar's tail twitched. Anxiety sparked in his fur. He'd never died before. What happened now?

Dovewing padded closer, her ears twitching. "How long does it take?" Her mew faded in the roar of the wind as snow swirled around her. When it cleared, the cats had moved. Jayfeather crouched near Bramblestar's body. Tigerstar stood beside Shadowpaw, eyeing the other cats. Bramblestar looked again at the sky. The clouds had shifted. How long had it been? Why hadn't he woken up yet? *Where's StarClan?* Was he supposed to face death alone? Had his ancestors deserted him?

"Bramblestar is dead. For good." Jayfeather's mew cut through the storm. Bramblestar stared at him. *No! I'm here! I'm ready to come back.* He strained to speak, but no words came, and Jayfeather went on. "StarClan has forgotten us."

The snowstorm engulfed him. Bramblestar struggled as wind tore at his fur and snow blinded him. It filled his nose and stung his ears. The ground seemed to give way. He snatched at it with his claws, his heart lurching as the blizzard swept him away. *Is this death?*

A moment later he was in the ThunderClan camp, staring at his body laid out for his vigil. The camp was dark. How much time had passed since he was on the moor? *They're going to bury me.* Panic flared like fire through his flesh. *I'm not dead! I'm here!*

Squirrelflight was speaking. Grief stole Bramblestar's breath as sorrow choked her mew. Something was very wrong. How could he be watching his own vigil? Had StarClan taken away *all* his lives? *Have I offended them?* He padded around his body as his Clanmates watched Squirrelflight, their eyes hollow with grief. Would StarClan take him soon? Above the camp he could see stars between the branches, cold and distant.

"May StarClan light your path, Bramblestar." Jayfeather dipped his head to Bramblestar's body. "May you find good hunting, swift running, and shelter when you sleep." As he spoke, Bramblestar saw a ripple run through his own corpse. He pricked his ears, eagerly. He was going to have another life after all. He braced himself, preparing to be swept into his old, familiar pelt, his heart melting with relief. He saw the corpse's legs twitch, then move. Then it opened its eyes.

*That's not me.* His body was moving without him. How could that be? He watched it roll onto its side, then push itself to its paws. It padded toward Squirrelflight and dipped its head. "Greetings," it meowed. "It's good to be with you again."

Bramblestar felt sick as Squirrelflight pressed herself against it.

"He's alive!" Bristlefrost's mew rang out among the gasps of his Clanmates. "StarClan hasn't forsaken us!"

Bramblestar backed away, unable to believe his eyes as he watched his body moving among his Clanmates. Something had gone terribly wrong. *That's not me!* He had to let some cat know. His mind raced. *Tree can speak to the dead!* The idea struck him like lightning. *Perhaps he can speak to me.* Pelt spiking with fear, Bramblestar fled into the forest. *I have to fix this!*

# CHAPTER 1

*Keep running! Rootpaw didn't dare look* over his shoulder.

"Wait! You have to help me! Please!" Bramblestar's plaintive wail echoed through the trees.

"Leave me alone!" Heart lurching, Rootpaw pushed his paws harder against the frozen forest floor. Why was the ThunderClan leader chasing him? What was Bramblestar doing on SkyClan land? And why did he look so much like a *ghost?*

Rootpaw's thoughts spiraled as his paws thrummed over the earth. *Bramblestar can't be a ghost. He's not dead!* He'd lost a life to fever. But he was a Clan leader; he had come back. He was alive. Then why had Rootpaw been able to see the forest through Bramblestar's shimmering pelt? Why hadn't he smelled ThunderClan scent? Why had his paws made no sound on the hard earth?

Something sinewy snagged Rootpaw's leg. It jerked from under him and he rolled, snatching it free as he thumped onto his side. The shock of his fall jolted him from his panic. Lying still for a moment, Rootpaw let his breath steady before scrambling to his paws. Pain flashed through the paw the root had caught. He glanced back the way he'd run. Something moved in the distance. *Bramblestar?* He stiffened, his belly tightening, then relaxed as he realized it was just bracken trembling in the breeze. He lifted his snagged paw, moving it gingerly. The pain softened and faded and he put his weight on it, relieved to find that it was okay.

He looked again for Bramblestar. The forest was deserted. He shook out his pelt. *Did I imagine it?* He'd been so sure he'd seen the ghostly ThunderClan leader. His breath caught in his throat. Perhaps Bramblestar had died again. Rootpaw shivered. Perhaps the fever that had killed him once had returned and killed him again. *But why would I see his ghost?* Dread crawled Rootpaw's belly. *Am I like Tree?* His father had always been able to see dead cats. Was it possible Rootpaw had inherited the skill?

Rootpaw shuddered. He didn't want to be strange like Tree. It was bad enough being Tree's son and having his Clanmates treat him like the kit of a five-legged squirrel. He just wanted to be like his denmates—a normal warrior, with normal warrior kin. He lifted his chin, irritated. He would go back to the clearing. If it had been the real Bramblestar, he might still be there. He could explain why he'd come. And if it turned out Rootpaw had imagined seeing the ThunderClan leader, he'd see that there was nothing to be scared of. The wind might have made the shadows shiver so they seemed like a tabby pelt.

Squaring his shoulders, Rootpaw marched back to the clearing. As he neared the tiny glade, he fluffed his fur against the cold, puffing out his chest as he padded down the slope and stopped in the middle. He looked around, pricking his ears, but saw no sign of Bramblestar, neither the warrior nor the ghost. There was no scent lingering in the air. Shadows rippled over the ground. Rootpaw shook his head. He had not seen Bramblestar's ghost. He'd imagined the whole thing.

He glanced at the sky, realizing that the sun had lifted high above the trees. His heart quickened. He was late. Dewspring would be expecting him for training. Rootpaw broke into a run and hared between the trees, heading back to camp.

"I'm glad you decided to turn up." Dewspring was waiting for him outside the fern entrance. He flicked his tail irritably as Rootpaw scrambled down the slope toward him.

"Sorry!" Rootpaw puffed.

"We're supposed to be stalking prey." Dewspring stared at him.

"We still can," Rootpaw mewed apologetically.

Dewspring huffed. "A warrior arrives on time."

"I got distracted." Rootpaw glanced at his paws. It was a lame excuse, but how could he tell his mentor that he thought he'd seen a ghost of a cat who wasn't even dead? Besides, he didn't want Dewspring to think he was as strange as Tree.

Dewspring whisked his tail. "Don't let it happen again," he mewed. "You've still got a lot to learn. If you want to become a warrior before greenleaf, we don't have time to waste."

As Rootpaw dipped his head, the frost-browned ferns rustled and Hawkwing pushed his way out of camp. Plumwillow and Nettlesplash followed at his heels.

"Hi, Dewspring." The SkyClan deputy paused beside the

gray tom. He glanced at Rootpaw. "How's your apprentice doing?"

"Not bad." Dewspring eyed Rootpaw sharply. Rootpaw tensed. Was his mentor going to tell Hawkwing that he'd been late for training? "He's a good hunter, and his battle skills are coming along well."

Relief washed over Rootpaw's pelt.

"I'm glad to hear it." Hawkwing nodded. "I'm taking a patrol to the ThunderClan border. The scent markers are a little stale toward the lake."

"That's a long trek," Dewspring observed.

"Yes," Hawkwing agreed. "But we need to make sure ShadowClan and ThunderClan respect that piece of territory. It's our only access to the shore."

As the warriors spoke, Rootpaw's thoughts quickened. ThunderClan would know if Bramblestar was dead. A ThunderClan patrol might share the news. Then he'd know if there was a chance he'd really seen Bramblestar's ghost. *I have to help mark the border.* He glanced at Dewspring. "It's been a while since I've been to the lakeshore," he mewed. Dewspring blinked at him, surprised, as Rootpaw went on. "Perhaps we could join the patrol and you could show me where the scent markers go again. I've forgotten."

Hawkwing pricked his ears. "Well, then, you'd better come along." He glanced at Dewspring. "Unless you had other plans."

Dewspring's tail twitched. "We were going to practice

stalking." He gazed curiously at Rootpaw. "But we can do that tomorrow."

"So we can go?" Rootpaw looked at his mentor eagerly.

"Sure."

Rootpaw dropped his gaze, worried that Dewspring might see his relief and wonder about his *real* interest in the ThunderClan border.

His paws ached by the time they reached the strip of land between ShadowClan and ThunderClan that led down to the lake. Dewspring had used the trek to teach him more about the forest. He'd pointed out prey trails and signs that birds were beginning to build nests in time for newleaf. Root-paw had tried hard to listen, but his thoughts had been on Bramblestar's ghost. The farther away he traveled from the sunny glade where he thought he'd see the apparition, the more certain he felt that he'd seen *something*. Perhaps StarClan had sent him a vision of the ThunderClan leader. But why send it to him? They hadn't shared with the Clans in moons. He felt sure that if they had a message, they'd share it with a medicine cat.

"Do you see that tree?" Dewspring's mew jerked him from his thoughts. His mentor had paused to point his muzzle toward a spreading ash, pale between the oaks.

Rootpaw stopped and followed Dewspring's gaze as Hawkwing, Nettlesplash, and Plumwillow continued along the narrow stretch of forest beside ThunderClan's land. "I see it," he mewed.

"Birds like to nest about halfway up." He nodded toward the branches. "There are nooks between the branches, and the trunk will give a lot of shelter once the leaves appear. And there are plenty of bugs to feed their young." Dewspring padded to the foot of the ash and pressed his forepaws against the trunk. "The bark is hard, but not too hard." He curled his claws into the wood. "It's easy to climb."

Rootpaw nodded, fixing his gaze on his mentor while his ears strained to hear sounds from the ThunderClan territory beyond. Were any patrols near the border? He struggled to keep his attention on Dewspring, relieved when the gray tom turned and followed his Clanmates. Rootpaw hesitated, peering across the scent line. He tasted the air. Was a ThunderClan patrol near?

"Stop dawdling!" Dewspring had stopped and was staring at him. He whisked his tail impatiently. "I thought you wanted to see where the scent markers should go."

Plumwillow was already leaving her scent on a patch of withered bracken while Nettlesplash rubbed his jaw along a jutting twig.

Dewspring nodded to a bramble spilling between two oaks. "Mark that tree," he told Rootpaw.

Rootpaw hurried to the brambles and left his scent, then quickly padded farther along the border where he could get a better view onto ThunderClan's land. There was no sign of a patrol. Frustration burned beneath his pelt. Perhaps ThunderClan was already sitting vigil for its leader.

He narrowed his eyes and peered deeper into the forest,

willing a ThunderClan patrol to appear. Just one look would be enough to tell him if something was wrong. *Please let him be alive.* Rootpaw's pelt prickled uncomfortably. *Let the ghost be my imagination.*

"Mark that patch, too." Plumwillow flicked her tail toward some bracken crowding along the border.

Rootpaw glanced past it, deeper into ThunderClan's forest. Was that a cat moving between the trees? He peered harder. It was! He glimpsed a pelt, and another, slipping through the undergrowth. *A patrol!* But it was heading away. Rootpaw's pads tingled with urgency. He had to get their attention before they disappeared. He lifted his muzzle. "Which bush did you want me to mark?" His mew rang among the trees, and he knew it would carry far into ThunderClan territory.

"Hush!" Dewspring glared at him. "You'll scare the prey."

"But we're not hunting," he mewed even more loudly. He met his mentor's gaze innocently. "I can't scare borders away."

Plumwillow grunted crossly. "You don't have to tell every Clan around the lake what we're doing!"

"Sorry." Rootpaw dropped his mew to a whisper, his heart quickening as he saw the ThunderClan cats' pelts turn and head toward the border. Bracken swished as they neared.

"Do you have to make so much noise?" Lionblaze slid from beneath a bramble and shook out his pelt. The ThunderClan warrior was frowning. "Even if you don't mind frightening your own prey, you don't have to scare ours."

Rootpaw searched the ThunderClan tom's gaze. Was there grief there? Or worry?

Sparkpelt and Cherryfall nosed their way out beside him and stared irritably across the border.

None of them seemed bothered by anything but Rootpaw's yowl. Was their leader still alive? Hope welled in his chest.

Plumwillow glanced crossly at Rootpaw. "Rootpaw is a little overenthusiastic today."

Dewspring brushed past Rootpaw. "I'm sorry. I thought I'd trained him to use his hunting voice no matter what patrol he was on."

Amusement flashed in Sparkpelt's eyes. "Apprentices don't always listen."

Rootpaw padded to the border and blinked at Lionblaze. "Sorry about being so loud," he apologized. "It won't happen again."

"You've probably just gotten used to your new territory." Lionblaze's gaze softened sympathetically. "Maybe you've forgotten what it's like to share borders on every side."

"I guess." Rootpaw held the golden warrior's gaze. "Is Bramblestar better now?" He didn't care if the question sounded odd. He needed to make sure that everything was okay in ThunderClan.

"Of course." Lionblaze narrowed his eyes, clearly surprised. "He's been better for days."

Rootpaw felt dizzy with relief. Bramblestar was alive and well. Which meant he hadn't seen a ghost. Everything was okay.

Dewspring hurried forward and nosed Rootpaw away from the border. "I'm sorry," he told Lionblaze again. "I don't know what's gotten into Rootpaw today."

"That's okay." Lionblaze looked toward the lake. "The scent of newleaf always makes young cats crazy."

Sparkpelt followed her Clanmate's gaze. "The ice is breaking up at the shore," she murmured.

Plumwillow swished her tail. "We could use a little warmth."

"And more prey," Nettlesplash added.

There was a glint in Sparkpelt's green eyes as she told the SkyClan patrol, "Maybe the Moonpool's finally thawing too!"

Lionblaze purred. "That would be a relief to us all."

As the warriors gazed dreamily into the distance, clearly imagining the return of StarClan and an end to the bitter leaf-bare that had gripped the forest, Rootpaw shook out his pelt. He wasn't like Tree after all. Whatever he'd seen in the forest, it hadn't been a ghost. Perhaps he'd dreamed it. Perhaps his imagination *had* turned a shadow into what he'd thought was a ghost. And yet, if it had only been a shadow, whose *voice* had he heard?

"Come on." Dewspring's mew jolted him back into the moment. The ThunderClan patrol was heading away, and Plumwillow and Nettlesplash were marking the border where they'd stood. "We'll finish marking here and head back to camp. This afternoon you can train with Needlepaw. Reed-claw wants her to practice battle moves with a cat her own size."

Rootpaw followed his mentor as he padded toward the shore. Leaves crunched beneath his paws. The breeze felt fresh in his fur and he lifted his muzzle, enjoying the scents rolling in from the lake. It would be fun to train with Needlepaw. She could be annoying, because she was faster than him and liked to rub it in, but she was his sister, after all, and she might show him a new move. It would be better than worrying about ghosts.

Needlepaw rolled into the soft grass at the edge of the clearing, her pelt ruffled with tiredness. "Bring me back a mouse."

"Okay." Rootpaw left his sister and padded toward the fresh-kill pile. The evening patrol was setting out while the rest of his Clanmates were still returning after their day's duties. Leafstar watched contentedly through half-closed eyes at one end of the clearing, Hawkwing at her side. Training had gone well, and Rootpaw was pleased that he'd managed to counter Needlepaw's battle moves with unusual speed. She'd pushed him hard while Reedclaw and Dewspring had called advice from the edge of the training clearing, but he'd matched her blow for blow and ducked and feinted with such skill that Dewspring had let them finish training early so they could take first pick from the fresh-kill pile when they got back to camp.

Rootpaw pulled a mouse from the middle of the pile and chose a shrew for himself. Grabbing the tails between his jaws, he headed back toward Needlepaw. He stiffened as he saw the air shimmer beside her. Was that the outline of a cat? *Please, don't let it be the ghost!* He could make out a tabby pelt and wide, round eyes. Rootpaw's heart dropped like a stone as, silently,

Bramblestar flickered into view. The fern wall behind the ThunderClan leader showed through his pale form. He was barely more than a shadow, and he was staring at Rootpaw, his eyes glittering with desperation. *I must be imagining it.* Rootpaw forced himself forward. *He can't be there.* He dropped the prey beside Needlepaw, avoiding Bramblestar's gaze. "Is this mouse big enough?" He stared at his sister as she looked up. Could she see Bramblestar's ghost standing beside her?

She blinked at him, then looked at the mouse approvingly. "It looks perfect." She shifted to make room beside her, and he sat down stiffly and pawed the shrew closer. *She can't see it.* His chest tightened as he felt Bramblestar's gaze burn his pelt. He glanced around the camp. Leafstar was chatting to Hawkwing. Plumwillow washed her face while Nettlesplash and Macgyver chose prey from the pile. No cat was looking at the transparent, scentless figure beside Rootpaw. *No cat can see him.* Panic flashed beneath his fur. *Only me!*

# CHAPTER 2

*Bristlefrost fluffed out her fur against* the morning chill, relieved
that the sun had risen high enough to flood the camp with
tepid sunshine. Greenleaf still seemed a long way off, but after
the hard leaf-bare, even the smallest trace of warmth was welcome.

"Help me pull this strand clear." Thriftear's mew made her
turn. Her sister was tugging hard at a shriveled length of honeysuckle dangling from the wall of the elders' den.

Bristlefrost hurried to help her and grabbed the stem with
her claws. Pulling together, she and Thriftear drew it out.

Graystripe peered out through the gap they'd left. "What
are you trying to do?" He ducked outside. "There'll be a draft
tonight, and you know how the cold makes Cloudtail's bones
ache."

"Don't worry." Stemleaf padded from behind the den,
where he'd been checking for more shriveled stalks. "I'll bring
bracken back from my patrol today and fix the holes before
sundown."

"I'll help too." Spotfur hurried to his side. She'd been helping Stemleaf behind the den, and honeysuckle sprigs stuck in

her pelt. "Stemleaf would never want an elder to be cold." She looked proudly at Stemleaf, as though it had been his idea to fix up the elders' den in the first place.

Stemleaf puffed out his chest happily.

Irritated, Bristlefrost forced her fur flat. She should be glad that her denmates had been eager to help. And she had to get used to Stemleaf and Spotfur being so close. Her crush on the white-and-orange tom had been mouse-brained. It was obvious now that he'd only ever seen her as a friend. So he liked Spotfur—so what? There were plenty more mice in the forest. Thriftear caught her eye and pulled a goofy face, mimicking Spotfur's wide-eyed admiration for Stemleaf. Her sister knew how she felt about the tom. Bristlefrost swallowed back a purr.

Spotfur blinked at her anxiously. "Did I say something wrong?"

"No!" Bristlefrost felt instantly guilty. It wasn't Spotfur's fault Stemleaf liked her. "I'm really glad you want to help fix up the elders' den."

Spotfur sat back on her haunches looking pleased. "We have to do *something* while we're waiting for Squirrelflight to assign patrols. If we just sat around, we'd get cold." She glanced around the camp, where her Clanmates were shifting their paws to keep warm, their breath billowing in the morning air.

Flamepaw and Finchpaw were nosing at the camp wall, sniffing for signs of prey, while Lilyheart and Cinderheart murmured quietly to each other. Flipclaw was playing mossball with Dewnose and Snaptooth nearby, lunging between his denmates to grab the tuft of moss they'd been chasing at the edge of the clearing. Bumblestripe and Lionblaze sheltered beneath the Highledge, while Rosepetal eyed the meager pawful of stale prey lying on the fresh-kill pile.

"When are we going out to train?" Across the clearing, Baypaw looked eagerly at Mousewhisker. "You promised to teach me about ShadowClan battle moves today."

The young tom's mentor glanced toward the Highledge. "We'll leave when I know Squirrelflight doesn't have other plans for us."

Squirrelflight had only emerged from Bramblestar's den for a few moments before dawn to assign the first patrol of the day. Bramblestar had called her back inside before she could organize the rest of the day's duties. Since he'd lost a life, the ThunderClan leader preferred the quiet of his den, and he seemed to need Squirrelflight's company more than a newborn kit. *I can't imagine losing a life,* Bristlefrost thought. She guessed it would take a while to get over—the first time, at least.

Brightheart padded stiffly from the elders' den. "Is any cat going to fix those holes?" She glanced ruefully at the gaps the young warriors had made in the walls of the honeysuckle den.

"Stemleaf and Spotfur are going to fetch bracken to fill them later," Graystripe told her.

Bristlefrost blinked eagerly at the old she-cat. "The bracken will keep you warm until fresh honeysuckle grows in." She felt sorry for the elders. They were too old to warm themselves up with a run through the forest.

"Good." Brightheart turned away. As she padded back inside, the camp entrance shivered. The dawn patrol had returned.

Its leader, Thornclaw, stopped at the edge of the clearing. Hollytuft, Plumstone, and Eaglewing halted beside him, their eyes widening with surprise as they saw their Clanmates still in camp. "Haven't the hunting patrols left yet?" Thornclaw eyed Lionblaze, puzzled.

Lionblaze shrugged. "We're waiting for Squirrelflight."

"I was looking forward to fresh prey when we got back." Thornclaw glanced disapprovingly at the Highledge before padding to the fresh-kill pile. "Don't expect much excitement when you go out," he told Lionblaze as he picked up a shriveled mouse. "The forest is quiet today." He carried to it to a patch of frost-scorched grass at the edge of the clearing, dropped it, and sat down. "But there are plenty of signs of prey on the WindClan border." He blinked at the golden warrior. "It won't take long to restock the fresh-kill pile."

Lionblaze sniffed. "It should be full by now."

"I'm not waiting any longer." Mousewhisker got to his paws. He beckoned Baypaw with a flick of his tail. "Come on. We can't sit around here all morning." As he led his apprentice out of camp, Lilyheart hurried after him.

Cinderheart nodded to Finchpaw and Flamepaw. "We'll go too," she told them. "Border patrols will have to wait."

As they padded out of camp, movement on the Highledge caught Bristlefrost's eye. Squirrelflight slid out of Bramble-star's den. She stood on the ledge and glanced down into the clearing, her gaze flicking toward the entrance as Finchpaw and Flamepaw filed out. "Are they going to train?" she called distractedly.

"Yes," Lionblaze called up to her. "I can fetch them back if you want them on patrol."

She shook her head. "No thanks." She scrambled down the rock tumble. "Training is the best thing they can do." She glanced around the clearing, as though focusing her thoughts.

Bristlefrost blinked at her eagerly, her pelt pricking with excitement as Bramblestar emerged from his den and made his way down the rock tumble to join Squirrelflight. The day could start properly now. She pricked her ears, wondering which patrol she would be assigned to.

"Lionblaze." As Squirrelflight nodded to the golden warrior, Bramblestar's gaze flitted curiously around camp. "Take Rosepetal, Bumblestripe, and Berrynose hunting."

Bristlefrost watched Bramblestar. Since he'd lost a life, Bramblestar seemed to find the camp intriguing, as though it had changed. Every now and then he'd wander around the edges, and yesterday his nose had twitched, as though he'd been surprised by the smell of herbs, when he'd gone into the medicine den. She wondered if losing a life made a leader forget the life before, so that everything afterward seemed strange.

"Thornclaw says there are signs of prey on the Wind-Clan border," Lionblaze told Squirrelflight. "Should we hunt there?"

"Yes." Squirrelflight gazed at the trees. "But be careful

not to chase prey across the scent line. Now that we've finally worked out the borders, we don't want to confuse them again." She nodded to Cherryfall. "Take Poppyfrost, Sparkpelt, and Stormcloud and refresh the border markers."

"The WindClan ones?" As Cherryfall blinked at Squirrelflight, Bramblestar padded closer to the fresh-kill pile.

"No. Start with SkyClan," Squirrelflight told her. "They refreshed their markers yesterday, and I want to make sure that our scent line is as clear as—"

"Is the fresh-kill pile always so poorly stocked?" Bramblestar interrupted her. He poked at the damp shrew that was all that was left of yesterday's prey.

Squirrelflight looked at him, her gaze gentle. "It's early," she mewed apologetically. "I haven't had time to organize the hunting patrols. It'll be well-stocked later." She turned back to Cherryfall. "Try and catch some prey while you're out. I'm afraid I'm a little behind—"

"Why are we repairing the elders' den?" Bramblestar had crossed the clearing and was sniffing at the withered stems Bristlefrost and Thriftear had tugged from the walls.

Bristlefrost's pelt prickled. Had it been a dumb idea to fix the elders' den? "We want to make sure they're warm," she told him quickly. "Until fresh honeysuckle grows in."

Bramblestar hardly looked at her, his gaze flashing toward the warriors' den. The brambles were torn on one side, where the leaf-bare snows had dragged them down. "It's the warriors who keep the Clan healthy and strong," he meowed. "We should take care of them first. Elders are tough enough to survive a draft or two."

Graystripe shifted beside Bristlefrost, a frown clouding his gaze. "Cloudtail's bones feel the cold," he grunted.

Bristlefrost shifted uneasily. Graystripe was right to remind the ThunderClan leader of that, but Bramblestar wouldn't suggest repairing the warriors' den instead without a good reason.

Bramblestar answered the old gray tom without looking at him. "Extra bedding will keep Cloudtail warm."

Bristlefrost felt relieved. See? Bramblestar was thinking of every cat.

Squirrelflight swished her tail. "We can take care of the dens once we've restocked the fresh-kill pile," she mewed briskly. "Let me finish organizing the hunting patrols and then I'll see about gathering extra bedding."

"Squirrelflight." Alderheart's mew made the ThunderClan deputy turn. The dark ginger medicine cat was hurrying from his den. "Do you need me this morning? I want to go out and check to see if there are signs of new herbs growing yet."

"I told you . . ." Jayfeather followed Alderheart out. "It'll be a moon before we see fresh herbs. We might as well make the most of the ones we've got. If we mix the dried leaves with some sap, it will preserve them for a while longer."

"I can collect some sap while I'm out," Alderheart suggested.

Squirrelflight didn't seem to be listening. Her gaze had drifted past them, growing sad as she stared at the bramble-covered entrance of the medicine cats' den. Bristlefrost's heart pricked with sympathy. That was where Leafpool had died. The whole Clan was still grieving her loss. Bristlefrost moved closer to Thriftear. She couldn't imagine losing a littermate.

Bramblestar padded to Squirrelflight's side and glared at the medicine cats. "I don't know why you're bothering the deputy with stuff that doesn't concern her," he told them sharply. "Decide for yourself whether you want sap or herbs."

As Jayfeather jerked his nose toward the ThunderClan leader, his face creasing in a frown, Bristlefrost blinked. "Why is he so angry with Jayfeather and Alderheart?" she whispered to Thriftear.

"Perhaps he blames them for letting him die," Thriftear whispered back.

Bristlefrost shivered. "I hope he never looks at me like that."

"Why would he?" Thriftear glanced at her.

Bristlefrost shrugged. "I don't know, but I'm going to try to be the best warrior in the Clan from now on." She was relieved to see Bramblestar's gaze soften as he turned back to Squirrelflight.

Stemleaf caught her eye. The white-and-orange tom looked puzzled. "Is it me, or is Bramblestar being weird?" he murmured under his breath.

"He's been weird since he lost a life," Spotfur agreed quietly.

"Losing a life must be hard," Bristlefrost told them. "We don't know what it's like."

"He'll feel better soon," Thriftear mewed.

"I hope so," Graystripe huffed. "Firestar never acted like this after he'd lost a life." With an irritable flick of his tail, the gray tom ducked into his den.

Flipclaw was crossing the clearing, Dewnose and Snaptooth at his heels. They stopped in front of Squirrelflight and Bramblestar. "Should we hunt in the beech grove?" Flipclaw offered. "I think I smelled a fresh mouse nest there yesterday."

Bramblestar frowned at the young tom. "Then why didn't you dig it up yesterday?"

Flipclaw blinked at him. "I'd already caught a squirrel," he mewed. "I thought it could wait."

Squirrelflight ran her tail along Bramblestar's spine. "It's best not to hunt too hard this early into newleaf," she mewed lightly. "Remember? We want some prey alive to make more prey so there's plenty by greenleaf."

Bramblestar's fur ruffled. "Of course I remember," he snapped. He hesitated as though realizing he'd been too sharp and touched his nose to Squirrelflight's ear. "But you're right to remind our younger warriors." He nodded to Dewnose. "You're training him well, Dewtail."

"Dewnose." Dewnose blinked at him. "I'm called Dewnose."

"Of course you are." Bramblestar grunted crossly. "I knew that."

Squirrelflight leaned against the ThunderClan leader, her eyes welling with pity. "You don't have to remember everything. Are you tired again? Perhaps you should rest."

As she steered him away, talking softly in his ear, Stemleaf leaned closer to Spotfur. "He *used* to remember everything," he grumbled.

Bristlefrost glared at the white-and-orange tom. Why was he being so hard on Bramblestar? She eyed her leader sympathetically, relieved he was too far away to hear Stemleaf's criticism. "Have you forgotten how sick he was?"

"He's healthy now," Stemleaf retorted.

"But he *died!*" Bristlefrost's pelt flushed with indignation. "It's bound to change things."

"If the Clan leaders changed personality every time they lost a life, the Clans would be a mess," Stemleaf pressed.

Spotfur nodded. "Even if Bramblestar's feeling weird, he doesn't have to stop Squirrelflight from organizing patrols. The fresh-kill pile is usually full by this time of day."

"Now you're blaming both of them!" Bristlefrost fluffed out her pelt.

"You must admit, things have been strange since Bramblestar started his new life," Thriftear breathed.

"So what? They're great warriors!" Bristlefrost jerked away from her sister. "We're lucky to have a leader like Bramblestar, and Squirrelflight is an awesome deputy. Why are you criticizing them? They're your Clanmates! You should be helping them."

Anger hardened her belly. She was grateful Bramblestar had come back to them. How would ThunderClan have survived without him? Squirrelflight and Bramblestar needed the support of their Clan. Puffing out her chest, she left her denmates and crossed the clearing. *She* was going to help

Bramblestar. It was what a honorable warrior would do.

Bramblestar and Squirrelflight stood beneath the Highledge. Bramblestar had clearly decided that he didn't need any more rest and stood watching as Squirrelflight gave orders to Flipclaw.

"Take Eaglewing with you," she told the young warrior. "Start at the beech grove, and then try the area beside the abandoned Twoleg den."

"What about the ancient oak?" Bramblestar chipped in. "There's always good hunting there."

"That's a good idea." Squirrelflight blinked at her mate gratefully. "But the hunting hasn't been so good there for the past few seasons. It might be best to wait till greenleaf to give prey a chance to return."

As Bristlefrost reached them, her ears grew hot. She'd only been a warrior for a moon. Was she allowed to approach her leader and offer help? She hesitated and looked nervously at Squirrelflight. "Excuse me."

The ThunderClan deputy dragged her gaze distractedly from Flipclaw. "Can it wait?" she asked. "I've got more patrols to organize."

"I—I just wanted to know if there was anything I could do to help," Bristlefrost's mouth felt dry as she met Squirrelflight's gaze.

"I suppose you can join your brother's patrol," Squirrelflight mewed thoughtfully. Her gaze was flitting around the camp, as though wondering who else to send hunting.

"Sure." Bristlefrost lifted her tail eagerly.

Bramblestar's eyes flashed with sudden interest. "Why send her out on patrol?" he mewed suddenly. "Leave that to the other warriors."

Bristlefrost chest tightened. Didn't he think she was good enough to hunt with her Clanmates?

Squirrelflight looked at him quizzically. "But she wanted to help," she mewed.

"She can help in a much more important way than that." Bramblestar's gaze rounded with warmth as he stared at Bristlefrost. Her pelt prickled self-consciously. What was he going to ask her to do? "She's clearly an intelligent and loyal warrior," he went on. "Who else has offered to help?" He flicked his tail dismissively. "Bristlefrost is the kind of warrior we want. We should give her more responsibility." He glanced critically around the Clan. "Rewarding her initiative might encourage her Clanmates to offer help when it's needed."

Squirrelflight's brow furrowed as she looked at Bramblestar. "She hasn't been a warrior for long," she cautioned.

"Then she won't be stuck in old warrior ways," Bramblestar meowed breezily. "From now on, Bristlefrost will organize the daily patrols." He looked at Squirrelflight. "After all, why should you waste your time on such mundane things? You're Clan deputy. You should learn to delegate, and I'm sure Bristlefrost will be great at it."

Bristlefrost flinched as his eager gaze switched back to her. Did he mean it? It seemed too good to be true.

"I s-suppose." Squirrelflight didn't sound as eager as Bramblestar.

At the edge of the clearing, Thornclaw got to his paws. "Do you think it's wise to give a young cat so much responsibility?"

"Of course," Bramblestar told him. "How else will our young Clanmates grow into warriors as strong and capable as you? Surely you see it'll be good for the Clan?" He held Thornclaw's gaze until the dark tabby dipped his head.

"I guess," Thornclaw murmured.

Excitement pricked through Bristlefrost's paws. "Thank you, Bramblestar!" she mewed before any of the other warriors could object. "I just want to help my Clan any way I can." She purred happily, ignoring the doubt shimmering in Squirrelflight's gaze.

"See?" Bramblestar blinked at Squirrelflight. "Energetic, enthusiastic young warriors will make ThunderClan stronger."

Squirrelflight returned his gaze. "Okay," she mewed softly. She looked at Bristlefrost. "Do you think you can handle it?"

Bristlefrost whisked her tail. "I'll do my best!"

# CHAPTER 3

*"Come on, Shadowpaw! The moon's rising* and your Clanmates are waiting to see you off." Puddleshine blinked at Shadowpaw from the medicine-den entrance, his pelt fluffed with pride.

Inside, Shadowpaw kept his eyes on the chervil he was shredding. He was supposed to be traveling to the Moonpool to receive his medicine-cat name. He knew he should be excited, but he couldn't help feeling he hadn't earned it yet. "I want to finish stripping these stems."

"They can wait." Puddleshine's tail twitched eagerly.

Shadowpaw's pelt itched with worry. He'd wanted to tell his mentor for days that he was uncertain about receiving his medicine-cat name, but the time had never seemed right. "But I'm not ready."

"Of course you're ready," Puddleshine sounded impatient. "You have your whiskers and tail. What else do you need?"

"I mean I'm not ready to be a medicine cat." Shadowpaw didn't dare look at his mentor. Was he letting Puddleshine down? "I haven't learned enough."

"You've learned plenty," Puddleshine told him.

"But there's so much I don't know yet."

"Medicine cats never stop learning. That doesn't mean they're not ready to help their Clanmates." Puddleshine padded nearer, until Shadowpaw felt his mentor's pelt brush his flank. "You're bound to be nervous, but it's okay. You can do this." He caught Shadowpaw's gaze warmly and held it. "I know I haven't always been sure about your visions in the past, Shadowpaw, but I've always believed that you were special. And now that you've saved Bramblestar, every cat knows it."

Shadowpaw's belly tightened as he remembered the dreadful vigil he'd sat beside the dying ThunderClan leader. StarClan had told him the only way to save Bramblestar from the fever that held him between life and death was to take him onto the frozen moor and expose him to the cold. The treatment had killed him, but it had made way for his next life. Now Bramblestar was healthy and strong again, and ThunderClan had its leader back. As his thoughts drifted, Shadowpaw realized that Puddleshine was still speaking. He jerked his attention back to his mentor.

"Your Clanmates feel lucky to have you as their medicine cat," Puddleshine mewed.

"I don't see why." Shadowpaw looked at the ground. "I'm just the same as I always was."

"But you've made ShadowClan special with your connection to StarClan. Our ancestors haven't spoken to any other medicine cat while the Moonpool's been frozen. After so many troubled moons, it feels as though ShadowClan has StarClan's blessing again. It's made all of us feel proud."

Shadowpaw shifted his paws self-consciously. "ShadowClan

should feel proud without me."

"I know it must feel like a big responsibility, but StarClan clearly thinks you're special, or they wouldn't have chosen you. They must think you're ready to be a full medicine cat."

Shadowpaw returned his gaze. "But are *you* sure?"

"I am," Puddleshine told him gently. "And you'll be sure too after tonight. The Moonpool will be thawing, and we'll finally be able to share with StarClan once more." He leaned closer. "Everything is going to be fine, once you've spoken with our ancestors—once we've *all* spoken with them again." Puddleshine padded to the den entrance, his tail fluffed happily. "Don't tell any cat I said this, but I was starting to worry that we'd offended them. But if we had, they wouldn't have spoken to you, would they?" He blinked brightly at Shadowpaw.

"I guess not." Unease wormed in Shadowpaw's belly as he followed his mentor out of the den. Would Puddleshine be so proud of him if he knew he was holding something back? Bramblestar's fever cure wasn't the only thing StarClan had shared with him. They'd also warned him about the code-breakers. *The Clans have forgotten the code,* a voice from StarClan had whispered. *It has been broken time and time again, and because of the codebreakers, every Clan must pay a price. They must suffer.* Images of Twigbranch and Lionblaze had flashed before him. Crowfeather, Squirrelflight, Mothwing, Jayfeather . . . Remembering this, Shadowpaw was frightened, his breath catching in his chest as he pictured again the last cat who'd appeared in his vision—Dovewing. How could his mother be a codebreaker? She was a good cat, wasn't she?

He had told Tigerstar about the vision, of course, and he remembered how his father's eyes had darkened when he'd heard Dovewing's name among the other cats. *You must keep it to yourself.* His father's words still rang in his head. Shadowpaw was sure StarClan wanted him to share this terrible vision, and yet he must obey his leader. He swallowed. *But I'm a medicine cat*—by dawn he'd have his full medicine-cat name. Wasn't his first duty to StarClan?

Shadowpaw shook out his fur as he followed Puddleshine into the clearing. His Clanmates clustered around the edge, murmuring excitedly as he walked past them. Pouncestep's and Lightleap's eyes shone. Strikestone puffed out his chest, while Scorchfur and Grassheart exchanged glances, as though agreeing with each other that they were lucky to have a medicine cat like Shadowpaw.

Shadowpaw's pelt felt hot. He avoided the gaze of his Clanmates. What would they say if they knew he was keeping a vision from them?

"Shadowpaw." Dovewing hurried to meet him as he crossed the clearing. "I'm so proud of you." Her eyes began to shimmer with emotion, and she licked the top of his head fiercely. "You're going to be a wonderful medicine cat."

"He already is." Tawnypelt padded toward him, purring. "He helped Bramblestar move safely to his next life." She stopped a tail-length away and blinked at him gratefully. "Bramblestar was my littermate. I don't know what I would have done if he'd never come back." With StarClan so oddly silent, the medicine cats had feared for a while that

Bramblestar wouldn't be able to return for his next life.

Shadowpaw forced himself to blink happily at Tawnypelt. Dovewing had stepped away and was gazing at him lovingly. How could he expose her as a codebreaker? She'd never hurt any cat.

Tigerstar was waiting at the entrance.

As Shadowpaw saw him, Puddleshine looked back expectantly. "We'd better hurry, Shadowpaw," he mewed. "The other medicine cats will be waiting. If the Moonpool really is thawing, we'll be able to commune with StarClan again—we don't want to miss that."

Shadowpaw quickened his pace, relieved to be leaving his Clanmates behind. Their admiration was making him uncomfortable. He nodded to Tigerstar, hoping that his father wouldn't want to make a fuss, but Tigerstar blocked his way. "You've earned your name," he mewed fondly. "I know you'll make a wise and loyal medicine cat who will always act in ShadowClan's best interest." He spoke slowly, and Shadowpaw could tell that Tigerstar wanted him to hear another meaning beneath his words. *He's warning me not to tell the other medicine cats about the vision.*

"I'll do my best, I promise." Nervously, he met his father's gaze, hoping Tigerstar couldn't hear the quiver in his voice.

Tigerstar purred and gently nudged Shadowpaw after his mentor. "I hope you like your new name," he called after him.

Shadowpaw hurried into the moonlit forest. He wondered what his new name would be. Had his father helped Puddleshine choose it? For the first time, excitement tingled in his paws. He was going to become a medicine cat. He'd dreamed of this moment since he was a kit. He just hoped that he could live up to the faith his Clanmates—and StarClan—had put in him.

The trek to the Moonpool was cold, but the air didn't have the stony chill of the past few moons, when the stream trickling down from the pool and even the Moonpool itself had been frozen. As he scrambled up the rocks after Puddleshine and leaped over the lip of the stone hollow, Shadowpaw's pelt rippled nervously. He hoped he wouldn't make any mistakes during the ceremony. What if he *didn't* like his new name?

The half-moon shone in a clear black sky. Shadowpaw could see silhouettes lined around the Moonpool, as still as rocks. The others were here. Puddleshine led him down the spiraling path, dimpled by countless moons of paw steps.

Jayfeather got to his paws first as they neared. "You're here." The blind medicine cat sounded pleased. Alderheart padded to his Clanmate's side and greeted Puddleshine and Shadowpaw with a nod.

Willowshine's eyes sparkled. "Are you nervous?" she asked Shadowpaw.

"A bit." Shadowpaw glanced at the Moonpool. Stretches of open water gleamed between white patches of ice.

Kestrelflight followed his gaze. "It's beginning to thaw." The WindClan medicine cat's pelt was fluffed. He sounded hopeful. "StarClan will be able to hear us tonight."

"They could *always* hear us," Jayfeather growled. "They just couldn't speak."

"They could speak to Shadowpaw," Puddleshine reminded him gently.

Shadowpaw noticed Frecklewish look away. Was that doubt in her gaze? Did she wonder why StarClan had picked him? He wasn't surprised. He'd wondered too. He blinked at the SkyClan medicine cat apologetically. "I'm sure they would have spoken to you if they could," he told her.

"StarClan knows best," Jayfeather mewed firmly. On the edge of the Moonpool, Mothwing stood, the dappled golden she-cat looking like she was biting her tongue while the others discussed their ancestors. Puddleshine had told Shadowpaw that, of all the medicine cats, Mothwing had the trickiest relationship with StarClan.

Frecklewish frowned. "It is strange that the only cat they could reach was the youngest and most inexperienced medicine cat."

Puddleshine flicked his tail. "Perhaps his youth makes him easier to talk to. He's not so bound by Clan tradition."

Frecklewish looked at the ShadowClan medicine cat. "Is that meant to be a good thing?"

"That's rich coming from a SkyClan cat," Willowshine put in. "You lived away from Clan traditions for moons. It didn't seem to do you any harm."

"This is supposed to be a celebration." Jayfeather padded between the cats, his pelt sleek in the moonlight. "Let's stop arguing about who StarClan is supposed to speak to and get on with Shadowpaw's ceremony. Then we can *all* share with StarClan at last."

Silently, Kestrelflight, Willowshine, and Alderheart fanned out around the pool. Jayfeather sat on the smooth, cold rock while Frecklewish and Fidgetflake moved closer, watching as Puddleshine led Shadowpaw to the water's edge.

Shadowpaw's heart quickened. He pricked his ears, trying to remember when he was supposed to speak.

"I, Puddleshine of ShadowClan, call upon my warrior ancestors to look down on this apprentice." His mentor raised his eyes to the sky, addressing the stars. *Can they see me?* Shadowpaw swallowed back anxiety as Puddleshine went on. "Shadowpaw has trained hard to understand the ways of a medicine cat, and with your help he will serve his Clan for many moons."

Puddleshine fixed Shadowpaw with his gaze. "Do you promise to uphold the ways of a medicine cat, to stand apart from rivalry between Clan and Clan . . ."

Shadowpaw's thoughts whirled. *What if StarClan is angry I haven't passed on their vision about the codebreakers? Will they stop me becoming a medicine cat?* Shadowpaw glanced at the sky, half expecting to see the stars blink out and disappear. But they glittered on. He realized Puddleshine was looking at him expectantly. *It's my turn!*

"I do!" he mewed quickly. His mew echoed around the rock walls of the hollow.

"Then by the powers of StarClan I give you your true name as a medicine cat. Shadowpaw, from this moment you will be known as Shadowsight. StarClan honors your insight, your courage, and your kindness, and we welcome you as a full medicine cat of ShadowClan." Puddleshine touched his nose to Shadowpaw's head, and Shadowpaw licked his mentor's shoulder gratefully.

Relief washed over his pelt. He was a medicine cat. The sky hadn't fallen in. Clouds hadn't billowed across the moon. Perhaps StarClan was happy that he had his medicine-cat name.

"Shadowsight!"

"Shadowsight!"

Around the Moonpool, the medicine cats lifted their voices and yowled into the night. Shadowsight blinked. How strange to be called by a new name. He liked it. He thought of the healer cat he'd once known, from the city. Spiresight had helped bring his family back to ShadowClan. Tigerstar must have told Puddleshine about him when they'd gotten back. How else could his mentor have known the name? Shadowsight had been a young kit during the journey, but he remembered the strange old cat well. He'd been wise and brave—he'd died saving Pouncekit's life—and he'd once said that Shadowsight would see into shadows. Did the old tom *know* that one day he'd share visions with StarClan? Shadowsight wasn't sure Spiresight even knew what StarClan was, but he was proud to share part of his name.

As the medicine cats' yowls faded into echoes, Willowshine hurried toward Shadowsight. "Do you feel any different?"

"I don't know." Shadowsight shook out his pelt, wondering if he *did* feel different. The rock still felt icy beneath his paws, and his tail still felt feathery and light. His anxiousness was gone. "I think I'm just pleased to be a medicine cat."

Willowshine's eyes sparkled. "It feels great, doesn't it? Wait till you get home. The older cats will start treating you with respect. And when you're busy in your den, apprentices will bring you prey." She purred. "There's more responsibility, of course, but Puddleshine will still help you. And learning new things is half the fun."

"Congratulations." Alderheart wove around him.

"StarClan will be pleased," Kestrelflight mewed, his gaze sparkling with approval.

Puddleshine blinked at Shadowsight. "Do you feel ready now?"

"I think so." As Shadowsight blinked at him happily, Jayfeather crouched at the edge of the Moonpool, where a clear stretch of water rippled against the stone. Alderheart ducked down beside him, and Kestrelflight padded to a patch on the far edge where the ice had thawed. Willowshine hurried to settle on his other side, fluffing out her pelt as she stretched her nose toward the water.

"Come on." Puddleshine nosed Shadowsight to the water's edge and crouched down. Shadowsight crouched next to him, closing his eyes as he stretched his muzzle forward and touched his nose to the surface of the Moonpool. Would StarClan greet him warmly? Would they tell him if he was supposed to share his vision about the codebreakers with the other medicine cats? He could ask them whether his loyalty should be to them or to his Clan leader. Hope flickered in his chest, and he squeezed his eyes tightly shut as the searing cold of the Moonpool stung his nose. He held it to the water as it grew colder and colder, wondering how long before StarClan would appear.

He willed them to come. *Please talk to me.* Was he doing it wrong? Perhaps StarClan didn't want to speak to him because he hadn't earned his medicine-cat name after all. He dipped his nose lower, holding his breath as the icy water engulfed his muzzle. Nothing happened. His heart lurched. Where was StarClan? Lifting his head, he shook the water from his nose. The other medicine cats were sitting up, gazing at one another with wide, frightened eyes.

"They didn't come." Willowshine was the first to speak. She looked hopefully around at the others, as though she thought they might explain. No cat spoke. Jayfeather's blind blue gaze was dark. Kestrelflight's pelt pricked nervously along his spine as Puddleshine glanced at the sky. Shadowsight forced his paws not to tremble. StarClan was still silent. The thawing of the Moonpool hadn't brought them back. Where were they? Why were they silent?

"Did they speak to you?" Puddleshine whispered.

"No." As Shadowsight answered, he saw Frecklewish staring at him. Her gaze seemed to burn in the darkness. Was that an accusation in her eyes?

Shadowsight shrank beneath his fur. He had been so sure that StarClan would return now that the Moonpool was thawing—they all had been. But their ancestors had stayed silent, not speaking to any cat. *Not even me.* Dizzy with fear, he tucked his paws closer beneath him. *Is this my fault?*

# CHAPTER 4

*"What are you staring at, Rootpaw?"* Needlepaw sounded exasperated as she stared at her brother. "It's like you're somewhere else. This is a Gathering, remember? We should be honored Leafstar let us come. Look!"

Rootpaw followed Needlepaw's gaze as it flashed around the island clearing, trying hard to focus his thoughts. Cats from every Clan crowded around them. Hawkwing and Macgyver were chatting with Cloverfoot. Violetshine had found Twigbranch and seemed to be peppering her with questions while her ThunderClan littermate blinked back at her, happily. Tree was deep in conversation with two RiverClan warriors. Rootpaw's tail twitched. His sister was right. He should be paying attention. Gatherings were meant to be exciting. But Rootpaw couldn't help scanning the clearing. Had Bramblestar's ghost come here too?

The apparition had plagued him for a half-moon, flitting into view every few days. Nowhere was safe. It would appear in the camp clearing while Rootpaw was trying to eat. Its shimmering pelt would catch Rootpaw's eye while he was hunting in the forest, glimmering between bushes as though tracking Rootpaw's patrol. One night, Rootpaw had woken up to find Bramblestar's ghost sitting silently beside his nest. Rootpaw's pelt prickled at the memory. Seeing the real Bramblestar beneath the Great Oak only unnerved Rootpaw more. How could the ThunderClan leader be dead and alive at the same time?

"Rootpaw!" Needlepaw nudged him. "Look over there." Her bright eyes were fixed on a group of young cats showing battle moves to one another at the edge of the clearing. Rootpaw stared at them mutely. He was still thinking about the ghost. What if it appeared here? Would any other cats see it? "You go talk to them." He nudged Needlepaw away. "You can tell me about them later."

Needlepaw narrowed her eyes. "What's wrong with you? You're acting weird again."

"Am I?" Rootpaw blinked at her innocently. He couldn't let her find out what was unnerving him. She'd think he had bees in his brain. Or worse. She'd think he was like Tree. "I guess I'm just worried about my assessment."

"You don't even know when it is. Why bother—" Needlepaw hesitated. She was staring at Bristlefrost moving toward them through the crowd. She gave Rootpaw a knowing look. "I understand now," she purred. "You want to talk to Bristlefrost." She shrugged and began to head toward the ThunderClan apprentices. "I'll leave you in peace," she teased. "But don't let Leafstar see. She doesn't approve of cats having mates in other Clans."

"She's not my mate!" Rootpaw's pelt felt hot as he yowled after his sister.

"Hey, Rootpaw." Bristlefrost's friendly mew made him jump. She had reached him already.

"Hi, Bristlefrost," he mewed quickly. "How's Thunder-Clan?"

"Good, I guess." She blinked at him. "How's your training going?" She tipped her head to one side kindly, as though asking a kit if they liked playing moss-ball.

"Fine." Rootpaw fluffed out his fur. "I'll probably be assessed soon."

"Really?" she looked surprised. "I thought you'd be training for moons yet."

"It might be any day." Rootpaw's pelt ruffled hotly along his spine. Did she think he was too young to become a warrior, or just mouse-brained?

She shifted her paws. "I mean," she corrected herself, suddenly self-conscious, "it seems so quick. I feel like I've only just gotten my warrior name."

"Maybe other Clans train their apprentices differently," he suggested. "But in SkyClan you don't have to be an apprentice to learn. Warriors learn new skills all the time."

"I guess." She looked at him thoughtfully. "Like, the other day, Blossomfall taught me how to track birds from the forest floor. I'd never tried it before. Have you?" She didn't wait for an answer before she began to explain. "You have to choose a bird and keep your eye on it. You can't stop watching for a moment. One blink and you could lose it among the leaves."

Rootpaw guessed she was just trying to be nice, but he didn't like being told something he knew already. "We track birds a lot in SkyClan."

"Really?" Bristlefrost didn't seem to hear him. Her attention had flitted to the Great Oak, where the leaders were scrambling onto the lowest branch. "I'd better go," she mewed. "Bramblestar's announcing Thriftear's and Flipclaw's warrior names. I want to be the first to yowl them out." Before he could say good-bye, she slipped into the crowd and disappeared.

Feeling unsatisfied, Rootpaw nosed his way between his Clanmates. He hadn't said anything clever or funny, but nor had Bristlefrost. Perhaps he didn't like her as much as he used to. It was for the best; after all, they were from different Clans.

Tree and Violetshine were at the edge of the clearing with Sandynose and Plumwillow. Rootpaw settled between them as Needlepaw arrived. When she reached Rootpaw, she was out of breath. "The new apprentices are called Myrtlepaw and Baypaw," she whispered. "Aren't ThunderClan names strange?"

"No stranger than Needlepaw." Rootpaw blinked at her.

Needlepaw looked worried. "Do you think Needlepaw is a strange name?"

"Of course not." He nudged her. "I was just teasing."

"Hush." Violetshine swished her tail at her kits and looked up at the oak.

Tigerstar had stepped to the edge of the branch. "Puddle-shine's apprentice has received his medicine-cat name." His mew rang out over the gathered cats. "From now on, he will be known as Shadowsight."

"Shadowsight!" The ShadowClan warriors chanted his name proudly. Kestrelflight, Alderheart, and Jayfeather joined in as Shadowsight shifted self-consciously beside them.

Rootpaw caught Shadowsight's eye and nodded. He'd met the medicine cat a few times in the forest, and he liked him. He seemed less intimidating than the older medicine cats.

As the yowling died away, Tigerstar went on. "Prey is beginning to return after the long leaf-bare. We will have full bellies within a moon." He looked toward Bramblestar as though inviting the ThunderClan leader to speak next.

Bramblestar bowed his head. "We have new warriors," he told the gathered cats. His gaze flitted toward his Clanmates, crowding at the far edge of the clearing. "Thriftear and Flip-claw passed their assessment. It won't be long before they're leading their own patrols." His gaze settled on Bristlefrost for a moment. "In ThunderClan, we believe in encouraging our younger warriors to take on new and challenging responsibilities as soon as they're able."

Bristlefrost glanced shyly at her paws.

*Has she been given special duties?* Rootpaw narrowed his eyes. Perhaps that was why she'd seemed distracted. His old affection for her filled his heart once again. How could he forget that she'd pulled him out of the frozen lake two moons ago and saved him from drowning? As he watched her, a familiar shape moved behind the ThunderClan cats. His heart sank as he recognized the shimmering outline, pale against the forest behind. *Bramblestar's ghost.* He jerked his muzzle back to the real Bramblestar, who was still speaking from the Great Oak.

"Our two new 'paws will soon be warriors," he told the Gathering confidently. "And ThunderClan will be stronger than ever."

Mistystar stepped forward. "RiverClan is strong too." Rootpaw looked away as she began to address the Clans. How could he concentrate on what they were saying when the ghost of a living cat was skulking at the edge of the clearing? He tried not to look at the apparition. He'd been avoiding its eye since the first time he'd seen it, pretending as hard as he could that he was as unaware of its presence as his Clanmates. He could see ghostly Bramblestar now, pacing impatiently, like a loner trapped in a kittypet den, his gaze flashing from the leaders to the warriors. Was it hoping some cat here would see it?

*I know how you feel.* Rootpaw scanned the gathered cats. Were any of them looking at Bramblestar's ghost? He glanced at Tree. Could his father see it? He hesitated. But Bramblestar *wasn't* dead. He was staring at the Gathering from the Great Oak. Rootpaw blinked hopefully at the medicine cats. Perhaps they could see the ghost? But their gazes were fixed on the leaders, unaware that anything was wrong.

"Rootpaw!" Violetshine hissed in his ear. "Stop staring around the clearing and concentrate. This is a Gathering. You need to pay attention." She nudged him sharply, and he dragged his gaze back to the Great Oak. Harestar was looking toward the medicine cats, lined beneath the branch. "Kestrelflight joined the other medicine cats for the half-moon meeting at the Moonpool." The WindClan leader's eyes glittered with worry as he looked expectantly at the mottled gray tom. "He wants to tell you what they saw."

Kestrelflight glanced at Frecklewish and Alderheart before he spoke. "The Moonpool has begun to thaw," he reported. "We expected to be able to share with StarClan." His ears twitched uncertainly. "But there was no word from them."

"Was there no vision at all?" Tawnypelt blinked from among the ShadowClan cats.

"We thought it was the ice that stopped you seeing StarClan!" Hootwhisker yowled, the fur rising along his spine. His Clanmates exchanged nervous glances.

Kestrelflight shrugged. "Perhaps they have nothing to share with us," he suggested.

Alderheart shifted beside him. "We've made it through leaf-bare," he agreed. "If there's no threat to the Clans, why would StarClan want to share with us?"

Hopeful murmurs of agreement rippled among the warriors.

"No news is good news," Sandynose meowed loudly.

"Perhaps they want to see if we can manage without them," Snowbird suggested.

"Why would they do that?" Tawnypelt looked unconvinced. "They've always shared with us in the past. Why would they suddenly stop?"

In the uneasy silence that followed, Bramblestar frowned. "Has Shadowsight heard anything?"

"None of us have," Kestrelflight told him.

"But Shadowsight has a special connection with StarClan," Bramblestar pressed. "He was the only medicine cat who shared with them during leaf-bare." His gaze fixed on the young ShadowClan medicine cat. "Are you sure you've heard nothing?"

Shadowsight stared at his paws, his fur pricking around his shoulders. "I'm sure," he mumbled.

Bramblestar swept his gaze around the Clans. "Perhaps StarClan is angry at us for not following the code."

Rootpaw stiffened as the gathered cats swapped uneasy glances. *Not this again.* Bramblestar had mentioned the code at the last Gathering too. His suggestion that cats should accuse one another of crimes against the code had made Tree wonder about leaving the Clans. Did the other Clans think the ThunderClan leader was right?

Could that be why Bramblestar's ghost was here now? Had StarClan somehow sent the ghost of his first life to support the living leader's message? *Should I tell some cat?* Rootpaw's pads tingled nervously. There was no way he was telling any cat he could see dead cats. He wasn't weird like Tree. He glanced at the apparition, wishing it would go away.

The dead Bramblestar was staring at the living Bramblestar, his ghostly pelt spiked with fury. Why was he angry? Wasn't he relieved to see he still had a body to return to? And yet how could he return to his body, when he was already in it? Rootpaw's head began to ache. This was too confusing. He glanced again at the medicine cats. They were trying to

contact StarClan, and here was a ghost, walking among them.
Surely one of them must see him!

He stiffened. Alderheart was staring at the apparition.
Could he see it? Rootpaw leaned forward eagerly. *Why not?*
Bramblestar was his father. The ThunderClan medicine cat
must have a closer connection with the ghost than any cat.
Leaves fluttered suddenly from a branch above Bramblestar's
ghost. Rootpaw glimpsed gray fur as a squirrel raced along it
and disappeared up the trunk. His heart dropped like a stone
as he saw Alderheart's gaze flash after the squirrel. *He was
watching* prey! Dismayed, Rootpaw swallowed back a sigh. *I'm
really the only cat who can see it.*

Feeling suddenly alone, Rootpaw stared at the gathered
cats. *Why me? It's not fair.*

"That's nonsense!" Dovewing's angry mew made him
jerk his muzzle toward her. Had he spoken out loud? The
ShadowClan cat was staring indignantly at the real Bramblestar. "StarClan would never *choose* to turn their tails on us,"
she called. "Something must be stopping them from making
contact."

"Well, it's not ice that's silencing them," Jayfeather grunted.
"The Moonpool is thawing."

Bramblestar stared fiercely back at Dovewing from the
Oak. "You just don't want to believe that StarClan is angry
with us for breaking the code," he snapped. "Because you're
one of the cats who broke it."

Tigerstar bristled beside the ThunderClan leader. "Don't
talk to her like that—"

Mistystar stepped between them. "Getting angry won't help."

Bramblestar puffed out his chest. "If we'd gotten angry earlier, we wouldn't have so many codebreakers in the Clans." His accusing gaze swept around the cats below him. "And StarClan might still be speaking to us."

As the gathered cats glanced nervously at each other, Crowfeather flattened his ears. "Do you really think StarClan wants us to start throwing around accusations? They want peace in the Clans, not arguments."

Bramblestar growled. His gaze flashed to the WindClan deputy. "You're just another codebreaker in denial about what's really going on!"

Shocked mews sounded from WindClan. ShadowClan cats were exchanging anxious looks. Rootpaw shifted closer to Needlepaw. Why was Bramblestar upsetting every cat? What made him so sure that StarClan was angry with them?

Bramblestar's gaze gleamed with determination. "StarClan is silent for a reason. It's perfectly clear to me what we have to do to bring them back. We must make sure the warrior code is respected and upheld."

As he spoke, ghostly fur flickered at the edge of Rootpaw's vision. Alarmed, he jerked his gaze toward it. Bramblestar's ghost was moving fast toward the Great Oak, ears flat, teeth bared. Was it going to attack the real Bramblestar? Rootpaw stared, fear sparking in his paws. The ghost suddenly turned, its spectral gaze locked with Rootpaw's so intensely that it seemed to burn deep into his thoughts. Panic shrilled through his fur. *It knows I can see him!* Blood roaring in his ears, Rootpaw turned and fled. He plunged into the long grass, then hared toward the tree-bridge. Pelt spiked with terror, he exploded from the grass. *I have to escape!* The tree-bridge was a few tail-lengths ahead. He made for it, his breath shallow, and leaped onto the fallen tree. The frost on the bark made his paws slip, and he jerked sideways to keep his balance

"You have to help me!" A voice sounded behind him. Rootpaw skidded to a clumsy halt on the tree-bridge. Dread weighted his paws. *I can't outrun a spirit.* He turned, trembling.

Bramblestar's ghost stood below him on the shore. Behind, the long grass was still shivering where Rootpaw had charged through it. The ghost eyed him, desperation in its pale gaze. "You're the only cat who can see me, and I don't know how long I can last like this." It took another stop forward.

Rootpaw scrabbled backward. "Stay away!" His paws slipped again. Alarm flared beneath his pelt as he slithered sideways and tumbled from the bridge. He hit the water with a splash. The cold snatched his breath as he sank. Flailing, he tried to keep his head above the surface as he reached for the lakebed with his hind paws. But there was only water beneath him, and he sank deeper into the chilly blackness.

Terror burned beneath his pelt. He churned his paws, hauling himself upward long enough to poke his muzzle into air. He gasped for breath, swallowing water as he sank again. *Help!* He remembered how he'd fallen into the lake before. Bristlefrost had fished him out, but she wasn't here now. His Clanmates were in the clearing. *Help!* He fought for the surface once more. As he broke it, he saw Bramblestar's ghost leaning down from the tree-bridge. A ghostly paw swung toward him.

"Grab it!" Bramblestar's faint mew echoed in the moonlight. Eyes stinging, heart pounding, Rootpaw thrust a foreleg above the surface, reaching for the apparition. His paw swished through the ghostly silhouette. *He can't touch me!* The hope that had flashed for a moment in Rootpaw's heart flickered out. With a wail he sank beneath the rippling water.

He struck out again, not for the surface this time, but forward. If he could push himself to the bank, he'd find the shallows. Lungs screaming for air, he thrashed the water, kicking out with every leg, hope rising again as he moved beneath the surface. His forepaw struck something hard. The lakebed. It was rising to meet the shore. He dug his claws into the sandy earth and hauled himself toward it until he felt solid ground beneath every paw, and felt the fresh night air bathe his head. Pulling himself forward, he gulped a desperate breath and staggered from the lake, trembling with terror and the cold. Teeth chattering, he shook out his pelt.

"Rootpaw!" Needlepaw dashed across the tree-bridge and landed on the shore behind him. "What happened? Are you okay?"

The Gathering must have ended, because the cats were leaving the island, pouring along the long grass and filing across the bridge. As he struggled to calm himself, his Clanmates streamed around him.

"How did you fall into the lake *again*?" Kitescratch stared at him, his whiskers trembling with amusement.

Needlepaw turned on the brown tom. "He could have drowned!"

Violetshine wove around Rootpaw. He could feel her pelt prickling with fear. "What happened?" she mewed.

"I slipped on the frozen bark," Rootpaw told her, rubbing water from his eyes with his paw.

Dewspring reached him. His mentor gazed at him sternly. "You shouldn't have run out of the Gathering like that. How does it look to the other Clans if one of our apprentices hares away for no reason?"

"Leave him alone!" Violetshine glared at Dewspring. "He could have drowned."

"Don't be mouse-brained," Dewspring snapped back. "There are only a few tail-lengths of water between the island and the shore. Even a mouse could have swum it." His gaze flitted back to Rootpaw. "Why did you run away?"

Rootpaw stared at his mentor. He couldn't tell him that he'd seen Bramblestar's ghost. He couldn't tell any cat. They'd think he was mouse-brained. Or lying. Or just weird, like Tree. "I'm sorry." He looked at the ground, trying to stop himself from trembling. At least his Clanmates were here now. Bramblestar's ghost wouldn't try to talk to him while they were here, would it?

"Come on." Violetshine nudged him along the shore. "Walking will warm you up." She pressed close beside him as they followed their campmates toward their border. Tree slid in on the other side, his gaze soft with concern, and Rootpaw was grateful for the warmth of their pelts.

As they neared the forest, he glimpsed a ghostly form in the trees. Was Bramblestar's ghost still following him? Dismayed, he pressed closer to Violetshine. He was going to have to do something about the apparition. But what could he do? *It wants my help.* But what could Rootpaw do? *I'm not even sure if it's real.* As his fur began to dry in the chilly night breeze, Rootpaw tried to think of a plan. His heart felt heavy.

If none of the other cats at the Gathering could see the ghost, it was up to him. Ignoring it wasn't working. Rootpaw was going to have to talk to the ghost.

The thought sent a chill through his whole body. *Maybe,* he thought, *I should talk to a medicine cat first.* . . .

# CHAPTER 5

*The dawn chill had already faded* by the time Bristlefrost followed Rosepetal, Dewnose, and Lionblaze into the beech grove. The sun glittered between the trees, warm now even though it was still a long while until sunhigh.

Bristlefrost tasted the air, relishing the hazy scents of coming newleaf. "Hurry up," she called to her sister.

Thriftear was trailing behind. "Aren't you tired after staying up past moonhigh?" They'd arrived home late after the Gathering and talked for a while before finally going to their nests.

"The fresh air has woken me up." Bristlefrost was happy to be out with her Clanmates.

Lionblaze glanced over his shoulder, his whiskers twitching with amusement. "Young cats need plenty of sleep," he teased.

"It's Thriftear who's tired, not me!" Bristlefrost lifted her tail indignantly. "I like getting up early. I was awake before dawn to send out the day's patrols."

"Show-off," Thriftear grumbled from behind.

"I'm not showing off," Bristlefrost told her, feeling hurt that Thriftear had missed the point. She guessed her sister was just crabby because she was sleepy. "I want to help Bramblestar. You heard him at the Gathering. We have to be the best warriors we can be. That's all I'm doing."

"I wish you'd assigned me to a later patrol," Thriftear sniffed.

Bristlefrost ignored her. There was no point in arguing with Thriftear when she was tired.

Rosepetal ducked under a low branch. "I think Bristlefrost has done a great job organizing the patrols."

Lionblaze followed her. "The borders will be marked and the fresh-kill pile full by midmorning."

Bristlefrost pricked her ears happily. "Do you really think I did okay?" She padded under the branch, letting the rough bark scrape her spine.

"Yes." Rosepetal blinked back at her. She'd been her mentor, and there was pride in her gaze. "You were polite and firm. And you matched your Clanmates well. Though I'm not sure Thornclaw will *enjoy* being out with younger cats."

Lionblaze purred. "He's going to have to work to keep up. Flipclaw and Stemleaf are as fast as hares."

Bristlefrost puffed her chest out, padding past the older warriors as they paused at the top of the slope. The trees thinned here, and the delicate branches of the beeches, still in bud, let sunshine stream onto the forest floor. Her paws scuffed over last leaf-fall's leaves, hardly more than dust now, as she scanned the trailing brambles. Bramblestar had been so sure of what the Clans had to do at last night's Gathering. They must uphold the warrior code so that StarClan would return. She was determined to do her best to help. She'd set an example to other cats. StarClan would have no choice but to return. She'd be the greatest warrior ThunderClan had ever known. She swallowed back a purr. She was lucky to have a leader like Bramblestar, who had faith in her and who knew exactly what to do. He'd lead the Clans down the right path, she was sure. Soon everything would be perfect thanks to him.

Mouse-scent touched her nose. She jerked her gaze toward an old beech, where tiny piles of freshly dug earth showed between the roots. She stopped, signaling to the others with a flick of her tail. As Lionblaze reached her, his paws barely made a noise on the forest floor.

Dewnose stopped beside him and followed Bristlefrost's gaze. "It looks like mice are nesting there," he whispered, as Rosepetal crept up to join them.

Thriftear caught up, her gaze sharpening with interest for the first time that morning. "There might be a whole family," she breathed softly.

"Let's surround the tree," Bristlefrost suggested. "They might have a secret way out. If we cover every side, we'll catch at least one."

"Good idea." Lionblaze nodded her forward. Clearly he wanted her to lead the way.

Bristlefrost crept quickly and silently toward the beech, crouching down behind it and waiting while her Clanmates fanned out around the roots, each covering a side.

"Thriftear." Lionblaze blinked at the dark gray she-cat as she dropped her belly to the earth. "You start digging them out. We'll be ready to catch any that try to escape."

Thriftear nodded and shuffled forward and began to claw away the crumbly soil, using first one paw, then both, until she was digging deep between the roots.

Bristlefrost pricked her ears. Was that a squeak? She tensed, every hair on her pelt bristling with excitement. A flash of brown fur darted from beneath the root. She slammed her paws down, but it was too fast. It shot away and disappeared beneath the roots of a neighboring tree. Another mouse shot from the nest, then more. Thriftear snatched one up. Lionblaze hooked another and gave it a killing bite. Dewnose leaped, triumph shining in his eyes as he pinned a mouse with each forepaw. He killed one and then the other and sat back on his haunches. "Good plan, Bristlefrost."

"We've caught a morning's worth," Lionblaze purred. "And the sun is hardly above the trees."

"Maybe getting up early wasn't so bad." Thriftear held up the mouse she'd caught and purred.

Bristlefrost shook out her pelt. She didn't care that she hadn't caught a mouse. She was happy her idea had worked. Her Clan would eat because of her.

"Let's bury them here and hunt some more," Lionblaze suggested. "We can pick them up on our way back to camp."

Thriftear hollowed out a space beneath the tree and Lionblaze and Dewspring dropped their catches into it. As Bristlefrost watched them, her pelt fluffed with satisfaction, she stiffened. A thought flashed across her mind. She'd been so proud of her idea that she'd forgotten it was StarClan who had guided her paws. They'd guided the *whole patrol's* paws. "We never thanked StarClan for the prey!" Alarm sparked beneath her pelt. Thanking StarClan was the first thing every kit learned. Worry crawled through her belly. She hadn't realized how easy it was to forget the warrior code. Her Clanmates could be breaking it all the time without even realizing. She looked around at her Clanmates, expecting to see their pelts bristle too. How could they have forgotten something so simple? "We must thank StarClan."

"I thanked StarClan." Dewnose shrugged. "Just not out loud."

Thriftear glanced at her paws. "Me too," she mewed quickly. "I said it to myself."

Bristlefrost narrowed her eyes. *Really?* She was unconvinced. Her sister always made excuses when there was something she should have done; it was easier to keep the peace than own up to mistakes. "Perhaps we should all say it out loud now, so we know we've done it." She couldn't let StarClan be mad at Thriftear.

Thriftear rolled her eyes. "We're not kits."

Bristlefrost blinked at her earnestly. "It's important,' she mewed. "You heard Bramblestar at the Gathering. We have to stop breaking the code if we want StarClan to talk to us again."

Rosepetal's ears twitched, as she and Lionblaze shared a glance. "Do you really think StarClan would stop talking to us because of something so small?"

"It's not small if every cat does it," Bristlefrost pointed out.

"I think we should all thank StarClan out loud from now on, after every catch. That way we can be sure we've done it, and we can remind any cat who forgets."

"We can't start yowling after every catch," Lionblaze mewed gruffly. "We'll scare off our next prey while thanking StarClan for our last."

Bristlefrost stared at him. Why were her Clanmates risking StarClan's anger over such a small thing? "Warriors have been giving thanks to StarClan for their prey since the warrior code was invented. It must be important."

The older warriors swapped glances.

"She has a point," Dewnose conceded. "There's a reason it's part of the code."

"Exactly." Bristlefrost looked hopefully at Lionblaze. Would he agree?

"Okay." The golden warrior dipped his head. "We'll thank StarClan out loud from now on."

"I'll mention it to Bramblestar so he can remind the other warriors," Rosepetal chimed.

Relief washed Bristlefrost's pelt. StarClan couldn't be angry with them now. She glanced at the prey buried in the fresh earth. "Let's start by thanking them for this catch."

"Thank you, StarClan, for sending us this prey." The older warriors mewed the words, and Thriftear mumbled along haltingly.

"Thank you, StarClan." Bristlefrost raised her muzzle to the sky. "It was a good catch and we're really grateful." Pride swelled in her chest. She was already showing her Clanmates how they could please StarClan. It wouldn't be long before their ancestors were speaking to them again.

As the sun reached high above the forest, spilling sunshine into the hollow, Bristlefrost followed Rosepetal, Dewnose and Lionblaze into the camp. She was carrying a rabbit between her jaws. It was so heavy that her neck ached, but she barely noticed; she couldn't help feeling that thanking StarClan for their prey had made a difference. After unearthing the mouse nest, they'd gone on to catch a rabbit and a squirrel. Thriftear had even trapped a shrew that had darted across her path on their way home. It felt as though StarClan had been sending prey toward them because they were so pleased that the warriors were following every part of the code.

She dropped the rabbit on the fresh-kill pile and looked around the clearing. Bramblestar and Squirrelflight lay beneath the Highledge. The deputy's rich, deep purr echoed around the camp as Bramblestar joined in. His eyes shone with affection as he gazed at Squirrelflight. Bristlefrost paused, pressing back a purr of her own. She hoped she'd find a mate who loved her as much as Bramblestar clearly loved Squirrelflight.

Squirrelflight started to get to her paws, but Bramblestar flicked his tail toward her. "Stay with me," he mewed.

"A Clan doesn't run itself." Squirrelflight looked at him, pretending to be stern. "I want to check the pile. It's barely newleaf and I want to make sure we're not hunting more young prey than we should. The forest can only provide so much."

"You can see the pile from here." Bramblestar gazed at her imploringly. Sparkpelt's patrol had already returned, and the pile was half full. "And there's another hunting patrol still out. Check the fresh-kill pile when they get back."

Squirrelflight gave him an exasperated look but lay down again beside him. "I guess it can wait a little."

Rosepetal dropped two mice beside Bristlefrost's rabbit. She tipped her head appreciatively. "I haven't seen such a haul in moons." She flicked her gaze toward Bristlefrost. "I'm going to tell Squirrelflight and Bramblestar about your idea."

"Which idea?" Bristlefrost blinked at her self-consciously. Did she mean her hunting strategy?

"About thanking StarClan out loud," she told her. "I think it might have helped."

Bristlefrost fluffed out her pelt proudly. "Do you really think so?" Should she tell her that she thought so too?

"Come on." She beckoned her with a jerk of her muzzle.

"Where?"

"To tell Bramblestar."

"Now?" She wanted to help her Clanmates be the best warriors they could be, but she hadn't imagined that her plan would make a difference so soon. She forced her fur to smooth. She didn't want Rosepetal to see how excited she was.

Rosepetal led her across the clearing and stopped in front of Bramblestar and Squirrelflight. Bramblestar didn't seem to notice them, only turning his muzzle when Squirrelflight sat up and greeted them with a dip of her head.

"It looks like the hunt went well." She nodded appreciatively toward the fresh-kill pile.

"Prey is returning," Rosepetal told her.

"We must be careful not to catch all of it," Squirrelflight warned. "We want some left for greenleaf."

"There's plenty left," Rosepetal promised. "The forest is so full of prey-scent, it's hard to know which trail to follow first."

Bramblestar's tail flicked impatiently. He looked past the dark cream she-cat, his gaze fixing on Bristlefrost. She straightened as he looked at her, conscious that her paws were still dusty from the hunt. "Are you enjoying organizing the patrols?" he asked.

"Yes," she told him eagerly. "It's a great honor."

"Good." He nodded curtly. "It saves Squirrelflight from getting up before dawn."

Rosepetal shifted her paws. "Bristlefrost had a good idea while we were out hunting."

Bramblestar's eyes widened. "What was it?"

"She suggested every cat say their thanks to StarClan after every catch, like the warrior code says, but out loud." Bristlefrost looked shyly at her paws as Rosepetal went on. "That way, no cat can forget."

Bristlefrost's heart seemed to stop in the pause that followed her mentor's words. She looked nervously up at Bramblestar. Did he think it was a dumb idea?

His eyes were shining. Relief washed her pelt.

"That's a great idea." Bramblestar blinked at her. "I'm glad to see you taking the warrior code so seriously."

"I remembered what you said last night," Bristlefrost told him eagerly. "About upholding the code so StarClan will come back."

Bramblestar tipped his head approvingly. "I'll make an announcement to the Clan this evening. If every cat follows your lead, Bristlefrost, StarClan will be back before we know it." He nodded to Rosepetal. "Thank you for sharing this with me." He flicked his tail toward the fresh-kill pile. "No doubt you'll want to taste some of the prey you helped catch."

"Yes." Rosepetal dipped her head politely and turned away. As Bristlefrost began to follow her, Bramblestar pricked his ears. "Wait, Bristlefrost," he mewed. "I want to talk to you about something."

Her heart quickened. She blinked at him excitedly. What did he want to say? Was he pleased with her? Was there something else she could help with?

Squirrelflight glanced at Bramblestar curiously. "Why not let her go with Rosepetal? She's been up since before dawn. She probably hasn't eaten. Let her go and get some prey."

"She can go in a moment," Bramblestar told her without taking his eyes from Bristlefrost. "But it's important our warriors know how we appreciate them."

Bristlefrost lifted her chin. Was he going to praise her again?

"You're doing exactly what I wanted you to do," he told her, his gaze warm with approval. "You're obviously a very dedicated warrior, and observant too."

Bristlefrost tried to stop her chest from puffing out more. "I'm just trying to do my best," she mumbled modestly. "I don't want StarClan to abandon us. I want . . ." Her mew trailed away, and her ears grew hot as Bramblestar stared at her thoughtfully.

"You've done so well assigning patrols," he meowed evenly. "And by noticing that your Clanmates haven't been thanking StarClan—"

"I'm sure they have." She interrupted, anxious they he'd think her Clanmates had been doing something wrong. "But in case they ever forget, I thought it would be a good idea—"

"Yes, of course." Bramblestar's mew was smooth as he pressed on. "Could you take on another special task?"

"Sure!" Bristlefrost answered immediately. She didn't care what it was. She was eager to help her Clan any way she could.

"I can't help feeling the whole Clan has been a bit sloppy when it comes to following the code," Bramblestar began.

Squirrelflight glanced at him sharply. "Our Clanmates are loyal and honorable warriors."

"Indeed they are," Bramblestar agreed. "But it's easy to become forgetful and to fall into bad habits. Even the most loyal and honorable warrior might overlook a small part of the code here and there. It's hard to remember all of it."

"I guess." Bristlefrost felt his gaze burn into her. Hurriedly she tried to remember any time she might have forgotten the code without realizing it.

"I can't fix what I don't see." Bramblestar blinked at her

innocently. "But if I know exactly how and when my Clan-mates might be breaking the code, I can help them."

"So can I!" Bristlefrost stretched her muzzle forward eagerly. If they both helped ThunderClan follow the code, StarClan would be back in no time!

Bramblestar's tail swept the earth. "I want you to be my eyes and ears in the Clan, Bristlefrost. You can see things I can't. I want you to report back to me if you see or hear any codebreaking."

Squirrelflight shifted her paws uneasily. "Is that fair?"

"Of course it's fair," Bramblestar told her. "She wants to help her Clanmates be better warriors."

Bristlefrost tipped her head. "I can tell them if they're breaking the code. I'm sure if they realized they were doing it, they'd stop."

"I guess." Bramblestar gaze drifted past her. "But it's impor-tant I know too. It's the best way to help our Clanmates."

Squirrelflight's ears twitched. "I don't think you should make Bristlefrost your spy. That can't be what StarClan wants."

Bramblestar looked at his mate. "She's not going to be my spy," he told her. "She's just going to make sure I know if there are any problems in the Clan."

"Isn't that spying?" Squirrelflight's fur ruffled along her spine.

Bristlefrost's chest tightened. *Is she angry with me?*

"Let's talk about this later," Bramblestar told Squirrelflight.

She stared at him defiantly. "What is there to talk about?"

"You're overreacting." Bramblestar eyed her calmly. "Are you worried she might see or hear *you* doing something wrong?"

"Of course not!"

Bramblestar didn't seem to hear. "Only a codebreaker would worry about being spied on."

Anger flashed for a moment in Squirrelflight's gaze. She looked away but didn't speak.

Bristlefrost wondered if she should leave them to finish their conversation in private. She began to edge away, hesitating as Bramblestar's gaze lingered on Squirrelflight. Was he going to change his mind?

"It's good to see you haven't lost your fire, Squirrelflight," he mewed silkily. "It reminds me of the old days. You used to stand up to me then too."

Squirrelflight looked at him, her gaze unreadable. Was she remembering when she and Bramblestar had been young? Or was she thinking about the argument she and her mate had had a few moons ago, when they had disagreed over whether to drive the Sisters off their territory so that SkyClan could claim it?

*They have been arguing quite a lot lately,* Bristlefrost realized.

"You can go."

Bristlefrost realized with a start that Bramblestar was looking at her again. "Y-yes. Of course." She backed away.

"I'm relying on you," he told her. "I know such a loyal and smart warrior won't let me down."

His words rang in her ears as she padded to the fresh-kill pile. She'd been given another special duty. Bramblestar must really trust her to ask her to keep an eye on the Clan. She pushed away the doubt itching in her paws. *I won't have to report any codebreaking,* she told herself. Her Clanmates were loyal warriors, and, if they followed the code, there'd be nothing to report. She hooked a shrew from the pile, imagining how pleased Bramblestar would be when she told him their Clanmates had been following the code. She fluffed out her fur. It wouldn't be long until StarClan returned, and then everything would be back to normal.

# CHAPTER 6

Shadowsight tucked a loose bracken stalk into the nest he'd woven and sat back to check his work. A rustle above him made him look up. Through the roof of the medicine den, he saw a bird swoop low, settling for a moment on the brambles before fluttering away. He pricked his ears hopefully. Was that the sign he'd been waiting for? He'd been on tenterhooks all morning, jumping at every sound and movement in case it turned out to be a message from StarClan. Above him, the bird had disappeared, leaving no trace. His heart sank. *It's not a sign. I'd have known if it was.*

He looked back to the nest. It was neat and, once he'd lined it with moss, would make a comfortable bed for an injured cat. As he gazed at the long, clean strands of bracken lit by the sunshine flooding through the entrance, his thoughts drifted to last night's Gathering. Bramblestar had asked him directly if he'd heard from StarClan. He'd hated lying, but he'd promised Tigerstar he wouldn't share his vision about the codebreakers. What he'd told Bramblestar had been partly true. StarClan hadn't shared with him when he'd visited the Moonpool with the other medicine cats, and hadn't spoken to him since.

Worry wormed beneath Shadowsight's pelt. He'd grown used to the idea of being StarClan's chosen cat. So why wouldn't they speak to him now? Had he done something wrong?

Puddleshine was on the other side of the den, pulling apart an old nest that had grown damp and moldy over the long leaf-bare. He caught Shadowsight's eye. "Don't just look at it," he told him as Shadowsight stared at the nest. "Put some moss in."

Shadowsight blinked at him, startled from his thoughts. "Sure." He reached for the moss piled beside him.

"Is everything okay?" Puddleshine tipped his head, concerned. "You've been distracted since we got back from the Gathering."

"Do you think Bramblestar's right?" Shadowsight ripped a wad of moss from the pile and began to press it into the nest. "About StarClan being angry at us for breaking the code?"

"I don't think it helps to try to second-guess StarClan." Puddleshine tore open a bunch of tangled stems. "They'll let us know if we're doing something wrong."

"What about my vision?" Shadowsight remembered with a shudder how he'd seen fire rise from the lake and reach out along the Clan boundaries, dividing the Clans with flame before spreading to consume all their land.

"It was scary." Puddleshine frowned thoughtfully. "But there's no reason to think it was anything to do with breaking the warrior code."

"I guess not." Shadowsight kept his gaze on his work, his pelt suddenly hot. *Puddleshine doesn't know what I know.* Guilt wormed in his belly as he tucked the moss between the bracken stems. *StarClan showed me the codebreakers.* What if the fire vision was a warning? Would the Clans burn if they didn't acknowledge the codebreakers? *I have to tell them!* But how could he betray his father? And what would happen to Dovewing if he did? She had been one of the cats in his codebreaker vision. His chest tightened. *Am I making everything worse by keeping quiet?*

He had to speak to Tigerstar. He couldn't keep ignoring the vision and hoping that everything would work itself out. There was too much at risk.

As he headed for the entrance, Puddleshine looked up. "Aren't you going to finish the nest?"

"I'll finish it when I get back." Shadowsight avoided Puddleshine's eye. He didn't want to explain where he was going. He ducked outside, relieved that he was a full medicine cat now and Puddleshine couldn't tell him what to do.

Outside, Tigerstar was rummaging through the fresh-kill pile. The patrols were gone for the morning, and the clearing was empty apart from the Clan leader. Shadowsight crossed it and stopped beside his father.

Tigerstar blinked at him distractedly, as though his thoughts were elsewhere. "Last night, the other Clans said prey was running well," he mewed. "But it's still thin on the ground here." He sat down, his tail flicking uneasily.

"Tigerstar." Shadowsight tried to catch his eye, but Tigerstar didn't seem to be listening.

"I wish I knew why," he murmured. "It's been cold, but no

colder than in WindClan or RiverClan territory."

Shadowsight tried to get his attention again, leaning closer. "I have to talk to you."

"I guess I could ask Cloverfoot to double up the hunting patrols." Tigerstar frowned, his gaze flitting around the deserted clearing. "But we're already sending out six patrols every day."

Frustration welled in Shadowsight's chest. His father needed to listen. "It's important," he pressed.

Tigerstar looked at him hazily. "What is?"

"I have to tell the Clans about the codebreakers."

Tigerstar's gaze suddenly focused. He stiffened. "No."

"But what if keeping quiet is making things worse?" Fear jabbed Shadowsight's belly.

Tigerstar squared his shoulders. "We've just survived the hardest leaf-bare any cat has ever known. Things are going to get better."

"But what about my vision about the fire? There could be a threat to all the Clans—"

"I know you're worried." Tigerstar blinked at him reassuringly. "But this is the best way, I promise."

"I'm not sure it is." Shadowsight dug his claws into the earth, wondering how his father would react to what he said next. "I want to protect Dovewing, too, but isn't that selfish? I can't keep this a secret from the Clans because I'm worried about my own kin."

Tigerstar narrowed his eyes. "You heard Bramblestar last night. He wants to make an example of any warrior who breaks the code. If you tell him that StarClan is worried about codebreakers, who knows what he'll do. ThunderClan has always thought it was better than the rest of us. They'll use this to make the lives of the other Clans miserable."

"You can't be sure of that," Shadowsight argued. "What if this means that Bramblestar's *right*? StarClan may not return until we deal with the codebreakers."

"'Deal with'?" Tigerstar's gaze hardened. "What do you mean, 'deal with'?" He didn't wait for an answer. "What do you think will happen to Dovewing—to any of the codebreakers—if we tell the Clans about your vision?"

"I'm sure StarClan just wants the codebreakers to acknowledge what they've done," Shadowsight mewed, hoping he was right. "I can't believe that StarClan would want to hurt any cat."

"It's not StarClan I'm worried about," Tigerstar mewed darkly. "You don't know what Bramblestar is like. He thinks he can use this to make ThunderClan stronger and the other Clans weaker. He'll hurt us if he gets the chance." He leaned closer to Shadowsight, fear flashing in his eyes. "You said it yourself—I don't want to risk Dovewing's safety, and I know you don't either. We both love her too much."

A chill ran along Shadowsight's spine. Was Tigerstar right? *Even if he is, can I risk the safety of all the Clans just to save one cat I love?* He blinked back at his father. "But—"

Tigerstar interrupted. "We have no choice," he meowed darkly. "This has to remain between you and me."

Shadowsight watched his father stalk away and disappear

into his den. His belly felt suddenly hollow. He understood why Tigerstar wanted to protect Dovewing. He wanted to protect her too. Bramblestar had seemed far too eager to accuse cats he believed were codebreakers. There had been little sympathy in the ThunderClan leader's call to expose them. What if he *did* want to exploit StarClan's silence to impose ThunderClan's authority over the rest of the Clans? *But StarClan sent me the vision.* Shadowsight couldn't ignore the feeling that his ancestors wanted him to share it.

His ears pricked. A panicked yowl rang outside camp. "Shadowsight!" He recognized Lightleap's mew. Pelt spiking with alarm, Shadowsight raced for the camp entrance.

Lightleap was pushing her way through with Flaxfoot. Snowbird limped between them.

The white she-cat's cat face was twisted with pain. She held her forepaw off the ground, and Shadowsight could see at once that it was badly twisted.

"She slipped." Lightleap pushed past him as she helped Snowbird toward the medicine den.

Puddleshine hurried out, his eyes round with concern. "What happened?"

"Snowbird hurt her paw." Shadowsight padded beside his sister, peering past her to see Snowbird's paw. It hung limply, pointing the wrong way. It must be broken.

"She slipped as we were jumping over a log," Flaxfoot told him. "She landed badly."

Snowbird closed her eyes and let out a long, agonized breath.

"I'll get some comfrey and poppy seeds." Puddleshine ducked back into the medicine den, and Shadowsight followed as Flaxfoot and Lightleap helped Snowbird inside behind him.

Shadowsight hurried past them and quickly piled the remaining moss into the nearly finished nest. He pressed it down quickly. It would have to do for now. "Lay her here," he told Lightleap.

Lightleap and Flaxfoot helped Snowbird to the nest and let her slump gently onto the moss. She grunted as she slid down.

Puddleshine padded to the nest, a wad of comfrey leaves between his jaws. He dropped and unrolled them to reveal a scattering of poppy seeds in the middle. After dabbing the seeds with his pad, he offered them to Snowbird. She licked them from his paw and lay back, her eyes glittering with pain. Puddleshine nudged Lightleap toward the entrance. "Go and finish your hunting," he told the brown tabby she-cat. "We'll take care of Snowbird."

"But I want to see that she's okay." Lightleap pricked her ears.

Puddleshine nosed Flaxfoot after her. "If you want to help"—he steered them toward the entrance—"go find four smooth, straight sticks we can use as a splint."

"Can't we wait here to see if her paw will be okay?" Lightleap looked pleadingly at Shadowsight.

"I'll come and find you when we've finished treating her," he promised. "I'll let you know how she's doing then."

"We need those sticks," Puddleshine told the two young

warriors as he ran a gentle paw over Snowbird's leg.

As Lightleap and Flaxfoot trailed reluctantly from the den, Shadowsight padded to Puddleshine's side. "Is it broken?" he asked softly.

Puddleshine nodded, avoiding Snowbird's gaze.

The white she-cat blinked at Shadowsight. "Can you fix it?"

It looked like a nasty break. Shadowsight glanced hopefully at Puddleshine.

Puddleshine began to wrap comfrey around Snowbird's paw. "The splints will help straighten it, but I don't want to set the bone until the poppy seeds have started working." He looked evenly at Snowbird. "I'm afraid it will hurt."

"I don't care." Snowbird lifted her muzzle defiantly. "Just fix it. I don't want to have a limp."

Shadowsight caught Puddleshine's eye. He saw darkness in the medicine cat's gaze. Would Snowbird's paw fully heal? Worry settled around his heart. Snowbird was a brave and loyal warrior. How could StarClan have let this happen to her?

Shadowsight hurried through the forest in search of Lightleap and Flaxfoot. They hadn't returned with the sticks yet. Snowbird was sleeping in the medicine den, her paw wrapped in thick layers of comfrey. He tasted the air, picking up Lightleap's trail. Flaxfoot's scent mingled with it. He followed the warriors' trail through the woods, where melting snow was still piled between roots and heaped on branches, dripping as the thaw set in for good. In a few days, the snow would be gone.

Perhaps he'd feel less worried when newleaf was here. There'd be as much prey for ShadowClan as for the other Clans, and, with a full belly again, he'd feel better. His conversation with Tigerstar still nagged at his thoughts. Perhaps his father was right and he should keep the secret of the codebreakers to himself. Everything might work itself out. StarClan would return soon. After all, StarClan had always helped in the past. Why would it stop now?

He paused and scanned the trees. There was no sign of Lightleap and Flaxfoot here. Had the two warriors found the sticks and headed back to camp? He turned and followed the scent trail back the way he'd come, wondering why he hadn't seen them. The trail veered and he quickened his step. A creak overhead made him look up. Above him, a heap of snow slithered from a branch and plummeted down. It hit him with a thud and engulfed him, knocking him off his paws. He struggled up and burst out of the drift, his eyes and ears filled with snow. Clambering onto the top of the pile, he shook out his fur and rubbed the snow from his face with a paw. Of all the trees in the forest, why did he have to be walking under this one? He glanced up indignantly, questions flashing in his mind. *Why me? Why now?* Why did ShadowClan have less prey than the other Clans? Why had Snowbird hurt her paw so badly?

His pelt pricked uneasily. Was StarClan trying to tell him something? He'd been hoping all day that they'd send him a sign. Perhaps this was it. If they didn't want to speak to the Clan through the Moonpool, there were other ways to communicate. Shadowsight felt suddenly cold, and not just because the melting snow was seeping into his pelt. He hurried toward camp. The sticks could wait. He wanted to check on Snowbird. What if StarClan thought he hadn't understood their message? Could they make her injury worse? *I can't believe that StarClan would want to hurt any cat.* As he remembered what he'd told his father, doubt tugged in his belly. Perhaps StarClan would let one cat suffer if it helped all the rest. Was this their way of telling him that they wanted him to share his vision?

His heart quickened as he neared camp. Anxious mews sounded from beyond the bramble wall. Puddleshine was issuing orders. "Take him to the medicine den! Fetch cobwebs!" Shadowsight tasted the air, panic flashing beneath his pelt as its iron tang touched his tongue. *Blood!* He raced into camp.

As he burst from the entrance, he saw Stonewing, Antfur, and Scorchfur limping toward the medicine den. Dovewing was with them, tufts of fur sticking out of her pelt.

"What happened?" He hurried toward them. Had foxes found the patrol? Had another Clan invaded? His pelt spiked with alarm. "Were you attacked?"

Dovewing turned to meet him, her eyes wide. "A branch fell." She was breathing rapidly. "It hit Antfur and Scorchfur."

"Are you hurt?" Shadowsight scanned his mother's pelt frantically. Despite the tufts of fur, she didn't look too badly injured, although one ear was torn.

"I'm okay," she told him. "Antfur got the worst of it." She glanced toward the small brown-and-black tom. His eyes were glazed as Stonewing and Puddleshine guided him into the medicine den. "He was knocked unconscious. We had to carry him back."

"And the others?" Shadowsight blinked at Scorchfur. The dark gray tom's pelt was ragged as he limped after his Clanmates as though every paw step hurt.

"Scorchfur is badly bruised," Dovewing told him. "I don't think any bones are broken, though. Stonewing's tail got trapped. We had to scoop out the earth underneath the branch to get him free."

As Dovewing's green eyes clouded with shock, Tigerstar padded from his den. He blinked as he saw Dovewing, his pelt bushing. "What hurt you?" He raced across the clearing, scrambling to a halt beside her and sniffing her pelt anxiously.

"A falling branch." Dovewing nodded toward the medicine-den entrance. "Antfur's been hurt, and Scorchfur. You'd better take a look."

Tigerstar stared at her. "Are you okay?"

She nodded shakily. "I just want to go to our den and rest."

"Of course." He guided her away. "I'll look in on the others once I've made sure you're comfortable." He looked at Shadowsight. "Will you take care of them while I see to your mother?"

"Of course." Shadowsight gave his mother an anxious glance.

"I'll be okay," Dovewing reassured him. "I just need to rest. Go help Puddleshine."

Nodding, Shadowsight ducked into the medicine den.

Snowbird was still asleep. Scorchfur lay in one of the old nests, his eyes closed, but breathing steadily. Stonewing was gingerly licking his battered tail. Puddleshine leaned into a nest at the far end of the den where Antfur sat up straight, staring blankly ahead.

"What's wrong with him?" Shadowsight hurried to his nest.

"No broken bones," Puddleshine told him without taking his eyes off Antfur. "But the branch caught him on the head."

There was a gash behind his ear, not that Antfur seemed to notice. He glanced strangely at Shadowsight. "Are you one of those forest cats?" He looked confused for a moment, then blinked and looked away. "I need to scavenge," he mewed to no cat in particular. "There are hungry cats here. I know where the scrapcans are."

Shadowsight frowned as he recognized the words from when he was a young kit. "He thinks he's back in the city," he whispered to Puddleshine.

"He's dazed." Puddleshine looked uneasily at the tom. "Rest might help."

Antfur tried to step out of the nest. "Let's go scavenging."

"We can scavenge later." Puddleshine nudged him back. "You have to rest now."

"Why is the den spinning so fast?" Antfur wobbled and collapsed into the bracken.

"I'll fetch some marigold," Shadowsight mewed. "We can treat the gash, at least." He turned away, fear opening like a bottomless pit in his belly. Another accident? On the same day? As he rummaged for marigold in the herb store, his thoughts whirled. StarClan *must* be trying to send him a message. *What do they want?* he thought desperately.

But he knew. His pelt prickled along his spine. As he took the marigold back to Antfur's nest, Tigerstar padded into the den.

"How are they?" he asked Shadowsight as he glanced from nest to nest.

"We don't know yet." Shadowsight laid the dried marigold petals beside the nest.

Tigerstar padded to Scorchfur's nest. "How did this happen?"

Scorchfur blinked at him, his pelt ruffled. "We were hunting and a branch just snapped above us." He looked puzzled. "It wasn't rotten," he mewed. "There was no reason why it should have fallen."

Shadowsight felt sick. It *must* be StarClan. He couldn't keep this secret anymore. What if Tigerstar was wrong?

He had to ask another cat for advice. He glanced at Puddleshine. "Can you manage while I check on Dovewing? I want to put some marigold on her torn ear."

"Okay." Puddleshine nodded. "But don't be long."

Shadowsight grabbed a mouthful of marigold petals and hurried to the entrance. Treating his mother's ear wasn't the only reason he wanted to see her. She could advise him. He crossed the clearing and ducked into her den. Dovewing lay in her nest, her eyes half-closed.

Shadowsight padded forward and dropped the marigold beside her. "How are you doing?"

She blinked at him drowsily. "Just tired," she told him. "How are the others?"

"Antfur's a bit confused." He didn't tell her that the tom didn't even know where he was. "Scorchfur will be fine with some rest."

"Good." Dovewing let her eyes close again.

Shadowsight took a few petals and chewed them into a pulp. He leaned into the nest and began gently to lap the ointment onto the torn edges of Dovewing's ear. She flinched but said nothing. When he'd finished, he sat back and looked at her. "What would you do if you had a secret that might help a lot of cats, but might hurt a few if you told it?"

Dovewing tipped her head to one side and looked at him thoughtfully. "If it were me," she mewed softly, "I'd tell the truth." She held his gaze, and Shadowsight wondered for a moment if she was going to ask him why he wanted to know. But she didn't. Instead she curled deeper into her nest. "You can never go wrong by telling the truth."

Shadowsight's pelt prickled uneasily. She was right. He *had* to tell the truth. The other medicine cats should know about the codebreakers. But how could he risk his mother's safety? His heart ached as he watched Dovewing close her eyes once more. She had no idea that telling the truth might mean trouble for her. He just hoped it wouldn't be as bad as Tigerstar feared.

# CHAPTER 7

*Rootpaw opened his eyes. Morning sunshine* streamed through the woven branches of the apprentices' den. He lifted his head, alarm jabbing his belly as he saw that Needlepaw's and Wrenpaw's nests were already empty. *I'm late.* He scrambled up. Where was Dewspring? Lately his mentor had been waking him each morning, sticking his head into the apprentices' den just after dawn to hurry Rootpaw out of his nest. Needlepaw and Wrenpaw had teased Rootpaw about his new habit of oversleeping, telling him that leaf-bare hibernation was over, but Rootpaw ignored them. It wasn't his fault. He hadn't been getting to sleep until close to dawn, worried that Bramblestar's ghost might be lurking nearby.

In the two days since the Gathering, Rootpaw hadn't had the chance to talk with the medicine cats. The ghost had been appearing more regularly, hanging around the edges of the camp, trying desperately to catch Rootpaw's eye. Rootpaw had steadfastly ignored it, but that hadn't driven it away. Last night it had approached him while he'd been eating a thrush beside Needlepaw. Pressing its muzzle close to Rootpaw's ear, it had demanded to be heard.

"You can see me!" it had growled. "Stop pretending you can't. I need help!"

Rootpaw had kept his eyes on his thrush. *Go away!* Did the ghost really expect him to answer when he was surrounded by his Clanmates? They'd think he was crazy. He'd carried on eating, pretending he couldn't hear, but the ghost kept pestering.

"I need to find out what's going on," it had pressed. "Some cat addressed the Gathering pretending to be me! Are there two of me now? Is StarClan going to make a new one of me every time I die?"

*Why is it just me who can see this ghost?* Rootpaw's pelt had prickled irritably along his spine. *I'm a warrior apprentice, not a medicine cat. Go bother some other cat!* he'd wanted to yowl at the ghost, but Needlepaw was already glancing at him out of the corner of her eye.

"You're being weird again," she'd mewed.

Rootpaw had shifted self-consciously. "How?"

"Your pelt keeps prickling, and you get this look." She demonstrated, widening her eyes and glancing around furtively. "Like you're in trouble and you're about to be found out."

"You're imagining it." He'd tried to wave Bramblestar's ghost away with his tail.

Needlepaw had looked at him for a moment longer, then retuned to her shrew.

Now, as birds sang their morning chorus, Rootpaw glanced around the den. The ghost wasn't here. *Good.* He hurried outside. Bright sunshine sparkled on the dewy clearing while his

Clanmates stretched and chatted, their breath billowing in the damp air. Rootpaw scanned the camp for his mentor.

"Are you looking for Dewspring?" Hawkwing called to him from beside the prey pile.

"I'm supposed to meet him for training," Rootpaw told him.

"He's in the medicine den." Hawkwing nodded toward the dogwood. "He's strained a paw."

Rootpaw nodded his thanks to the SkyClan deputy and wandered to the bush where warriors had hollowed out a shallow dip to form a wide, shady den. Anxiety bristled through his fur, and it wasn't just that he was worried Dewspring might be badly hurt. But this might also be his chance to ask a medicine cat about the ghost.

He ducked inside and saw his mentor lying beside a nest. Fidgetflake had swathed his paw in comfrey and was dripping water from a ball of moss onto the dressing, while Frecklewish sorted herbs at the back of the den.

Dewspring looked up as Rootpaw padded in. "Don't worry," he told him before he could speak. "I just landed badly while we were hunting yesterday. I thought the pain would ease after a night's sleep, but it swelled instead."

Rootpaw padded to his side. "Will it be okay?"

"I hope so." Dewspring glanced at Fidgetflake.

The medicine cat blinked back. "If you rest it today, it'll be fine by tomorrow."

"Rootpaw has his assessment soon," Dewspring told Fidgetflake. "He won't want to miss any training."

"I could go out with Wrenpaw or Needlepaw today," Root-paw offered.

"They left at dawn," Dewspring told him. "They're hunting on the lakeshore."

Normally, Rootpaw's heart would have sunk at the idea of being stuck in camp all day, dodging Bramblestar's ghost. But today it lifted. "I could help out around here." He looked hopefully at Fidgetflake. If Bramblestar's ghost bothered him in the medicine den, Fidgetflake or Frecklewish might see it. They were used to seeing dead cats. And if *they* could see Bramblestar, then the ghost wouldn't be Rootpaw's problem anymore.

Fidgetflake dropped the moss and patted the comfrey around Dewspring's paw. "I'm going out to gather herbs soon," he told Rootpaw. "Want to help me?"

"Okay." Rootpaw blinked at him eagerly. It would give him time to talk to the medicine cat alone.

Dewspring settled onto his belly and laid his injured paw gently on the ground. "You might as well make yourself useful," he meowed.

Rootpaw looked hopefully at Fidgetflake. "Should we go now?" If they left at once, the apparition might not know where he went.

Fidgetflake purred. "If you like." He nodded to Freckle-wish. "I'm going to gather horsetail. Is there anything else we need?"

"See if the marigold is sprouting," she told him. "We're running a little low."

Outside camp Rootpaw led the way uphill, slipping between boulders and only pausing when he reached the top. He gazed across the rolling hills, relieved to be free for a while from Bramblestar's ghost. Stretches of snow still lay in shadows between the hills, but around them green fields unfurled beneath a bright blue sky, and trees flung up their branches in an emerald haze.

Fidgetflake stopped beside him and pointed his nose toward the valley below. A stream sparkled at the bottom. "There's horsetail down there," he told Rootpaw, heading downhill.

Rootpaw followed, relishing the breeze in his pelt. It was chilly, despite the sunshine, and he could see his breath. Preyscent touched his nose, and he wished he were hunting with Dewspring instead of gathering herbs. But this was his chance to find out if Bramblestar's ghost was unusual. He knew it was different for medicine cats because they saw StarClan cats, not ghosts who hadn't found their way to StarClan like the ones Tree saw. But Bramblestar was *nearly* a StarClan cat; perhaps he *already* was a StarClan cat and just didn't know it. Whatever—Fidgetflake must have some useful advice.

He caught up to Fidgetflake as the black-and-white tom nosed his way into a patch of horsetail and began to reach up and snap the tips with his teeth. Rootpaw copied him, wincing as bitter sap bathed his tongue. He spat it out. "What's it like, talking to dead cats?" he asked, trying to sound casual. He had no intention of telling Fidgetflake about seeing Bramblestar's ghost. But the medicine cat might know the answers to

Bramblestar's questions. *Was* it possible to be dead and alive at the same time?

"Why do you ask?" Fidgetflake glanced at him as he snapped a fresh stem. He dropped it on the ground. "'Paws aren't usually interested in dead cats."

"I was just wondering." Rootpaw shrugged. "Do you see dead cats out here in the forest, like Tree does?"

"We only see StarClan cats," Fidgetflake explained. "They appear to us in visions. Tree sees cats who are left behind in the forest." He paused, tipping his head. "At least I think he does."

"So spirits wandering in the forest are never StarClan cats?" Rootpaw pressed. Couldn't Bramblestar get to StarClan? Was he stuck?

"StarClan cats usually stay in their own hunting grounds," Fidgetflake told him. "There's no reason to come back to the forest. They can share with us at the Moonpool."

So why had Bramblestar come back? Rootpaw's tail twitched uneasily. "If one did come back to the forest, would you speak to it?"

"Of course." Fidgetflake had stopped picking horsetail. He was staring at Rootpaw curiously.

Rootpaw reached up for another stem. He quickly snapped off the tip with his teeth and laid it with the others, avoiding Fidgetflake's eye.

"You're not thinking of becoming a medicine cat, are you?" Fidgetflake blinked at him.

"No," Rootpaw told him quickly. "I was just talking about

ghosts at the Gathering," he lied. "Some of the other apprentices were interested. One said they'd seen the ghost of a
Clan cat."

Fidgetflake pricked his ears. "When?"

"I don't know." Rootpaw's heart quickened. He didn't want
Fidgetflake asking too many questions. "Ages ago. He said . . .
he said he saw the ghost of a cat who was still alive."

Fidgetflake looked disappointed. "It sounds like he was
making it up. A living cat can't have a ghost."

Rootpaw's heart sank. "So it's impossible, right?"

"Totally."

Rootpaw frowned. He wasn't ready to give up entirely.
There was another question that had been nagging him since
Bramblestar's ghost had appeared. Why had the apparition
chosen him and not a cat from his own Clan? "Do you ever
speak to StarClan cats who aren't from SkyClan?"

"We do now that we live beside the lake," Fidgetflake told
him. "We had our own StarClan beside the gorge. But now we
see all our ancestors, and once a cat is in StarClan, they talk
to any cat they like."

"So it's okay for dead cats to speak to cats from other Clans."

"Of course."

Rootpaw felt a glimmer of relief. At least something about
this was normal.

Fidgetflake went on. "It doesn't matter which Clan a warrior comes from," he mewed. "Or if they come from StarClan
at all. If a dead cat has a message to pass on, we must listen to
it and do our best to honor their wishes."

*Am I supposed to honor Bramblestar's wishes?* Rootpaw shifted uneasily. He wasn't even sure what they were.

The horsetail shivered a few tail-lengths away. Rootpaw jerked his muzzle around to see what was moving there.

"Hey!" Tree pushed through the stems toward them. His paws were wet and water dripped from his belly. "I was seeing if it's possible to catch fish in the stream."

"Any luck?" Fidgetflake asked.

"No." Tree stopped as he reached them. "Fish are too slippery. I can't hold on to one even with my claws out. RiverClan must have burrs on their paws. I can't see how else they can catch them." He blinked at Rootpaw. "Where's Dewspring?"

"He's sprained a paw."

"No training today?" Tree's gaze rounded.

"No," Rootpaw told him. "I'm helping Frecklewish gather herbs instead."

"I thought your assessment was coming up." Tree looked worried.

"It is, but I'll be okay," Rootpaw reassured him.

"Come with me," Tree mewed cheerily. "I can teach you some of my hunting skills."

Rootpaw hesitated. His father's skills would be strange. "I'm not sure Dewspring wants me learning new skills somewhere else."

"Nonsense." Tree swished his tail. "You can't have too many skills." He glanced at the pile of horsetail stems Rootpaw had gathered. "If you can learn how to gather herbs, you can learn a few of my hunting tricks."

Rootpaw's tail drooped.

"Can I take him away?" Tree asked Fidgetflake.

"Of course." Fidgetflake dipped his head to Rootpaw. "Thanks for the help."

"No problem." Rootpaw followed his father as Tree led the way across the meadow to an alder grove. Perhaps it was better to leave the medicine cat in peace. If he asked any more questions, Fidgetflake might start to get suspicious.

Tree padded among the pale trunks and stopped. "Have I shown you how to be a bush?"

"'Be a bush'?" Rootpaw stared at his father. He loved him very much, but did he have to be weird about everything?

"If you're a bush, prey doesn't know you're there," Tree told him.

"But I'm a cat." Rootpaw blinked at him, confused.

"You can *pretend* to be a bush." Tree crouched and rolled, one way, then the other, until his fur was flecked with leaf litter. He got to his paws. "The first thing you have to do is smell like a bush." He nodded toward the patch he'd rolled in. "Try it."

Reluctantly, Rootpaw rolled in the leaf litter until he could feel his fur itching with it. He got to his paws, resisting the urge to shake his pelt out.

"We need to find a shady place where we can hide." Tree led Rootpaw between the trees until they reached a spot where a sprawling bramble spilled between the alders. He crouched beside it, hunching down in its shadow. "Now we just sit quietly until the prey comes," he whispered.

Rootpaw ducked and squeezed in beside him. "Wouldn't it be quicker to find a prey trail and track it?"

"Sometimes it's better to let prey come to you." Tree's litter-specked pelt brushed Rootpaw's as he shifted to get more comfortable. "Warriors insist on making everything harder than it should be."

Rootpaw bristled. Why did Tree have to criticize Clan cats all the time? "They just want to be the best warriors they can be. Is there something wrong with that?"

"Nothing." Tree purred. "But it's nice just to sit around with another cat while you're pretending to be a bush." He glanced at Rootpaw. "It's a good excuse to talk."

*Does he know something?* Rootpaw wondered, dread tingling in his belly. *Is that why Tree brought me here? To talk?* He glanced suspiciously at his father. "What about?"

"Leaving the Clans."

Alarm pricked in Rootpaw's pelt. "But . . . I'm about to become a warrior," he mewed. "I've been training for moons." Tree had talked about leaving the forest after the last Gathering when Bramblestar had suggested that cats should start accusing one another of crimes that could get them expelled. He'd been worried that it was the sort of rule Darktail would have made. Rootpaw had heard all about Darktail and the Kin and how they had taken over ShadowClan first, then the other Clans, and killed and starved any warrior who'd stood in their way. Tree had said that it would be safer to live as rogues than to live with Clans who behaved like rogues.

Tree gazed thoughtfully into the distance. "I'm not saying

we have to leave now. But this Gathering wasn't any better than the last one. I don't think Bramblestar is going to let go of this codebreaking issue any time soon. The Clans are changing, and I think that you, Needlepaw, Violetshine, and I need to be prepared to walk our own path if we have to."

Rootpaw frowned. Bramblestar's ghost would leave him alone if he left the Clan. That would be good. But was it worth becoming a rogue? "I think we should stick it out. Isn't that what being a warrior is all about?"

"Maybe, but I'm not sure staying would be good for any of us." Tree glanced at Rootpaw anxiously. "Why did you run away after the Gathering? It's not like you."

Rootpaw felt hot. "I saw something that startled me, that's all."

"What startled you?" Tree's gaze darkened.

"It doesn't matter." Rootpaw wished his father would stop questioning him. What could he say? That he'd seen a ghost? What if Tree was proud that he shared the same weirdness?

Tree shifted beside him. "If there's anything you're worried about, you can always talk to me," he mewed softly.

"I know." Rootpaw felt a flood of affection for his father. He wasn't like other Clan cats, but he never hid how much he loved Rootpaw, Needlepaw, and Violetshine. Rootpaw felt suddenly lucky to have him. He wished he could tell him about Bramblestar's ghost. But how would it help? His heart lurched as a pelt shimmered among the alders. He recognized the ghostly fur. Bramblestar had found him and was pacing between the trees a few tail-lengths away. *At least the ghost isn't trying to get my attention.* Rootpaw watched Bramblestar out of the corner of his eye as the ThunderClan leader paused and seemed to taste the air. *Perhaps my bush disguise worked,* he thought. *Perhaps it can't see me.* Disappointment pierced his chest as Bramblestar stiffened, his eyes brightening as he caught sight of Rootpaw. *Mouse dung!*

"Did you learn anything from Fidgetflake?" Bramblestar padded nearer and stared at Rootpaw eagerly. "Do you know who the other Bramblestar is yet?"

Rootpaw blinked back at the ghost helplessly. Did it really expect him to speak? *Are you blind? Tree's sitting right next to me!* Rootpaw stiffened as an idea flashed in his mind. Would Tree be able to see the apparition here? "Look," he mewed loudly, nudging Tree with a paw. A bird was hopping along the branch above Bramblestar's head. "Should we catch it?"

As Tree stared thoughtfully at the bird, Rootpaw willed him to notice the ghost standing underneath.

"It looks jumpy," Tree mewed. "It'll fly away the moment it sees us move."

Rootpaw's heart sank. His father still couldn't see Bramblestar's ghost. *Why not?* Frustration welled in his chest. *If you can see ghosts, why not this one?*

Tree got to his paws and shook the leaf litter from his pelt. He blinked at Rootpaw. "Would you think about leaving the Clans if things get worse?"

Rootpaw shrugged, feeling Bramblestar's gaze on his pelt. "I don't know. I want to be a warrior."

"Think about it," Tree told him. "I know it's complicated,

but with every Gathering, I can't help feeling more sure it would be for the best. I don't like where Bramblestar is leading the Clans. If he pushes this codebreaker talk much further, I think we ought to go."

Rootpaw saw Bramblestar's ghost shift uneasily. He wanted to tell his father everything. Tree might know a way to get rid of the apparition. He hesitated. But if Tree knew there were *two* Bramblestars causing trouble, would he insist on leaving straight away? Rootpaw couldn't risk it. He wasn't ready to give up his chance to become a SkyClan warrior. He would have to make this ghost go away by himself. He looked into his father's eyes. "It will work out," he mewed earnestly. "I know it will. The Clans won't let anything really bad happen."

Tree narrowed his gaze. "I hope so," he mewed darkly. "But I've seen more of life than you. Sometimes things don't work out the way we want." He brushed leaf litter from Rootpaw's pelt with his tail. "Are you coming back to camp?"

"I'll stay here and practice some hunting moves," Rootpaw told him. He was going to talk to the ghost. The time had come, and even if he couldn't answer its questions, he could find out what it wanted and, like Fidgetflake had told him, try to figure out a way to honor its wishes. He blinked at his father. "I want to be ready for my assessment."

"See you later." Tree touched his nose to Rootpaw's ear, his breath billowing in the chilly air, then headed between the trees.

The ghost turned its head to watch the yellow tom disappear, then slumped onto the ground. Resting its chin on its forepaws, it stared blankly at Rootpaw. "I don't know what's happening," it murmured. "But if warriors are thinking about leaving the Clans already, it can't be good."

Rootpaw stared at Bramblestar. Was he giving up? "You must have some idea what's going on."

Bramblestar started in surprise. This was the first time Rootpaw had addressed him. "I'm just as confused as you are," the ghost confessed.

Rootpaw frowned, thinking. "Perhaps you just need to go back to StarClan."

"I don't know how," Bramblestar told him. "I haven't seen a single StarClan cat since I died. I'm stuck in the forest."

"Why can't you go back to your body?"

"There's some other cat in it, or haven't you noticed?"

"Who?" Rootpaw began to pace.

"I don't know."

Rootpaw stared at the ghost cat. "Do you think I can do something about it?" he asked. "Because I can't. I'm not a medicine cat. I'm not even a warrior yet. I don't even know why you keep following me. There must be another cat who can help you."

"I've tried to find one," Bramblestar told him. "But you're the only cat who can see me."

Rootpaw sat down. "Why me?"

Bramblestar shrugged. "Perhaps you're the only one who can help me."

"But how?" Rootpaw huffed, exasperated. "There's nothing I can do."

Bramblestar sat up. "You have to get a message to Squirrelflight."

"*Me?*" Rootpaw cringed. Squirrelflight was ThunderClan deputy. Even if he could find his way through ThunderClan territory and speak to her, she wasn't going to listen to a SkyClan apprentice, especially if he tried to tell her that he had a message from Bramblestar's ghost. "How?"

Bramblestar stared at him, giving a sharp mew. "Find a way."

*If a dead cat has a message to pass on, we must listen to it and do our best to honor their wishes.* As he remembered Fidgetflake's words, a shiver raced along Rootpaw's spine. Bramblestar was asking the impossible.

He closed his eyes. *You want to be a warrior,* he told himself sternly. *Then do what Bramblestar says and find a way.*

# CHAPTER 8

*A cold wind swirled around the* hollow, and pigeon-gray clouds hung heavily above the camp. Bristlefrost fluffed her fur out to keep herself warm as she tugged a young bramble shoot that was creeping toward the elders' den. Prickles jabbed her paws, and she leaned down to bite through the young stem where it disappeared into the camp wall. She picked the stem up gingerly between her teeth and carried it to the pile she had made. Finleap and Stormcloud were clearing brambles farther along the wall.

Bristlefrost had organized the dawn patrols, but Squirrelflight had gone back to deciding the patrols for the rest of the day—without telling Bramblestar. So Bristlefrost was busying herself, along with her Clanmates, tidying the camp while she waited for the ThunderClan deputy to emerge from her den. Lionblaze and Spotfur were clearing dusty bedding and old leaves from the nursery while Daisy wove fresh bracken into the roof. Ivypool and Fernsong stripped withered strands of bracken from the walls of the warriors' den, and Thornclaw and Blossomfall looked for gaps that needed patching in the sides of the apprentices' den.

Pride warmed Bristlefrost's pelt. StarClan would be pleased to see ThunderClan working so hard. She wondered if they were watching.

"Bristlefrost!" Finleap called to her. He nodded to a thick bramble snaking past him. Stormcloud was already tugging it with his teeth. "Help us with this one."

Bristlefrost hurried to join them and grasped the stem carefully between her teeth.

"Pull!" Finleap grabbed it farther along, and together they tugged until, with a jerk, it came away from its root.

As it snapped, pain pierced Bristlefrost's lip. As Stormcloud dragged the stem to the pile, she sat up, licking blood where a thorn had spiked her. Finleap glanced up at the Highledge.

"Every cat's working except our leader," he muttered.

Bristlefrost glanced sharply at the brown tom. Was he criticizing Bramblestar?

Outside the elders' den, Jayfeather pricked his ears. The blind medicine cat was rubbing goldenrod pulp into Cloudtail's hind leg to ease an ache. "Perhaps he forgot he was a warrior when he died," he mewed sourly.

Cloudtail's eyes glittered nervously. "Careful what you say." He glanced toward Finleap. "Bramblestar hasn't been in the best of moods since he lost a life."

Across the clearing, Lionblaze snorted. "That's an understatement. I've never seen him act like this before. I hope he's okay."

"Of course he's okay." Stormcloud dropped the bramble

stem onto the pile. "Losing a life must be hard, that's all. We can't imagine what it's like."

Bristlefrost blinked gratefully at the gray tabby. "He just wants us to be the best warriors we can be." She looked at Finleap. "So StarClan will come back."

Finleap shrugged. "Bramblestar's always wanted us to be the best warriors we can be. He's just going about it in a funny way these days." He turned and began to tug another bramble stem.

Bristlefrost's pelt prickled uneasily. Surely Finleap shouldn't question his leader. StarClan had given Bramblestar nine lives. Wasn't arguing with him like arguing with StarClan? And since StarClan was still silent, shouldn't they listen to Bramblestar even more?

On the Highledge, ginger fur rippled at the entrance to Bramblestar's den. Lionblaze turned quickly back to his work as Squirrelflight padded out and leaped down the rock tumble. She stopped in the clearing and looked around the camp. "Good work, every cat." As her Clanmates turned to listen, she glanced at the empty fresh-kill pile. "I want two more patrols to go hunting, and another to check the SkyClan border."

"I'll go." Stormcloud hurried toward her.

"Me too." Ivypool padded from the warriors' den, Fernsong at her heels.

"I'd be happy to go," the yellow tom mewed eagerly.

Bristlefrost was pleased to see ThunderClan so keen to support Squirrelflight.

"Happy to go where?" Bramblestar slid out of his den.

Fernsong stiffened as the ThunderClan leader leaped from the Highledge and crossed to Squirrelflight's side.

"Hunting," Fernsong told him.

"Checking the border," Ivypool chimed. "Squirrelflight wants to send three more patrols out."

Bramblestar's eyes rounded as he looked at Squirrelflight. "Are you organizing patrols again?" He didn't wait for an answer. "I thought we were letting Bristlefrost deal with that."

Bristlefrost looked up, surprised. Did Bramblestar want her to organize *all* the patrols? She could if he wanted. As she padded forward to offer, Squirrelflight swished her tail. "Bristlefrost already has enough to do," she told Bramblestar.

"Then let some cat else organize it," Bramblestar mewed.

"It's my responsibility," Squirrelflight insisted.

"The Clan doesn't need you to fuss over it like a mother bird," Bramblestar told her. "A well-run Clan runs itself. Your duty is to support me, your leader." He gazed into her eyes. "And your mate."

Squirrelflight's pelt ruffled along her spine. "I can't spend every moment cooped up in our den like an elder."

"What's the point in being leader and deputy if we have to spend every moment organizing patrols?" Bramblestar's ears twitched.

Squirrelflight's gaze hardened. "Our Clan is part of us," she snapped. "And we're part of it. Organizing patrols is the least we should do."

Bristlefrost's chest tightened as she saw fury flash in Bramblestar's eyes. It was not so long ago that he and

Squirrelflight had had serious disagreements over how to deal with the Sisters, a group of she-cats who'd settled in unclaimed territory that she was scouting as a possible new home for SkyClan. The whole Clan had been worried that their leader and deputy would never recover.

But now Bramblestar's fury vanished as quickly as it had come, and he dipped his head politely. "I know you worry about our Clanmates," he mewed smoothly. "But you should have more faith in them. And you really shouldn't wear yourself out unnecessarily. You went out on two patrols yesterday, and one the day before that. From now on, I want you to stay in camp with me. Leave patrolling to your Clanmates."

Squirrelflight bristled. "But I *like* going on patrol. Being a warrior isn't a chore; it's an honor. I enjoy it." She looked at him as though for a moment she didn't recognize him. "You used to feel the same way."

"I haven't changed," he told her. "But I know now that there are more important things in life than patrolling."

"The less we do," Squirrelflight told him, "the more our Clanmates have to do."

"So?" Bramblestar looked puzzled. "If being a warrior is an honor, let them enjoy it. From now on, spend more time in camp with me."

Squirrelflight stared at him wordlessly, her tail twitching.

Bramblestar shrugged. "You'd better get used to it."

As Bramblestar turned away, the camp entrance rattled. Berrynose and Poppyfrost led Cinderheart, Finchpaw, and Rosepetal into camp. Each warrior held prey in their jaws.

They carried it to the empty fresh-kill pile and laid it down.

Cloudtail's eyes lit up eagerly. "At last," he mewed. "I'm starving." He began to get to his paws.

Bramblestar narrowed his eyes. "Wait." He nodded toward the elder.

Bristlefrost pricked her ears. Bramblestar was looking thoughtful. Did he have an idea?

"Elders must wait for their prey." Bramblestar swung his gaze around the Clan.

Lionblaze frowned, looking puzzled. Thornclaw, who had just dropped a fat thrush on the pile, looked up, his fur prickling uneasily. Around the clearing, the Clan cats exchanged glances.

"Why should the elders wait?" Blossomfall stepped forward, looking from Bramblestar to Cloudtail and back. "The code says that queens and elders must eat before warriors, as a show of respect."

"Before warriors, maybe." Bramblestar gazed steadily at the she-cat. "But it says nothing about leaders."

Bristlefrost saw Lionblaze's claws curl into the ground.

"Are you saying that *you* should eat before elders and queens?" The golden warrior looked directly at Bramblestar, a challenge in his eyes.

Bramblestar stared back. "Not just me," he mewed. "The deputy too." He moved closer to Squirrelflight, who seemed to flinch.

Her gaze flitted uncertainly around her Clanmates. "Bramblestar. I don't—"

Bramblestar didn't let her finish. "What good is it to give the best prey to our weakest Clanmates?" His gaze was still fixed on Lionblaze. "If we're under attack, will our elders protect the Clan?"

Thornclaw stared at the ThunderClan leader as though he couldn't believe his ears. Lionblaze's eyes narrowed ominously as Bramblestar went on.

"*They* will be the ones who need help, and who will help them? Warriors. And who will lead them against whatever hardship or enemy we might face?" He looked around, as though challenging his Clanmates to answer.

No cat spoke. Bristlefrost shifted her paws awkwardly. Did Bramblestar think trouble was coming? Did he know something they didn't? He must be trying to prepare the Clan for something. She lifted her muzzle. "You will lead us through any hardship, Bramblestar," she ventured nervously.

"Precisely!" His gaze fixed on her eagerly. "Squirrelflight and I must be stronger than you all because we are the ones who will guide you through whatever hardship might face us. So we should eat first."

"But we've always shown respect to the elders and queens," Lionblaze objected.

"There are other ways to show respect." Bramblestar blinked at the golden warrior. "Would you break the code by defying me?"

"Aren't you breaking the code by eating before the elders?" Lionblaze pressed.

Bramblestar held his gaze. "I am your leader." His growl

was so soft that Bristlefrost could barely hear. "I decide what the code is."

Her Clanmates stared at Bramblestar, their gazes clouded with uncertainty. Lionblaze's tail flicked harder but he didn't speak as Bramblestar padded to the fresh-kill pile and lifted the fat thrush from the top. He carried it back to Squirrelflight and nudged her toward the rock tumble. She followed him onto the Highledge as Bramblestar took the thrush into their den, but she glanced uneasily back at her Clanmates before disappearing inside.

Lionblaze picked two shrews from the fresh-kill pile and carried them to the elders' den. Cloudtail nodded his thanks as the golden warrior dropped them at his paws, his gaze flitting toward the Highledge. Neither tom spoke, but Bristlefrost could see from their ruffled fur that they were troubled.

In the clearing, Stormcloud and Fernsong glanced at each other.

"Should we go hunting?" Fernsong wondered.

Stormcloud shrugged.

Bristlefrost suddenly realized that Squirrelflight hadn't finished organizing the afternoon's hunting patrol. *Am I supposed to do it now?* Fernsong was looking at her expectantly. "I'll check with Squirrelflight." She scrambled up the rock tumble. Perhaps she should organize *three* hunting patrols. If there was plenty of prey in camp, the Clan might not worry about the new rule. Eating before the elders and queens sounded like a strange decision, but Bramblestar must know what he was doing. He was Clan leader. Perhaps he was just testing his

Clanmates' willingness to follow the warrior code.

On the Highledge, she padded to the den entrance, hesitating as she heard a hiss from inside.

"Do you really think this is the best way to run a Clan?" Squirrelflight sounded angry. "After the leaf-bare we've had, do you think you'll improve morale by pushing cats around and stealing the best prey for yourself?"

Bramblestar's reply was silky, but she couldn't make out the words. She backed away. She didn't need to talk to Squirrelflight right now. She could organize the patrols herself and report back later. Squirrelflight would probably thank her for taking the initiative.

As she slithered down the slope, stones cracking beneath her paws, a chill ran along Bristlefrost's spine. If Squirrelflight didn't agree with Bramblestar's prey rule, would any cat? At the bottom, she shook out her fur.

Fernsong looked at her expectantly. "What did she say?"

"She was busy," Bristlefrost told him. "You might as well go hunting. I'm sure that's what she wanted."

Stormcloud blinked at Bristlefrost. "Do you want to come with us?"

"I want to organize some more patrols," she told him. She also wanted to stay close to camp. Something was different about Bramblestar, and it was starting to make her uneasy. If she stayed close, she might find out what it was. Losing a life had changed him. Was something wrong?

She pushed the thought away. *Of course not.* He was still Bramblestar. So what if he was sterner now? He was just trying to make sure his warriors obeyed the code so that StarClan would come back. He wanted the best for his Clan, and that was enough. Flicking her tail, Bristlefrost padded to the camp wall and began to tug another stray bramble. She was sure everything would work out.

Bristlefrost shivered as rain pierced her pelt. Yesterday's clouds had brought a storm. It had begun in the night and was still falling as she followed Lionblaze and Spotfur toward the edge of the forest.

"Let's patrol the SkyClan border first," she called to the golden warrior as he followed a stale prey trail. "It's more sheltered beneath the trees."

"She has a point." Spotfur eyed Lionblaze hopefully. "It might stop raining. Then we could check the WindClan border without getting drenched."

Lionblaze glanced up at the canopy, where rain was dripping steadily between the branches. "We're going to get drenched anyway," he mewed. "We might as well check the scent line before it's completely washed away."

Bristlefrost flattened her ears, bracing herself for a soaking as Lionblaze broke from the trees ahead of her. She followed him out, narrowing her eyes against the rain. As Spotfur fluffed out her fur and moved closer to Lionblaze, Bristlefrost pricked her ears. She'd hung back all the way from the camp, wondering if the two warriors would mention Bramblestar's new rule. She'd been aware of murmuring among her

Clanmates last night as they'd shared tongues around the clearing, but she hadn't heard any cat directly criticize their leader. They'd seemed more puzzled than angry, glancing occasionally at the Highledge as though wondering why Bramblestar had changed a long-standing Clan tradition.

"It's good to see rain instead of snow," Spotfur mewed.

"I think I prefer snow." Lionblaze flicked water from his ears.

"At least there's warmth in the air," Spotfur argued.

"Not much." Lionblaze crossed the grass that stretched toward the moor. "But the prey's returning, which is worth a little rain."

"Thank StarClan." Spotfur glanced at the sky.

"You're wasting your breath," Lionblaze grunted. "We don't even know that they're listening anymore."

Spotfur blinked at him. "Of course they are. The thaw has set in properly now. There's no reason why they can't."

"It might take a while for them to reach us again."

Worry wormed beneath Bristlefrost's pelt. "Perhaps they're waiting for us to follow the warrior code properly."

Lionblaze glanced back at her sharply. "We've always followed the warrior code." He hesitated. "At least, some of us have."

Bristlefrost frowned. Was he thinking of any cat in particular?

"I can smell rabbit." Spotfur stopped and lifted her muzzle.

Lionblaze tasted the air. His wet pelt spiked excitedly.

"So can I." Pricking his ears, he glanced across the stretch of heather that led to the WindClan border. Gray fur bobbed between two bushes.

Bristlefrost's heart quickened. *Rabbit!* She licked her lips eagerly and dropped into a hunting crouch as Spotfur and Lionblaze began to stalk toward their quarry. She crept after them, keeping her belly close to the ground. Her pelt tingled with excitement as the rabbit shot suddenly from the heather and Lionblaze chased after it. It saw him and veered away, panic sparking in its round black eyes. Plunging back into the heather, it disappeared. Lionblaze wove between the bushes, Spotfur at his heels.

Bristlefrost straightened, alarm flashing in her belly as she saw the heather tremble. Lionblaze and Spotfur were heading straight toward the border.

"Watch out!" she yowled. They mustn't catch the rabbit on WindClan land! She froze as she saw the two warriors break from the heather and chase the rabbit past the line of gorse that marked the border. Lionblaze drove the rabbit down a few tail-lengths beyond it. He killed it and she saw him raise his muzzle to mew a quick thanks to StarClan before picking it up and carrying back onto ThunderClan territory.

Bristlefrost raced to meet them, dread hollowing her belly. "You caught that on WindClan land!" She stopped as she reached them and stared at Lionblaze. Catching prey on another Clan's territory was against the warrior code. She searched his gaze, expecting to see alarm there. What if StarClan *was* watching? They'd never come back at this rate.

Lionblaze dropped the rabbit onto the grass, looking around. When his eyes widened, Bristlefrost knew he had realized where they were. "We couldn't help it," he mewed, sounding as if he was speaking to himself. *Convincing* himself.

Spotfur stopped beside him and sniffed the rabbit. She nodded in agreement. "It was only on WindClan land because we chased it there."

"But you've broken the code." Bristlefrost could hardly believe her ears. Didn't they care if StarClan never came back?

"It doesn't hurt any cat," Lionblaze told her. "And in this rain, WindClan will never know we crossed the border."

"StarClan will know," Bristlefrost mewed desperately.

"StarClan would never be angry at a warrior for feeding his Clan." Lionblaze nudged the rabbit. "This will make a good meal for Graystripe, Cloudtail, and Brightheart."

Lionblaze picked up the rabbit and headed along the scent line.

"Are we going to mark the border?" Bristlefrost blinked at Spotfur.

"Of course." Spotfur padded to a gorse bush and rubbed her jaw along a spiny branch. "But I doubt our scent will stay for long in this rain."

Pelt prickling uneasily, Bristlefrost marked the next bush. Neither warrior seemed to care that they'd broken the warrior code. And she couldn't help feeling that marking a border right after they'd crossed it might make StarClan even angrier.

\* \* \*

The rain had eased by the time they reached camp. Bristlefrost's paws ached from the long trek around the borders.

"Bristlefrost."

She looked up as Bramblestar called her from the Highledge. He beckoned her to join him. She felt the gazes of her Clanmates on her pelt as she climbed the rock tumble and followed him into his den. Squirrelflight wasn't there, though her scent still lingered in the warm, dank air. Had she gone on patrol despite Bramblestar telling her she couldn't?

Bramblestar sat down and dipped his head. "Did you check all the borders?"

"Yes." Bristlefrost felt nervous. She hadn't been alone with Bramblestar before. She shifted her paws self-consciously, hoping her pelt wasn't too spiky from the rain. She wanted to shake it out, but she was scared of soaking Bramblestar. Raindrops dripped onto the sandy stone around her. "SkyClan renewed their marks quite recently, although it was hard to tell in the rain. But it seemed like—"

"I'm sure the other Clans are taking good care of their borders." Bramblestar's gaze bored into hers. "How were Lionblaze and Spotfur?"

Bristlefrost stiffened. Had he found out that they'd crossed the border? She dropped her gaze. "They were okay."

"Did they say anything about the new prey rule?" His mew was smooth but firm.

"Nothing." She met his gaze again, relieved that she could answer with the truth.

"And the rest of the Clan?"

Bristlefrost's ears twitched. "I've haven't heard anything," she told him honestly. "But I get the feeling they find it confusing."

"Confusing?" Bramblestar tipped his head to one side. "I thought I'd made it clear."

"You did," she told him quickly. "They're just confused about why you made a new prey rule."

"Has some cat said something?"

"No," Bristlefrost told him. "It's just a feeling I have."

Bramblestar's eyes brightened. "Good." He sounded relieved. "So nothing's happened to upset StarClan." His statement was a question.

"I don't think so." Bristlefrost hesitated. "Except . . ."

Bramblestar narrowed his eyes. "What?" He leaned closer.

Bristlefrost met his gaze uncertainly. She didn't want to tell on any cat, but Lionblaze and Spotfur *had* crossed the border. StarClan would be angry, maybe even angrier if she kept it a secret from her leader.

"You can tell me anything," he mewed softly. "Remember, you're helping me keep the Clan safe. I need to know if anything's happened so I can protect it."

Bristlefrost took a breath. "Lionblaze and Spotfur accidently crossed the WindClan border while they were hunting."

Bramblestar didn't move. His gaze lingered on her until she felt her pelt burning.

"Only a little way," she mewed quickly. "They didn't realize until I told them."

Bramblestar leaned back, his fur smoothing around his

shoulders. He looked relieved that she'd told him. Happiness flickered in her chest. She'd done the right thing. He could fix it now and StarClan wouldn't have to be angry. She wasn't sure how he could fix it, but he was leader. He'd find a way.

Suddenly a shadow seemed to fall across Bramblestar's face as his gaze darkened. Bristlefrost flinched as he bared his teeth for a moment. Then he stood and brushed past her, striding out of the den.

She hurried after him, alarm sparking beneath her pelt. What was he going to do? Outside, on the Highledge, Bramblestar yowled across the camp. "Lionblaze! Spotfur!"

He leaped down the stone tumble as Lionblaze and Spotfur looked up. Their eyes glittered with curiosity as they met him at the bottom. Bristlefrost stopped a tail-length away. Fear tightened her chest. Were they in trouble?

"Is it true?" Bramblestar glared at Lionblaze.

"True?" The golden warrior looked puzzled.

Bramblestar's gaze flicked toward Spotfur. "Did you cross the border into WindClan territory?"

Spotfur and Lionblaze glanced past Bramblestar. Bristlefrost felt their gazes as sharp as thorns as they saw her. It was obvious that she'd told Bramblestar what they'd done. She shrank beneath her pelt, wishing Bramblestar hadn't accused them so directly.

Around the clearing, the other ThunderClan warriors were gathering, their pelts prickling nervously. Stemleaf stared at Spotfur in dismay. Cinderheart and Fernsong moved closer, exchanging nervous glances.

Bramblestar curled his claws into the earth. "Well, did you?"

Lionblaze lifted his chin. "We did, but it was an accident and no cat saw us. WindClan won't ever know."

"Oh, *really?*" Bramblestar curled his lip. "You're sure of that, are you? Did you lick your scent off the grass?"

Lionblaze stared at him. "It was raining!"

Spotfur nodded. "If it hadn't been, we'd have smelled the border. We probably would never have crossed it."

"So what are you saying?" Bramblestar's eyes flashed with rage. "That WindClan didn't mark their border strongly enough?"

Lionblaze gave a frustrated huff. "That's not what we—"

"If Harestar comes here," Bramblestar hissed, cutting him off, "and accuses us of invading his land, is *that* what you're going to tell him? That you wouldn't have done it if he kept his borders better marked?"

Lionblaze's pelt ruffled. "Harestar isn't going to accuse us of anything," he snapped. "Warriors have crossed borders by accident before. It happens. We all know that." He glanced around at his Clanmates. They returned his gaze blankly, as though they didn't want to take sides.

Bramblestar narrowed his eyes. "You know StarClan has been silent these past moons. We're supposed to be following the warrior code so that they'll come back. How do you think they'll feel about warriors crossing borders without permission? Do you think they'll come back if we can't even obey such a simple rule?"

"StarClan isn't going to abandon us just because I crossed

the WindClan border." Lionblaze growled.

"Did they tell you that?" Bramblestar mewed sarcastically. "Are you our new link with StarClan?"

"Of course not." Exasperation glittered in Lionblaze's eyes.

Bramblestar flattened his ears. "Then don't tell me what StarClan is thinking. You broke the code even though I've told you it must be followed."

Spotfur bristled. "Every cat here has broken the code at some point." She glared angrily at Bramblestar. "Some of us worse than others."

"What's that supposed to mean?" Bramblestar flexed his claws.

"I mean that Squirrelflight once lied to every cat, pretending her sister's kits—her sister the *medicine cat's* kits—were hers. She lied on purpose and she lied for moons. If you can overlook that, then you can overlook us crossing a border without realizing."

Bramblestar stared at the spotted tabby she-cat. His hackles lifted menacingly. Bristlefrost swallowed back fear. Was the ThunderClan leader going to attack one of his own warriors? As she held her breath, Bramblestar shifted his paws. His pelt smoothed as he seemed to regain control of his temper.

"Don't concern yourself with Squirrelflight," he meowed coldly. "As deputy, she's served her Clan selflessly. I'm Clan leader and I decide who deserves punishment. Unless you think being granted nine lives by StarClan doesn't mean anything?"

Spotfur dropped her gaze. She looked defeated. Lionblaze moved closer to her, as if to protect her from Bramblestar's rage. Bristlefrost glanced at her Clanmates. Graystripe had padded from the elders' den and was staring at Bramblestar as though he barely knew him. Thornclaw watched with interest, his gaze dark. As Bramblestar stared at Spotfur, the camp was so silent that Bristlefrost wondered if the birds had stopped singing. Then she realized that her heart was pounding so loudly in her ears that she could barely hear anything.

"For the next quarter moon," Bramblestar began, "no cat is to talk to Spotfur."

Spotfur lifted her head sharply and stared at the Thunder-Clan leader. Bristlefrost felt cold. Was this a normal way to punish Clanmates? She glanced at Graystripe. He'd know, surely. But the old warrior looked as surprised as she felt.

Bramblestar's gaze moved to Lionblaze. "*You* are banished from the camp for a quarter moon."

Cinderheart stepped forward. "You can't do that. . . ." She stared at Bramblestar. "He's a ThunderClan warrior. We protect each other!"

Bramblestar looked coolly at Lionblaze's mate. "He has broken the warrior code, and questioned me for trying to uphold it. I will not let any cat undermine me or my Clan like that." He returned his gaze to Lionblaze, who was staring at him in amazement. "You're a seasoned warrior. You should know better."

Lionblaze's gaze cleared. He blinked in disbelief but didn't speak.

Bramblestar curled his lip. "Surely you can stand living like a rogue for a quarter moon?"

Lionblaze didn't answer. Bristlefrost felt sick. She'd caused this. Would Lionblaze ever forgive her?

Bramblestar went on. "If your scent is caught on Clan land—*any* Clan land—you will be treated like an invader and you won't *ever* be allowed to return."

Lionblaze squared his shoulders. He looked around at his Clanmates, his gaze furious. Then he walked to the entrance and padded out of camp.

Bristlefrost's paws trembled. *I was only trying to help.* Her belly was hard with dread. She backed toward the shelter of the Highledge. *Oh, StarClan! What have I done?*

Bristlefrost blinked open her eyes. The ground beneath her was damp. The sky had cleared, and stars glittered above her head. Night had swallowed the camp while she'd slept. She'd tried to escape her misery in sleep after Lionblaze had left. As she remembered with a jolt what had happened earlier that day, guilt seared her pelt once more. She lifted her head and gazed around the camp. Her Clanmates were sharing their evening meal, no more than shadows around the clearing, their mews hushed. Bramblestar was nowhere to be seen, and she guessed he was in his den with Squirrelflight.

She pricked her ears as two shapes shifted behind the nursery. Their pelts gleamed in the moonlight as they sat a mouse-length away from each other. She recognized them at once. *Stemleaf and Spotfur.* Bristlefrost stiffened and sat up slowly, keeping her head low. She didn't want to be noticed. Stemleaf and Spotfur were clearly hiding from their Clanmates. Their mouths were moving. Were they talking to each other? Had Stemleaf forgotten that no cat was supposed to speak to Spotfur for a quarter moon? Her heart quickened. What if Bramblestar found out? Would he banish Spotfur as he'd banished Lionblaze? She pricked her ears, her heart sinking when she heard their hushed whispers. After getting to her paws, she moved softly through the shadows, skirting the edge of the camp.

"You can't do this!" she breathed.

Stemleaf swung his muzzle toward her. "Haven't you caused enough trouble?"

"Are you going to report us to Bramblestar?" Spotfur's eyes flashed angrily.

"No!" Did they really think she wanted to see them in trouble? "But what if some other cat sees you or hears you?" Bristlefrost's belly churned with anxiety. Did they think rules didn't apply to them? No wonder StarClan had turned their tails on the living cats. "You're not supposed to be talking."

"Do you think that's fair?" Stemleaf stared at her defiantly.

"It doesn't matter whether it's fair or not," Bristlefrost whispered urgently. "Bramblestar gave an order. You're breaking the warrior code if you ignore it."

Spotfur's ears flattened. "But his orders are dumb!"

"Don't say that!" Bristlefrost's pelt spiked. "He's our leader."

"He hasn't been much of a leader since he lost a life," Stemleaf growled under his breath.

"It was his first life," Bristlefrost reminded him. "He's just getting used to it, and while he does, we just need to follow orders."

"Even if they're wrong?" Stemleaf flexed his claws in frustration.

"How will StarClan come back if we keep breaking the code?" Bristlefrost stared at him. Why didn't he understand?

Spotfur snorted. "Do you really think they'll come back if no cat talks to me for a quarter moon?"

"Not just that," Bristlefrost argued. "It's lots of things. I never realized how much we break the code without thinking. Every cat has to obey orders."

Stemleaf narrowed his eyes. "And you're going to make sure that we do?" he mewed bitterly.

"I'm just trying to stop you from getting into trouble like Spotfur," Bristlefrost breathed. "You don't want Bramblestar to stop your Clanmates from talking to you too."

Stemleaf stared at her, his eyes glittering with starlight. "You don't get it, do you? There's more at stake here than whether we're allowed to talk to each other. Something is very wrong." He stretched his muzzle closer. "I always thought you were a good cat. Soon we're going to have to make choices. I just hope you'll be ready to make the right ones." He stalked away.

Spotfur blinked at her, her eyes glistening with anger, then slid past her and headed toward the clearing.

Alone in the dark, Bristlefrost glanced around the camp. No cat paid any attention to Spotfur as she settled outside the warriors' den and Stemleaf sat down between Dewnose and Bumblestripe. A dark sense of foreboding seemed to enfold her as Stemleaf's words rang in her head. *Soon we're going to have to make choices.*

She shivered. What in StarClan did he mean?

# CHAPTER 9

Early morning light seeped through the medicine-den entrance as
Shadowsight crept from his nest and crossed to Antfur's. He
hoped that Antfur would be his old self today. For three days,
Shadowsight had padded to the injured cat's nest in the medicine den and checked his eyes for cloudiness and asked him
questions, hoping that he'd recovered enough to answer them
sensibly. But each time Antfur had been confused, unsure
where he was and answering questions as though he were still
a guardian cat in the city.

Shadowsight's heart seemed to beat too loudly in the quiet
dawn. Snowbird was curled in her nest, eyes closed. At least
the pain in her broken paw had eased enough for her to sleep
through the night, and the swelling in Stonewing's tail had
gone down enough to reassure Shadowsight that he wouldn't
lose the tip. Their Clanmates were healing quickly. Shadowsight couldn't help feeling that he and Puddleshine had done
well. Scorchfur's bruising was still tender, but Puddleshine
had sent him back to his nest in the warriors' den when he'd
complained that the smell of herbs was making him queasy.
"If he's well enough to complain," Puddleshine had said, "he's

well enough to sleep in his own nest." Perhaps ShadowClan hadn't been cursed with bad luck after all.

And yet, as Shadowsight stopped beside the warrior's nest, doubt tugged at his belly. *Please let Antfur be better today.* He wondered if it was any use appealing to StarClan. He still wasn't sure they hadn't *caused* all this. Shadowsight leaned into the nest.

"Antfur?" He nudged the sleeping cat with a paw.

Antfur lifted his head, blinking in the half-light. He looked at Shadowsight, puzzled. "Is that you, Mittens?"

Shadowsight's heart sank. "It's me, Shadowsight."

Puddleshine's nest rustled at the back of the den as the medicine cat climbed out of it. "Why did you wake him?" Puddleshine breathed softly as he crossed the den toward Shadowsight.

"I wanted to see how he was," Shadowsight murmured.

"Any better?" Puddleshine stopped beside him and looked at Antfur hopefully.

"He's still confused," Shadowsight told him.

"He just woke up." Puddleshine peered into Antfur's eyes. "He's bound to be confused."

Antfur blinked at him. "What's happened? Is something wrong?" His gaze flicked toward the pale light at the den entrance. "Am I supposed to be on patrol?"

"No," Puddleshine told the warrior. "You're supposed to be resting. We're just checking on you." He sat back on his haunches and looked at Shadowsight. "His eyes seem clearer."

"Do they?" Shadowsight was blocking the light from the

entrance. He moved until pale sunlight fell past him and glistened in Antfur's amber gaze. Hope flickered in Shadowsight's chest. Puddleshine was right; the haziness that had shrouded his eyes since the branch hit him had cleared.

Antfur blinked at them. "Why are you both staring at me?"

"Do you know who I am?" Puddleshine asked him.

"Of course." Antfur stared at him as though he'd asked if birds could fly. "You're Puddleshine."

*He recognizes us.* Shadowsight's paws tingled eagerly. "Do you know why you're in the medicine den?"

"I got hit by a branch," Antfur told him.

"Who was with you?" Shadowsight pressed.

Antfur stood up and shook out his fur. "Dovewing, Scorchfur, and Stonewing."

Shadowsight glanced at Puddleshine. Relief washed over his pelt. He'd been a bit confused when he first woke, but now Antfur seemed to be as sharp as he'd been before the accident.

Puddleshine puffed out his chest. "It's good to see you feeling better," he told Antfur happily.

Antfur pricked his ears. "Can I get back to my warrior duties now?"

"Maybe," Puddleshine told him.

Shadowsight looked at his old mentor. "Are you sure? This is only the first time he's seemed to know what's going on. He called me Mittens earlier."

"He'd just woken up."

"Don't you think we should watch him for a day or two to make sure he's okay?"

"If he feels well enough . . ." Puddleshine's mew trailed away as Antfur hopped out of his nest.

"I might have been confused before, but I'm fine now. I haven't broken anything," the warrior told him. "And my bruises are feeling a lot better."

The den entrance shivered. Tigerstar padded in, his gaze flitting toward Snowbird's nest first as the white she-cat lifted her head. Her eyes were bleary with sleep.

"How's the paw?" Tigerstar padded toward her.

"Only a little better." Snowbird lifted it with a grimace. It was still swathed in comfrey and held stiff by four smooth, straight sticks.

"Keep resting it," Tigerstar told her brightly. "You'll be hunting again in no time." He crossed the den and stopped beside Puddleshine, his tail high. Shadowsight wondered if his father really felt as cheerful as he was acting. Perhaps he was just trying to keep his wounded warriors' spirits high. "And how are you?" Tigerstar looked at Antfur.

"Ready for patrol," the tom told him, standing up straight.

"Patrol?" Tigerstar looked surprised. "Already?"

"I think he should rest for a couple of days," Shadowsight mewed.

Puddleshine tipped his head thoughtfully. "But going on normal patrols again could be good for him."

Shadowsight saw Antfur's muscular legs begin to quiver. The brown-and-black tom grimaced a little. Shadowsight darted toward him, pressing his flank against Antfur's to steady him as he began to sway. "Are you dizzy?"

"A little," Antfur confessed. "But that's okay. I should get back to my warrior duties."

"You need to rest." Shadowsight was supporting most of the warrior's weight as he leaned against him. Antfur seemed hardly able stand on his own four paws. How could he be ready for patrols?

Antfur pulled away from him. "I've already rested for three days," he pointed out.

Tigerstar swished his tail. "He just needs some exercise. A warrior's place is out there, in the forest."

"Besides, Mittens was going to show me a shrew nest," Antfur meowed eagerly.

"*Mittens?*" Tigerstar frowned.

Antfur frowned, clearly realizing he'd said the wrong name. He tried to correct himself. "I mean Blaze."

Shadowsight's paws pricked anxiously. "You mean Blaze-*fire*, right?" Had he forgotten his friend's warrior name?

"Of course." Antfur lifted his chin.

Tigerstar's gaze darkened. "Perhaps you should stay in the medicine den for another day or two."

Antfur's eyes widened indignantly. "I don't want to be treated like a kit, or an elder. I joined ShadowClan so I could be a warrior. I'm perfectly okay. I should be taking care of my Clanmates. They shouldn't be taking care of me."

Tigerstar caught Shadowsight's eye. "What do you think?"

"I'd like to keep an eye on him."

"Puddleshine?" Tigerstar looked at the other medicine cat.

"Shadowsight is right. Another day in the medicine den

might be best," Puddleshine mewed.

"No!" Antfur's pelt bristled. "I'm as fit as a hare." He padded around the den, swishing his tail. "I'm perfectly capable of hunting." He stared at Tigerstar.

"But what if you get dizzy again while you're out of camp?" Shadowsight felt unconvinced.

"I won't be on my own," Antfur told him. "I'll have a patrol with me, and my Clanmates won't let anything happen."

Shadowsight still wasn't sure. As long as he was keeping the secret of the codebreaker vision, he couldn't let any cat take risks. If StarClan really had let Antfur get hurt to send him a message, they might decide to send another. "He should stay here."

Tigerstar frowned thoughtfully. "But Antfur has a point," he murmured. "He won't be on his own."

Puddleshine nodded. He padded around Antfur, sniffing his pelt. "There's no swelling or stiffness. If he gets dizzy, he can rest until it passes."

"What if he gets confused again?" Shadowsight stared at Puddleshine.

"He'll be with his Clanmates." Puddleshine looked decided. "They'll help him."

Antfur shifted his paws impatiently. "Can I go?" he asked Tigerstar. "The dawn hunting patrol will be heading out soon."

Tigerstar nodded. "Okay, but take it easy."

"Of course I will." Antfur ducked out of the den.

Shadowsight watched him go. Would StarClan watch over

him? Or would Antfur be in danger until Shadowsight shared the codebreaking vision with the Clans? *I hear you, okay?* He glanced upward, anger welling in his chest. *I'm just trying to do what's best.*

As Tigerstar left the den and Puddleshine fetched herbs from the store for Snowbird, Shadowsight gazed into the pale dawn light. Perhaps the run of bad luck had nothing to do with StarClan. Antfur would be fine. Fresh air and company would make him better, wouldn't it? He tried to push his nagging doubt away. *StarClan, I know what you're trying to tell me!* Worry itched beneath his pelt. *Please protect Antfur.*

The morning passed slowly. Shadowsight made poultices for his Clanmates' injuries: oak leaf and goldenrod for Stonewing's tail, nettle for Scorchfur's bruises, and marigold for Dovewing's ear. He kept his ears pricked, listening for Antfur's return. The small brown-and-black tom was probably having fun, relieved to escape the gloom of the medicine den and feeling like his old self again.

As Shadowsight crossed the clearing, his paws still green with the nettle juice he'd smeared on Scorchfur's injuries, paw steps sounded at the entrance. A patrol was returning.

Whorlpelt and Flowerstem looked up from the mouse they were sharing. Flowerstem's nose twitched nervously as she tasted the air. Outside the apprentices' den, Cinnamontail dropped the brambles she'd been threading into the wall. She looked toward the entrance, her pelt ruffling along her spine.

Shadowsight followed her gaze nervously. What had put his

Clanmates on edge? Through the thrumming of paw steps, he could hear fur brushing the forest floor, as though the patrol had caught a large rabbit and was dragging it back to share with their Clanmates. The entrance shivered as Snaketooth padded in. Shadowsight's breath caught in his throat as he saw grief in the tabby she-cat's gaze. Blazefire and Gullswoop followed her. They were hauling something behind them, their claws hooked into dark brown fur.

Shadowsight froze. Horror swamped him like ice water as he recognized the body they'd brought back. It wasn't a rabbit. It was Antfur, and the warrior was clearly dead. He swallowed back nausea as Blazefire pulled his Clanmate's body into the clearing and let it drop to the ground.

Cinnamontail raced from the apprentices' den, her eyes wide with shock. "What happened?" She crouched beside Antfur and stared at Blazefire.

"We told him to say close." The white-and-ginger tom sounded numb. "But he chased a squirrel up a tree. I followed him, but he was too fast. He'd cornered it at the top before I reached him, and he got dizzy." Blazefire's mew broke. "He fell."

"There was nothing we could do." Gullswoop stared bleakly at Antfur's body.

Cinnamontail stared at her dead friend. Like Blazefire, she'd shared a den with the tom when they'd lived in the city, before they joined the Clan. They'd known each other since kithood. Her eyes glistened with grief. "He was injured so recently. He should never have gone out."

"He wanted to hunt with his Clan," Blazefire mumbled.

"He wanted to be a warrior the moment he knew what one was," Cinnamontail wailed. "He was always first to spot prey and first to chase it. He wanted to help make his Clan as strong and healthy as it could be. And in the end, it killed him."

Dovewing padded from her den. When she saw Antfur's body and heard Cinnamontail's sob, she limped across the clearing. Pressing her cheek to Cinnamontail's, she looked at Shadowsight. He stiffened. Could she see his guilt? It was searing his belly like fire. *I should have made Tigerstar keep him in camp!* He dropped his gaze. Would it have changed anything? Antfur had only been hurt in the first place because StarClan was trying to send Shadowsight a message. His death proved it. This couldn't just be a run of bad luck. Shadowsight's paws felt as heavy as stone. *It was a message from StarClan.* And he knew, with a sense of dread that made the ground seem to shift beneath his paws, that the injuries and deaths would keep happening until he stopped them. He glanced guilty toward Tigerstar's den. No matter what his father had said, he couldn't risk keeping the secret anymore. He had to warn the other medicine cats.

# CHAPTER 10

*Rootpaw hunched his shoulders miserably as* he followed Dewspring down the steep trail toward camp, despair clinging to his fur like heavy rain. Another training session with his mentor, and another day where Rootpaw seemed to mess up everything.

Dewspring's tail flicked crossly. "I don't know what's wrong with you, but you need to snap out of it. It's like trying to train a kit. You're always watching something else when you should be listening to me. How will you ever learn if you don't focus? You should be ready for your assessment by now, but I don't trust you not to wander off in the middle of it and forget what you're doing."

Pelt prickling with frustration, Rootpaw padded into camp after his mentor. At this rate, he was never going to pass his assessment and show Leafstar and Dewspring that he *could* be a good warrior. He felt a twinge of annoyance in his belly fur. His training would surely be going better if he didn't have Bramblestar's ghost on his tail all the time, pestering him to take a message to Squirrelflight.

*How, exactly, am I supposed do that?* There was no way Thunder-Clan's deputy would believe the story Rootpaw had to tell her.

Especially if she heard it from a SkyClan apprentice. He'd just cause more trouble for the Clans, and for what?

Dewspring stopped at the edge of the clearing, gazing at him so intently, Rootpaw couldn't help staring down at the ground. He was keenly aware of his Clanmates relaxing in the midday sunshine. Needlepaw was chattering with Wrenpaw and Kitescratch. Tree was hooking mice from the fresh-kill pile and inspecting them carefully, as though looking for one he liked. Violetshine and Palesky watched Pigeonfoot, who was demonstrating how he'd caught a bat mid-flight yesterday evening. Every cat seemed happy except Rootpaw. He looked at Dewspring, wishing he could explain that there was a good reason he was messing up in training so much. But even if he told his mentor what it was, he felt sure it would sound like nothing but a desperate excuse. "I'll try harder," he mumbled.

His heart sank even deeper as he saw Leafstar look toward him.

Her eyes were dark as she exchanged glances with Dewspring. *Has he warned her how badly I'm doing?*

The SkyClan leader crossed the clearing and stopped beside them. "Again?" she mewed heavily, her gaze resting on Rootpaw.

*He has told her.* Rootpaw wished he could melt into the earth as Dewspring sighed.

"He's still not concentrating," the gray tom growled.

"Rootpaw." Leafstar stared at him sternly. "I don't mind if apprentices find their training challenging. I *expect* it to be challenging. Learning is hard. But Dewspring told me you had promise. I thought I'd be giving you your warrior name by now. You certainly have the ability, but you can't be spending your training sessions mooning over some cat who doesn't even live in our Clan. It's a waste of your time—yours and your mentor's."

Rootpaw blinked at her. "I'm not mooning."

"Really?" She sounded unconvinced. "I can't think why else Dewspring would tell me you spend most of your training staring into the trees when you should be watching prey."

Rootpaw tried not to see the disappointment in her eyes. It was bad enough that Dewspring was looking at him like he'd caught a beetle instead of a mouse.

"The Clans are on edge," Leafstar went on. "Who knows what will happen next? We've had no word from StarClan. Bramblestar is spreading panic and fear, throwing around accusations about codebreakers. If he's trying to use StarClan's silence to make ThunderClan more powerful, we need to be on the alert. SkyClan needs strong, reliable warriors. There's no time for your antics. You need to try harder. You owe it to your Clan, to your mentor, and to yourself."

He met her gaze, longing to explain that he could be a good warrior if only a certain dead cat would leave him in peace. Did Bramblestar's ghost realize how much trouble it was causing? It should be here now, watching this. "I'm sorry," Rootpaw mumbled.

"'Sorry' catches no prey." Leafstar whisked her tail angrily. "I want to see some changes." She stalked away, her pelt ruffling along her spine.

Rootpaw looked apologetically at Dewspring. His mentor was staring at him with undisguised exasperation. "I'm really sorry," Rootpaw mumbled again.

Dewspring flattened his ears. "Don't waste your breath," he growled. "Just try harder." He followed Leafstar back to her den and stopped beside her. They talked softly, leaning close, and Rootpaw could tell they were discussing him, his paw pads tingling with a mix of guilt and embarrassment. He wasn't sure what he was more afraid of—failing his warrior assessment, or his leader and mentor finding out why he was doing so badly at his training.

Was there *any* way that he would be able to get rid of the ghost? He'd consulted Fidgetflake; he'd tried to get Tree to see it. Nothing had helped. He glanced at his father, who'd plucked a skinny mouse from the fresh-kill pile and was carrying it toward the shady patch beside the dogwood where he liked to eat alone. *I have to tell him.* He needed to share his secret before it got him into more trouble. Tree was the only cat in SkyClan who might understand what it was like to be plagued by a dead cat. And Tree was his father. He *had* to believe him, didn't he?

His paws felt heavy as he padded across the grass. His father looked up as he neared, his eyes rounding. "Hey, Rootpaw. Is everything okay?" He tipped his head to one side. "I saw Leafstar was talking to you. She looked kind of angry. Did you forget a battle move? Or catch the wrong sort of mouse?"

"No." Rootpaw's pelt ruffled with irritation. He knew his father hadn't wanted to be a warrior himself, but could he not take his own son's ambition seriously?

Tree pushed the mouse toward him. "Sit down and have a bite," he mewed gently. "You can tell me why you look like a sparrow that's lost its chick."

Rootpaw glanced over his shoulder. Leafstar and Dewspring were still talking. Leafstar's gaze flitted toward him. He shifted his paws self-consciously. "Can we talk about it outside?" he asked Tree.

Tree eyed his mouse, then met Rootpaw's gaze. "I guess this can wait." He got to his paws, his eyes glittering suddenly with worry. "It sounds important," he mewed. "Should I ask Violetshine to join us?"

"Violetshine won't be able to help with this." Rootpaw headed for the entrance.

Tree padded beside him, his fur fluffed. Rootpaw glanced at his father. *Is he pleased I'm asking him for help?* He slid after Tree through the ferns at the entrance to the camp and climbed up the steep slope between the boulders, pausing as he reached the top.

Ahead of him, hills rolled toward the mountains. He took a deep breath of crisp, clean air and faced his father. "I keep seeing a ghost," he blurted. He waited for his father's eyes to light up. *He'll be proud that I'm like him.* His pelt ruffled irritably.

Tree eyed him thoughtfully without speaking.

"I thought you'd understand," Rootpaw pressed. Why wasn't Tree saying anything? *Doesn't he believe me?* His chest tightened. "Except it's not a ghost. It's *Bramblestar's* ghost. But it can't be, because Bramblestar is alive. Am I imagining it? Is it normal? It's driving me crazy." His heart quickened as Tree frowned. "Perhaps I am crazy. I'm the only one who can see him. And he's started talking to me. Asking me to help him. How can I help a dead cat? I'm not even—"

"Slow down." Tree moved closer, his gaze fixed on Rootpaw's.

"But you think I'm crazy, right? I can tell by the way you're looking at me." Panic began to spiral in Rootpaw's belly. The ground seemed to sway beneath his paws. If *Tree* thought he was crazy, perhaps he *was* crazy.

"You're not crazy," Tree mewed firmly. "I don't know how you're seeing the ghost of a living cat. But I believe you, and we're going to sort this out."

Rootpaw's throat tightened. He felt an overwhelming desire to bury his muzzle in Tree's fur, as he'd done when he was a kit. He was relieved that the ghost wasn't his secret anymore. And Tree believed him. He blinked at his father. "It's been happening since before the Gathering. That's why I ran out. I saw him looking at me. He knew I could see him. It freaked me out when he wanted to talk to me."

"That must have been very scary." Tree ran his tail along Rootpaw's spine. "Do you think Bramblestar's ghost wants to hurt you?"

"No," Rootpaw told him quickly. "He seems as confused as I am. He just wants to understand why he's a ghost when his body is still leader of ThunderClan. He says it's been stolen, and he doesn't know what to do. I'm the only cat who can see, and he wants me to help him."

Tree sat down and gazed across the hilltops. "So a ghost can take over another cat's body?" He frowned, clearly puzzled.

"It only took over when Bramblestar died on the moor." Rootpaw told Tree what the ghost had told him.

"I've never heard of such a thing before."

"But it's happened now."

Tree paused for a moment, then tipped his head thoughtfully to one side. "I guess it explains why Bramblestar has been behaving so strangely. But who would want to take over his body?" He looked at Rootpaw. "If it's not Bramblestar, who is it?"

Rootpaw shrugged.

"It must have something to do with all this nonsense about codebreakers," Tree went on. "Whoever it is, they're clearly trying to stir up trouble in the Clans." He narrowed his eyes. "We're going to have to tread carefully."

"But if we warn the other Clans what's happening, it'll help, won't it?" Rootpaw's ears pricked with hope.

"Most warriors don't see dead cats," Tree told him. "They're going to find this hard to believe. Can you imagine old warriors like Thornclaw or Emberfoot swallowing the idea of two Bramblestars—one dead and one alive?"

"But they believe in StarClan. And they fought alongside dead cats in the Great Battle, didn't they?"

"That was moons ago," Tree told him. "Before SkyClan even came here. And they *all* saw those dead cats. I'm not sure any cat will want to believe that a SkyClan apprentice, and you alone, can see the ghost of a living warrior. They might think we're causing trouble for trouble's sake." His tail twitched uneasily. "If this living Bramblestar is trying to hurt the Clans, telling any cat that he's a fake might just give him something new to sharpen his claws on."

Rootpaw stared at him, his paws heavy with disappointment. He'd thought Tree might be able to help. *He's as powerless as I am.* He blinked at his father. *Or maybe not!* Hope sparked suddenly from his desperation. "But you're Clan mediator," he mewed eagerly. "They'd believe you, wouldn't they? Bramblestar wanted me to tell Squirrelflight. But I'm just an apprentice. I've got no reason to cross their border. *You* can visit ThunderClan easily. Just say it's important Clan business and tell Squirrelflight that Bramblestar's a fake."

Tree gazed at him solemnly. "I can't use my position like that," he mewed gently. "If she doesn't believe me, it will reflect badly on SkyClan. Squirrelflight could say that I'm trying to undermine ThunderClan. It could go very wrong. It might even start a battle. We can't risk that until we're sure of our facts."

Rootpaw's pelt tingled. He felt sure another pair of eyes was watching him. He turned around, his heart lurching as Bramblestar's ghost padded toward him.

"Can he see me?" The ghost nodded toward Tree.

Rootpaw shook his head. "But I've told him about you."

"Does he believe you?" Bramblestar's eyes narrowed.

"Yes." Rootpaw nudged his father. "Bramblestar's ghost is here."

Tree stiffened, looking around. "Where?"

"Over there." Rootpaw flicked his tail toward the apparition. Its ghostly pelt was rippling like water in the sunshine.

Tree stared blankly at the patch of grass Rootpaw had
pointed out.

"Can you see it now?" Rootpaw asked eagerly. Perhaps if he
tried harder, now that he knew where the ghost was . . .

Tree shrugged. "I can't see *every* dead cat." He blinked at
Rootpaw. "I wouldn't want to."

Bramblestar's ghost was staring excitedly at Tree. "Is he
going to help you speak to Squirrelflight?"

"He can't," Rootpaw told it. "Not without getting SkyClan
in trouble with the other Clans."

Bramblestar's gaze darkened. "He could try."

Rootpaw stretched his muzzle toward his father. "He wants
you to try to talk to Squirrelflight," he explained.

"I can't." Tree stared blankly into space, clearly trying to
focus on the spot where he thought Bramblestar's ghost stood.
"This needs to come from Rootpaw. He's the only cat who
can help her speak to you, if she asks—which she certainly
will, because she will want proof. And if she figures out that
I'm lying, she might think it's some kind of SkyClan plot. It
could cause all sorts of trouble. . . ."

The ghost looked thoughtful. "I guess Rootpaw would
sound more genuine."

Rootpaw's pelt bristled. "But I'm just an apprentice!" He
shifted uncomfortably as Tree and Bramblestar's ghost looked
at him. "How am I even supposed to get into the Thunder-
Clan camp?"

Tree narrowed his eyes thoughtfully. "You have a friend there, don't you?"

Rootpaw fluffed out his fur indignantly. "Bristlefrost is not a *friend*. She's just a cat I know."

The ghost's eyes sparked with hope. "You can visit her, though."

"Not without getting into trouble!" Rootpaw glared at it.

Tree pricked his ears. "What did Bramblestar say?"

Rootpaw had forgotten that his father couldn't hear Bramblestar's ghost. "He thinks I should visit Bristlefrost."

"Maybe not visit her, exactly," Tree mewed. "But she might be able to help when you get there."

"How do I get there?" Rootpaw's heart was pounding. They were both acting like this was easy.

"You'll have to sneak in," Bramblestar's ghost told him.

"*Sneak in?*" Rootpaw stared at the ghost, hardly able to believe his ears. A Clan leader was telling him to break the warrior code.

"I can help you," the ghost pressed. "I know the territory. I can show you how to get to the camp without being seen." It turned and headed along the hilltop. "Come on. We should go now. There's no time to waste."

Rootpaw blinked desperately at his father. "He wants me to go to the ThunderClan camp now," he breathed. "He says he can help me get there without being seen."

"You should go," Tree told him. "If another spirit is using Bramblestar's body, the Clans might be in danger." He fixed Rootpaw's gaze solemnly. "I know he's asking you to do something dangerous and difficult, but I think you should try. If you get in trouble, I'll do everything I can to help you. But I know you can do this. Squirrelflight needs to know, and if any cat can persuade her, you can."

Rootpaw stared into Tree's eyes, his heart pounding. Tree was right. If Bramblestar's ghost needed help, he should help it. He nodded to his father. "I'll do it."

Bramblestar's ghost was already disappearing over the crest of the hill. "Hurry up!" he yowled.

"Take care of yourself!"

Tree's mew rang out across the grass as Rootpaw bounded to follow Bramblestar's ghost downslope.

Rootpaw's ears twitched nervously as he stepped across the ThunderClan border.

"This way." Bramblestar's ghost was barely visible in the shadowy forest as it hurried past a wide swath of brambles and stopped where the forest floor sloped into a lake of bracken.

Rootpaw hurried after it, keeping close as the apparition led him among the stems.

His nose twitched as ThunderClan scents bathed his muzzle. "Is there a patrol nearby?"

"I'll scout ahead." Bramblestar's ghost signaled for him to stay where he was with a flick of its tail and disappeared. Rootpaw waited, his breath shallow with fear until the ghost finally returned. "It's clear all the way to the bluebell glade. Quick."

As Bramblestar moved silently through the stems, Rootpaw

followed, wishing his pelt didn't make them rustle.

"Stop." The ghost's order sent alarm spiking through Root-paw's chest. He froze as the ghost pulled up and peered from the undergrowth. "Patrol."

Rootpaw pressed his belly to the earth, holding his breath as paw steps sounded in the distance. He was trembling by the time they'd passed and faded.

"Up here." Bramblestar's ghost climbed effortlessly into an oak and disappeared among the branches. Rootpaw followed, scanning the forest as he heaved himself up. The ghost's pelt was barely visible in the shadows as Rootpaw followed it along a branch, and he watched, alarmed, as it leaped into the next tree. Teetering on the end, Rootpaw stared at the forest floor. He mustn't fall. There was no cat here to help him. He bunched up his muscles, then leaped, digging his claws deep into the bark as he landed. The branch trembled beneath him, and he clung on tight until it stopped shaking.

Bramblestar's ghost was already hurrying along it, past the trunk and onto the next branch. Rootpaw's heart was pound-ing as he followed the apparition from one tree to the next, thankful for his SkyClan training. He'd never traveled so far in trees before, and by the time he finally leaped down onto the forest floor, his pelt was spiked with fear.

"The camp's not far," Bramblestar told him.

Rootpaw swallowed back his dread. If this was scary, what would it be like to sneak into ThunderClan's camp? He hur-ried after the ghost as it ducked beneath a bramble.

"Squeeze under here," it ordered. Rootpaw ducked down

and hauled himself beneath the low bush, wincing as the prickles snagged his fur. He was sharply aware of the branches pressing around him. He was so far from home. His fear started to spiral. *What am I doing?* What if his fur got caught? Who'd drag him to safety? Not the ghost. The ghost couldn't touch him. Panicking, he scrabbled forward, desperate to be out in the open. At least there he would be able to see where he was.

"Slow down!" The ghost's fur shimmered among the stems. Alarm edged its mew.

"I've got to get out of here." Blood roared in Rootpaw's ears. He could hardly breathe beneath this dusty bush. Why had he agreed to such a dangerous mission? *You'll be okay,* he told himself. *You're not trying to hurt any cat. This isn't your fault.* He saw open forest and made for it. As he hauled himself out, relief swept through him. He gulped in fresh air.

"Wait!" The ghost's cry rang in his ears as sharp, strong ThunderClan scent bathed his tongue.

"What are you doing here?" He heard Molewhisker's mew, his pelt spiking as he jerked around and found himself facing a ThunderClan patrol. Bristlefrost, Finleap, and Molewhisker were staring at him with wide, round eyes.

Molewhisker flattened his ears. Finleap's pelt bristled with hostility. As Bristlefrost blinked at him, Rootpaw shrank away, his heart sinking like a stone in his chest. This wasn't how it was supposed to happen. He hadn't even made it to the ThunderClan camp. He stared helplessly at Molewhisker, feeling Bristlefrost's gaze burning his pelt. He looked around quickly for Bramblestar's ghost but saw nothing. Turning back to Molewhisker, he tried to stop himself from shaking. "I'm sorry," he mewed.

Molewhisker glanced at Bristlefrost, accusation flashing in his eyes. "Did you know he was coming?"

Bristlefrost stiffened. "No! I'd never break the code like that."

Molewhisker nodded curtly and looked back at Rootpaw. The anger in his gaze made Rootpaw's pads prick with fear. "We'd better take you to Bramblestar," the ThunderClan warrior growled. "You can explain to *him* what you're doing on our land." He nudged Rootpaw forward roughly.

Rootpaw padded stiffly ahead, aware of the eyes of the ThunderClan patrol burning into his pelt as they fanned out around him. Dread gripped his belly. Why had he listened to his father and the ghost? They weren't the ones who'd have to face Bramblestar. He forced himself not to tremble, suddenly aware that he'd made a terrible mistake.

# CHAPTER 11

Bristlefrost followed Molewhisker and Finleap as her Clanmates escorted Rootpaw toward camp. Her pelt rippled uneasily along her spine. She didn't want to walk too close to the Sky-Clan apprentice in case they thought she'd had something to do with his sudden appearance on ThunderClan territory. Why in StarClan had he come? It had been uncomfortable enough last time, when Leafstar had allowed him to bring her prey as thanks for saving him from the lake. Bristlefrost had hoped that would be the last time he'd do anything so mouse-brained, but clearly his crush on her was worse than she'd thought. Her ears twitched self-consciously. She liked him, he was nice enough, but they were from different Clans. And he was only an apprentice. She could never have any special feelings for him.

She fluffed out her fur. What would Bramblestar say? He'd been trying to stop the Clans from breaking the warrior code, and Rootpaw had broken one of the most important rules of all. This was ThunderClan land. He shouldn't be here. She hoped with an anxious shiver that Bramblestar wouldn't jump to the same conclusion as Molewhisker and assume that she'd asked him to meet her here.

No cat spoke as the patrol neared the camp entrance. Rootpaw's tail was bushed, and she guessed he was scared. She hoped he had a good reason for being here. As she slid through the shadowy entrance tunnel and emerged into sunshine, Bramblestar got up from where he'd been lying beneath the Highledge. Squirrelflight was beside him, her tail flicking absently until she saw the patrol. Then she leaped to her paws, her gaze brightening with interest. She followed Bramblestar as he crossed the clearing and stopped in front of the patrol.

The ThunderClan leader's gaze flitted over Rootpaw before settling on Molewhisker. "What is he doing here?" His mew was sharp with anger.

"He won't say." Molewhisker told the ThunderClan leader. "Bristlefrost knows him better than I do." He looked pointedly at Bristlefrost. "Perhaps she can explain."

*This has nothing to do with me!* Her heart quickened as Squirrelflight padded closer, narrowing her eyes. Around the camp, ThunderClan warriors turned to watch, their gazes flashing with curiosity. Outside the elders' den Cloudtail and Brackenfur exchanged glances. Fernsong padded from a patch of long grass, while Spotfur looked up from the mouse she'd been eating beside the rock tumble.

Bristlefrost lifted her chin defensively. "I don't know why he's here," she told Bramblestar. "He was hiding under a bramble near our camp."

"By trespassing on our territory, he's broken the code." Bramblestar's eyes flashed dangerously. "If we want StarClan to come back, the code must be followed exactly!"

Rootpaw seemed to shrink beneath his pelt.

*Say something!* She wished Rootpaw would defend himself. He must have a reason for coming here. "He's just an apprentice," she mewed, hoping Bramblestar would go easy on him. "He probably just made a mistake."

Bramblestar's ears flattened. "It's a long way to come for a mistake."

Squirrelflight whisked her tail. "Why don't we try asking?"

Rootpaw suddenly straightened and turned his head as though he'd just spotted prey beside him. He pricked his ears, his attention focused on the empty air. Had he forgotten where he was? Didn't he realize Bramblestar was expecting an explanation?

"Well?" Bramblestar glared at the SkyClan apprentice. "What are you doing on my land?"

Rootpaw jerked his muzzle toward the ThunderClan leader, but Bristlefrost couldn't help noticing that his ears were still turned toward the patch of empty air, as though he were listening for something. He hesitated, staring distractedly at Bramblestar while above the camp a starling's call rang in the silence.

Bramblestar shifted his paws, his gaze growing darker.

At last, Rootpaw seemed to focus. "I thought I smelled rogues on the edge of our border. I was worried they might cause trouble." He didn't take his gaze from Bramblestar. Bristlefrost frowned. What was he going on about? Why did rogues on SkyClan's border mean he had to visit ThunderClan?

Bramblestar was never going to believe such a vague story. Rootpaw pressed on. "It's not long since you helped chase off that group of she-cats . . ." He hesitated, frowning. "What were they called? I can't remember the name."

Bristlefrost's tail twitched uneasily. *The Sisters!* How could any cat forget their name? Especially Rootpaw! They'd lived in his camp after the battle.

Rootpaw was staring expectantly at Bramblestar. "Were they called the Queens?" He blinked at the ThunderClan leader. It sounded like he was testing him, Bristlefrost realized. "Was that the name? Their leader was called Moonlight. . . ."

"What in StarClan are you babbling on about?" Bramblestar growled.

Rootpaw's fur prickled. "I was just trying to remember the name of those cats—"

"What does that have to do with your being on Thunder-Clan territory?"

"I—I just thought you'd know since . . ." Rootpaw's mew trailed away as Bramblestar stared at the SkyClan apprentice, his dark gaze glittering with fury.

Squirrelflight blinked at Bramblestar in surprise. "Surely you remember, Bramblestar."

Bristlefrost shifted her paws. It did seem strange that Bramblestar had forgotten. Squirrelflight's support of the Sisters had caused such a rift between her and Bramblestar that the whole Clan had felt the strain.

"I can't remember *everything* that happens!" Bramblestar

snapped. He turned back to Rootpaw. "You're living on their land. If you can't remember their name, why should I?"

Bristlefrost stepped forward. "The Sisters," she mewed. "They called themselves Sisters."

Around the camp, she saw her Clanmates shift nervously. Spotfur hooked her mouse closer, her tail twitching. Molewhisker glanced at the ground as though embarrassed for his leader.

Rootpaw looked relieved. "The Sisters. Of course. I thought you'd want to know they could still be hanging around."

Bramblestar's ears were flat. Hostility burned in his eyes. "Why not tell your own leader?" he snarled.

Rootpaw pricked his ears innocently, but his tail was still bushed. Bristlefrost could see he was scared. "I know how close Squirrelflight was to them," he offered.

Bramblestar looked perplexed.

Rootpaw went on. "I thought I'd be doing you a favor."

"Doing me a favor?" Bramblestar padded closer to Rootpaw, his hackles lifting. Bristlefrost held her breath. He looked like he might attack the SkyClan apprentice. "You trespass on my land and question me in my own camp, and then you tell me you're doing me a favor?"

Rootpaw flinched away, alarm flashing in his eyes.

Molewhisker padded forward and stood beside the young tom. "He's just making up stories to explain why he's here." He eyed Bramblestar nervously. The ThunderClan leader looked ready to fight. "It's probably the same reason he came last time. Every cat knows he has a crush on Bristlefrost. He probably just wanted to see her."

Shame seared Bristlefrost's pelt. "That's not true!" she meowed hotly.

Molewhisker stared at the SkyClan apprentice encouragingly. "Even if Bristlefrost knew nothing about it, you know what young cats are like when they like some cat. They act first and think later."

Bramblestar's hackles lowered a little. "Is it true?" he asked Rootpaw. "Did you come to see Bristlefrost?"

Rootpaw blinked at him as though he were staring into the eyes of a Thunderpath monster. "Y-yes," he stammered. "That's it. I just wanted to say hi to Bristlefrost."

Bristlefrost stiffened with rage as her Clanmates' gaze focused on her. She could see Finleap's whiskers trembling with amusement. Bristlefrost felt so humiliated that she wanted to hide in her den. She glared at Rootpaw. Why did he have to embarrass her like this, and in front of her leader? Did he think a stunt like this would make her like him? Did he have bees in his brain?

Squirrelflight padded to Bramblestar's side and ran her tail along his spiked pelt. "He's just a foolish apprentice," she told him. "We all do dumb stuff when we're young. Go easy on him. Let's just escort him off our territory and forget about it."

Bramblestar growled softly, his expression still as dark as when he had punished Spotfur and Lionblaze. If he could be so hard on his own warriors, what would he do to a cat from another Clan?

"It's not against the code to have feelings," Squirrelflight pressed. "And that's all it is. I'm sure Rootpaw and Bristlefrost haven't *done* anything—"

"Of course not!" Bristlefrost snapped. "It's *his* crush, not mine! And I'd never break the warrior code." She looked earnestly at Bramblestar, ignoring Rootpaw's tail as it drooped.

Bramblestar frowned, but his pelt was smoothing where Squirrelflight had stroked it. "Okay," he grunted. "I'll let him off this time. But Molewhisker and Finleap can go to the SkyClan border and get word to Leafstar that she'll need to send a patrol to fetch him. I'm not letting him slink home. His Clanmates can come here and explain why they let an apprentice trespass on *our* land."

Molewhisker blinked at Bramblestar. "We could just escort him home. I can tell Leafstar what he's done while I'm there."

"They can come *here*," Bramblestar insisted. "I'm not making this easy on SkyClan. They should have more control over their apprentices."

Molewhisker dipped his head and turned toward the entrance, beckoning Finleap to follow with a flick of his tail. As they disappeared, Bramblestar glared at Bristlefrost. "Since you brought him here, you can guard him until his Clanmates arrive."

*I didn't bring him here!* Bristlefrost puffed out her pelt, but she didn't argue as Bramblestar stalked back to the shade of the Highledge, his tail flicking ominously. She looked at Rootpaw. "What were you thinking?" she hissed as she steered him toward the nursery. She nudged him into the shelter of its wall, where her Clanmates couldn't hear them. "You can't just wander onto another Clan's territory. And why did you have to tell them that you came here because of me? Bramblestar was just starting to take me seriously. Now he'll think I'm no better than a mouse-brained apprentice. Couldn't you have lied?"

"I did." Rootpaw blinked at her solemnly.

"What?" Had he just come here to embarrass her?

Rootpaw looked furtively around the camp. Then he fixed his gaze on her firmly as though making a decision. "I couldn't tell them the real reason why I came."

"What about the Sisters?" Bristlefrost demanded.

"That was a lie too." He glanced to one side, as though he'd spotted prey again, then mewed pointedly, "And it was a mouse-brained one. Who reports rogues to another Clan? It was a *really* dumb idea." His ears twitched irritably.

Bristlefrost stared at him. "So you didn't come here to see me?"

"No," he mewed, his gaze still distracted.

Bristlefrost tried to ignore the disappointment tugging in her belly. *I don't care,* she told herself. *I'm glad.* And yet it had been reassuring after Stemleaf's rejection to think that *some* cat liked her, even if it was a hare-brained apprentice from another Clan.

Rootpaw turned suddenly toward his invisible prey. "I'm *really* sorry," he told it earnestly. "If there'd been another way to do it, I would have."

"Do what?" She felt mystified. What was he going on about? Why was he talking to thin air?

Rootpaw turned back and stared at her for a moment as

though trying to work out what to say.

"Well?" she prompted, her tail flicking sternly.

Determination hardened his gaze. "You know Tree can see dead cats," he mewed.

"So I've heard." What was he talking about now? "What does Tree have to do with this? Or dead cats?"

"I can see one as well." Rootpaw glanced at his paws, his ears twitching uncomfortably. Then he sat down with a hopeless sigh. "He brought me here."

"Who brought you here?"

"A dead cat," Rootpaw told her. "He showed me the way."

Rootpaw was even more hare-brained than she'd thought. "So a dead cat brought you to ThunderClan territory?" She narrowed her eyes. "Do you really expect me to believe that?"

"No," Rootpaw mewed. "I don't expect any cat to believe it. Why would they? And the dead cat's not even dead. He's alive. But I'm still seeing his ghost."

Bristlefrost tried to understand. Rootpaw had never been this dumb. There had to be some sense in his story. She stared at him harder. "You're seeing a living cat's ghost?"

"Yes." He sounded as though he believed it. He turned in a slow circle, looking toward the entrance to the nursery. Like he was making sure that no cat was nearby. Then he turned back to her. "Bramblestar's ghost has been following me around the forest for a moon. No cat can see him but me, but I know he's real. He's the one who wanted me to come here. He says the Bramblestar who leads your Clan is an impostor. He stole his body when Bramblestar lost a life, and now the real Bramblestar can't get back in."

Bristlefrost's gaze flitted toward the Highledge. Bramble-star was lying in the shade, Squirrelflight sitting stiffly beside him. Of course he wasn't an impostor! Rootpaw must have had a bad dream. "That's impossible."

"I wish it were." Rootpaw's shoulders sagged.

Bristlefrost's paws pricked crossly. The day had been going so well. She'd caught a rabbit on her first patrol and marked the whole WindClan border. She knew Bramblestar must be impressed by what a good warrior she was becoming. And now Rootpaw had to spoil it, humiliating her in front of her Clanmates and telling her a nursery story as though she were a kit who'd believe anything. "Why are you telling me this?"

"Because this is too important for me to leave without tell-ing some cat," Rootpaw mewed. "I trust you more than any cat in ThunderClan, and I thought we were friends."

Bristlefrost looked away guiltily, then hesitated. What did she have to feel guilty about? "I'm a ThunderClan warrior," she snapped. "My first loyalty is to my Clan and my leader. Why should I believe a SkyClan apprentice's lies?"

"Because ThunderClan is in danger," Rootpaw pressed. "Who knows what this impostor is planning or why he stole Bramblestar's body?" He searched her gaze hopefully.

She sniffed. "This is nonsense! It's not possible to steal another cat's body."

Rootpaw's shoulders drooped. "I know it sounds crazy, and I understand why you don't believe it." He stared at her, his tail lying limply behind him. "But can you do one thing for me?"

"What?" She glared at him. What did he want now?

"Bramblestar's ghost brought me here so I could warn Squirrelflight," Rootpaw told her. "He wants me to pass on his message. I'm supposed to say, 'I don't know who that is in my body, but it's not me.'" His eyes rounded imploringly. "Can you tell her that? Please?"

Bristlefrost shook out her fur angrily. "I'm not telling Squirrelflight such a ridiculous thing! Are you trying to ruin my reputation completely?"

Rootpaw dropped his gaze. "I'd never do that."

Bristlefrost turned away and stared intently across the clearing. If Rootpaw was going to lie to her and try to make her feel guilty, then she wasn't going to listen to him.

She heard him sigh. Then he settled beside her and gazed miserably at the camp entrance. It was going to be a long, awkward wait until his Clanmates arrived.

Bristlefrost watched Dewspring and Plumwillow escort Rootpaw from the camp. The young yellow tom padded between them, tail down and shoulders drooping. Bramblestar had used the opportunity to give the SkyClan warriors a lecture on how to discipline their apprentices, and she could tell they were furious at being humiliated by the Thunder-Clan leader. She felt a twinge of pity for Rootpaw. He was going to be in serious trouble when he got back to camp.

She tried not to think about the punishment Rootpaw might face, just as she tried not to think about the dumb story he'd told her. Why couldn't he have been honest about why he'd come to ThunderClan territory? Had he come to see her after all and simply been too embarrassed to admit it to her face? She padded to the fresh-kill pile. It had been a long day, and she wasn't going to think about Rootpaw anymore. She'd eat a mouse and go to her nest early so she'd be up in time to organize the dawn patrols.

Dusk was settling over the camp and her Clanmates were already sharing prey, talking softly in the twilight. Bramblestar was dozing beneath the Highledge, and Squirrelflight had taken the opportunity to move among her Clanmates, weaving around the clearing and stopping to talk here and there. Bristlefrost watched as the ThunderClan deputy stood beside Thornclaw, listening as he told her about the rabbit tracks he'd found in the beech grove. On the other side of the clearing, Alderheart was sharing a thrush with Sparkpelt and Finchpaw, while Stemleaf sat a tail-length away, throwing a reassuring glance toward Spotfur as the spotted tabby she-cat sat alone beside the warriors' den.

Bristlefrost lifted a mouse from the pile and carried it toward Thriftear, who was already eating with Lilyheart and Flamepaw. As she neared, Stemleaf padded toward her and nosed her away.

She dropped the mouse and blinked at him. "What?"

"I wanted to talk to you." Stemleaf stretched his muzzle closer and lowered his voice. "You shouldn't encourage Rootpaw," he whispered. "Or he'll keep coming back."

Bristlefrost pulled away sharply. "I didn't encourage him!" Anger flared beneath her pelt.

"You probably don't mean to, but he came here today, didn't he? You need to let him know that nothing can ever happen between you. Relationships with cats from other Clans never work, and we're supposed to be sticking to the warrior code."

"I *am* sticking to the warrior code." Her hackles lifted. How dare he suggest she might break it? She was the one who was trying to enforce it! "Rootpaw didn't come here to see me."

"That's not what he said," Stemleaf murmured. He glanced around the Clan. "Cloudtail said that he wanted to see you."

"He was lying!"

Stemleaf's eyes rounded with interest. "Then why *did* he come here?"

Bristlefrost stared at him. She couldn't repeat Rootpaw's story. It was too absurd. "It's none of your business." She lashed her tail crossly. "Just leave me alone." She picked up her mouse and carried it to Thriftear, where she laid it on the ground and settled beside it.

Thriftear blinked at her, concern showing in her pale amber eyes. "What did Stemleaf say to you?"

"Nothing." Bristlefrost forced her pelt to smooth and took a bite.

Thriftear frowned but, clearly guessing that Bristlefrost didn't want to talk about it, returned to her conversation with Lilyheart.

Bristlefrost chewed the mouse, barely tasting it. Her thoughts were whirling. Why did Rootpaw have to tell her such a mouse-brained story? She couldn't even repeat it to her Clanmates. It was bizarre. And impossible. They'd think she was dumb for even listening to it. And yet why would he ask her to tell such a story to Squirrelflight? He clearly knew how crazy it sounded. Perhaps he'd gotten some sort of coded message from StarClan and didn't realize it. Maybe if she passed it on, it would make sense to Squirrelflight. The Thunder-Clan deputy might understand something in the message that she and Rootpaw didn't.

She took another bite and chewed it unenthusiastically. She wasn't even hungry. She swallowed and sat up, butterflies fluttering in her belly. Perhaps she should pass on the message. Squirrelflight would know whether it was important or not. She glanced at the ThunderClan deputy. Bramblestar had woken up and was blinking sleepily. Bristlefrost didn't want to repeat the story in front of him. Who knew how he'd react? He was probably still angry with Rootpaw. This would make him angrier.

Bristlefrost pricked her ears as Bramblestar got up and padded to the dirtplace tunnel. As he disappeared, she scrambled to her paws. *I'll tell Squirrelflight. It's what a loyal warrior would do. If it's nonsense, so what?* Squirrelflight could ignore it. But at least she'd know what rumors might be flying around the other Clans.

Squirrelflight looked up as she reached her. "Bristlefrost." She acknowledged her with a nod.

"I'm sorry to bother you." Bristlefrost eyed the Thunder-Clan deputy nervously, hoping that she wasn't going to sound like a complete mouse-brain. "But I wanted to talk about Rootpaw."

Squirrelflight's ears twitched uneasily. "I was hoping you'd forget about him," she mewed. "Cross-Clan relationships are dangerous, especially now."

"No!" Bristlefrost blinked in alarm. "I don't mean I want to talk about him in *that* way." Her paws felt hot. "It's just he *told* me something."

Squirrelflight's gaze sharpened. "What?"

"He wanted me to pass on a message to you."

Squirrelflight leaned closer. "Tell me."

Bristlefrost took a breath. "I know this is going to sound crazy—it sounded crazy to me, and he probably made it up, but I thought I'd tell you anyway, because if Rootpaw told me, he might tell some other cat, and it'll be a rumor in no time, and I—"

Squirrelflight cut her off. "Just tell me."

"Rootpaw says that Bramblestar's ghost has been following him around for a moon." Bristlefrost shrank beneath her pelt but forced herself to keep going. "He said the ghost wanted him to give you a message, and that's why he came here today."

"What's the message?" Squirrelflight's gaze flicked to the dirtplace tunnel.

Bristlefrost followed it, her heart lurching. Was Bramblestar coming back?

"He said, 'I don't know who that is in my body, but it's not me.'"

Squirrelflight seemed to freeze, staring at Bristlefrost for a moment. Then she looked away. "What nonsense." She fluffed out her fur. "I'm glad you didn't let Bramblestar hear that. That's the most ridiculous thing I've ever heard. Did

Rootpaw think any cat would believe it?"

Bristlefrost shifted her paws nervously. "He didn't, actually. He just said I had to tell you."

"I'm glad you did." Squirrelflight eyes glittered uneasily. Bristlefrost's chest tightened. Did Squirrelflight think there could be any truth to the story? But then the deputy's gaze cleared. "It's best to know what's going on in other Clans. And now that you've told me, we can both forget about it. Rootpaw is clearly as strange as his father."

"It's a crazy story, right?"

"Yes." Squirrelflight nodded. "Crazy. Perhaps Rootpaw really does believe it. Maybe he dreamed it and thinks it's a message from StarClan. Most likely, he was trying to cover his real reason for coming here." She looked pointedly at Bristlefrost. Bristlefrost's pelt pricked self-consciously as she went on. "Every cat knows he has a crush on you. But it's best we don't even think about it. It's got nothing to do with ThunderClan." She nodded Bristlefrost away. "Go and finish your mouse."

Bristlefrost nodded gratefully to Squirrelflight. She felt relieved. She'd done the right thing in telling her. She didn't think Rootpaw would lie, but he might believe he'd had a message from StarClan if it gave him an excuse to visit her. Nothing else made sense. She padded back to her mouse, suddenly hungry. She wasn't going to think about Rootpaw or ghosts anymore. She'd forget him and focus on her duties. Bramblestar and Squirrelflight were relying on her to be the best warrior she could be.

# CHAPTER 12

Shadowsight shivered as a cold breeze whisked around him. In the distance, the Moonpool's hollow was lit from above. It glowed against the dark moor. He couldn't help feeling that it was waiting for him, that it knew he was coming to share his vision of the codebreakers at last. He tried to ignore the doubt that had been shadowing the edges of his thoughts for the last three days. What would StarClan demand from the cats it had shown him—from Dovewing—to make amends?

He followed Puddleshine along the stream and up the rocks as they steepened. Scrambling from paw hold to paw hold, he was breathless by the time he reached the top and hauled himself into the silver moonlight of the hollow. The other medicine cats sat like stones at the bottom, the Moonpool shining beside them.

Puddleshine paused at his side. He glanced at Shadowsight. "You've been quiet tonight."

"I'm worried about leaving Snowbird," he told him. It was a half-truth, but what else could he say? He hadn't told Puddleshine what he was planning to reveal at the meeting. "Her paw isn't healing as well as I'd hoped." He thought of the injured she-cat, and of Scorchfur, whose pelt was still slicked with ointment to soothe his injuries, and of Dovewing's torn ear and the kink in Stonewing's tail. Antfur had been buried three days ago, and the Clan was still in mourning. He *had* to share his vision about the codebreakers. It was the only way to protect his Clan from StarClan's anger.

As he padded down the dimpled rock, he realized the Moonpool was unfrozen. Its water was as black as the night sky, but no stars reflected in its glossy surface. StarClan still seemed very far away.

Frecklewish got to her paws as the ShadowClan cats neared, padding to greet them with a nod. "Do you think StarClan will share with us tonight?"

Puddleshine's gaze was dark. "I hope so."

Beside the pool, Jayfeather stared blindly ahead. "If StarClan wishes to share, they will."

Alderheart glanced at the blank water. "Is it me, or does the Moonpool seem different tonight?"

"It looks darker than usual." Kestrelflight's ears twitched uneasily.

"It's only water," Mothwing mewed briskly. "Why don't we see what happens." She crouched at the edge, beckoning Willowshine closer with a flick of her tail.

Shadowsight fought to stop his paws trembling. He had to speak before they touched their noses to the water. They had to know what was wrong before they faced another silence. He took a breath. What would they say when he told them?

"I think I know why StarClan has stopped sharing with us," he blurted out.

Kestrelflight jerked his muzzle toward him. "Why should *you* know what we don't?"

"StarClan sent me a vision that I haven't told you about." Shadowsight pressed on as the others blinked at him in surprise. "When we were here a few moons ago, a voice spoke to me. It said the Clans had forgotten the code." He closed his eyes, quoting the words. "'The code has been broken time and time again, and because of the codebreakers, every Clan must pay a price. They must suffer.'"

"'Suffer'?" Frecklewish stared at him. "StarClan has never wanted us to suffer before. They want to help us."

Shadowsight pressed on. "This is what they told me," he insisted. "They showed me a vision of the cats who have broken the code."

Kestrelflight's ears flattened. "Which cats?" he demanded.

"Crowfeather, Squirrelflight, Jayfeather—"

Jayfeather stiffened as Shadowsight said his name. "Me? Why?"

Shadowsight looked at him. "I don't know."

"Who else?" Alderheart asked nervously.

"Dovewing." The name caught in Shadowsight's throat. He was naming his mother as a codebreaker. He felt dizzy as he forced himself to go on. "Lionblaze, Twigbranch, and Mothwing." He avoided the RiverClan medicine cat's gaze, guilt washing his pelt.

Puddleshine was staring at him. Anger flashed in his eyes. "Why didn't you tell me this before?"

"I couldn't." Shadowsight looked at his paws. "Tigerstar wanted me to keep it secret. He was scared for Dovewing." He glanced at the medicine cats. They were staring at him wordlessly. "He was scared for all the codebreakers."

Jayfeather growled. "He was right to be scared. Bramblestar has already been calling for any cat who breaks the code to be punished."

"Perhaps Bramblestar's right," Shadowsight mewed softly. "The vision says the Clans will suffer for what the codebreakers have done. But perhaps if the codebreakers make amends, the rest of us will be spared."

Mothwing lashed her tail angrily. "This is nonsense! This proves what I've always thought. We shouldn't let our ancestors guide us. Why should every cat suffer because a few have made mistakes?"

"We can't turn away from StarClan when we disagree with them." Willowshine blinked at her former mentor. "They see everything. They have more knowledge than us."

As Mothwing grunted crossly, Shadowsight met her gaze. "There have been a lot of injuries in ShadowClan recently. If it's StarClan's doing, we can't let it go on. We have to make things right."

"Injuries are a part of life," Mothwing retorted. "If we believed StarClan was angry with us every time a warrior gets hurt, then we'd have to believe they were angry with us all the time!"

"This is different," Alderheart mewed softly. "This is the first time StarClan has ever stopped speaking to us." He nodded to the still, black water. "Can you remember a time when there were no stars glittering in the Moonpool? Something has changed, and if Shadowsight has had a vision that tells us what's wrong, we must listen to it." His dark ginger fur rippled nervously.

Shadowsight felt a wave of sympathy. Alderheart's mother was on the list of codebreakers, too. He knew how hard it was to admit that the codebreakers might be the reason for StarClan's silence. "I can't let my Clanmates suffer."

Kestrelflight glared suddenly at Shadowsight. "Are you sure you heard the vision right?"

"I told you everything I saw and heard," Shadowsight told him.

"But how can we be sure you remembered right?" Kestrelflight looked around the other cats. "He's the youngest of us. Why should we trust a cat with so little experience?"

Puddleshine padded to Shadowsight's side. "He's been having visions since he was a kit," he mewed firmly. "And he's trying to do the right thing."

Frecklewish nodded. "The vision sounds pretty clear. I don't see how Shadowsight could have gotten it wrong."

Kestrelflight frowned. "But it doesn't make sense," he mewed. "Why is Dovewing named and not Tigerstar? They both fell in love with cats from different Clans. They both ran away. Why should only Dovewing be held responsible? It doesn't seem fair."

Jayfeather whisked his tail angrily. "Why am *I* named? Or Lionblaze? When have *we* broken the code?"

"We've all probably broken the code at some point," Kestrelflight pointed out. "Without even realizing."

"Then why isn't every cat named?" Jayfeather snapped. "Am I going to be punished because my mother broke the code? She was the one who had kits with a cat from another Clan, not me!"

Frecklewish blinked at Jayfeather. "StarClan has spoken," she mewed. "We have to obey."

Jayfeather snorted. "That's easy for you to say. You're not named! No SkyClan cat is!"

Alderheart was frowning. "I don't understand why StarClan has decided these codebreakers should be punished *now*. Why not sooner? Warriors have been breaking the code for generations. Long before we were born. StarClan has never asked the Clans to suffer for it until now."

Shadowsight's pelt prickled uneasily. Why were the other medicine cats questioning his vision? They should act, not talk. "We're wasting time," he mewed. "We should be deciding what to do next."

"Should we tell our Clans about the vision?" Willowshine's eyes glittered darkly in the moonlight.

"No!" Jayfeather's bind blue gaze swung toward her. "Can you imagine what Bramblestar will do when he knows who to blame?"

"We can't keep it to ourselves," Alderheart argued. "It's too important."

Frecklewish nodded. "It affects every cat in the Clans."

Shadowsight's belly tightened. "We have to tell them." His Clanmates had already suffered too much because of his silence.

Kestrelflight nodded. "If it's true, our Clanmates must know."

"They should have known sooner," Puddleshine murmured.

Shadowsight felt the sting of his denmate's words. *He's angry because I kept the vision to myself.*

Alderheart swished his tail. "The sooner the codebreakers atone, the sooner the Clans will be safe."

Frecklewish lifted her muzzle. "Let's go home and tell our leaders what we've learned."

Willowshine's ears twitched. "Let's hope they know what to do."

The chill of the hollow cut through Shadowsight's pelt. He had a second confession to make. He braced himself. He'd known from the start the next one would be harder: he was going to have to tell Tigerstar that he'd broken his promise and told the other medicine cats. He tried not to picture his father's anger, but he knew he was going to have to face it eventually. Fear fluttered in his chest, and yet he still felt relieved. He'd shared his vision at last. Now the Clans could take action and his Clanmates' suffering could end.

He watched Jayfeather settle beside the Moonpool. The blind medicine cat touched his nose to the water. Did he still hope that StarClan would share with him tonight? As

Jayfeather closed his eyes, the ThunderClan medicine cat's words rang in Shadowsight's ears. *Can you imagine what Bramblestar will do when he knows who to blame?* Shadowsight stifled a shudder. Would his vision end his Clanmates' suffering, or make it worse?

Shadowsight waited until dawn. He'd given up trying to sleep and was watching anxiously from his nest. At last, as pale light began to loosen the shadows, he heard the paw steps of the dawn patrol gathering in the clearing. Heart quickening, he crept from his nest and waited until Snaketooth, Yarrowleaf, Conefoot, and Gullswoop headed out of camp, then ducked outside and crossed to his father's den.

"Tigerstar," he whispered into the darkness, his heart pounding so hard that he felt his body pulse with its beat. Puddleshine had offered to come with him to tell Tigerstar about last night's meeting, but this was something Shadowsight wanted to do alone. He was the one who had betrayed his father's trust.

Bracken rustled inside, and Shadowsight stepped back as he heard paw steps cross the den.

His father emerged, blinking, into the clearing. "Is something wrong?" His eyes rounded with worry as he scanned the sleeping camp.

"The Clan is safe," Shadowsight reassured him.

Dovewing slid past Tigerstar and looked anxiously at Shadowsight. "It's early," she mewed. "Is everything okay?"

"I have something to tell you." Shadowsight glanced over his shoulder to make sure no cat was listening. "About the half-moon meeting."

Tigerstar's gaze darkened. Had he guessed?

Dovewing tipped her head seriously. "It sounds serious."

"It is." Shadowsight held his father's gaze, his breath shallow. "I told the other medicine cats about my vision."

Anger flashed in Tigerstar's eyes.

Dovewing looked puzzled. "What vision?"

"The one StarClan sent me." Shadowsight dragged his gaze to his mother. "It told me that there are codebreakers in the Clans, and that the Clans must suffer because of them."

Dovewing's ears pricked. "Codebreakers?"

"They named cats who have broken the warrior code." His throat tightened. He had to force himself not to look away. "You were one of them."

Dovewing seemed to flinch. She looked anxiously at Tigerstar. "And your father?"

"They didn't name him."

"Who else?" Fear sharpened Dovewing's mew.

"Crowfeather and Squirrelflight." Shadowsight didn't dare look at Tigerstar. From the corner of his eye, he could see his father's breath billowing in the cold morning air. He wanted to ask for forgiveness for what he'd done. Instead he pressed on. "Jayfeather, Twigbranch, Lionblaze, and Mothwing."

"Is that all?" His mother stared at him.

"That's all they showed me."

"We can't be the *only* warriors who have broken the code." Dovewing swung her muzzle toward Tigerstar. "You broke it too. Why aren't you named?"

Tigerstar was staring at Shadowsight. "You shouldn't have told them," he growled. His tail flicked ominously.

"I had to." Shadowsight held his ground. "Bad things kept happening to our Clanmates. Antfur *died*. It was a sign from StarClan, don't you see? They warned me that cats would have to pay a price, that they would have to suffer. . . . I had to tell the others so terrible things would stop happening."

Tigerstar flattened his ears. "What if knowing who the codebreakers are causes *more* suffering?"

"I had to do something," Shadowsight insisted. "I couldn't sit by and let anything else happen to my Clanmates."

Tigerstar narrowed his eyes. "So Jayfeather and Alderheart are going to tell Bramblestar?"

"Yes." Shadowsight swallowed. "They have to."

"Why aren't you named?" Dovewing asked Tigerstar again.

Tigerstar looked at her grimly. "StarClan might accuse more cats. If they don't, I'm sure Bramblestar will."

Shadowsight's heart lurched. Was this just the beginning? Would the Clans tear themselves apart with accusations? The ground seemed to tremble beneath his paws as he realized what he'd started. "I'm sorry," he blurted. "I wanted to protect our Clan. I had to tell them about my vision."

Tigerstar scowled at him. "No matter who it hurt?" Rage hardened his mew.

"Be kind." Dovewing touched Tigerstar's tail with hers.

"We raised him to be honest, didn't we?" She blinked at Shadowsight. "I told him only a few days ago to tell the truth." Shadowsight's heart seemed to break. His mother clearly realized that it had been her words that had encouraged him to betray her to the other medicine cats. He felt ashamed as he saw love glisten in her green gaze. "I'm proud of him," she mewed. "And I *did* break the code. If StarClan wants to punish me, then I have to face up to it." She lifted her chin, her pelt smoothing. "We must obey their word."

Tigerstar's pelt spiked with rage. "Look what you've done!" he snarled at Shadowsight. "Once the other leaders hear this, who knows where the accusations will end? What will happen to ShadowClan if they accuse *me*? I won't be able to protect your mother then."

Shadowsight straightened. Shame seemed to loosen its grip around his heart. He'd done the right thing. He was sure of it. He met his father's gaze determinedly. "It is every warrior's duty to be honest and loyal. You've always done your best for your Clan. ShadowClan is only still *here* because of you. No cat could accuse you"—he glanced at Dovewing—"either of you of being bad warriors."

Dovewing pressed her flank to Tigerstar's. "He's right," she murmured. "We may have broken the code, but so has nearly every warrior at some point in their lives. We have to trust StarClan to be fair."

"But why accuse the codebreakers *now*?" Tigerstar blinked at her. "We're no worse than all the warriors that have gone before us. Why should *we* be punished?"

"I don't know," Dovewing whispered. "But if I can save ShadowClan by atoning for the things that I have done, then that's what I will do."

Foreboding darkened the edges of Shadowsight's thoughts. He swallowed back fear. He knew he'd been right to tell the other medicine cats, but what would happen now? Was Dovewing going to have to suffer to save her Clan? Tigerstar had a point. Why had StarClan named *these* cats? Why now? His heart began to quicken. *StarClan, have pity. I've done what you wanted.* He glanced at the watery dawn sky, hoping they could hear. *Don't let Dovewing suffer for my honesty.*

# CHAPTER 13

*Rootpaw dragged a pile of moss* across the den floor and pawed it to the edge of the clearing. Leafstar had put him on nest-cleaning duty since Dewspring and Plumwillow had escorted him from the ThunderClan camp, and he was determined to prove to that he was the best nest cleaner in the Clan. Right now he was the only one. Shaking the dust from his pelt, he headed back into the warriors' den. Bramblestar's ghost watched him as he began to pluck stale heather from Sagenose's nest. He'd been working all morning and the ghost hadn't left his side.

Rootpaw sat back on his haunches. "If you can't help, do you have to keep hanging around?"

"What else can I do?" Bramblestar padded to the entrance and peered out. "You're the only cat who can see me."

Irritably, Rootpaw rubbed heather sprigs out of his whiskers. His fur was full of leaf dust and it itched. The ghost stuck close nearly all the time now, but at least Rootpaw had persuaded it to stay away while he was training. He'd finally made it understand that he needed Leafstar and Dewspring to trust him again, and the best way to do that was to show them that he was serious about becoming a warrior. The ghost hadn't been pleased, but it had reluctantly agreed, grateful that Rootpaw had at least tried to pass on its message to Squirrelflight. They could do nothing now but wait and see what happened next.

"Rootpaw!" Bramblestar's ghost hissed from the entrance.

Rootpaw looked up, his paws full of crushed heather. "What?"

"Leafstar's calling a Clan meeting!" Bramblestar slid out of the den. "Hurry!"

Rootpaw brushed the leaves from his paws and followed the ghost, wondering what the meeting was about.

His Clanmates were already crowding around the grassy clearing as he reached the edge. Leafstar stood in the middle, her gaze calm as Frecklewish and Fidgetflake padded to her side.

Bramblestar's ghost paced around Rootpaw as he scanned his Clanmates.

"What's going on?" Rootpaw whispered to Macgyver, who had stopped beside him.

Macgyver shrugged. "I don't know."

The ghost slid between them, eyeing the medicine cats. "Do you think there's been word from StarClan?"

Last night had been the half-moon meeting. But why would StarClan send a message now, when they'd been silent for so long? Rootpaw shook out his fur. He had three more nests to clean, and training later, and he wished he could have just a few moments without the ghost asking him questions. Being haunted was hard work.

Bramblestar's ghost blinked eagerly at Frecklewish. "Perhaps Squirrelflight told the medicine cats about my message."

"Clanmates." Leafstar's gaze flashed around the clearing. "Frecklewish has brought me news from the half-moon meeting." She nodded to the mottled brown tabby cat who stepped forward and addressed the Clan.

"Shadowsight had a vision from StarClan," Frecklewish began. Surprised murmurs rippled around the Clan. "They told him that the Clans have forgotten the warrior code, and they showed him the codebreakers. Because of them, they said the Clans would suffer."

Harrybrook pricked his ears. "It's just like Bramblestar said," he mewed.

A low growl rumbled in the ghost's throat. Rootpaw ignored it. He wanted to hear what else the medicine cat had to say. He blinked at Frecklewish expectantly.

Across the clearing, Plumwillow whisked her tail. "Why must we suffer? SkyClan has always respected the warrior code."

As the warriors exchanged anxious glances, Sparrowpelt looked at Frecklewish. "Who did StarClan say broke the code?" he demanded.

"They named Lionblaze." Frecklewish began to list warriors. "Crowfeather, Squirrelflight, Jayfeather, Dovewing—"

Macgyver cut her off before she could finish her list. "No cat from SkyClan?"

"Does that mean we don't have to suffer?" Harrybrook stared hopefully at the medicine cat.

"I don't know." Frecklewish shifted her paws. "But it's

true—none of the named cats were from SkyClan."

Around the clearing, SkyClan seemed to relax. Their pelts smoothed and their tails softened. Rootpaw glanced at the ghost. Several of the named cats were in ThunderClan. The ghost's tail was twitching angrily. "Why would StarClan agree with that impostor?" he growled. "Don't they realize he's just trying to cause trouble in the Clans?"

"Hush." Rootpaw whispered under his breath. He stiffened as Macgyver glanced at him, and hurriedly turned his gaze back to Frecklewish.

The medicine cat's eyes glittered uneasily. "StarClan didn't say how we could fix this. Or how much we must suffer."

Harrybrook looked at Leafstar. "If Bramblestar's right, we have to make sure we respect the warrior code."

Plumwillow glared at him. "But we do!"

Sparrowpelt nodded beside her. "That's why we haven't been named."

"The codebreakers must apologize and make amends," Harrybrook insisted. "So StarClan can come back."

Bramblestar's ghost bristled. "He sounds just like the impostor." He stared at Rootpaw, his eyes glittering with alarm. "Why is every cat listening to that liar?"

Rootpaw ignored him.

Hawkwing narrowed his eyes. "What does StarClan want from us?" he mewed. "We can't do more than we're already doing."

Leafstar shrugged. "I guess we have to wait and see what the other Clans do."

Tree stepped forward. "What about Bramblestar?" he meowed grimly.

"He must deal with his codebreakers as he thinks fit," Leafstar answered.

"But you've seen him at the Gatherings," Tree pressed. "He's been accusing any cat who speaks out against him of being a codebreaker. I don't trust him. He's using StarClan to turn the Clans against one another."

The ghost pricked his ears. "Tree understands!" He blinked gratefully at the yellow tom. "The impostor is trying to divide the Clans by making them accuse one another. Why is he the only cat who can see that?"

Rootpaw tried to keep his fur from ruffling. Tree and the ghost were seeing problems that might never happen. The message from StarClan had made it clear that the codebreakers were the problem.

Leafstar blinked at Tree. "Bramblestar has been aggressive in calling out codebreakers," she conceded. "But now that he knows which ones StarClan is concerned about, he might relax."

"Does she really believe that?" The ghost stared in disbelief.

Leafstar gazed at her warriors. "This will be a difficult time for the other Clans," she told them. "Our home is beside the lake now, and even if StarClan's message doesn't include us, we must support every Clan in whatever they decide."

"Support them by standing up to that impostor!" The ghost's pelt bristled as Leafstar followed Frecklewish and

Fidgetflake to the medicine den and SkyClan's warriors returned to their duties.

Rootpaw headed back to the warriors' den, beckoning the ghost to follow with a flick of his tail. "Perhaps StarClan will let you go back to your body when the codebreakers have been dealt with," he whispered as soon as they were clear of his Clanmates.

The ghost stared at him in amazement. "Do you think StarClan let an impostor take my place on *purpose?*"

"Not exactly." Rootpaw dropped his gaze. "But Squirrel-flight was named as a codebreaker," he pointed out. "Maybe StarClan thought it would be easier for some other cat to deal with them."

The ghost flexed its claws. "No. The impostor is the one using StarClan. We have to stop him before it's too late."

"How can he use StarClan?" Rootpaw met his gaze, puzzled. "They're more powerful than any cat."

The ghost stared at him, his gaze shimmering with frustration. "Something is very wrong," he murmured darkly. He turned away, his tail quivering.

"Rootpaw." Violetshine was heading toward him, her gaze sharp with worry. "You must promise not to see Bristlefrost again," she mewed urgently.

He blinked at her. "I wasn't planning to."

"I know," she mewed, only half listening. "But if StarClan is worried about codebreakers, you have to behave. No more sneaking away to ThunderClan. No SkyClan cat has been named yet, and I don't want you to be the first." She looked scared. "And I don't want you mixed up with a Thunder-Clan cat. Bramblestar's going to use this to cause trouble, whatever Leafstar says." Her ears twitched nervously. "I just hope Twigbranch is okay. She switched Clans before you were born." Violetshine looked worried. "Does that count as code-breaking?"

Rootpaw shrugged. "Frecklewish didn't mention her."

Violetshine looked at him anxiously. "Do you promise you won't try to see Bristlefrost?"

"I promise." He touched his nose to her cheek. It wasn't a lie, but he wasn't sure it was a promise he could keep. If this news was going to bring trouble to ThunderClan, Bristlefrost might need help.

Rootpaw fluffed out his fur. The night was cold and a sharp breeze was blowing across the island. Bramblestar had called an emergency Gathering the day after the medicine cats had shared the news of Shadowsight's vision. Rootpaw nosed his way among his Clanmates and settled between Violetshine and Tree. Over the heads of the other cats he could see that Bramblestar was already on the lowest branch of the Great Oak.

The ThunderClan leader lifted his muzzle. "Let's begin!"

Tigerstar and Mistystar were still hurrying toward the tree as their Clanmates gathered in its shadow. As the two leaders scrambled up the trunk, Harestar and Leafstar shifted to let them take their places on the branch.

Bramblestar's ghost was watching from the edge of the

clearing. Rootpaw could hardly see it from where he was at the center of the throng. The ghost had been restless since Frecklewish had announced the vision, pestering Rootpaw for reassurance that he'd do something to stop the living Bramblestar from using the vision to harm the Clans. Rootpaw had tried to keep an open mind. ThunderClan's current leader hadn't actually harmed any cat yet. Rootpaw wanted StarClan to stop being angry and come back, and if that meant putting up with an impostor for a while, maybe that was okay.

"You've all heard about Shadowsight's vision by now." Bramblestar's gaze burned in the starlight. The gathered cats glanced warily at each other. "What I've been saying all along is true. StarClan is angry that so many warriors have broken the code. They've even given us a list of the worst offenders." His gaze flashed from Dovewing to Crowfeather, flickered angrily over Mothwing and Jayfeather. Rootpaw wondered if he was angry with Squirrelflight too. She was on the list, and yet the ThunderClan leader didn't look at his mate as she sat stiffly among the other deputies. Instead he pressed on. "I have a plan." As he narrowed his eyes, the Clans seemed to lean closer, pricking their ears. "The codebreakers must publicly take responsibility for their wrongdoings. They must atone!"

Tigerstar bristled beside the ThunderClan leader. "'Atone'?" he snapped. "What does that mean, exactly?"

Below, Dovewing sat unmoving while her Clanmates shifted nervously around her. Rootpaw noticed Tigerstar's gaze flick nervously toward his mate before snapping back to Bramblestar.

Bramblestar swung his muzzle toward the ShadowClan leader. "They must be punished, of course."

"How?" Tigerstar demanded.

Bramblestar held his gaze. "That's what this Gathering is for," he mewed smoothly. "StarClan won't return until the codebreakers have suffered for their crimes."

Squirrelflight glanced up at him, her eyes dark. "Are you sure StarClan wants them to suffer?" she mewed nervously. "They only said that every Clan must pay a price. Perhaps we must all suffer together rather than target individual cats."

Bramblestar's gaze flashed toward her. "They named the codebreakers!" he snapped. "They clearly want them punished."

Squirrelflight looked at her paws, seeming to shrink beneath her pelt. Rootpaw frowned. Was she going to back down so easily? As she stared at her paws, the ThunderClan leader looked around at the gathered cats once more.

"We must decide how the codebreakers suffer," he growled.

"'We'?" Tigerstar flattened his ears, his mew outraged. "Don't you mean *you*? You've wanted cats to suffer since this began. You're using StarClan's silence as a way to divide the Clans!"

Rootpaw saw the ghost padding closer to the oak, its pelt prickling excitedly as it stared at Tigerstar.

Bramblestar leaned down over his branch, his lip curling with menace. "But StarClan isn't silent any longer. They've sent us this vision. They've made it clear exactly who the codebreakers are and why they should be punished. They won't come back until amends have been made. In Thunder-Clan, we've already begun giving out stricter punishments to cats who break the code. You'll notice that Lionblaze is not here. . . ."

A murmur rippled through the gathered cats as, one by one, they realized that the golden tabby tom was nowhere to be seen. Cats let out nervous rumbles and exchanged surprised glances. Lionblaze had been a ThunderClan warrior for moons, and had fought in great battles that took place long before Rootpaw had been born—not that this seemed to matter to Bramblestar.

"He has not yet returned from his exile," the ThunderClan leader went on. "But he betrayed the code, and he accepted that he had to pay a price. Spotfur, too"—he gestured with his tail at the spotted tabby she-cat, standing at the edge of the Gathering with Stemleaf—"was very grateful to be ignored by all her Clanmates for a quarter moon. Weren't you, Spotfur?"

Spotfur said nothing. Bramblestar purred contentedly—something about the sound made Rootpaw's flesh prickle beneath his pelt. "StarClan will appreciate us for this, you'll see."

Tree shifted uneasily beside Rootpaw. "He's using this to turn the Clans into a bunch of vengeful rogues," he breathed into Rootpaw's ear. "This impostor is no better than Darktail. He will destroy the Clans if he's not careful."

Rootpaw blinked at his father. "Perhaps he's just trying to help."

"How can making cats suffer help anything?"

"It might bring StarClan back," Rootpaw insisted even as doubt pricked in his paws.

"Do you *want* StarClan back if they only want to watch us suffer?" Tree stared at Rootpaw, his eyes glistening.

Rootpaw had no answer. Panic fluttered in his chest. Had this Gathering finally persuaded Tree that he should leave the Clans and take his family with him?

Tigerstar's pelt was spiked. "You have no right to decide the fate of cats from other Clans," he snarled at Bramblestar.

"And you have no right to defend codebreakers when one is your mate!" Bramblestar hissed back.

"Your mate is a codebreaker too!" Tigerstar's gaze flashed toward Squirrelflight. She seemed to flinch for a moment before lifting her chin defiantly.

"I will deal with her myself," Bramblestar mewed. "And I'll deal with the other codebreakers in my Clan as harshly as I expect you to deal with yours. Lionblaze, Jayfeather, Twigbranch." His eyes flashed menacingly toward his Clanmates. "They will all *atone*."

*Twigbranch!* Rootpaw's heart lurched. He glanced at Violetshine. Her sister had been named after all. Violetshine's gaze had darted toward Twigbranch. The ThunderClan she-cat sat hunched among her Clanmates, her eyes wide. A cold chill ran along Rootpaw's spine. Now that StarClan's threat of suffering was aimed at Twigbranch, he realized how other cats, in other Clans, must have been feeling all along. A flush of heat settled in his gut. *Would I ever have spoken up for them if my own kin weren't being threatened?*

Rootpaw glanced toward the ghost. It was pacing agitatedly, its hackles high. It caught Rootpaw's eye, panic flashing in its gaze. Rootpaw pushed his way through the crowd and slid into the space at the edge of the clearing where the ghost was pacing. He led it away from the gathered cats. "You're right," he breathed softly. "The impostor just wants to hurt cats. He doesn't care what it does to the Clans."

Bramblestar's ghost looked relieved. "Thank you," he murmured. "Thank you for believing me. Maybe you can convince others. . . ."

His voice trailed off as he turned back to the Great Oak, seeing Harestar step warily forward to the edge of the branch, and meet the impostor's gaze. "How do we know what sort of punishment StarClan wants?" he asked nervously.

"StarClan clearly trusts us to decide," Bramblestar told the WindClan leader.

Mistystar narrowed her eyes. "Are we sure this vision came from StarClan?"

"Of course it did!" Bramblestar swung his muzzle toward Tigerstar. His gaze hardened. "Your son wouldn't lie, would he?"

"Of course he wouldn't!" Tigerstar's fur ruffled.

Bramblestar turned his gaze back to Mistystar. "A medicine cat has brought us a vision from StarClan. Would you deny that?"

"No," Mistystar told him. "But I want to be very sure of what we're doing before we start punishing cats."

"They broke the code, didn't they?" Bramblestar stared at her. "What good is a code if it's not enforced?" He didn't wait for an answer. Instead he looked at Leafstar. "You've been very quiet. Are you going to object to upholding the warrior code too?"

Mistystar bristled. "I didn't obj—"

Bramblestar cut her off, still staring at the SkyClan leader. "*Leafstar*, do you agree the codebreakers should be punished?"

Leafstar curled her tail around her paws. "SkyClan has not been accused of codebreaking. What the other Clans do about *their* codebreakers is up to them."

Bramblestar dipped his head. "Very well. Then all we have to do now is decide on a fitting punishment." He turned back to the gathered cats. "Does any cat have a suggestion?"

Rootpaw felt queasy as Bramblestar's gaze raked the Clans.

The ghost paced around Rootpaw. "Why doesn't some cat challenge him?"

Rootpaw held his tongue, aware of the silence that had fallen over the Clans.

"You have to do something!"

"What can I do?" Rootpaw hissed, one eye on the crowd beside him. The cats were staring at Bramblestar as though hypnotized.

"Speak up! Say something! You can't let this happen!" The ghost lashed its tail. "Whoever's in my body up there, this is just the start."

Rootpaw tried to ignore him, moving closer to the crowd. It would be useless to speak out now. He'd only get in trouble again.

The ghost thrust its muzzle closer. "He's going to destroy the Clans!" it yowled. "He'll turn the Clans against one another, and then he'll turn each Clan against itself."

Frustration welled in Rootpaw's chest. *Don't yell at me! I'm as helpless as you are!* He ducked away from the ghost.

It darted after him and stood close, its nose a whisker from Rootpaw's face. "Some cat has to speak out!"

"Shut up!" The words burst from Rootpaw before he could stop himself.

He saw countless faces turn toward him, eyes flashing in the moonlight. His pelt burned as the living Bramblestar stared at him from the Great Oak.

"What did you say?" the ThunderClan leader growled slowly.

Rootpaw stared back at him, his mouth dry. He wanted to run away, but he felt as though his paws had sunk deep into the ground. "I'm sorry," he mumbled. "I was thinking about something else. I didn't mean to speak. I was distracted."

Bramblestar eyed Rootpaw for a moment, then turned his gaze back to the crowd. "So?" He dismissed Rootpaw's interruption with a flick of his tail. "Has any cat come up with a suggestion?"

As Bramblestar waited for an answer, Rootpaw noticed that Stemleaf and Spotfur were still staring at him. They stood at the edge of their Clan, almost separate from the other warriors. Spotfur still looked a little timid and chastened after being singled out by Bramblestar—but her eyes, like Stemleaf's, were bright with interest as they regarded Rootpaw. He dropped his gaze, self-conscious.

In the crowd, Scorchfur lifted his muzzle uncertainly. "We should think before we act."

Agreement rippled through the crowd.

"It's an important decision," Hootwhisker agreed. "We should discuss it first."

Mistystar padded to Bramblestar's side. "They're right," she mewed. "Let's return to our camps and talk about the best way forward. This Gathering is at an end."

As she spoke, the crowd shifted and began to break up. The taut knot of gathered cats unraveled as they turned away from the Great Oak and began to head toward the long grass. Tigerstar jumped from the branch and hurried toward Dovewing, pressing against her protectively when he reached her. Leafstar slithered down the trunk and padded quickly toward her Clanmates.

In the oak, Bramblestar was still glaring at Mistystar. "Am I the only cat trying to do as StarClan wishes?" Indignation shone in his eyes.

"We all want to do as StarClan wishes," she answered evenly.

Harestar padded to the RiverClan leader's side. "You can't just bully every cat into agreeing with you."

"I was the last one of us to see StarClan," Bramblestar snapped. "I lost a life, don't forget. I speak for StarClan more than any cat here."

Rootpaw saw orange fur slipping through the crowd. His heart quickened. Squirrelflight was hurrying toward him. He tensed as she stopped in front of him. "Quick," she hissed, glancing back at Bramblestar. "I don't have long. Were you telling the truth about Bramblestar's message?"

As Rootpaw stared at her, the ghost fluffed out its fur excitedly at the edge of his vision.

"Tell me!" She looked scared.

"Y-yes," he blurted.

"Why should I believe you?" She searched his gaze desperately.

Bramblestar's ghost whisked its tail. "Tell her that after the battle with the Sisters, we sat here in this clearing, looking up at the stars, wondering which one was Leafpool. She said it didn't matter, because Leafpool would always be watching over ThunderClan."

Rootpaw glanced at him, then at the impostor still in the Great Oak. Was this going to get him into more trouble?

"Don't just stare into space!" Anger hardened Squirrelflight's mew. "Tell me why I should believe you!"

"After the battle you . . ." He paused, trying to remember the words. "You were here with Bramblestar and you were looking at the stars, wondering which one was Leafpool, but it didn't matter because she would always be watching over you." He spoke so fast he nearly tripped over the words.

Squirrelflight stared at him, amazed. "He's really a ghost?"

"He's here now," Rootpaw told her quickly.

She scanned the empty air.

"He can't get back into his body because some other spirit is there," Rootpaw told her. Hope flickered in his chest. Perhaps she could make everything right again.

"Squirrelflight!" The impostor's yowl cut through the night air. "We're leaving."

Squirrelflight scanned the air once more, then turned and hurried away. She caught up with Bramblestar as he marched out of the clearing and pushed his way through the long grass, his pelt bristling angrily. The ghost watched her go, and she shot a longing look over her shoulder. Rootpaw searched the thinning crowd for his family. What would Tree say after the impostor's behavior tonight? If he'd thought about leaving before, tonight must have convinced him that the Clans had changed, and not for the better.

Two ThunderClan warriors were pushing through the crowd, heading toward Rootpaw. He stiffened when he recognized Spotfur and Stemleaf. Were they coming to accuse him of disrespecting their leader?

"It was an accident—" he began as they reached him.

"What was?" Spotfur stopped and tipped her head, looking puzzled.

"Telling Bramblestar to shut up," he mewed apologetically.

"We're not here to talk about that." Stemleaf glanced furtively over his shoulder. "We just wanted to tell you that we're planning a secret meeting."

He blinked at the white-and-orange tom. "What does that have to do with me?"

"It's for cats who are worried about the way things are going in the Clans," Stemleaf dropped his mew to a whisper. "We thought you might be interested."

"Because you told Bramblestar to shut up," Spotfur chimed.

"I wasn't talking about *him*," Rootpaw mumbled.

Stemleaf wasn't listening. He seemed in too much of a hurry. "We're going to see if we can stop Bramblestar from trying to punish so many cats."

"We're meeting at the greenleaf Twolegplace," Spotfur whispered.

"Three nights from now," Stemleaf added. "At moonhigh."

They turned and hurried after their Clanmates before Rootpaw could speak. His pelt prickled along his spine.

"You're going to go, aren't you?" The ghost's mew made him jump. He'd forgotten it was there.

He blinked at it. "I'm still in trouble for sneaking out last time," he pointed out.

"But cats are finally realizing something is wrong!" The ghost was staring at him eagerly.

"If I get caught attending a secret meeting, I might never become a warrior!"

"You might never become a warrior if Tree decides to take you away from the Clans," the ghost growled darkly. "And he will if the impostor carries on about making cats suffer."

Rootpaw didn't know what to say. Bramblestar's ghost was right.

"You have to go." The ghost stared at him. "You and Tree are the only ones who know about the impostor. You might be able to save the Clans."

Rootpaw stared wordlessly at Bramblestar's ghost. He felt suddenly small beneath the wide, black sky. He wasn't even a warrior yet, and the whole fate of the Clans seemed to rest on his shoulders. If he acted, he might get in trouble. But if he did nothing, Tree might take their family away. He could stay, without his kin, but what if the impostor's accusations tore the Clans apart? He'd have no family *and* no Clan.

He blinked helplessly at the ghost. "Okay," he mewed. "I'll go."

# CHAPTER 14

*Bristlefrost poked a honeysuckle stem into* the wall of the elders' den and tugged to secure it.

"I can see the hole," Flamepaw called to her from the roof. The young tom was balancing carefully on the delicate canopy of stems, a bracken frond in his paw.

"Can you reach it?" Bristlefrost called back.

"Yes." Flamepaw began to thread the bracken into the woven honeysuckle.

Bristlefrost sat back on her haunches, relieved to be patching the final holes in the den at last. The sun was high, and ThunderClan had sent out two large patrols. Bristlefrost had asked Lilyheart if Flamepaw could stay in camp to help fix the den. He was nimble and light enough to work on the roof without crashing through it.

Lilyheart had taken the opportunity to clean out her nest and was hauling heather into the warriors' den while Birchfall, Cinderheart, and Finchpaw rewove loose strands of brambles around the entrance tunnel. Alderheart and Jayfeather were sorting herbs in the medicine den. Poppyfrost was helping

Cloudtail and Graystripe line their nests with fresh moss. It was rare these days to see a ThunderClan warrior resting. They preferred to work, which pleased Bristlefrost. StarClan would surely approve of their efforts. Even now, Sparkpelt, Spotfur, and Stemleaf were clearing old ferns from the patch beside the medicine den to give the young ferns more room to grow.

Below the Highledge, Bramblestar got up sleepily from his favorite patch of grass and padded toward the dirtplace tunnel. Squirrelflight scrambled to her paws as he disappeared and hurried across the clearing. Bristlefrost stiffened. Squirrelflight was heading toward her, her eyes glittering with worry.

She nosed Bristlefrost away from the den, away from their Clanmates. "I have to speak to you," she whispered.

Bristlefrost's pelt prickled. "Is everything okay?"

"Remember what Rootpaw said?" Squirrelflight told her urgently. "At the Gathering? That's *not* Bramblestar." She glanced nervously toward the dirtplace tunnel.

"Of course it is." Bristlefrost blinked at her. "Who else could it be?"

"I know it sounds crazy," Squirrelflight hissed. "But Bramblestar is my mate. I can *tell*. I had a feeling something was wrong . . . I just told myself it was because he'd lost a life. Now I think it's more than that. I've been paying close attention to him today. He's . . . *different*."

"But he's our leader." Bristlefrost lifted her chin. "And he's obeying StarClan." How could he be any cat but Bramble-star? Things had been going too well. The Clan was following the warrior code more closely than ever. Prey was plentiful. StarClan must be pleased. Bramblestar was making Thunder-Clan the best Clan in the forest.

Squirrelflight stared at her, her gaze suddenly unreadable. Then she headed back to the Highledge, settling into the spot she'd left just as Bramblestar padded into camp.

"Bristlefrost." The ThunderClan leader beckoned her with a flick of his tail.

She hurried to meet him, shaking out her fur smartly as she reached him. She narrowed her eyes. He *looked* like Bramble-star. His mew was exactly as it had always been. She glanced at Squirrelflight, puzzled. How had an apprentice from another Clan managed to convince her that her mate was some other cat? "What is it?" She blinked at him eagerly. Did he have another special duty for her?

"I want a word in private." He padded slowly around the clearing and stopped at the far side, a distance from their Clanmates. "The camp is in good order." He nodded toward Flamepaw, who was still weaving bracken. "And our Clan-mates seem to be following the code. You've been a really big help making sure the Clan does its best."

Bristlefrost's pelt warmed with pride. She dropped her gaze shyly. "I want StarClan to come back, that's all."

"Of course." Bramblestar's gaze drifted toward the forest. "Prey has been running well, which is a good sign. I'm pleased to see the fresh-kill pile so full, but I think our warriors could be doing better." He swung his gaze back to Bristlefrost. "Don't you agree?"

She blinked at him. Was he about to criticize her? Had she let him down? Anxiety burrowed beneath her fur. "I—I guess?" She searched his gaze, trying to guess what he was thinking.

"I've been out in the forest, and I've seen prey trails that haven't been followed and undisturbed mouse nests. I'm worried that some of our warriors aren't pulling their weight."

Relief swamped Bristlefrost. She'd been hunting more diligently than ever before. He couldn't be blaming her. "I think every cat is trying," she told him earnestly. Her Clanmates had been working hard too. She didn't want Bramblestar to be disappointed in them.

"Every cat?" He tipped his head to one side.

She met his gaze. "Every cat."

"Are you sure?"

As he stared at her she hesitated. *Am I sure?* She tried to remember, feeling less sure by the moment. Had every warrior on her patrols hunted as hard as she had? She frowned as she remembered yesterday's patrol with Sparkpelt, Spotfur, and Thornclaw. Sparkpelt hadn't caught as much prey as usual, even though she'd ventured deeper into the forest than the others. Bristlefrost could feel Bramblestar's gaze boring into her. It couldn't do any harm to mention Sparkpelt. After all, she was Bramblestar's kit. If she was having trouble keeping up with her Clanmates, surely he'd just want to help her. "Sparkpelt went off by herself during yesterday's patrol," she mewed. "She said she knew a good hunting spot near the edge of our territory, but she didn't bring any prey back."

"None?" Bramblestar narrowed his eyes.

"She caught a mouse later and a shrew on the way home," Bristlefrost told him quickly. "She's a really good hunter. I think she was just having a bad day."

She held her breath as Bramblestar's eyes clouded in thought. This was the sort of information he wanted, right? So his warriors could please StarClan. She stiffened as he stalked away, his tail twitching ominously.

"Sparkpelt!" He yowled his daughter's name, and she turned and blinked at him.

Bristlefrost's belly tightened. She crept around the clearing so she could see Bramblestar's expression. Was he as angry as he sounded?

"What is it?" When she saw her father's face, her emerald gaze sharpened. She glanced toward Squirrelflight.

"Don't look at her." Bramblestar snapped. "*I'm* your leader."

Bristlefrost's pads itched with foreboding. Should she have kept quiet?

Squirrelflight got to her paws slowly as Sparkpelt crossed the clearing.

"Is something wrong?" Sparkpelt stopped in front of Bramblestar. Bristlefrost hung back at the edge of the clearing, her fur pricking with fear.

"You disappeared during your hunting patrol yesterday," Bramblestar growled. "Where did you go?"

Sparkpelt stuck out her chest. "I was hunting," she told him.

"I wanted to check the territory near the border. We hadn't hunted there for a while."

Bramblestar held her gaze. "Why didn't the rest of the patrol go with you?"

"I don't know," she told him. "I didn't ask. I didn't realize I had to *ask*. I've hunted alone before. We all have."

"But things are different now," Bramblestar growled. "StarClan is angry. We have to be careful what we do. We must stay with our Clanmates."

"How will that make StarClan happy?" Sparkpelt's ears twitched.

"It will make *me* happy," Bramblestar snapped. "And while StarClan is silent, I'm their voice in the forest. They gave me nine lives. I think they must trust me to care for my Clan, don't you?" He leaned closer to Sparkpelt. "Or do you think you know better than StarClan?"

"Of course I don't!" Sparkpelt bristled.

"Where did you go?" Bramblestar snarled.

"I was hunting!"

"Then why didn't you bring any prey back? Did you forget how to catch it?"

"No!" Sparkpelt was angry now. As her hackles lifted, Squirrelflight padded closer. Flamepaw slid quietly from the elders' roof and watched, his eyes rounding with alarm.

Bristlefrost glanced guiltily at the apprentice. She hadn't meant to get his mother into trouble. She'd only wanted to help Bramblestar take care of the Clan.

"Where did you go?" Bramblestar demanded again.

Sparkpelt glared at him. "I went to look for Lionblaze, okay? Has StarClan made a rule against caring about our Clanmates now?"

Bristlefrost's heart quickened with fear. She hadn't known Sparkpelt had been looking for Lionblaze. If she had, would she have told Bramblestar about his daughter's disappearance? Had Sparkpelt broken the code? She no longer knew.

She glanced at the ThunderClan leader, seeing that his ears had flattened. "How dare you!" he snarled at Sparkpelt. "I banished Lionblaze. You had no business going after him."

"I didn't go after him. The quarter moon was up two days ago, and he's still not back yet. I went to see if he might be on his way home."

As Sparkpelt stood her ground, Bramblestar stared at her. Around them, the Clan had fallen silent. They were watching, pelts ruffled with unease.

Squirrelflight padded softly to Bramblestar's side. "She only went to check on a Clanmate," she mewed.

He rounded on her. "This has nothing to do with you. Keep your whiskers out of it."

"She's my kit!" Squirrelflight snapped.

"She's a ThunderClan warrior and she broke the rules!" Bramblestar snapped back.

"What rules?" Squirrelflight demanded.

Bramblestar bared his teeth. "She left her patrol without permission and she went to look for a codebreaker I banished!"

Sparkpelt stared at her father, her gaze glittering suddenly with fear as he loomed over Squirrelflight. "I'm sorry," she blurted. "Okay? It was wrong of me and I won't do it again."

Bristlefrost flinched as Bramblestar turned back to his daughter. He looked ready to rake her muzzle with his claws. She held her breath, relief swamping her as the ThunderClan leader's fur finally began to smooth.

Flamepaw was shivering as he watched his mother. Sparkpelt seemed suddenly small as she blinked at Bramblestar. "Don't banish me too," she mewed quietly. "I can't leave my Clan, and my kits are still only apprentices. They need me."

Bramblestar stared calmly at Sparkpelt. Bristlefrost pressed back a shudder. Was he enjoying the look of fear on his daughter's face? *Of course not. He's not a fox-heart.* But if she'd known he'd react like this, she'd never have told him. And yet Sparkpelt had broken the rules, hadn't she? Bramblestar was only making sure his Clan was obeying StarClan. It was more important than ever now that Shadowsight had shared his vision about the codebreakers.

Slowly, Bramblestar turned his head. "Alderheart, are we running low on catmint?" His yowl rang across the clearing.

*Catmint?* Bristlefrost blinked at her leader. What did that have to do with anything?

Alderheart stuck his head out of the medicine den, looking puzzled. "I guess we're a little low, but we don't really need any at the moment."

Bramblestar looked back at Sparkpelt. "But it doesn't do any harm to make sure we have enough."

Alderheart frowned. "I'm not sure it will be growing yet. It might be best to wait another moon."

Bramblestar was still staring at Sparkpelt. "Do you want to wait another moon until your Clan has enough catmint?"

Sparkpelt looked puzzled. "N-no."

"Then why don't you go to the abandoned Twoleg nest and check whether the catmint is growing yet?" Bramblestar's tail swished over the ground.

"If you want me to." Sparkpelt glanced at her mother uneasily.

Bramblestar padded closer. "It would be a good way to prove to your Clanmates that you're more interested in helping them than in wandering off on your own private missions." He glanced ominously at Flamepaw. "A mother who's so worried about taking care of her kits would want to set them a good example."

Bristlefrost felt suddenly cold, unnerved by the threat in Bramblestar's mew.

"Sure." Sparkpelt nodded. "If that would help."

"Go on, then." Bramblestar nodded toward the camp entrance. "Off you go."

Sparkpelt headed away, glancing back nervously as she crossed the clearing.

But Bramblestar had already turned to pad to his spot beneath the Highledge. He settled down and looked expectantly at Squirrelflight.

The ThunderClan deputy watched her daughter leave the camp, then flashed a look at Bristlefrost, which seemed to say, *See? It's not him.*

A chill slid beneath Bristlefrost's fur. *It has to be him! Who else could it be?* She pushed back a tingle of foreboding as Squirrel-flight joined Bramblestar, her pelt rippling along her spine.

Bristlefrost glanced again at the camp entrance. Spark-pelt had been gone all afternoon. Would she be back soon? Most of the patrols had returned, and Flamepaw had finished patching the elders' roof.

Bristlefrost's belly growled and she headed toward the fresh-kill pile. As she took a shrew from the top and headed to the patch of grass where Thriftear was sharing a mouse with Twigbranch, paw steps sounded at the entrance. Her heart leaped as Lionblaze padded into camp. His pelt was unkempt and his eyes hollow. He crossed the clearing, his head high as he stopped in front of Bramblestar.

His Clanmates turned to watch, relief showing in their eyes, but no cat spoke as Lionblaze faced Bramblestar.

"The quarter moon is up," the golden warrior mewed. "I've come home to take care of my Clan."

"The quarter moon was up two days ago," Bramblestar grumbled. "What took you so long?"

Lionblaze stared down at his paws. "I didn't want to hunt close to Clan territory," he growled, "so I ended up farther and farther away from the lake. I ran into a Clan of Twolegs, whose mouse-brained kits seemed intent on making me their kittypet. They wouldn't stop chasing me! I managed to lose them, but I lost track of my way home, too."

Bramblestar snorted a laugh as he got to his paws. Bristle-frost searched his gaze. Was he relieved to see Lionblaze home and safe? His face gave nothing away.

"He looks thin," Thriftear whispered, looking at Lionblaze.

"But he's safe now." Bristlefrost shifted guiltily. If she hadn't reported him, he'd never have been exiled. *Is he really safe now?* She remembered Bramblestar's warning at the Gathering. He'd said the codebreakers must atone. And Lionblaze had been named. Perhaps the ThunderClan leader was planning to punish Lionblaze again.

Bramblestar's gaze flitted over Lionblaze. "It looks like your time away will make you appreciate your life here," he meowed.

Lionblaze shook out his pelt. "A warrior is not meant to live without a Clan," he answered. "But I'm home now and ready to return to my duties."

Bramblestar narrowed his eyes. "Not so fast."

Bristlefrost pricked her ears. Was he going to send Lionblaze away again?

"While you were away, StarClan named you as a codebreaker." Bramblestar stared darkly at the tom.

Lionblaze stiffened. "What?"

"Shadowsight had a vision," Bramblestar explained. "It named all the codebreakers in the Clans. They must atone, or their Clans will suffer."

"Who's suffering?" Lionblaze looked pointedly around his Clanmates, then at the fully stocked fresh-kill pile.

Bramblestar narrowed his eyes. "The suffering hasn't started yet," he mewed ominously.

"You believe the word of a ShadowClan cat over your

own Clanmate's honor?" Lionblaze squared his shoulders. "I haven't broken any code!"

"What about crossing the WindClan border?" Bramblestar growled.

"I've paid for that." Lionblaze glared at him.

Squirrelflight got to her paws, her fur ruffled. "I was named too," she told Lionblaze, as though she wanted to reassure him. "So was Jayfeather and—"

"Jayfeather?" Lionblaze's gaze flashed toward the medicine den. "What's he ever done but help his Clan?"

Squirrelflight looked at the ground. "I think you are paying for my mistake."

"Because you and Leafpool lied about who our mother was?" Lionblaze sounded as though he couldn't believe his ears.

She nodded meekly.

"But that was moons ago!" Lionblaze snapped. "Why should StarClan drag that up now? And what has it got to do with me and Jayfeather? Did we break the code by being *born?*"

Bramblestar shrugged. "It's pointless arguing," he mewed smoothly. "StarClan has spoken. We must obey them."

"How?" Lionblaze snapped. "Am I supposed to apologize for being alive?"

"No." Bramblestar padded to the middle of the clearing and looked around at his Clanmates. "But I think it's time we began to atone."

Bristlefrost glanced at Thriftear. She was staring at

Bramblestar, her eyes round with worry. Around the clearing, her Clanmates exchanged uneasy glances.

Lionblaze padded after Bramblestar. "How do we 'atone'?"

"The codebreakers must make things right."

Bristlefrost's belly tightened. What was he going to demand of the named cats? She glanced nervously at Twigbranch. The gray she-cat sat up, her ears twitching.

Bramblestar looked at Lionblaze. "The codebreakers must swear an oath."

*Is that all?* Relief swamped Bristlefrost's pelt. Beside her, Thriftear's shoulders loosened. Twigbranch let out a long breath. Around the clearing, their Clanmates seemed to relax, their pelts smoothing.

"Okay." Lionblaze lifted his chin. "Whatever you want, if it will get this over with. If StarClan thinks I'm a codebreaker, then I'll atone."

Twigbranch got to her paws and padded into the clearing. "So will I."

Bramblestar lifted his muzzle. "Jayfeather!"

A few moments later, Jayfeather hurried from the medicine den. Flecks of herbs were caught in his pelt. "What is it?" He blinked blindly toward the camp entrance. "Is Sparkpelt back?" His nose twitched suddenly. "Lionblaze!" He hurried to the clearing as he smelled his brother's scent and, purring, touched his nose to Lionblaze's cheek. "Are you well? Have you had enough to eat?" He sniffed Lionblaze anxiously.

"I'm fine," Lionblaze promised.

"I want you to come to the medicine den so I can check you

over properly," Jayfeather told him. "You smell a bit sour."

"That's just from sleeping on strange bracken," Lionblaze told him.

Bramblestar flicked his tail. "You can have your reunion later. First you must swear your oath."

"Oath?" Jayfeather's eyes widened.

"He wants us to make amends to StarClan for breaking the code," Lionblaze explained.

Jayfeather snorted. "If I've broken the code then I'm sorry for it, but every cat knows I'm loyal. I don't need to swear an oath."

"Just do it," Lionblaze told him. "Then perhaps we can get back to normal."

Bramblestar's pelt twitched. "We can get back to normal when I say so," he growled. "This oath is just so that your Clanmates can see that you're sorry and that you are committed to obeying the code from now on."

"Next time," Lionblaze muttered, "I'll check who my parents are before I'm born."

Bristlefrost's heart sank in her chest when she saw Bramblestar's eyes light up with rage. Why was Lionblaze provoking him? The ThunderClan leader looked ready to spit something back at the warrior, but Squirrelflight hurried forward before he could speak.

Her eyes flashed with guilt. "Do I have to take the oath too?"

Bramblestar waved her away with a flick of his tail. "You've spent time in StarClan recently. Our ancestors sent you back to us." Bristlefrost had been told the story of how the deputy, and her medicine-cat sister, Leafpool, both went to StarClan after being injured in a landslide. Squirrelflight returned, but Leafpool did not.

"They have clearly forgiven you," Bramblestar went on. "There's no need for you to take the oath."

Squirrelflight stared at him, surprised.

*You see!* Bristlefrost felt a rush of happiness. *Bramblestar hasn't changed. He's still fair.* She blinked expectantly at Jayfeather, Lionblaze, and Twigbranch. What would the oath be? This would help their ancestors forgive them, she was sure. *I hope you're listening, StarClan.*

Bramblestar turned to face Jayfeather, Lionblaze and Twigbranch. "Repeat after me," he ordered. "'StarClan, forgive me for breaking your code.'"

Haltingly, the three cats echoed his words. Lionblaze shifted his paws awkwardly as Bramblestar went on.

"'I promise I will always obey my leader without question.'" The ThunderClan leader paused to let them repeat it. "'And I will do whatever I'm asked for the good of the Clan.'"

"As if we didn't before," Jayfeather mumbled when he'd finished saying the words.

Bramblestar grunted. "Just repeat it," he growled. "You don't need to comment. This is for the good of the Clan—to bring StarClan back." He pressed on. "'I will hunt only for my Clan. I will protect my Clanmates with my life. . . .'"

As the rules went on, Bristlefrost glanced at the entrance.

Sparkpelt still wasn't back. She wondered if the she-cat had found no catmint at the Twolegplace and had gone farther in search of new growth. She looked back at the clearing. Jayfeather, Lionblaze, and Twigbranch were repeating the last words of their oath.

"'If I break the code again, I will be exiled from my Clan to protect them from StarClan's anger.'"

*Exiled?* Bristlefrost frowned, noticing her Clanmates glancing at one another questioningly. She knew they were thinking the same thing she was—would this exile be permanent?

Thornclaw padded forward. "Surely a cat must do more than break the code to be exiled."

Bramblestar eyed the dark warrior accusingly. "If a cat chooses to break the warrior code again, they must be prepared to face the consequences."

"But—" As Thornclaw began to object, a groan sounded at the entrance. Bristlefrost jerked her muzzle toward the noise, heart lurching as she smelled blood. A moment later Sparkpelt staggered into camp. Blood showed on her pelt. Tufts of fur were missing. Every stumbling paw step seemed to take more strength than she had.

Squirrelflight raced forward, reaching her as she dropped to the ground.

Jayfeather rushed to Sparkpelt's side. "Alderheart! Bring cobwebs," he yowled across the clearing.

"What happened?" Squirrelflight pressed her muzzle to Sparkpelt's ear.

"There were dogs," Sparkpelt gasped. "At the abandoned Twoleg den. They attacked me. . . ." Jayfeather quickly sniffed along her flank.

Bristlefrost leaped to her paws. How could this have happened? She looked at Bramblestar. He must feel terrible that he'd sent Sparkpelt to the Twolegplace. But when she spotted the leader, she froze. Shock pulsed through her. The Thunder-Clan leader was watching Sparkpelt coldly, as though staring at a piece of prey. As Sparkpelt's Clanmates clustered around her and began to help her to the medicine den, Bramblestar sat down and began washing his face.

Bristlefrost stared at him, a chill running through her body. She backed away, ducking behind the elders' den, and caught her breath. What was wrong with Bramblestar? Dogs had just attacked his daughter. Didn't he care?

She headed for the entrance. If *he* didn't care, she did! She was going to find out what those dogs were doing on Thunder-Clan territory. If they'd made a home there, the Clan needed to know. No cat should risk being attacked by them again.

Outside camp, she broke into a run. Dusk was seeping through the forest, darkening the shadows. She raced through them, her pelt bushed, her nose twitching. She was breathless by the time she neared the abandoned Twoleg den. She slowed, tasting the air. There were dog scents here, but they were stale. There was no sound of movement as she crept around the crumbling stones and sniffed the ground. Sparkpelt's scent was here too, but there was another scent, just as familiar. Bristlefrost padded toward it, her whiskers twitching.

The earth beside the stone walls of the den was soaked with blood. It wasn't Sparkpelt's blood, or a dog's. She sniffed it. *Prey blood.* This spot smelled like fresh-kill. Her thoughts quickened. Some cat had made a fresh-kill pile here.

She frowned. Rogues didn't gather their prey. They ate it as they caught it. Only Clan cats made fresh-kill piles. Had Lionblaze sheltered here on his way back to the Clan?

She sniffed the stone walls around the blood-stained earth, but smelled only dog-scent. Lionblaze couldn't have stayed here. It would have been too dangerous.

She stiffened as a thought flashed through her mind. Had some cat gathered prey here on purpose? Had they *wanted* to lure dogs here? The earth seemed to shift beneath her paws, and she pictured Bramblestar washing his face while Squirrel-flight helped their daughter to the medicine den. Not only had he not been concerned, but he'd seemed unsurprised that she'd returned to camp injured. Had he known about the dogs when he sent her here? She felt sick. Squirrelflight's warning rang in her ears. *Rootpaw was right. It's not Bramblestar.* Had she been wrong to dismiss it? She leaned against the wall, her paws trembling.

Had Bramblestar tried to murder his own daughter?

# CHAPTER 15

As dusk softened the shadows of the pine forest, Shadowsight scratched delicately at the earth and leaned down to sniff a crack where new shoots were pushing open the soil. The fresh scent of marigold leaves touched his nose, and he sat up, satisfaction warming his belly. It had been more than three days since Bramblestar's impromptu Gathering, and new plants were now growing a short walk from camp. For a moment he thought only about herbs and the ointments he'd be able to mix once newleaf coaxed the first sign of fresh growth into full leaf. But as he gazed into the shadowy woods, his doubts returned. The satisfaction he'd felt at the sprouting marigold faded, and a chill crept through his fur.

Had he been right to tell the other medicine cats about his vision? Nothing had changed. There was still no sign of StarClan, and since the Gathering, prey hadn't been running any better in ShadowClan's part of the forest. Snowbird's broken paw was healing just as slowly. What had he expected? For StarClan to send him a vision congratulating him? He got to his paws. Of course there'd be no vision. But he had expected to feel a sense of relief at having shared the names of the codebreakers with the other Clans. Instead he only seemed to have succeeded in putting Dovewing in danger, just as Tigerstar has predicted. Bramblestar seemed determined to exact some sort of punishment on the codebreakers. There had been no talk of forgiveness.

"Shadowsight." Dovewing's call jerked him from his thoughts. His mother was padding through the forest toward him, her eyes warm with affection. "There you are." She stopped beside him and touched her nose to his ear.

Shadowsight blinked at her, worried. Why was she looking for him? He hadn't been out of camp long. "Does Puddleshine need me?"

"No." Dovewing glanced around the forest. "I was worried about you, that's all. You've seemed distracted since the Gathering."

"I'm fine." Shadowsight brushed loose soil gently over the crack in the earth to protect the new shoots and began to pad back to camp.

Dovewing fell in beside him. "You're worried about your vision, aren't you?"

"I'm not sure I should have shared it," he admitted. "I think it might have caused more trouble than it solved."

"You did what you thought was right," Dovewing told him gently.

"Tigerstar didn't think it was right." His father had hardly spoken to him since he'd shared the vision.

"He'll come around. He'll see that you did the right thing." Dovewing's pelt brushed Shadowsight's. "Eventually."

"But what if I didn't?" Shadowsight glanced at his mother. "I got you in trouble, maybe even Tigerstar. Bramblestar wouldn't even listen to him at the Gathering."

"Bramblestar has just got a burr in his pelt about codebreakers," she told him. "He didn't want to listen to *any* cat."

"But he must have been thinking that if you're a codebreaker, Tigerstar is too."

"Your father is a loyal and honorable warrior," she reminded him. "He only broke the code when he had no other choice— and no cat could do more than he has done to uphold it since."

"But what if he's named too?" Shadowsight's tail twitched nervously. "Will he be allowed to remain ShadowClan's leader?"

"Let's not get ahead of ourselves," she soothed. "The Clan respects him. Without him, there might be no ShadowClan. No cat's going to stop him being leader."

"But surely you've heard the whispers." Shadowsight lowered his voice as they neared the camp entrance. "Scorchfur was telling Yarrowleaf that StarClan might be angrier at ShadowClan than any other Clan because of you and Tigerstar."

"I hope you told him that's nonsense," Dovewing mewed sharply. "If StarClan is angry with me and Tigerstar, they won't punish our Clanmates for it." She ducked through the bramble tunnel. Shadowsight watched her go, wondering what it was going to take for her to really listen to him.

As Shadowsight followed her in, he was aware of their Clanmates eyeing him. Berryheart looked up from the mouse she was eating and narrowed her eyes. Snaketooth followed her gaze, her ears twitching. Shadowsight's pelt prickled self-consciously. He knew that they thought he was a traitor for betraying one of their Clanmates in the list of codebreakers.

He lowered his gaze as he headed toward the medicine den, relieved that Dovewing was with him. "*They* think I made the wrong choice," he murmured to Dovewing, pointing his muzzle toward the two warriors.

"Whorlpelt thinks you did the right thing." Dovewing dipped her head politely to the gray-and-white tom as they passed him. "Plenty of your Clanmates think we need to atone so that StarClan can come back."

"But not all." Resentment jabbed at Shadowsight's belly. "They were happy enough when I was the only medicine cat who was hearing from StarClan. But now that I've brought news they don't like, they say I'm too inexperienced to understand."

Dovewing paused as they reached the medicine den and ran her tail along his spine. "I know it hurts to have your Clanmates say mean things about you. But you mustn't listen to whispers. Warriors will always have an opinion. The most important thing is that you did what you thought was right. And you told the truth. In the end, it's lies that tear a Clan apart, not the truth." She gazed at him affectionately. "I wish you had as much faith in yourself as I do."

"Even though I got you in trouble?" Shadowsight blinked at her guiltily.

"It's not so bad," she told him. "If atoning for my

codebreaking will help, I'm happy to do it. There's no harm in admitting mistakes."

Her courage reassured him. As he blinked at her gratefully, a long, deep groan sounded from the medicine den. He stiffened. A cat was in pain.

Shadowsight darted inside, his heart lurching as he saw Pouncestep lying in a nest. Her eyes glittered with distress. Tawnypelt stood stiffly beside her, as though unsure what to do, while Puddleshine leaned over the nest, running his paws gently over Pouncestep's flank.

"What happened?" As Shadowsight crouched beside the nest, his sister groaned again.

Tawnypelt's eyes were round. "She fell from a tree after she disturbed a wasps' nest."

Dovewing hurried to Tawnypelt's side. Her gaze flicked in alarm from her injured kit to Puddleshine. "What's wrong with her?"

Puddleshine's paws traced a line along Pouncestep's flank. "It feels like she's broken a rib, but I can't feel any swelling. There's no bleeding inside." He looked at Tawnypelt. "Did she land on her paws?"

Before Tawnypelt could answer, Pouncestep lifted her head weakly. "I panicked. I didn't manage to turn in time." She groaned and lay back in her nest.

Shadowsight could see swelling around one eye and on her muzzle where the wasps had stung her. "I'll get some ointment." He hurried to the store, relieved that Pouncestep's injuries, while painful, weren't life-threatening. The stings would go down with a little dock and honey, and the rib would mend.

And yet he couldn't shake the feeling that something was wrong. It was another accident. He'd hoped that by sharing his vision, he'd fix ShadowClan's run of bad luck. Had he waited so long that StarClan was still angry? He pulled a leaf from the store and unfolded it. The honey he'd managed to gather a few moons earlier was still sticky. He reached in for a pawful of dock and some poppy seeds and carried them back to Pouncestep's nest.

"You can come back later." Puddleshine was shooing Tawnypelt and Dovewing away.

Tawnypelt eyed her denmate anxiously. "She'll be all right, won't she?"

"She'll be fine," Puddleshine told her. "She just needs to rest."

Dovewing touched her kit's ear with her nose. "I'll be back soon," she promised.

Pouncestep blinked at her gratefully. "I'll be okay."

As the two warriors ducked out of the den, Shadowsight tore a piece of dock leaf and chewed it up. He spat the pulp into the honey and mixed it, while Puddleshine gave Pouncestep the poppy seeds.

The gray tabby she-cat closed her eyes. "It hurts to breathe," she whispered.

"It will for a while," Puddleshine told her. "But you'll be okay."

As Pouncestep closed her eyes, Shadowsight rubbed the

ointment gently into her stings. A few moments later, her breath grew deeper as she slipped into sleep.

Shadowsight glanced at Puddleshine anxiously. "Should we wake her?" He didn't want her slipping into too deep a slumber.

Puddleshine shook his head. "Sleep will do her good."

Shadowsight blinked at him. "I thought the accidents would stop when I shared my vision."

"This could have happened at any time," Puddleshine told him. "It may have nothing to do with StarClan."

But doubt tugged at Shadowsight's belly. "Maybe I should have shared my vision earlier," he mewed. "Or maybe Tigerstar was right, and I shouldn't have shared it at all."

"It's pointless second-guessing StarClan." Puddleshine's gaze was clear and round. "You can only do what you think is best." He tipped his head. "Have you had any more visions?"

"Nothing." Shadowsight dropped his gaze. "They've stopped talking to me." He felt suddenly lost. Even during the long leaf-bare, when StarClan had been silent for the other medicine cats, they'd spoken to *him*. "Why are they silent now? I've done everything they asked."

Puddleshine held his gaze solemnly. "Are you sure your visions have been from StarClan?" he asked suddenly.

Shadowsight stared at him. "Of course they are!" Did Puddleshine think he'd dreamed them up?

"It does seem strange that they only spoke to one cat." Puddleshine looked thoughtful.

"They were *visions*, I promise," Shadowsight mewed

fervently. "I didn't imagine them."

"I know." Puddleshine frowned. "But I can't help think-ing that the Clans shouldn't act on any more visions until StarClan starts sharing with all the medicine cats again."

Shadowsight felt queasy. "Do you think I've done some-thing wrong?"

"No," Puddleshine mewed quickly. "But every vision seems to have pushed the Clans deeper into conflict. I don't see why StarClan would want to lead us down that path."

Shadowsight stared at him. Did Puddleshine also believe that he should have protected ShadowClan by keeping the vision to himself? Feeling hollow, he headed for the entrance.

"Where are you going?" Puddleshine called after him.

"I have to think," he answered. "I'm going for a walk."

Night had fallen, and the camp was dark as he crossed the clearing. His Clanmates were sharing tongues beside their dens. He avoided their glances as he headed for the entrance and slipped into the forest.

Puddleshine's words had unsettled him. Could it be true that he'd misinterpreted StarClan's signs? Were his ancestors trying to send him a deeper message that he was too mouse-brained to understand? Instinctively he headed for the edge of the forest and the stream that would lead him to the Moon-pool. Perhaps they'd talk to him now, if he confessed that he didn't understand their visions and begged them to just tell him what they wanted.

The moon was high by the time he pulled himself over the lip of the hollow and followed the dimpled rock down to the pool. The black surface reflected no stars, and the dark water made him nervous. Was StarClan determined not to listen? His heart quickened as he crouched at the edge. *Please, StarClan, speak to me. I only want to make things right, for you and for the Clans.* Surely they'd hear the longing in his heart and respond? The Moonpool was cold, but the thawed water rippled as he touched his nose to it. He let his mind clear, waiting for the wide green meadows of StarClan to open before him and the voices of cats he'd only known in visions to speak to him.

He saw only endless darkness. The chill of the stone beneath his paws seemed to reach through him, until he felt as cold as ice. Fear trickled along his spine, and he shivered, suddenly unnerved. The weight of another cat's gaze seemed to press into his pelt. Was some cat watching him? He lifted his head sharply and blinked open his eyes. In the silence of the night, he could sense another presence in the hollow. He fluffed out his fur, feeling suddenly vulnerable in the Moonpool's wide stone basin beneath the endless black sky. Fear wormed beneath his pelt and, keeping low, he crept away from the water and hurried up the spiraling path to the lip of the hollow. He scrambled over the edge, relieved as the shadows swallowed him.

He had felt nothing of StarClan in the hollow, and as he padded quickly along the stream that cut through the moor and led back toward the forest, his pelt prickled with foreboding. He realized with a sense of dread that none of the visions had swept him to the sun-drenched meadows of StarClan. There had been no glittering pelts, only a single disembodied voice swathed in shadow. That voice had told him to take Bramblestar onto the moor to let him die. It had told him that the Clans must suffer until the codebreakers were punished.

Puddleshine's words rang again in his head. *Every vision seems to have pushed the Clans deeper into conflict.* His mentor was right. Each time he'd shared what he'd seen, the Clans had grown more frightened and more defensive. *I don't see why StarClan would want to lead us down that path.* StarClan had only ever wanted the Clans to be safe and happy. Why would they demand suffering now?

He glanced back toward the hollow, no more than a silhouette against the starry sky. He'd gone to the Moonpool to find clarity. And he had, but not in the way he'd expected. Certainty sat like a rock in his belly. The voice, which had told him to cure Bramblestar by letting him die and had shown him the codebreakers, belonged to a spirit that knew the Clans. But he knew now, with a sureness that filled him with horror, that the voice had never been the voice of StarClan.

# CHAPTER 16

*Rootpaw peered from the den entrance* and tasted the damp night air. Musty forest scents bathed his tongue. The dark clearing was deserted. He pricked his ears and heard only the call of an owl far away in the forest. Anxiety fluttered in his belly as he glanced at the moon. It was already high in the raven-black sky. His Clanmates had taken ages to settle into their dens and go to sleep. *I'm going to be late for the meeting!*

Bracken rustled behind him, and he jerked his muzzle around, alarm sparking in his pelt. Had one of his denmates woken? In the shadows, he saw Wrenpaw curl tighter in her nest and settle deeper into the moss. Needlepaw was still snoring softly beside her.

Holding his breath, Rootpaw slipped outside, skirting the clearing as he made for the entrance. He quickened his step. Once he was out in the forest, he would only have to worry about being seen by foxes and badgers. For once, he wished that Bramblestar's ghost were with him. He didn't like being alone in the woods at night, and another pair of eyes would be useful. But the ghost had disappeared last night and Rootpaw hadn't seen it since. Perhaps it had gone to keep an eye on

Squirrelflight. She'd looked pretty scared when she'd found out her mate was an impostor.

"Rootpaw?" A whisper from the shadows made him freeze. Fur spiking, he glanced around, his heart sinking as he recognized his father's yellow pelt glowing in the moonlight.

Tree padded from the darkness beside the camp wall. "You're up late."

"So are you." Irritation hardened Rootpaw's belly. Why couldn't his father be asleep in his nest like the rest of the Clan? "What are you doing here?"

"I like to watch the stars when every cat is sleeping." Tree glanced at the sky. "It's nice to have some time to myself." He glanced back at Rootpaw. "Why aren't you asleep?"

Rootpaw shifted his paws self-consciously. "I was on my way to the dirtplace."

Tree looked unconvinced. "Why not use the dirtplace tunnel?" He nodded across the clearing.

"I . . . wanted to stretch my legs." Rootpaw blinked, his thoughts whirling. How could he get rid of Tree? The meeting would be starting soon.

Tree's eyes rounded. "I thought Leafstar told you not to leave camp without permission after your trip to Thunder-Clan."

Rootpaw flicked his tail crossly. Tree wasn't going to make this easy. "There's somewhere I have to be," he snapped.

"Where?" Tree tipped his head to one side.

"A meeting, *okay*?" Why couldn't Tree just let him go?

"Does this have something to do with the ghost?" Tree

leaned closer, concern darkening his eyes.

"No," Rootpaw told him. "I haven't seen it all day."

"Are you meeting Bristlefrost?" Tree blinked at him.

"No!" Rootpaw stuck out his chin. "Spotfur and Stemleaf invited me to a meeting of cats who are worried about what's going on in the Clans."

Tree pricked his ears. "Other cats are worried too?" He sounded relieved.

"Of course they are." Rootpaw's shoulders drooped. He was going to have to tell Tree everything. "Stemleaf and Spotfur invited me when we were leaving the Gathering. They're going to see if there's something they can do to stop what's happening."

Tree whisked his tail. "Then I'd better come with you."

"No!" Rootpaw stared at him, dismayed. What would the other cats think if he turned up with his father?

"Why not?" Tree looked surprised. "You know I've been worried about the direction the Clans are heading. If other cats are meeting to discuss it, I want to be there."

Rootpaw realized it would be pointless to object. Tree was never going to let him sneak out if he didn't get to come too. "Okay," he muttered. "But we have to hurry. The meeting starts at moonhigh."

Tree glanced at the sky. "Come on, then."

Rootpaw padded after his father as Tree hurried out of camp. He fluffed out his fur. *At least I have that other pair of eyes now.* As the forest stretched away into darkness on every side, he forced back a shiver. The journey suddenly felt dangerous.

want the codebreakers punished too."

Stemleaf's gaze darkened. "I know," he mewed grimly. "If we stand up to Bramblestar, we'll be challenging StarClan."

Rootpaw shifted his paws. "Perhaps StarClan doesn't want the codebreakers to suffer as much as Bramblestar does," he ventured. "Perhaps they only want them to acknowledge that they've broken the code."

Spotfur frowned. "Not every codebreaker knows what they've done wrong."

Twigbranch's ears twitched. "I wish I knew exactly what *I've* done wrong," she mewed. "I'd happily own up to it if I did. I've only ever wanted to be a loyal warrior."

Cloverfoot met her gaze. "*All* the codebreakers want to be loyal warriors. I don't understand why they must be punished."

"Bramblestar seems intent on making life miserable for the codebreakers in ThunderClan," Finleap mewed, shaking his head.

"Banishing cats!" Outrage edged Cloverfoot's mew. "Clans are supposed to stick together, not turn their backs on their Clanmates."

"We're meant to support one another through good times and bad," Sneezecloud mewed.

Slightfoot's pelt twitched. "Warriors are honorable because they *want* to be, not because they're scared of being punished!"

"We look after our Clanmates because we care about them," Whorlpelt chimed. "Not just because we're obeying rules."

Frecklewish frowned. "But StarClan does want us to follow the rules," she mewed.

"Well, if Bramblestar weren't yowling about punishment all the time, the Clans could find a better way to deal with the codebreakers," Stemleaf replied, annoyed.

Cloverfoot's eyes narrowed. "What are you suggesting?"

Stemleaf lifted his chin. "Bramblestar is trying to make us act like Darktail's Kin. He wants us to turn on one another. But warriors aren't cruel. They never have been. Bramblestar must have bees in his brain. We have to get rid of him before he spoils the Clans forever."

Rootpaw's chest tightened. Was a ThunderClan cat really suggesting the Clans turn on his leader?

"If we try to get rid of Bramblestar, we'll be breaking the code in the worst way possible," Cloverfoot argued.

Frecklewish's eyes widened. "What would StarClan think about that?"

Stemleaf stared at the SkyClan medicine cat. "We have to do something! StarClan can't really want us to turn our backs on one another. If Bramblestar wants to banish cats, I say we should banish *him*!" He gazed around at the cats, and Rootpaw saw Sneezecloud, Slightfoot, and Breezepelt nod in agreement.

*What would the ghost say if it were here?* thought Rootpaw. *It'd want me to tell them that the ThunderClan leader is an impostor.* Rootpaw curled his claws into the ground. It would be so much simpler for these cats if they knew they were rebelling against an intruder and not a Clanmate. Tree was looking at him. He could read his father's expression clearly. *Tell them,* it urged. Rootpaw tried to force himself to say the words, but he couldn't. Shame washed his pelt. What if they thought he was crazy? What if they accused him of lying?

Cloverfoot shook her head. "How could we banish the leader of ThunderClan?" Her gaze flashed around the cats. "There aren't enough of us."

Sneezecloud nodded. "And we're from different Clans. Even if we could each persuade our own Clans that what we're doing is for the best, what could we do—invade Thunder-Clan's camp?"

"We could end up causing a war," Cloverfoot agreed.

"Not if enough cats agree that Bramblestar has to go," Stemleaf argued.

Breezepelt snorted. "When was the last time the Clans agreed on anything without fighting about it first?"

The cats looked at one another, hesitating.

Tree raised his muzzle. "Is it really worth fighting about? Doesn't it make more sense to leave the Clans if you don't like them?" He looked around at the gathered cats.

Cloverfoot's ears flattened. Finleap's tail flicked danger-ously as Tree went on.

"You could make your own Clan. Or be free to live how you like. I lived alone for a long time and it was great. Why let some crazy cat tell you what to do if you don't agree with them?"

Rootpaw's head drooped. Didn't Tree realize what he was saying? Did he really understand so little about being a war-rior? He nudged Tree, but his father hadn't finished.

"I think we should show Bramblestar what we think of his

codebreaking rules by leaving—"

Rootpaw stepped forward, cutting Tree off. "Leaving isn't an option." He looked pointedly at Tree. "If we can't drive Bramblestar away by force, we have to find another way to deal with him." His thoughts quickened. This was his chance to help the others see that something was wrong with the ThunderClan leader. "Haven't you noticed how much he's changed since he lost a life?" He looked questioningly at the cats, relieved to see some of them nodding. "Losing a life is scary, but is it supposed to change you *completely*?"

"It didn't change Leafstar," Blossomheart mewed.

Rootpaw's pelt spiked. Had Leafstar lost a life? He'd thought she still had nine. Perhaps Blossomheart was mistaken.

Frecklewish flashed a warning look at Blossomheart, and the ginger-and-white she-cat quickly dropped her gaze.

Cloverfoot was frowning. "Tigerstar didn't change when he lost a life. I don't see why any cat would. Surely one life is the same as another, and Bramblestar still has eight left, which is more than most leaders."

Finleap flicked his tail. "The old Bramblestar would never have acted like this."

*The old Bramblestar.* Rootpaw blinked at the ThunderClan tom. Had he guessed that his leader was an impostor?

"I wish he'd pull himself together and be normal again," Finleap went on.

Rootpaw's heart sank. Finleap clearly had no idea. "Perhaps he can't be normal again. Perhaps something happened while he was dead." He blinked at the others, willing them to guess. He could feel Tree staring at him. He knew his father was urging him to speak, but he avoided catching his eye. *Just tell them!* The words were on his tongue, but he couldn't bring himself to speak.

Spotfur stared at him, puzzled. "Do you think StarClan said something to him while he was dead?"

Tree padded forward. "Something happened while he was dead, but I don't think it was anything to do with StarClan." The other cats stared at him, ears pricking as Tree went on. "The cat that came back isn't Bramblestar."

"What do you mean?" Stemleaf looked puzzled.

"It can't be Bramblestar," Tree told him. "Because I've seen Bramblestar's ghost in the forest. I've spoken to it."

Stemleaf's eyes widened. "You saw his ghost?"

"You *spoke* to it?" Spotfur stared at Tree in disbelief.

Gratitude flooded beneath Rootpaw's fur. The truth was out. And he didn't have to admit to seeing dead cats. They'd have to do something now, wouldn't they?

Frecklewish frowned. "But Bramblestar is alive. He *can't* be a ghost."

"The Bramblestar who came back isn't the *real* Bramble-star," Tree told her. "Some cat is using his body to harm the Clans. The real Bramblestar is a ghost. He can see what's going on, but he can't contact StarClan. I'm the only cat he can talk to."

Frecklewish's pelt was bristling as she stared at Tree. "Do you mean that the leader of ThunderClan is an impostor?"

Tree nodded.

Rootpaw saw the cats exchange glances. Their eyes were wide with confusion.

"A cat *stole* another cat's body. . . ." Whorlpelt stared, open-mouthed, as his mew trailed away, clearly struggling to believe what he was saying.

Breezepelt's ear twitched. "How can that be? Surely no cat could steal a body?"

Tree shrugged. "All I know is that Bramblestar's ghost is trapped in the forest and his body is being used by some other cat."

"It's too crazy to believe," Cloverfoot breathed.

Rootpaw leaned forward eagerly. *You have to believe him!*

As the cats eyed one another doubtfully, Tree whisked his tail. "If you don't want to believe me, then don't. But how would you explain the way Bramblestar has changed?"

Stemleaf and Spotfur exchanged glances. Breezepelt frowned. Rootpaw felt queasy. Were they going to reject Tree's claim?

Twigbranch padded forward. "The Bramblestar who's lead-ing the Clan is not the Bramblestar any of us grew up with." Her eyes glittered anxiously. "Since he made his new rule that he and Squirrelflight can take prey from the fresh-kill pile before the elders and queens, he's become even more strict."

Breezepelt blinked in surprise. "Did Squirrelflight *agree* with this rule?"

Twigbranch shifted, uncomfortable. "She didn't seem happy," she murmured.

Breezepelt's hackles lifted. "How could any warrior take

prey before elders and queens?"

"What a fox-heart!" Cloverfoot hissed.

Frecklewish's eyes flashed. "I think we need to speak to Shadowsight."

"Why Shadowsight?" Stemleaf looked at her.

"He's the one who told ThunderClan to take Bramblestar to the moor when he was sick," Frecklewish explained. "He was there when Bramblestar got his second life. Didn't he say that StarClan had told him what to do?"

"Do you think Shadowsight's behind this?" Cloverfoot looked scared.

Rootpaw searched Frecklewish's gaze. *Was* Shadowsight helping the impostor? He leaned forward as the SkyClan medicine cat's eyes darkened.

"He's very young," she mewed thoughtfully. "I was surprised that StarClan put so much trust in him. But if he *is* involved, I don't think he realizes what he's doing. It's strange that he's the only medicine cat StarClan has shared with all leaf-bare. There might be more to their messages than he thinks." She looked at Cloverfoot. "Can you ask him about his vision?"

Cloverfoot shifted her paws uneasily. "He's Tigerstar's son. How would it look if the ShadowClan deputy questioned him? ShadowClan is still fragile after Darktail. I don't want to cause doubt. Besides, it might scare him into trying to cover his tracks."

"So you think he *has* been up to something?" Stemleaf flicked his tail.

"I don't think Shadowsight is capable of doing anything dishonest, but he might have made a mistake," Cloverfoot mewed.

"I'll speak to him." Frecklewish lifted her chin. "I'm a medicine cat. I can ask him about his visions without it seeming strange. There might be something he's missing."

"I'll help you." Rootpaw blinked at the SkyClan medicine cat. "We're kind of friends. He might open up if I'm there."

"Okay." Stemleaf lifted his tail. "We'll find out more about Shadowsight's visions before we decide what to do next." As the other cats nodded, Stemleaf headed for the bushes. "We'd better get back to our Clans before any cat notices we're missing."

Rootpaw felt relieved. Other cats, besides him and Tree, knew about the impostor. *It isn't just my problem anymore.* He blinked gratefully at Tree as they crossed the hollow. If they left now, they'd be home long before their Clanmates woke.

Rootpaw stiffened, his heart lurching. The branches rustled on the far side of the hollow. A shape was slinking from the shadows. Had the meeting been discovered? His breath caught in his throat as he recognized the pale gray fur. *Bristlefrost!* What was she doing here?

"Run!" Twigbranch's pelt spiked with panic. "It's Bramblestar's spy! Get out of here. She'll report us!"

Rootpaw froze as the others scrambled for the bushes. He stared at Bristlefrost. *Bramblestar's spy?* His throat tightened. Was she helping the impostor?

# CHAPTER 17

*Bristlefrost blinked in dismay. Did they* really believe she'd betray them? "I won't report you!" Panic sparked through her fur. "I came here to . . ." Her words trailed away as the cats hesitated, stopping and turning to look back at her, staring at her like prey watching a patrol. Why was she here? She hadn't even been sure she should come. Was she really ready to turn on Bramblestar? Guilt tugged at her belly. He trusted her more than he trusted any other cat in ThunderClan. But something was very wrong with her leader. He'd tried to kill his own daughter. Rootpaw had been right. She'd heard it with her own ears. Bramblestar wasn't himself. She lifted her muzzle. "I came here to join you."

Stemleaf looked suspicious. "Join us?"

Around him, the other cats shifted uneasily. Spotfur narrowed her eyes. Sneezecloud and Dappletuft moved closer together, eyeing her distrustfully. Breezepelt flattened his ears.

"I'm worried about Bramblestar," Bristlefrost blurted. She didn't want to admit she'd been eavesdropping, but she wanted ThunderClan to go back to normal.

"How long have you been here?" Stemleaf's hackles lifted.

"Not long," she told him. "I just heard the last bit," she told him. "I know Bramblestar's not really Bramblestar." She searched Stemleaf's gaze. Would he believe her? "You want to get rid of him."

Stemleaf frowned as though trying to decide if he could trust her.

Spotfur pushed past him, her ears twitching angrily. "How did you find out about this meeting?"

"I heard you talking about it with Stemleaf," Bristlefrost told her.

"So you were spying again?" Spotfur's mew was hard.

*Again.* The word stung. Did her Clanmates really think she was a spy? She'd only been trying to help Bramblestar make sure ThunderClan was following the warrior code. "Not spying," Bristlefrost mewed. "I was coming back from the dirtplace and I heard you telling Twigbranch and Finleap about it. I didn't mean to overhear."

Twigbranch padded closer. "Why did you come?"

"I told you." Bristlefrost swallowed. A small part of her had believed her Clanmates would be pleased to see her. She was disappointed to see that they weren't. "I'm worried about Bramblestar. He's been acting weird. But you say it's *not* Bramblestar. And that makes sense. Bramblestar was always kind. He always wanted the best for his Clan, but I think this Bramblestar wants to hurt ThunderClan." She remembered the scent of fresh-kill at the abandoned Twoleg den. "He doesn't care who suffers."

The other cats were creeping closer, circling her. Their tails flicked uneasily, but there was interest in their gazes. She noticed Rootpaw and felt her chest loosen. He'd trust her, wouldn't he? They were friends.

"We're going to ask Shadowsight about his visions," Rootpaw told her. "He might be able to give us a clue about who the impostor is."

Bristlefrost thought it was a good plan, but she had a better one. "Then what?" She didn't wait for an answer. "We have to expose Bramblestar. It's the only way we'll be safe. We need the support of more powerful cats."

"More powerful?" Frecklewish swished her tail. "Shadowsight is a *medicine cat*. So am I. Leaders listen to us."

"But Shadowsight is a ShadowClan cat, and you're SkyClan. We need more support in ThunderClan." Bristlefrost glanced around at the watching cats, relieved as their fur smoothed. They believed she was here to help. She went on. "There's a cat in ThunderClan who already suspects Bramblestar's not Bramblestar. If we can persuade her to join us, we might be able to get rid of the impostor without a fight."

Spotfur pricked her ears. "Who are you talking about?"

Bristlefrost met her gaze. *Squirrelflight.* She hesitated, swallowing back the name. Would telling them undo the little trust she'd gained? *They might not believe me.* Squirrelflight was Bramblestar's deputy. And his mate. She lifted her chin. She had to tell them. The ThunderClan deputy might be their strongest ally. "Squirrelflight."

"Squirrelflight?" Stemleaf blinked in surprise. "She's his

mate. Why would she turn against him?"

Spotfur nodded. "What if she accuses us of treason?"

Rootpaw stiffened. "She'd never do that!"

Bristlefrost saw his pelt ruffle along his spine. She met his gaze hopefully as the other cats stared at him.

Stemleaf narrowed his eyes. "What makes you so sure?"

"I took her a message from the ghost," Rootpaw mewed softly.

The cats' gazes widened.

Tree stepped forward. "I asked him to," he told them. "The ghost told me I needed to get a message to Squirrelflight, and it was easier for Rootpaw to sneak into the ThunderClan camp without causing suspicion."

Bristlefrost frowned at Tree in confusion. "The ghost told *you*?" Hadn't Rootpaw told her the ghost had spoken to him, not Tree?

"Yes," Tree answered.

Rootpaw blinked at her imploringly. "Tree can see dead cats," he mewed. "So the ghost talked to him."

She hesitated. Rootpaw clearly wanted her to go along with this story. Tree was staring at her too. There had to be a good reason why they were lying about which one of them could see the ghost. She swished her tail. "He's telling the truth," she mewed.

Frecklewish narrowed her eyes. "What message did you give her?" she asked Rootpaw.

"What did the ghost want to tell her?" Whorlpelt added.

Bristlefrost glanced at Rootpaw. She remembered the

message as though it were burned into her thoughts.

Rootpaw was staring solemnly at Whorlpelt. "He wanted to tell her that he didn't know who was in his body, but it wasn't him."

The gathered cats exchanged glances, unease glittering in their eyes.

"She didn't believe it at first," Bristlefrost added. "But with how strangely Bramblestar's been acting, she couldn't deny it for long."

Breezepelt tipped his head thoughtfully. "But even if she believes it now, she can't just get rid of him. She'd need the support of her Clanmates. It could be dangerous."

Stemleaf nodded. "We don't want our Clanmates fighting one another," he agreed.

"And we can't risk Bramblestar getting hurt," Spotfur chimed. "Bramblestar's ghost will want his body back."

Stemleaf gazed around at the other cats. They swapped anxious glances as silence filled the hollow.

Bristlefrost puffed out her chest, frustrated. "We have to do something," she pressed. "The impostor tried to kill Sparkpelt."

Twigbranch's pelt spiked. "What?"

"The dogs that attacked her weren't there by accident," Bristlefrost looked around at the other cats. "Bramblestar sent Sparkpelt to search for catmint beside the abandoned Twoleg den on our land," she explained. "She was attacked by dogs while she was looking for it. I went to investigate and found that some cat had been storing fresh-kill inside the old den. I think it was Bramblestar. I think he'd been luring dogs there for days before he sent Sparkpelt to fetch the catmint."

"How do you know it was Bramblestar?" Frecklewish asked.

"Who else could it have been?" Bristlefrost blinked at her. "He was angry with her because she'd tried to find Lionblaze. So he sent her there even after Alderheart told him that catmint wouldn't be growing yet."

Twigbranch padded closer to Finleap, her tail twitching nervously. "Are any of us safe?"

"I don't think so." Bristlefrost blinked at her. "That's why we have to persuade Squirrelflight to join us. I don't think it will be hard. She must want the real Bramblestar back, too."

Spotfur's gaze glittered warily. "Why should we believe you really want to help? You could be spying for Bramblestar."

"Why would I spy for an impostor?" Bristlefrost squared her shoulders. "You *have* to trust me. I only tried to help Bramblestar before I knew what he was. But now that I know he's not Bramblestar, I want to protect my Clan. I'll do anything you ask."

Stemleaf eyed her suspiciously. "Do you think you can persuade Squirrelflight to join us?"

"Of course!" Bristlefrost blinked at him eagerly.

Spotfur pricked her ears. "Joining us isn't enough. She has to tell the other leaders that Bramblestar's an impostor."

"I can ask her."

"You have to *convince* her," Spotfur pressed. "It's the only way we can save the Clans from Bramblestar."

"I'll try." Bristlefrost's paws pricked excitedly. She was

going to help make everything okay again.

Spotfur looked around at the cats. "If Squirrelflight tells the other Clans what's going on, they'll have to help us."

Frecklewish's ears twitched uneasily. "What if they don't believe her?" she mewed. "After all, she's one of the code-breakers."

Sneezecloud nodded. "Bramblestar has only been trying to make sure the Clans follow StarClan's message about the codebreakers. It's going to be hard convincing every cat that he's an impostor when StarClan's on his side."

"We have to have faith in our Clanmates," Stemleaf told the RiverClan warrior. "They'll recognize the truth when they hear it, just like Squirrelflight did. And the more Clans that know the truth, the less power he'll have."

Breezepelt grunted. "Won't it just seem like she's stirring up trouble?"

"Trouble has already been stirred up!" Spotfur glared at him. "Do you want to stand by while this impostor banishes some poor cat forever, or tries to send more of his Clanmates to their deaths?"

Breezepelt whisked his tail. "Of course not. But we can't think this is going to be easy."

Bristlefrost lifted her muzzle. "Squirrelflight can do it."

Frecklewish's gaze darkened. "I hope so."

Dawn was already lighting the edge of the sky by the time Bristlefrost reached camp. She'd trailed behind Stemleaf and Spotfur, keeping her distance, unsure if they'd forgiven her for helping Bramblestar. Besides, the other two warriors were so close now, she felt awkward around them. She'd put her feelings for Stemleaf aside, but it didn't mean that seeing him and Spotfur together didn't hurt. They'd gone to their nests by the time she reached the hollow, and she crouched below the Highledge and waited for her Clanmates to wake up.

As daylight filtered through the trees, she got to her paws, shaking out the chill that had reached through her pelt. Thornclaw was the first cat to wake. He padded, blinking, from the warriors' den, nodding as he saw Bristlefrost cross the clearing. "Should I lead the first patrol?" he asked.

"Yes." She blinked at him gratefully. She'd forgotten she was supposed to organize the dawn patrols. "You can decide who to take with you."

"Okay." As Thornclaw ducked back into the den to wake his denmates, stones cracked on the rock tumble.

Bristlefrost jerked her muzzle toward it, relieved to see Squirrelflight scrambling into the clearing.

She stopped beside Bristlefrost. "Have you organized the first patrol?"

Bristlefrost nodded. "Thornclaw is leading it," she mewed. "I told him to take whoever he wants."

"Good." Squirrelflight glanced back toward the Highledge. "Bramblestar is still sleeping. He'll want to see his Clanmates hard at work when he wakes."

Bristlefrost looked at her solemnly. "Can I talk to you?" she asked. "In private?"

Squirrelflight narrowed her eyes. "Sure." She led Bristlefrost to the edge of the camp, and as Thornclaw led Lionblaze, Mousewhisker, and Birchfall from the den, she faced Bristle-frost, her eyes sparkling with curiosity. "What is it?"

Bristlefrost hesitated, waiting for the patrol to head out into the forest. As soon as the last warrior had disappeared, she met Squirrelflight's gaze. "I've come from a meeting," she began.

"Just now?" Squirrelflight's ears twitched.

"A few cats from every Clan met to discuss Bramblestar." She glanced nervously at Highledge. "They know he's an impostor."

"How?" Squirrelflight shifted her paws.

"Tree told them," Bristlefrost explained. "I guess Rootpaw must have told him."

"What are they planning to do?" Squirrelflight leaned closer.

"They can't do anything until they have more support," Bristlefrost told her. "They want you to talk to the other lead-ers and tell them about Bramblestar. We need to stand up to him, but we can't until other cats are willing to stand beside us." She searched the ThunderClan deputy's gaze hopefully. It would be a big risk to share what she knew about Bramble-star with other leaders. What if they took advantage of ThunderClan's vulnerability? What if they didn't believe her and reported her to Bramblestar as a traitor? Her pelt pricked anxiously.

Squirrelflight's eyes gleamed in the early morning light. She glanced at the Highledge, then met Bristlefrost's gaze.

"I'll do it," she mewed. "I'll go to Leafstar first. I think she'll listen. SkyClan hasn't been accused of codebreaking. That makes her freer to decide what to do."

"What if she doesn't believe you?" Bristlefrost asked. "The impostor has StarClan on his side."

"I can only tell her what I know," Squirrelflight mewed. "Each warrior will have to decide for themselves. But every cat has seen how Bramblestar's been acting."

"Some cats think he's right," Bristlefrost pointed out. "They agree that the codebreakers must atone to bring StarClan back. Standing up to Bramblestar might mean war."

"No true warrior would knowingly bring suffering on the Clans." Squirrelflight held her gaze. "If we can persuade the leaders and the medicine cats that Bramblestar is an impostor and must be stopped, a war won't last for long."

Bristlefrost stiffened as a shadow flitted along the Highledge. Bramblestar was heading toward the rock tumble. "He's coming." She swallowed back panic.

"It's okay." Squirrelflight straightened. "He doesn't know we know."

"How will you get to Leafstar?" Bristlefrost asked. "He won't let you out of the camp."

"I'm a codebreaker, aren't I?" Squirrelflight winked at her, then turned to face Bramblestar as he leaped down the rock tumble.

Bristlefrost struggled to keep her fur flat. Butterflies were fluttering in her belly. Could they really get away with this? Her heart lurched as Bramblestar called out to Squirrelflight.

"I woke up and you weren't there." He crossed the clearing. He sounded hurt. "I wondered where you'd gone."

"I wanted to discuss the patrols with Bristlefrost before I left," Squirrelflight told him smoothly.

"Left?" Bramblestar's eyes widened. "You know I want you to stay here."

Bristlefrost's heart quickened. Squirrelflight clearly had a plan.

"I've been thinking about StarClan's message," Squirrelflight told him. "I think I need to atone for my codebreaking."

Bristlefrost pricked her ears. What was Squirrelflight talking about?

Bramblestar's ears twitched. "But you've spoken to StarClan. They've forgiven you."

"Perhaps," Squirrelflight mewed. "But we must obey StarClan's message, and more important, the other Clans must *see* us obeying it. How else can we expect others to follow StarClan's orders? I must show them all that I am willing to atone."

"You could take the oath Lionblaze and Jayfeather took," Bramblestar suggested.

"No." Squirrelflight's gaze was firm. "Lionblaze had to leave the Clan as punishment for breaking the code. I must do the same."

Excitement fizzed in Bristlefrost's paws as she suddenly understood Squirrelflight's plan. She was going to use the excuse of atoning to travel to the other Clans and warn them!

"I'll leave for a few days to make my peace with StarClan,"

Squirrelflight went on. "They can see for themselves that I am sorry for breaking the code. If they're going to come back, they must see *every* codebreaker atone. No warrior is above the code—not even a deputy."

Bristlefrost glanced at Bramblestar. His fur was pricking uneasily along his spine. Was he convinced? "It would impress the Clan if Squirrelflight atoned," she mewed quickly. "They'll try even harder to follow the code, and StarClan will come back sooner." She stared at him, willing him to agree to Squirrelflight's plan.

Bramblestar's gaze flicked from Bristlefrost to Squirrelflight. "I guess," he murmured.

"I won't be gone for long, and when I get back, I'll be an even better deputy," Squirrelflight pressed.

Bramblestar flicked his tail. "Okay," he mewed. "You can go."

"If I go straight away, I can come back sooner." Squirrelflight turned to Bristlefrost. "Can you organize all the patrols while I'm gone?"

"I'll do my best," Bristlefrost promised.

Squirrelflight touched her nose to Bramblestar's muzzle. "I'll miss you," she murmured.

Bristlefrost saw the ThunderClan deputy's tail twitch. *It must be hard for her to pretend that the impostor is Bramblestar.* She dipped her head politely as Squirrelflight headed toward the entrance. Bramblestar stared after his mate. He looked forlorn.

Bristlefrost's belly tightened. He might take his mood out on ThunderClan. She needed to soothe him. "Don't worry," she mewed awkwardly. "She won't be gone long. Why don't you go back to sleep?" Nests were rustling. The rest of the Clan was waking up. She wanted Bramblestar safely in his den before he could accuse more cats of codebreaking. She nodded toward the empty fresh-kill pile. "There's no prey, and there's nothing to do except organize the first hunting patrol."

"I guess," he grunted. "The sun's hardly up."

Relief washed her pelt as Bramblestar headed toward the rock tumble and scrambled up it.

Graystripe padded sleepily from the elders' den. He eyed Bramblestar as the ThunderClan leader disappeared into his den. "Why is he up so early?"

"Squirrelflight's gone to atone," Bristlefrost told him. "He was saying good-bye."

As Graystripe's eyes widened with surprise, she pressed back hope. The old warrior had no idea that Squirrelflight hadn't really gone to make peace with StarClan. Nor did Bramblestar. The ThunderClan deputy had gone to tell every Clan that her leader was an impostor and they needed to get rid of him. Her paws tingled. *I just hope they believe her.*

# CHAPTER 18

Dawn washed the forest with gray light as Shadowsight headed back to camp. The long walk home from the Moonpool hadn't eased his sense of foreboding. The feeling that he had been watched as he tried to share with StarClan still prickled uncomfortably in his fur. He'd passed on their messages to the Clans, and the Clans had listened. But everything had gone so wrong after that, he was sure it couldn't have been StarClan that had spoken to him. But if it had not been StarClan, then who was it? *What have I done?*

The Clan would still be asleep when he got back, but he had to warn them as soon as possible. *StarClan's not guiding them. Some other cat is!* He broke into a run as he neared the camp, raced through the entrance, and scrambled to a halt. Alarm jabbed his belly. Scorchfur and Yarrowleaf were in the clearing. Snaketooth and Puddleshine stood with them, blinking anxiously at Tigerstar. Why were they up so early . . . and why did they look scared?

"What's happened?" Shadowsight blinked at his father.

Tigerstar pricked his ears, clearly surprised. "Where have you been?"

He hesitated. Was he allowed to travel so far from camp by himself? He pushed the thought away crossly. *I'm a medicine cat! Of course I am.* "The Moonpool." Shadowsight searched his father's gaze. Was that fear glittering there? "I wanted to talk to StarClan, but—"

Tigerstar cut him off. "Dovewing's gone to atone."

"What?" Foreboding pulsed through Shadowsight.

"She's left Clan territory for three days to atone for her . . . *codebreaking.*" Tigerstar growled, clearly irked by the idea that Dovewing needed to atone.

"Why didn't you stop her?" Shadowsight could hardly believe his ears.

"She *wanted* to go," Tigerstar told him.

Puddleshine's gaze was solemn. "She said she couldn't stay while her Clan suffered. She had to do something to let StarClan know she was sorry."

Snaketooth glared pointedly at Shadowsight. "She wouldn't *have* to atone if *you* hadn't named her," she grunted.

Scorchfur's ears twitched. "Even if she hadn't been named, it's no secret that she's a codebreaker," he pointed out. "Shadowsight is living proof of that. If she's atoning, she's protecting her Clan," Scorchfur mewed. "StarClan is clearly angry with us. Too many warriors have been injured."

Yarrowleaf nodded. "If she atones, we might have better luck."

The bushes around the entrance tunnel trembled. Hope flashed in Shadowsight's chest. Had Dovewing changed her mind and come home? His heart sank as Whorlpelt, Blazefire, and Cloverfoot padded into camp. Why had they been out so early?

Cloverfoot pricked her ears as she saw Tigerstar. "You're awake."

Tigerstar glanced at the ShadowClan deputy. "Where have you been?"

"We went hunting," Whorlpelt mewed quickly.

Cloverfoot whisked her tail. "We thought we'd try a night hunt since there's been so little prey during the day."

Scorchfur's gaze flicked over her. "Where's your catch?"

Blazefire shrugged. "It must still be too cold for night prey."

Tigerstar didn't question them further. He was clearly distracted. "Dovewing's gone to atone."

Cloverfoot's ears twitched. *"Gone?"*

"She's left Clan territory for three days," Tigerstar told her.

Shadowsight noticed the ShadowClan deputy glance nervously at Whorlpelt, who looked away. Why were they behaving so furtively? He pushed the thought out of his mind. There wasn't time to worry about it now. "We have to find Dovewing," he told his father.

"Why?" Tigerstar tipped his head.

"It's dangerous for her on her own."

"I wish she hadn't gone," Tigerstar told him. "But don't forget your mother is a warrior. She can take care of herself."

"She might get hurt!" Shadowsight flicked his tail.

"She needs to atone," Scorchfur growled.

As Shadowsight glared at the dark gray warrior, Tigerstar

padded closer. "StarClan will watch over her," his father mewed.

"They won't!" Shadowsight's heart began to race. Why wouldn't they listen? "I'm not even sure they *can*."

Puddleshine stiffened. "What do you mean?"

Scorchfur pricked his ragged ears. "Has something happened to StarClan?"

"They're silent, remember?" Shadowsight snapped.

"They've been talking to you," Scorchfur reminded him.

"But they haven't! That's the point." Shame washed Shadowsight's pelt. He'd been so wrong.

Puddleshine nosed him away from his Clanmates. "You must be tired." He glanced back at Scorchfur as he guided Shadowsight toward the medicine den. "I'll make sure he gets some rest."

Tigerstar hurried after them, lowering his mew. "What do you mean, *they haven't been talking to you?*"

Shadowsight faced his father. They were out of earshot of their Clanmates. "They're gone. They've been gone for moons. Since the Moonpool froze."

Puddleshine's ears flattened. "What are you talking about?"

"But they've spoken to you," Tigerstar mewed. "They've sent you visions."

"It wasn't them!" Shadowsight hissed. "All the visions came from somewhere else. The voice that told me to take Bramblestar to the moor wasn't StarClan. Neither was the message about the codebreakers. Some cat is trying to control the Clans."

Tigerstar's pelt bristled. "Who?"

"I don't know, but they want to harm us," Shadowsight told him.

"How do you know this?" Puddleshine padded closer. His gaze burned into Shadowsight's.

"I felt it," Shadowsight told him, his mew rising with panic. "Tonight I realized—I haven't seen any StarClan cats in my visions. I haven't been to their hunting grounds. I just hear a voice. And see shadows. I can't really explain, but I felt a presence while I was at the Moonpool." He looked at Tigerstar and Puddleshine, hoping they'd understand. "It was watching me. It made my fur crawl. I don't know what it was, but it felt too . . ." He hesitated. How *had* it felt? He shivered at the memory. "Too *evil* to be StarClan. And I've let it guide me. It's been guiding me all along."

"Keep your mew down," Puddleshine ordered. "We can't let the Clan know. They trusted you and they've done what you told them."

Shadowsight's throat tightened. "I know."

Tigerstar ran his tail along Shadowsight's spine. "Slow down," he mewed. "We can fix this."

"Fix it?" Puddleshine blinked at the ShadowClan leader. "Bramblestar lost a life because of Shadowsight's visions. The Clans are turning on one another because of the codebreakers. What will they say if they find out Shadowsight's been mistaken all along? They won't just blame him—they'll blame all of ShadowClan."

Dread hollowed Shadowsight's belly. "I'm sorry." He gazed

desperately at Puddleshine. "I thought I was helping."

"We can't let this get out," Puddleshine warned Tigerstar.

Shadowsight stiffened. "But we have to! We have to warn them."

"And have every Clan turn against us?" Puddleshine's hackles lifted.

Tigerstar flicked his tail. "Let me worry about that," he told Puddleshine. "We have to do what's best for the Clans. If StarClan's not guiding us, the Clans are in danger."

Shadowsight nodded. "Whoever named the codebreakers must mean them harm."

Tigerstar's eyes widened. "Dovewing is out there on her own."

"We have to find her." Shadowsight blinked at his father, but Tigerstar was already heading for the camp entrance.

"Where are you going?" Cloverfoot called as he passed.

"I'm going to fetch Dovewing," Tigerstar told her. "She should be with her Clan."

"But she has to atone!" Scorchfur called after him.

Shadowsight raced after Tigerstar, his heart pounding as he ducked through the tunnel and followed him into the forest.

Tigerstar halted and sniffed the ground, mouth open as he searched for scents. "This way." He headed along a trail that led toward the Clan border. Shadowsight fell in beside him, panting as he fought to keep up. Tigerstar leaped over the ditches that cut through the pine forest like claw marks. Shadowsight followed him, scrambling to keep his footing on the slippery forest floor. His lungs burned as they neared the Thunderpath and began to follow it as it snaked toward the sunrise. The sun burned orange through the trees, setting the forest aflame. As they raced silently side by side, the birds began to chatter, their calls growing louder, sounding the alarm as Tigerstar and Shadowsight passed.

The roar of a monster howled beyond the trees, and Shadowsight's pelt prickled nervously. "Are we going to cross the Thunderpath?" he puffed, glancing sideways at Tigerstar.

"We will if that's where her trail leads." Tigerstar pulled up and sniffed the ground.

Shadowsight opened his mouth. He could taste his mother's scent. It was as clear here as it had been back at camp. Tigerstar hadn't lost it for a paw step, and this was the first time he'd stopped to check that they were still heading in the right direction.

"How can you follow Dovewing's scent so easily?" he mewed.

"I once followed it for a moon, when she traveled to the city," Tigerstar told him, scanning the trees. "It smells like she's heading for a Twolegplace again." He padded forward, moving slower this time, and Shadowsight was relieved at the chance to get his breath back. Tigerstar kept his gaze ahead. "Are you sure those messages didn't come from StarClan?"

"Yes." Shadowsight shivered as he remembered the presence at the Moonpool. "Some cat has been pretending to be StarClan," he mewed. "I think they chose me to pass on their messages because I'm not as experienced as the other medicine cats." Shame burned his pelt. "I shouldn't have been so eager to listen."

Tigerstar sniffed. "Experience has nothing to do with it. Any medicine cat would have been eager to hear from StarClan when they'd been silent for so long." He let his pelt brush Shadowsight's. "Don't be so hard on yourself. You believed you were doing the right thing."

This was the first time Tigerstar had spoken to him kindly since Shadowsight had shared his vision with the other medicine cats against his father's wishes. "I'm sorry I didn't listen to you and keep the vision to myself," Shadowsight murmured.

"What's done is done." Tigerstar whisked his tail.

"But Dovewing wouldn't be out here on her own if I hadn't shared it." Shadowsight mewed guiltily.

"We wouldn't be trying to find her if you hadn't told us you were wrong," Tigerstar told him. "A true warrior admits their mistakes."

Shadowsight glanced gratefully at his father, and he remembered his mother's words too. *There's no harm in admitting mistakes.* Gratitude swelled in his chest. He was lucky to have Dovewing and Tigerstar as parents.

Tigerstar broke into a run. "I can see Twoleg nests ahead. Beyond the trees."

Shadowsight followed his father, struggling to keep up as the trees thinned and large square dens cut into the early morning sunshine. High walls blocked their way, and Tigerstar veered closer to the Thunderpath, ducking past the tattered bushes that lined it. They followed the strip of stone as it curved past the Twoleg dens, stopping as it stretched away across a wide, barren meadow.

Tigerstar lifted his muzzle to taste the air. As his father's ears pricked uneasily, a new scent touched Shadowsight's nose. Fear pricked in his belly. He could smell the stale scent of dogs. This place was dangerous. He scanned the meadow. It was brown, the grass dead, pitted with small hollows and dotted with Twoleg clutter and mounds of dirt. High mesh walls enclosed it, rattling each time a monster roared along the Thunderpath. Around the mesh, Twoleg dens stretched out in identical rows.

Why had Dovewing chosen such a filthy place? Shadowsight flattened his ears against a low rumble that seemed to shake the air. He remembered the sound from his kithood. Monsters were patrolling the Thunderpaths between the Twoleg nests. "Why did she come here?"

"Perhaps she thought StarClan would forgive her if she made her atonement as hard as possible." Tigerstar began to cross the dried-up meadow, picking his way between piles of trash Twolegs must have left behind.

Shadowsight followed, keeping close as they scanned the meadow for a sign of Dovewing. He tasted the air, but the stench of monsters and Twolegs fouled his tongue. "How will we find her?" Panic began to spiral in his chest. What if she'd gone deep into the Twolegplace, or kept traveling? They might not catch up to her until it was too late.

"Look." Tigerstar halted and sniffed a smudged paw print beside a dirty puddle.

"Is it Dovewing's?" Shadowsight stared at his father, hope piercing his heart, almost too sharp to bear.

Tigerstar frowned. "I don't know. The stench here drowns out every scent."

"Are you sure she didn't go *around* the Twolegplace?" Shadowsight blinked anxiously at his father.

"Her scent led here," Tigerstar told him. "We left not long after her. She has to be nearby." As he spoke, a clatter split the air. Shadowsight turned, his heart bursting with fear, as he saw a scrapcan rolling along the ground, its top bowling away and spinning until it tumbled onto its side. An orange cat streaked away from it, bristling, while a black-and-white tom raced after it, ears flat and tail down.

"Scavengers." Tigerstar stared after them, the fur prickling along his spine.

Shadowsight felt sick. Dovewing was here somewhere, among loners and rogues. He moved closer to Tigerstar. "We have to find her."

Tigerstar had stiffened. He was staring toward the scrapcan.

Shadowsight followed his gaze. Gray fur moved in the shadows beneath a pile of Twoleg clutter. He recognized the pelt. "Dovewing!" Joy bursting in his chest, he raced across toward her, his paws sliding on the slimy earth.

As he neared, Dovewing slid out of the darkness, her eyes wide. "Shadowsight! What are you doing here?" Her gaze slid past him to Tigerstar. "Is something wrong in ShadowClan?"

"No." Shadowsight slithered to a halt in front of her and thrust his muzzle against her cheek as Tigerstar pulled up beside them and blinked happily at Dovewing.

"You have to come home," Tigerstar mewed.

"But I haven't finished my atonement," Dovewing told him.

"You don't have to atone," Shadowsight told her, quickly explaining that it had not been StarClan sending him visions, but some other cat.

When he'd finished, Dovewing met his gaze. "If you're lying to protect me, you don't have to."

"I'm not," he mewed earnestly. "You told me to always tell the truth. This *is* the truth. I can feel it in my heart."

Tigerstar padded to his side. "I believe him," he mewed. "Some cat wants to hurt the Clans, and they've used Shadowsight to reach us. It's too dangerous for any of us to be away from our Clanmates. Until we find out what's happening, we need to stick together."

Dovewing glanced back at the pile of Twoleg trash where she'd been sheltering. She flicked her tail decisively. "In that case, we'd better go home."

Shadowsight took a long, deep breath. Dovewing was safe. Once they were home, they could figure out what was going on and come up with a plan to deal with it. As Tigerstar and Dovewing began to pick their way across the grimy meadow, he slid between them. With or without StarClan, they'd always be with him. He shivered as foreboding pricked his pelt. Unless it was too late, and the visions he'd shared with the Clans were already enough to destroy them.

# CHAPTER 19

*Rootpaw eagerly scanned the island clearing.* A bright full moon shone
in the crow-black sky. The other Clans had already arrived and
were moving like ripples on the lake, their pelts glossy in the
moonlight as they dipped their heads in greeting and shared
gossip. He saw Squirrelflight standing beside Crowfeather
and Cloverfoot. Had the ThunderClan deputy managed to
speak to the leaders of the other Clans and warn them that
Bramblestar was an impostor? He searched Crowfeather's
gaze. Did the WindClan deputy know? Frustration prickled
beneath Rootpaw's pelt. It was impossible to tell. He'd have
to wait until the meeting began to see if they would challenge
Bramblestar.

Tree and Violetshine pushed their way among the gathered
cats while Leafstar and Hawkwing headed for the Great Oak.
Bramblestar's ghost skirted the clearing, heading toward the
far side, its gaze fixed on the false Bramblestar as the Thunder-
Clan leader leaped into the Oak. The ghost had shadowed
the SkyClan patrol as they'd traveled to the island. Rootpaw
was relieved it was keeping its distance, finally understanding

that Rootpaw couldn't acknowledge it when he was with his Clanmates.

Frecklewish's pelt brushed Rootpaw's. "We need to speak with Shadowsight."

Rootpaw nodded. He hadn't forgotten his promise at the secret meeting. He and Frecklewish were going to ask Shadowsight about his visions. Did the ShadowClan medicine cat have any idea that Bramblestar was an impostor? He kept close to Frecklewish as she nosed her way between the gathered warriors to where Shadowsight stood, close to Tigerstar.

"Hi, Frecklewish." Alderheart greeted her warmly before they reached him.

Frecklewish slowed. "Hey, Alderheart."

Rootpaw could tell she was trying to keep her mew light, but her gaze was flashing anxiously toward the young Shadow-Clan medicine cat.

"How's SkyClan?" Alderheart asked. "Any sickness?"

"Not at the moment." Frecklewish dipped her head politely and tried to move on.

Alderheart was clearly eager to chat. "Has marigold started sprouting in your territory?" he mewed.

"Not yet," Frecklewish told him.

"There're signs of some in the beech grove," Alderheart told her. "But it'll be another moon before we can pick it."

"Hurry," Rootpaw whispered in Frecklewish's ear. "It looks like the Gathering's about to start." Bramblestar was staring expectantly from the lowest branch of the oak.

Frecklewish dipped her head again to Alderheart. "I just need to speak with Shadowsight before the meeting starts."

"Really?" Alderheart looked puzzled. "Is there anything I should—"

Frecklewish hurried away before he could finish. Rootpaw glanced at the ThunderClan medicine cat apologetically as he followed his Clanmate.

Frecklewish and Rootpaw both nodded a greeting as they stopped beside Shadowsight, but the ShadowClan medicine cat seemed on edge, his gaze glittering in the moonlight. "Hi," he said, barely meeting Frecklewish's gaze.

"I wanted to speak to you," Frecklewish told him. She glanced at Tigerstar. "In private."

Tigerstar moved closer to his kit. "The meeting is about to start," he meowed formally. "Perhaps you could speak to him afterward."

As Shadowsight flashed his father a look, Rootpaw narrowed his eyes. Why was Tigerstar being so protective?

"I really need to speak to him now." Frecklewish stared intently at Shadowsight.

"Maybe later." Shadowsight dropped his gaze, shifting his paws self-consciously.

"Frecklewish!" Alderheart had followed them through the crowd. "What's so important?" He looked anxiously from Frecklewish to Shadowsight. "Do you have news?"

"Nothing important." Frecklewish's pelt prickled, and Rootpaw could sense her frustration as Leafstar leaped into the oak. Mistystar and Harestar were hurrying to take their places. Tigerstar hesitated beside Shadowsight, clearly unwilling to leave him.

Frecklewish nodded to Rootpaw. "You'd better join your Clanmates," she told him. "It looks like the Gathering's about to start."

Reluctantly, Rootpaw turned away and headed through the crowd. Glancing back, he saw Frecklewish take her place beneath the oak as Alderheart, Jayfeather, Mothwing, and Willowshine settled beside her. Only after Kestrelflight had settled down beside the SkyClan medicine cat, with Shadowsight and Puddleshine on his other side, did Tigerstar scramble up the trunk of the Great Oak.

Slipping between the Clans, Rootpaw noticed warriors glancing warily at one another. They seemed nervous. He could smell fear-scent in the air. Pelts prickled around him, and he was relieved to reach his Clanmates and settle next to Tree.

"What do you think will happen when the other leaders accuse Bramblestar of being an impostor?" he whispered to his father.

Tree glanced around at the gathered cats. "I don't think it'd be wise of any cat to accuse him of anything yet," he murmured.

"Why not?" Rootpaw blinked at him.

"While StarClan stays silent, Bramblestar can accuse any cat of codebreaking."

Rootpaw frowned. "But why would any cat listen to an impostor?"

"Not every cat will believe that he is," Tree murmured,

moving closer. "Especially if he seems to speak for StarClan. Now watch and listen."

In the Great Oak, Harestar and Mistystar hung back on the wide branch while Bramblestar stood at the front. Tiger-star was eyeing Bramblestar uneasily. Had Squirrelflight warned him? Rootpaw had seen her arrive at his own camp a few days ago, but Leafstar still hadn't told the Clan why she'd come. Rootpaw's tail twitched expectantly. Perhaps Leafstar was waiting until she could accuse Bramblestar directly.

The impostor swished his tail, glaring severely at the Clans until silence swept the clearing. "Last time we met," he began, "no Clan would say how the codebreakers should be punished. I hope you have all decided now."

"Exile!" Emberfoot called from WindClan.

Hootwhisker swished his tail eagerly. "The codebreakers must leave their Clans and atone before they can return."

Bramblestar's eyes glowed with satisfaction. "I'm glad some of you have begun to see sense. Atonement is the only way we'll end StarClan's silence, and exile is the best way for code-breakers to atone."

Hootwhisker stared pointedly at Crowfeather. "Some of the codebreakers have refused," he growled.

Rootpaw's heart quickened. Had the WindClan deputy refused because Squirrelflight had managed to warn him and Harestar? Were they going to stand up to the ThunderClan leader?

Crowfeather's hackles lifted. "Until I hear from StarClan, I'm not going anywhere."

Bramblestar narrowed his eyes. "We've *heard* from StarClan. They say that the Clans will suffer until the codebreakers atone."

Crowfeather scowled. "Why should we believe you?"

"I speak for StarClan!" Bramblestar showed his teeth.

Harestar padded to the edge of the branch. "Why won't StarClan speak for themselves?"

Bramblestar rounded on him. "Because the codebreakers haven't been punished yet!"

"Exile them!" Scorchfur called from among the Shadow-Clan cats.

"The codebreakers must atone!" Mallownose's call was echoed by angry yowls from his Clanmates.

Around the clearing, warriors lifted their voices in agreement.

Rootpaw pressed back a shiver. He moved closer to Tree. "Why are so many cats agreeing with Bramblestar?" he breathed to his father.

"They're frightened by StarClan's silence," Tree answered softly. "They'll do anything to bring them back."

Rootpaw scanned the crowd, relieved when he spotted Sneezecloud and Bristlefrost. Cloverfoot was standing beside the other deputies. Spotfur and Stemleaf watched quietly among their Clanmates. *They* knew that Bramblestar was an impostor. He glanced at Tree. "The other cats from the secret meeting are here. Do you think they'll speak out?"

"Would you?" Tree eyed him grimly as the calls of the Clan

cats rang around the clearing.

Rootpaw swallowed. *We're outnumbered.*

Bramblestar gazed approvingly over the Clans. "I'm glad I'm no longer the only cat who sees that StarClan won't return until the codebreakers have atoned."

Mistystar's eyes glittered nervously as she looked at Bramblestar. "It's strange that you knew what StarClan wanted *before* Shadowsight shared their codebreaking message with the Clans."

Bramblestar glared at her coldly. "I lost a life, remember? I was the last leader to commune with StarClan. It was clear to me then what they wanted. Shadowsight's vision simply confirmed it for the rest of you."

Shadowsight glanced nervously into the Great Oak. "I'm not sure my vision was from StarClan," he mewed.

Rootpaw stiffened as Puddleshine shot Shadowsight a warning look. Was the older ShadowClan medicine cat trying to keep him quiet? But Shadowsight pressed on.

"I may have misunderstood the message."

Bramblestar swished his tail. "Why would you doubt yourself? Your vision cured my fever."

"My vision made you lose a life." Shadowsight shifted his paws uneasily. "And StarClan hasn't spoken since they told me the Clans would suffer. Why would they send me a vision that would turn Clanmates against one another and then not speak? They're supposed to help us."

Bramblestar leaned over the edge of the branch and stared

at Shadowsight like a hunter eyeing prey. He flexed his claws, a threat in his gaze. Rootpaw edged forward, his breath catching in his throat. The ShadowClan medicine cat looked suddenly small. Was Bramblestar going to *attack* him?

Bramblestar's fur smoothed. The menace faded from his eyes and he dipped his head. "You are young," he mewed indulgently. "You were still an apprentice when your visions started. I'm not surprised you have trouble telling truth from imagination. But the visions you've shared with us have been clear. They spoke to you, named the codebreakers . . . and some of those codebreakers were cats you could never have known about." His gaze drifted around at the gathered cats as he went on. "Would any cat deny that those named in his vision have broken the code?"

Tigerstar pricked his ears angrily. "*Every* cat has broken the code at some time, whether they meant to or not. What is important is a warrior's heart. If a warrior is loyal and honorable, who cares if they made a mistake in the past?"

"StarClan does." Bramblestar faced the ShadowClan leader. "Their message was very clear."

"The message *was* clear." Shadowsight padded farther forward, craning his neck to stare at Bramblestar. "But I don't think it came from StarClan."

"Nonsense!" Bramblestar's pelt twitched. "Who else could it have come from?"

Berrynose gazed eagerly at his leader. "Only StarClan would care about the warrior code!"

"StarClan makes rules for a reason!" Mallownose yowled

from among the RiverClan cats. "We must obey them."

"The code has been broken!" Scorchfur glanced up from the ShadowClan warriors.

Rootpaw caught Bristlefrost's eye. She looked at him helplessly as, once more, yowls of agreement rose from every Clan. Stemleaf and Spotfur moved closer together. Cloverfoot stared somberly at the gathered cats.

"The codebreakers must atone!" Harrybrook lashed his tail.

Sparrowpelt pricked his ears. "We must bring StarClan back," he called. "They are silent for a reason."

Rootpaw shrank from his Clanmates. Were *SkyClan* cats siding with Bramblestar? He glanced to the edge of the clearing, where the ghost watched in dismay, pressing his belly to the earth like a cornered rabbit. Rootpaw's heart felt heavy with dread. *The ghost must realize the danger.* If warriors from every Clan believed atonement was the only way to bring StarClan back, to stand against them could mean war. Would the ghost want to get rid of the impostor if it meant Clanmate fighting Clanmate?

Scorchfur padded to the foot of the oak and looked up at Bramblestar. "Dovewing left ShadowClan to atone, but Tigerstar brought her back before she finished." His gaze flicked accusingly to his leader. "Hasn't ShadowClan suffered enough?" he asked Tigerstar.

Tigerstar puffed out his fur. "I couldn't let Dovewing risk her safety."

"Instead you risk the safety of the whole Clan!" Scorchfur held his gaze.

Bramblestar jerked his muzzle toward Tigerstar. "Is this true? Did you prevent a codebreaker from atoning?"

Tigerstar's ears twitched. "I am leader of ShadowClan. I say what happens there."

Bramblestar didn't move. "Are you going against the laws of StarClan?"

"That is for StarClan to decide." Tigerstar's tail flicked ominously. "Not you."

Bramblestar turned his gaze back to the gathered cats. "The only way to bring StarClan back is to stand together. Codebreakers must atone no matter what Clan they're from." He glanced scornfully at Dovewing. "Squirrelflight has atoned—why not Dovewing?" He didn't wait for an answer. "Any leader who can't enforce the law of StarClan has no right to be a leader."

Around the clearing, warriors glanced at one another uneasily. Then Berrynose raised his muzzle. "StarClan won't come back if the law isn't enforced."

"Leaders must lead!" Yarrowleaf yowled at Tigerstar.

"They owe it to their Clan!" Harrybrook mewed loudly.

As murmurs of agreement rippled through the crowd, Bramblestar swung his gaze back to Tigerstar. "If you can't lead ShadowClan, perhaps Cloverfoot should take your place."

Rootpaw's pelt bristled as he looked at Cloverfoot. She knew Bramblestar was an impostor. Surely she wouldn't agree to his demand! The ShadowClan deputy shifted nervously, then padded forward. "I stand by Tigerstar," she meowed slowly. "I would never take his place. And I won't let another Clan tell us what to do." Her hackles lifted as she met Bramblestar's gaze.

Bramblestar snorted and looked back to the crowd. "ShadowClan's warriors shouldn't suffer while their code-breakers go unpunished." His gaze fixed on Scorchfur. "If neither ShadowClan's leader nor its deputy is ready to follow StarClan's laws, perhaps we should find them new leadership."

Scorchfur's ears twitched nervously. He backed away into the crowd, but around him a soft murmuring echoed Bramble-star's suggestion.

"We need leaders who will make StarClan come back." Emberfoot's mew sounded from the WindClan cats.

Panic began to spark in Rootpaw's chest. This wasn't how the Gathering was meant to go. Bramblestar was supposed to be revealed as an impostor so the Clans could unite against him. Instead the Clans seemed to be supporting him more than ever. To call him an impostor now might start a battle. Rootpaw blinked at Bristlefrost desperately. She returned his gaze, her eyes round with alarm. He turned to Frecklewish. Perhaps a medicine cat could speak out. But she only stared grimly ahead as though trying to hide what she felt. Was no cat going to speak? Even the ghost seemed to have given up. It still crouched in the shadows, its translucent pelt so pale that it seemed hardly more than a dab of moonlight. *I have to do something!* Pelt bristling, Rootpaw lifted his chin. "Would our ancestors approve of one Clan turning on another?"

His voice sounded no more than a whisper, but the crowd seemed to grow still around him.

"What was that?" Jayfeather turned toward Rootpaw. "Speak up, apprentice! Don't make me think I'm deaf as well as blind."

As the gazes of the Clans turned toward him, Rootpaw's pelt burned. He forced himself to speak. He looked at the ghost. *I'm saying this for you!* "Even when the spirits of dead cats can't speak to those they love . . ." He willed the ghost to get to its paws. "They can still see us." If Bramblestar's spirit was defeated, what hope was there for the cats who wanted to stand up to the impostor? "They surround us all the time. How would they feel if they saw us turn on one another in their name?"

He felt Bramblestar's gaze sear his pelt and met it, sticking out his chest. He searched it, wondering who was behind those burning eyes. If it wasn't the real Bramblestar staring at him, who was it?

"You're Tree's kit, aren't you?" Bramblestar's snarl was as sharp as a fox's.

Rootpaw forced himself not to flinch. "Yes, I am."

"Your father thinks the forest is full of dead cats, but a true warrior knows that dead cats go to StarClan. No spirits *surround* us." Suspicion flared in his gaze. "Why are you arguing against enforcing the warrior code? Are you a codebreaker too?"

Rootpaw felt Tree stiffen beside him. "My kit is no codebreaker," he snapped. "A dead cat can walk where it likes. Just because you're a Clan leader doesn't give you the power to decide where they put their paws. I saw my father in the forest after he died, and my mate's mother returned to speak to her kits." He glanced across the heads of his Clanmates to where Twigbranch stood. "Isn't that right?"

She met his gaze uneasily but nodded. "It's true."

Violetshine moved closer to Tree. "I saw her too, *and* I saw Needletail after she died. She's the one who led me to Tree in the first place."

Murmurs of agreement rippled through the gathered cats.

"Plenty of us saw cats from StarClan and the Dark Forest fight at our sides." Crowfeather stared at the crowd, as though challenging them to deny it. "Surely you remember the Great Battle?" His Clanmates began to nod, and among the other Clans, warriors dipped their heads in agreement.

Bramblestar flicked his tail impatiently. "Let's not waste time reminiscing!" he growled. "So some of you have seen dead cats. It doesn't change anything. Rootpaw is just trying to stir up trouble. We know what our ancestors want. They want the codebreakers to atone."

Tree flattened his ears. "I thought it was *you* who wanted the codebreakers to atone," he mewed acidly.

Rootpaw glanced at his father, panic sparking in his fur. *Hush!* It was dangerous to provoke the ThunderClan leader any more. What if Tree got himself exiled? His father had already been talking about leaving the Clans. Would he ever come back?

Fury flashed in Bramblestar's eyes. "I speak for *StarClan*! It's our ancestors who want the codebreakers punished. And the fact that you're trying to stop me shows you're a codebreaker."

He thrust his muzzle forward. "*You* should atone!"

Violetshine's eyes flashed with alarm. As she laid her tail protectively across Tree's spine, Squirrelflight slid from the shadow beneath the Great Oak and looked up at Bramblestar.

"This is a SkyClan affair," she meowed evenly.

Tigerstar's ears pricked. "Like that ever matters to Bramblestar," he growled. He's always telling other Clans what to do."

Bramblestar bristled. "I'm doing this for the good of all the Clans! And if the other leaders won't do what is necessary, it's up to me to make sure StarClan's laws are enforced!" He swung his gaze back to Tree. "You've been questioning our ways for too long. It's time you proved you're one of us, rather than a loner who lives off our prey."

Leafstar lashed her tail angrily. "*I* discipline SkyClan warriors, not you!" She glared at Bramblestar.

Harrybrook looked at his leader questioningly. "But Bramblestar is right. Tree still prefers hunting for his own prey, even now. He never takes from the fresh-kill pile."

"He adds to it!" Violetshine snapped indignantly.

Berrynose called from among the ThunderClan cats. "We've all heard him question our traditions."

Rootpaw's heart began to pound as murmurs of agreement spread among the Clans. Surely the cats who'd been at the secret meeting would stand up for Tree. He was one of them! He looked hopefully at Bristlefrost. When she dropped her gaze, he looked at Stemleaf and then Spotfur. Stemleaf and Spotfur exchanged glances, then looked away. They weren't going to defend him! Rootpaw shifted his paws uncomfortably. Was it because Tree had suggested that any cat who didn't agree with Bramblestar should leave the Clans? Why did his father have to be so independent? Would he ever understand that loyalty was a warrior's first duty?

Bramblestar looked on with satisfaction as the murmurs spread. Then he fixed his gaze on Tree. "You must atone to show StarClan that you accept the warrior code."

"Atone!" Berrynose pushed his way through the Thunder-Clan cats and stared at Tree.

Harrybrook turned on his Clanmate. "Atone!"

"Atone!"

Violetshine pressed herself to her mate. "Leave him alone! He's done nothing to harm any cat."

"Are you a codebreaker too?" Bramblestar glared at her.

Tree nosed her away. "Violetshine's broken no code."

Rootpaw wanted to move closer to his father as the cry rose from the Clans, but fear rooted his paws to the earth. He didn't want to be named a codebreaker too. He couldn't risk being exiled. Who would protect Violetshine and Needle-paw? How could he protect his Clan, or help the ghost? He pressed against his mother and blinked apologetically at Tree. *I'm sorry!*

Tree gazed back at him gently, as though he understood.

Bramblestar lifted his voice above the yowls. "Tree must go into exile for three days to atone."

Leafstar's hackles lifted. "No ThunderClan cat tells my warriors what to do!"

Violetshine's pelt was bristling with fear, but Tree gazed

calmly at Bramblestar. "I'll spend three days in exile." He shrugged. "It won't be hard. I was a loner for many moons. I might even enjoy the solitude, especially if it puts this matter to rest once and for all."

Bramblestar narrowed his eyes. "Atonement should allow you to think about your mistakes," he told Tree. "Perhaps you'll find more reflection in spending the time visiting each Clan and persuading their leaders to accept StarClan's laws."

"We already accept them!" Leafstar snapped.

"Not enough to enforce the warrior code and make your warriors atone." Bramblestar turned his icy gaze on the Sky-Clan leader. "It seems that our warriors understand that atonement is the only way to bring StarClan back, but their leaders are dragging their paws. They clearly think they're above StarClan. They don't want to make their Clanmates atone." His mew grew silky as he scanned the leaders beside him on the branch. "But Tree is supposed to be persuasive. You call him your mediator. Perhaps he can convince each of you that it's in your Clan's best interest to send your codebreakers into exile until they have earned StarClan's forgiveness."

Tree's ears flattened. "What if I refuse?"

Bramblestar swung his muzzle toward the yellow tom. "The Clans have shown already that they don't trust your loyalty. What will they think if you refuse to help them now?" His eyes darkened menacingly as he went on. "There might be unpleasant consequences, don't you think? Not just for you, but for your kin."

At the edge of the clearing, the ghost got to its paws, its

gaze shimmering anxiously in the moonlight. Rootpaw forced his fur to remain flat as a chill reached to his bones. Bramble-star was threatening him and Violetshine too. He glanced at Frecklewish, hoping for reassurance, but she looked as scared as he felt. Sneezecloud, Cloverfoot, Breezepelt, and Stemleaf seemed to shrink. None of the cats from the secret meeting seemed ready to stand up for him or Tree. Disappointment jabbed his heart. Had they been all talk? Was no cat going to act? He gazed desperately at Bristlefrost. She must understand how unfair this was. Tree had only tried to help the Clans, but the impostor was making him look like a traitor.

*Do something!* he pleaded. She stared back at him helplessly. What *could* she do? What could *either* of them do when they were so outnumbered?

"Hey!" Berrynose growled from among the ThunderClan cats. "Why's Rootpaw staring at Bristlefrost?"

Rootpaw froze as the gazes of the Clans jerked toward him.

"They've been looking at each other since the Gathering began," Yarrowleaf growled.

"What are you up to?" Harrybrook glared suspiciously at Rootpaw.

Rootpaw stared back wordlessly. Guilt spiked his belly as he remembered the meeting at the greenleaf Twolegplace. He dropped his gaze, frightened that he'd betray his secret.

"Bristlefrost is one of Bramblestar's most loyal warriors." Berrynose's gaze was sharp with accusation. "Perhaps he's try-ing to turn her against our leader."

Bristlefrost whisked her tail. "No cat could turn me against my Clan," she mewed. "Especially not an apprentice from another Clan."

Macgyver shrugged. "Rootpaw's not trying anything of the sort. He's *always* looking at Bristlefrost. He's got a crush on her, remember?"

The gazes of the Clan seemed to soften, but Rootpaw's pelt began to burn.

Bristlefrost's shifted awkwardly. "If he's got a crush on me, that's *his* problem, not mine. He's not my Clanmate." Rootpaw tried not to flinch. Her words sliced through his heart as she went on. "I don't care anything about him. Besides, I'd never break the code."

Berrynose frowned. "Then why have you been looking at him?"

Rootpaw's ears twitched as silence gripped the clearing. Berrynose seemed determined to see treachery in their looks. Rootpaw blinked at the ThunderClan warrior, pushing the hurt away. He needed to stop this now. No cat could know that they'd been at the meeting. "I still like her, okay? Is that against the code?"

Berrynose stared at him for a moment, then shrugged. "So long as you don't act on it."

"Of course I won't." Rootpaw fluffed out his fur. "It's hopeless. I'd never break the code, nor would Bristlefrost. But it doesn't stop me liking her. She's the bravest, most loyal warrior I know."

Embarrassment squirmed in his belly as he heard indulgent

mews ripple through the crowd. *They think it's cute.* He glanced at Bristlefrost apologetically. It was the only way to protect her. As he looked away, his heart quickened. Was that fondness he'd seen in her gaze?

Bramblestar lashed his tail. "Enough of this!" As the gathered cats turned back to the impostor, he glared at them impatiently. "We didn't meet here to talk about apprentice crushes. We need to bring StarClan back, and the only way to do that is to stick to the code and exile any cat who breaks it." He glared at the other leaders. "And if you can't accept that now, I hope Tree will be able to change your minds."

Rootpaw glanced up at the impostor. Did he really think Tree would try to persuade another cat to believe something he didn't believe himself? Hope glimmered in his heart. The impostor was arrogant enough to think he could force any warrior to do anything. He might push the Clans too far. No matter how scared they were of losing StarClan, nothing could make a warrior abandon their honor.

"Let's go." Tree's mew nudged him from his thoughts. The crowd was melting away as the Clans headed for the long grass.

While Leafstar led her Clanmates toward the tree-bridge, Frecklewish crossed the clearing and blocked Tree's path. "What will you do?" she mewed.

Tree stared at her solemnly as Rootpaw and Violetshine stopped beside him. "Bramblestar was right about me," he told Frecklewish. "I've never truly believed in Clan life. I think it's time I left and took my family with me."

Rootpaw fought back panic. They couldn't leave. Not when the Clans were in so much trouble. Needlepaw wouldn't want to leave either. She was as committed as he was to being a great warrior.

The ghost hurried to Rootpaw's side. "You can't let him take you away!"

Frecklewish dipped her head. "I understand how you feel, Tree. The impostor has made this a dangerous place to be." She blinked at him. "Especially for you. But we need you."

"You can help the Clans." Rootpaw blinked desperately at his father.

Violetshine nodded. "We can't just abandon cats we care about," she mewed. "What about Twigbranch?"

"Twigbranch has Finleap and her Clanmates," Tree told her. "We have no choice. You heard Bramblestar. If I don't do what he says, he'll turn the Clans against us. We won't be safe anywhere."

Rootpaw refused to believe his Clanmates would really turn against Tree. "No true warrior would hurt us."

Tree looked at him. "I think some of the Clans have forgotten what a true warrior is."

Frecklewish's ears twitched. "There might be another way."

Tree frowned at her. "What?"

"You can travel around the Clans and speak to the leaders, just as Bramblestar ordered," the medicine cat told him. "But you don't need to persuade them to follow his rules. You can warn them what's really going on."

"But hasn't Squirrelflight already told them that Bramble-star's an impostor?" Tree reminded her.

"If she did, she clearly failed to persuade them," Freckle-wish pressed. "You might do better."

The ghost padded nearer. "Another voice might convince them that they're not alone."

"You can talk to the ghost," Frecklewish told Tree. "Squirrelflight couldn't do that."

Rootpaw's belly tightened. Tree couldn't talk to the ghost any more than Squirrelflight could. His paws pricked nervously as Frecklewish went on.

"You can pass on the ghost's message. You can encourage the Clans to fight for the real StarClan, not the StarClan the impostor represents."

"But I can't argue with StarClan's silence," Tree pointed out. "The silence is real. It's scared too many warriors. They'll do anything to end it, even if it means defying their leaders."

"But if you leave," Frecklewish argued, "nothing will change. The impostor will get stronger. If you stay, you might help us undermine him just enough to win back the Clans."

Rootpaw stared desperately at his father. He *couldn't* leave the Clans. Who knew what the impostor would do next? And who would be left to speak for the ghost?

Breath like mist touched his ear fur. "Make him stay," the ghost whispered.

Rootpaw placed his muzzle against Tree's cheek. "Let us stay," he begged. "We owe it to the Clans and to Bramblestar's ghost. If we leave, no cat will hear it. It may never find its way back to its body."

Tree started to speak, then stopped, gazing down at the ground, his eyes wide and helpless. Rootpaw could tell that his father had no idea what to do.

He saw the ghost's translucent pelt from the corner of his eye and turned to meet its gaze. *I tried,* he told it silently. *I can't do any more than that.*

# CHAPTER 20

*Bristlefrost nosed a sparrow from the* top of the fresh-kill pile and
sniffed unenthusiastically at the prey underneath. She wasn't
hungry, but her Clanmates were eating after a busy day patrolling. All she wanted was to settle into the soft grass beneath the
Highledge and think. Last night's Gathering had unnerved
her. There had been no challenge to Bramblestar. Squirrelflight had returned from her self-imposed exile, admitting
that she hadn't managed to speak to the other leaders. She'd
made it to the SkyClan camp, but Leafstar had warned her
that WindClan, RiverClan, and ShadowClan might not be so
welcoming. Squirrelflight had decided to visit them anyway,
but when Harestar had seemed unconvinced by her report,
she had returned to ThunderClan.

Bristlefrost pressed back a shiver and grabbed a shrew from
the pile. She carried it to the shelter of the Highledge. No cat
had stood up for Tigerstar. The Clans were clearly prepared
to allow Bramblestar to decide who should lead another Clan.
Didn't they realize how dangerous that was? And how wrong?
Without StarClan, the Clans seemed to be falling apart.

She dropped the shrew and circled on the grass beside it,

smoothing a place to sit. As she settled down, an angry hiss sounded from the Highledge. She looked up, heart pounding. Squirrelflight was up there with Bramblestar. The Thunder-Clan leader had summoned her to his den when she'd returned from patrol.

Then came a muffled snarl. Bristlefrost glanced at her Clanmates. Had they heard it? Sparkpelt was sharing a thrush with Stormcloud outside the warriors' den. Bumblestripe and Berrynose lay near the nursery, picking over the bones of a pigeon. Lilyheart, Stemleaf, and Spotfur were watching as Finleap demonstrated a hunting move. Thornclaw and Birchfall were eating with the elders, listening as Graystripe and Brackenfur told tales of when they were apprentices in ThunderClan's old home beyond the mountains. None of them seemed to notice the noise from their leader's den. Perhaps they were pretending not to hear. If Bramblestar and his mate were arguing, maybe they thought it was polite to ignore it.

Bristlefrost's belly fluttered anxiously. She picked up her shrew. If she took it to Bramblestar's den, she could ask if he or Squirrelflight was hungry and check that Squirrelflight was okay.

Scrambling up the rock tumble, she hopped onto the ledge and padded warily to Bramblestar's den. Through the leaves covering the entrance she heard Bramblestar's growl.

"Where did you go?" Anger hardened his mew.

"I told you," Squirrelflight sounded indignant. "I went to the horseplace and traveled over the meadows from there."

"What did you eat?"

"Whatever I could catch."

"And what did you do when you weren't hunting?"

Squirrelflight's mew was smooth. "I sat quietly and thought about the warrior code and how I could be a better deputy."

Bristlefrost's pelt pricked. She knew Squirrelflight was lying, and she still sounded convincing. Perhaps everything would be okay after all.

"So you'll be sure to follow it from now on?" Bramblestar sounded unsatisfied.

"Yes," Squirrelflight mewed. "I understand why you're determined to follow it so closely now."

"And why's that?" Bramblestar demanded acidly.

"The Clans have fallen away from the code. But it's all that stands between warriors and rogues. We must honor StarClan by following it exactly." Squirrelflight sounded sincere, but Bristlefrost guessed she was only acting to put Bramblestar at ease.

Bristlefrost glanced down at her Clanmates. They were busy talking and eating and didn't seem interested in why she was standing outside Bramblestar's den. She leaned closer to the entrance, pricking her ears, her heart pounding as she listened.

"Why did you break the code in the first place?" Bramblestar's mew grew harder.

"What do you mean?" For the first time, Squirrelflight sounded shaken.

"Why did you pretend Leafpool's kits were yours?"

"That was moons ago." Squirrelflight's mew was taut. Bramblestar had clearly touched a nerve.

"Your sister was a liar, and she made a liar out of you!" Bramblestar's hiss caught Bristlefrost by surprise.

"My sister was brave." Squirrelflight's mew cracked.

"She was a codebreaker!"

"I know." Squirrelflight hesitated as though trying to regain her composure. "I should have helped her tell the truth. But she was scared and I was weak."

"You *were* weak." Bramblestar's snarl made Bristlefrost freeze. "You still are." He sounded dangerous. "Did you think about your weakness while you were at the horseplace?" Squirrelflight gave a yelp. Bristlefrost's heart seemed to stop. Was Bramblestar hurting her? "Did you *atone* for it?" he hissed.

"I atoned for everything!" Squirrelflight's mew was taut with pain.

Bristlefrost's pelt spiked as Bramblestar snarled again. "I gave you one last chance to tell the truth and you didn't!" Her eyes widened. *Whose voice was that?* It didn't seem to belong to Bramblestar. Was another cat in the den with them? Bristlefrost held her breath, straining to recognize the mew. It didn't sound like any cat she'd ever heard before.

She heard paws scuff the floor of the den and she scrambled away, leaping down the rock tumble as the leaves shivered at the entrance and Bramblestar backed out. In the clearing, she stared up at the Highledge, her breath catching as she saw Bramblestar drag Squirrelflight from his den with his teeth in her scruff. He hauled her roughly down the rock tumble, letting go as she fought her way to her paws at the bottom.

She leaped away from him, hissing viciously.

Around the camp, the ThunderClan cats leaped to their paws, their backs arching as Squirrelflight faced Bramblestar, her lips drawn back into a snarl.

Bramblestar's gaze swept over them, anger glittering in his eyes. "There's a codebreaker among us!" he hissed. "And it pains me to punish her—but if we ever hope to hear from StarClan again, I must." He turned on Squirrelflight once more. "You," he snarled. "My own deputy. My *mate*! You don't belong in ThunderClan anymore. You don't deserve a place here."

Squirrelflight stared at him, fear showing in her eyes as Alderheart and Jayfeather padded from the medicine den, their ears twitching.

Bristlefrost stared in panic at the ThunderClan deputy. Had Bramblestar discovered that she'd lied? *How?* She hadn't noticed him leaving camp much lately. How could he know where Squirrelflight had gone?

Graystripe stared at Bramblestar. "She's Firestar's daughter," he mewed in disbelief. "You can't exile her."

Thornclaw padded forwarded. Shock showed in his pale blue eyes. "What has she done?"

"She's a liar." Bramblestar rounded on the two warriors, his eyes blazing. "She pretended to atone, but she wasn't trying to make her peace with StarClan. She was breaking the code *again!*"

Thornclaw blinked questioningly at Squirrelflight.

Bramblestar padded closer to his deputy, hissing. "Where did you go when you left ThunderClan?"

"I told you!" Squirrelflight lifted her chin. "I went to the horseplace."

"You're lying!" Bramblestar thrust his muzzle closer to hers. "I know because I sent a Clanmate to follow you."

Bristlefrost felt the gazes of her Clanmates flit toward her. She stiffened, feeling sick. *It wasn't me.*

Bramblestar nodded toward Bumblestripe. "I sent a *loyal* warrior to see where you went," the ThunderClan leader growled.

Fear spread beneath Bristlefrost's pelt, as cold as ice, as Bumblestripe padded forward, puffing out his chest.

"Squirrelflight didn't go to the horseplace," he mewed. "She went to SkyClan."

"SkyClan?" Thornclaw looked confused. "Why did she go there?"

Bumblestripe curled his lip. "She went to persuade Sky-Clan to rise up against ThunderClan."

Sparkpelt and Stormcloud stared at Squirrelflight in disbelief.

Berrynose curled his lip. "Traitor!"

The word rang around the camp. Lilyheart and Hollytuft echoed it. Bristlefrost stared at them. They didn't believe Squirrelflight would want to harm them, surely? Didn't they realize she wouldn't turn to another Clan unless there was a good reason?

Squirrelflight eyed Bramblestar, her tail flicking danger-
ously over the ground.

Blood roared in Bristlefrost's ears. What else did Bumblestripe know? Was he about to turn on *her*? Did he know
about the secret meetings? That she was a traitor too? She
wanted to look at Stemleaf and Spotfur for reassurance, but
she didn't dare. What if looking at them gave her away?

Sparkpelt padded forward and stared at her mother. Her
green eyes were wide with disbelief. "Is it true?"

Squirrelflight's tail fell still. She stared back at her daughter, but she didn't speak. Her eyes grew dull as though a fire
had been extinguished. Slowly, she straightened and looked
around at her Clanmates. "I'll leave," she mewed softly. "But
there's something you must know. My mate would never
behave like this. You must know in your hearts that *this
cat*"—she stared scornfully at Bramblestar—"has none of the
courage, honor, and honesty of the real Bramblestar. *This*
Bramblestar is an impostor."

Bristlefrost searched the gazes of her Clanmates. Did they
believe her? She watched them stare at Squirrelflight. Was
that pity in their eyes? *They don't understand!* Her Clanmates
seemed to hear Squirrelflight's words as no more than spite
from a cat whose mate had rejected her. The truth was clearly
too far-fetched to believe.

This time she couldn't stop herself from looking at Stemleaf, pleading with her eyes. *We have to do something!* As though
reading her thoughts, he shook his head, too subtly for their
Clanmates to notice.

"Bristlefrost!" Bramblestar's growl made her jump.

She stared at him, guilt searing her pelt. Was he about to accuse her?

His gaze was hard. "I want you, Twigbranch, and Lionblaze to escort Squirrelflight off our land."

Bristlefrost straightened. Was he sending her a message? Was escorting Squirrelflight off ThunderClan territory meant to warn her that she could be next?

Bramblestar nodded to Stormcloud and Birchfall. "Go with them."

Bristlefrost eyed the toms warily. Were they spies too? She tried not to tremble as she padded toward Squirrelflight. The ThunderClan deputy was already heading toward the entrance.

Bramblestar didn't even look at his mate. Instead he looked calmly around at the Clan. "ThunderClan needs a new deputy."

Bristlefrost paused at the edge of the clearing. Was he going to choose one *now*? After everything that just happened?

Bumblestripe quickly stepped forward. "I want to defend the warrior code as much as you do. I'd be honored if you'd consider me for deputy."

Berrynose brushed past him. "You know I'd do my best to be a loyal and brave deputy to ThunderClan," he told Bramblestar. "You were my mentor." He cast a sly glance at Bumblestripe. "So you *know* you can trust me."

Bristlefrost shuddered. She hurried to catch up to Squirrelflight, relieved to be heading out of camp. She didn't want to see her Clanmates behaving like fox-hearts. She followed Birchfall and Stormcloud through the entrance tunnel. As the two toms fanned out around Squirrelflight, Bristlefrost trailed behind with Lionblaze and Twigbranch. She glanced at them nervously.

Twigbranch looked shaken. "He can't banish her," the gray she-cat whispered as soon as they were clear of the camp. "Why's he doing this?"

Lionblaze padded closer, his ears twitching. "Isn't it obvious?" he growled darkly. "If his deputy and mate isn't safe, then no cat is. He wants to make that clear."

Dread dropped like a stone in Bristlefrost's belly. How could they stand up to Bramblestar now? He clearly had plenty of allies in ThunderClan, as well as the support of warriors in every other Clan. There could be no more secret meetings. Any cat could be spying on them. She glanced back at the camp. Were Berrynose and Bumblestripe still competing to see who could be ThunderClan's new deputy? She felt sick. Whoever was posing as Bramblestar was far more clever and ruthless than she'd ever imagined.

# CHAPTER 21

*Shadowsight padded into the medicine den,* relishing its shelter.
Outside, the wind was cold. He glanced at the empty nests,
relieved that there hadn't been more injuries. Snowbird had
returned to her nest in the warriors' den. Her paw was still
swathed in comfrey, but she'd grown gloomy in the medicine
den by herself as it became increasingly clear that, although
the bones were healing, her paw would never be as strong and
straight as it had been, and she'd always have a limp.

Shadowsight's shoulders drooped. Since yesterday's Gathering, he'd felt gloomy too. He'd hoped his confession to the
Clans would stop Bramblestar's ruthless persecution of the
codebreakers. If the visions hadn't come from StarClan, there
was no need to punish any cat. But his outburst seemed to
have made Bramblestar more determined to carry on. Didn't
the ThunderClan leader see that it couldn't be StarClan who
wanted the Clans to suffer?

Paw steps scuffed the earth, and he looked up as Yarrowleaf
padded in, her face crumpled with pain.

He hurried to meet her. "What happened?"

"A bee stung me." She turned her head to show a swelling on her neck.

"This early in the season?" Shadowsight frowned. Was StarClan still trying to let him know something was wrong? *I've done everything I can,* he told them silently. Perhaps it wasn't StarClan. After all, he knew they were silent now. Perhaps it was whoever had sent the visions. He pushed the thought away. What good did it do to speculate? He could only treat his Clanmates and hope StarClan returned soon.

Yarrowleaf sat down in the middle of the den and winced. "I disturbed a nest while I was digging into a rabbit hole."

Shadowsight examined the wound, looking closely to see if the stinger was still there. The ginger she-cat had clearly pulled it out in a panic; Shadowsight could see claw marks around the sting. "I'll fetch honey."

He headed for the herb store, relieved that he still had a little left. Honey would draw poison from the wound, and he had some lavender that would soothe it afterward. As he pulled out a bundle of herbs, their fragrant scents comforted him. He didn't have a special link with StarClan, but he still knew how to heal. He would focus on treating his Clanmates' injuries until StarClan returned. He could do no more than that.

He picked up the folded leaf, enclosing the honey along with a few stems of lavender, and turned from the herb store. His ears twitched. Puddleshine had come into the den and was checking Yarrowleaf's wound.

The brown medicine cat nodded to him. "I'll take care of this," he mewed briskly.

Shadowsight dropped his herbs beside Yarrowleaf. "But I've got honey and lavender."

Puddleshine padded past him and stopped beside the herb store. "Nettle juice and marigold will be the best treatment," he mewed. "And a few poppy seeds to help with the pain."

Yarrowleaf blinked gratefully at Puddleshine. "It really hurts," she mewed forlornly.

Shadowsight's heart sank as Puddleshine gathered up herbs and returned to Yarrowleaf. Nosing Shadowsight away, he chewed the dried nettle leaves and marigold petals into a pulp and smeared it onto the ginger she-cat's neck. Then he dabbed his paw onto the poppy seeds and offered them to Yarrowleaf. As she lapped them up, Puddleshine sat back on his haunches.

"How does that feel?"

"A bit better." Yarrowleaf turned her head gingerly.

"Go and rest," Puddleshine told her. "The poppy seeds will start to work soon. Come back if the pain gets worse, or if you start wheezing."

"Thanks." Yarrowleaf nodded to the brown medicine cat and padded outside.

Shadowsight bristled as soon as she was gone. "Don't you trust me to treat sick cats?" He stared at Puddleshine angrily.

"Of course I do," Puddleshine told him. "But I've been doing it for longer. I have more experience."

"But I have to learn!" Was Puddleshine going to stop him? He froze as a thought sparked in his mind. Did Puddleshine doubt him now that he knew his visions weren't from StarClan? Alarm jabbed his belly. "Do you think I'm not meant to be a medicine cat?"

Puddleshine hesitated for a moment; then he blinked at Shadowsight. "Don't be mouse-brained."

The hesitation sliced like claws through Shadowsight's heart. *He's not sure!* He stared at Puddleshine as his mentor went on.

"Of course you're meant to be a medicine cat. You've always been special."

*Special.* The word suddenly sounded more like an insult than a compliment. Shadowsight looked away. He couldn't stand the thought that he'd lost Puddleshine's trust.

A growl sounded outside. Shadowsight pricked his ears. "What's going on?"

Puddleshine turned toward the entrance. "I smell Sky-Clan." As the medicine cat hurried out, Shadowsight followed.

Rootpaw and Tree were in the clearing, flanked by Gullswoop and Blazefire.

Shadowsight's pelt rippled with surprise. Had Tree agreed to follow Bramblestar's orders?

Dovewing, who was eating beside the fresh-kill pile, got to her paws. Around the clearing, Snaketooth and Berryheart turned their heads to stare at the visitors. Scorchfur's hackles lifted.

Tigerstar padded from his den and glared at Tree and Rootpaw. "What are you doing here?"

Tree dipped his head. "You heard Bramblestar's order," he

mewed. "I'm to visit every Clan as part of my atonement."

Tigerstar curled his lip. "Do you really think you can convince me to make my warriors atone because Bramblestar tells me I should?"

Yarrowleaf blinked at her leader, pain still showing in her eyes. "Perhaps we should listen to him."

Scorchfur padded forward. "You want StarClan to come back, don't you?"

Tigerstar turned on him. "Your first loyalty is to your Clan, not to Bramblestar!" he snapped. "I decide if we atone, not him."

Scorchfur backed away, his tail flicking uneasily.

Shadowsight's pelt tingled with relief. Tigerstar was going to keep standing up to Bramblestar, even if it meant disagreeing with his own Clanmates.

Tigerstar padded closer to Tree. "You'd better get out of here," he hissed. "Before I have you dragged out by your scruff."

Tree's eyes rounded. "But I've come to talk to you about Squirrelflight's message."

Tigerstar narrowed his eyes. "What message?"

Tree started, looking confused. "Squirrelflight . . . she didn't visit?"

"No," Tigerstar hissed. "We've had no visit from Thunder-Clan—and even if we had, I'd have told her what I'm telling you. I don't want to hear anything you have to say!"

Tree glanced hopefully around the camp. "Is Cloverfoot

here? Maybe I can speak to her."

"Get out!" Tigerstar lunged at him, stopping a whisker away.

Tree recoiled, his pelt spiking. Rootpaw pressed close to his father and glared defiantly at Tigerstar.

Dovewing padded from the edge of the camp. "You should go," she told Tree softly. "Tigerstar won't change his mind. Bramblestar went too far at the Gathering. StarClan gave Tigerstar nine lives. No cat but them can take his leadership away."

"But I might be able to help you." Tree's gaze stayed on Tigerstar. "There's something you should know." He looked around at the ShadowClan warriors. "Something you should *all* know."

Shadowsight pricked his ears. What did he mean?

"Leave." Dovewing slid between Tree and Tigerstar as the ShadowClan leader uncurled his claws. "Before some cat gets hurt."

Tail flicking, Tree turned and headed for the entrance. Rootpaw hesitated. His gaze flitted around the camp, lighting up as it reached Shadowsight.

Shadowsight stiffened. *Me?* Rootpaw was staring at him eagerly. *What does he want me to do?* Shadowsight shifted his paws self-consciously as Rootpaw's eyes widened. *He's trying to tell me something.* He returned Rootpaw's gaze helplessly. Then Rootpaw turned and headed for the entrance, his tail twitching sharply. Shadowsight watched him go. *Was that tail flick meant for me?*

Cinnamontail brushed past Rootpaw as she padded into camp. She glanced over her shoulder as he disappeared. "What were they doing here?"

Dovewing met the tabby's gaze. "Bramblestar wanted them to come and persuade Tigerstar to exile the codebreakers."

Cinnamontail sniffed. "Since when does a ThunderClan leader tell ShadowClan what to do?" She padded toward the medicine den and stopped in front of Puddleshine. "I've been feeling queasy all morning," she told him. "I think I ate a bad mouse."

"Come with me." Puddleshine headed into the den. "I've got some watermint that will help." He paused and looked at Shadowsight. "Do you want to treat Cinnamontail?"

Shadowsight could see that the medicine cat was trying to prove that he still trusted him. He shook out his fur. "Can you give him the watermint? I want to check on the marigold I found near camp." Before Puddleshine could comment, he hurried across the clearing. It was a lie. He wasn't interested in the marigold right now. He wanted to catch Tree and Rootpaw before they crossed the border. Rootpaw had made it clear that they had more to share than Bramblestar's orders.

He ducked out of camp and scanned the forest, relieved when he glimpsed Tree's yellow pelt through the undergrowth. He chased after him, his paws thrumming against the earth as he raced to catch up. "Wait!" He skidded to a halt beside the two SkyClan cats.

Rootpaw turned first, his eyes lighting as he saw Shadowsight.

Tree's whiskers twitched with surprise. "I thought ShadowClan didn't want to hear my message."

"They didn't want to hear *Bramblestar's* message," Shadowsight told him. "But you came to tell us something else, didn't you?"

Tree blinked at him. "You said at the Gathering that your visions hadn't come from StarClan."

"Yes!" Shadowsight told him eagerly. He was relieved that some cat had heard him. "They came from some other cat."

"Who?" Rootpaw's eyes widened.

"I don't know," Shadowsight confessed. "I just know it wasn't StarClan."

Tree's gaze was solemn. "Did you know that Bramblestar isn't Bramblestar?"

"What?" Shadowsight froze. "How can he not be Bramblestar?"

"When he lost a life," Tree explained, "some other cat's spirit took his body. The real Bramblestar is a ghost. He can't get back into his body and he can't find StarClan."

Rootpaw's eyes were dark. "Whoever's leading ThunderClan is an impostor."

"An impostor?" Shadowsight's thoughts whirled, the earth seeming to shift beneath his paws. First StarClan wasn't StarClan and now Bramblestar wasn't Bramblestar. "What's going on?"

"We don't know yet." Rootpaw padded closer, his eyes bright. "But if your visions didn't come from StarClan, where did they come from?"

"I told you, I don't know," Shadowsight mewed. "I just know it was a voice."

Tree frowned. "Do you think it could have been Bramblestar's voice?"

Shadowsight felt confused. *"Bramblestar?"*

"The impostor." Rootpaw whisked his tail. "He's the one who's been yowling about codebreakers since this began, and your visions have agreed with him. Perhaps he the one who's been speaking to you."

Shadowsight's heart pounded. Some cat had stolen Bramblestar's identity and was trying to control the Clans through his visions. "How do you know Bramblestar is a ghost?"

Rootpaw and Tree exchanged glances.

"I've seen him," Tree mewed. "I can help you see him too, if you like."

Rootpaw's eyes widened. "Can you?"

Tree fluffed out his fur. "It's not easy, but I can make dead cats visible to the living—for a while at least," he told them. "I did it for ShadowClan when some of their warriors went missing after Darktail took over." He eyed Shadowsight somberly. "Are you ready?"

"Yes." Shadowsight nodded.

"I'm not." Rootpaw blinked at his father.

Tree met Rootpaw's gaze. "It'll be okay." He nosed Rootpaw away and whispered in his ear for a few moments.

Rootpaw drew back and stared at his father in disbelief.

Shadowsight stiffened. What had Tree told him? He padded closer. "Is summoning the ghost dangerous?"

"Not at all." Tree swished his tail. "It's just hard, that's all. Especially when you haven't done it"—he hesitated, glancing at Rootpaw—"for a while."

Rootpaw was still staring at his father as Tree closed his eyes. Shadowsight's pelt prickled uneasily. Why did the Sky-Clan apprentice seem so scared? *I guess he's never seen a ghost before.* As Rootpaw closed his eyes, Shadowsight wondered if he should do the same, but he was too curious to stop watching.

Tree's ears flattened and his tail quivered. Shadowsight pressed his paws hard against the earth as Tree began to tremble. Suddenly, pale fur shimmered between the trees. Shadowsight's breath caught in his throat as he recognized Bramblestar's tabby pelt. It glistened like water a few tail-lengths away.

The ghost's eyes widened in surprise as Shadowsight met its gaze. It lifted its tail. "You must help me." Its yowl was faint, as though carried away by a breeze. Then it vanished.

Tree jerked and staggered, as though trying to find his footing. He opened his eyes. "Did you see it?" he asked Shadowsight shakily.

"Yes." Shadowsight swallowed. There really *was* a ghost-Bramblestar, separate from the cat who was leading ThunderClan. "We have to fix this."

"I know." Tree took a shuddering breath. "We know Bramblestar is an impostor and some cat is sending you false visions. I think we can be pretty sure that the impostor is the one who's been talking to you."

"It makes sense." Shadowsight nodded, his eye falling on Rootpaw. The SkyClan apprentice was trembling, his eyes glittering with shock. "Is he okay?" Shadowsight asked Tree. Seeing a ghost had clearly shocked the young cat.

"He'll be fine in a moment." Tree wove around his son, smoothing his ruffled pelt with his tail. "We need to find a way to get rid of the impostor," he told Shadowsight.

"But how?" Shadowsight could picture the ghost's eyes burning desperately between the trees. "If the Clans chase him away, how will Bramblestar get back into his body?"

Tree nodded. "And if we kill him, there'll be no body for Bramblestar to go back to."

Shadowsight hesitated. It seemed impossible. Without StarClan he felt powerless.

Rootpaw seemed to pull himself together. He lifted his chin. "We need to tell as many cats as we can."

"You saw what it was like at the Gathering," Shadowsight argued. "I tried to tell them about my visions, but no cat wanted to believe me. Bramblestar's convinced them that StarClan is on his side."

"Squirrelflight believes us, and Frecklewish," Tree told him. "There are already a few cats in every Clan who know that Bramblestar's not himself. But we need to convince the medicine cats. They can tell the leaders. Does Puddleshine know that your visions aren't from StarClan?"

"Yes, but he doesn't know that Bramblestar's an impostor," Shadowsight mewed.

Rootpaw thrust his muzzle closer. "You must tell him."

Shadowsight hesitated. Would Puddleshine believe him? He couldn't get rid of the feeling that his former mentor didn't trust him anymore. *You've always been special.* Shadowsight pressed back a shudder as the words rang in his head. And even if Puddleshine did believe him, would he let him tell the rest of the Clan? He hadn't wanted to alarm the Clan with the idea that Shadowsight's visions weren't from StarClan. Maybe he'd want to keep this secret too.

Shadowsight blinked at Tree. "No. You have to tell Tigerstar. He's the only one who can stand up to Bramblestar."

"We've already tried," Tree reminded him. "You saw what happened. He sent us away."

"Come back with me now," Shadowsight pleaded.

Tree glanced at Rootpaw. "Do you want to go back?"

Rootpaw's ears twitched uneasily. "Tigerstar seemed ready to claw our ears off last time."

"We have to spread the word," Tree pressed. "The Clans are in danger."

Shadowsight swished his tail. "I'll make sure he doesn't hurt either of you."

Rootpaw looked unconvinced. "But will he listen?"

"I'll *make* him listen," Shadowsight promised.

Rootpaw dipped his head. "Okay. We'll come."

Hope flashed in Shadowsight's chest. At last, he could

start to fix everything. He hurried toward camp and ducked through the tunnel, freezing as he reached the clearing. "Squirrelflight?" He stared in disbelief at the ThunderClan deputy.

She was standing in front of Tigerstar, her pelt ruffled and unkempt. She shifted her paws, her gaze darting nervously around the camp. "I'm sorry to come here," she mewed. "But I had no choice. I've come to ask for sanctuary."

## CHAPTER 22

❧

*Rootpaw frowned. Why would Squirrelflight come* to Tigerstar for sanctuary?

The ShadowClan cats looked puzzled too. Flowerstem and Whorlpelt got slowly to their paws. Scorchfur exchanged glances with Snaketooth as Puddleshine slid from his den, his tail twitching nervously.

Tigerstar was staring at Squirrelflight, as though lost for words. "Sanctuary?" he echoed.

As Dovewing hurried to his side, Tawnypelt padded into camp, a mouse dangling from her jaws. The tortoiseshell stopped as she saw Squirrelflight, her gaze widening. "What's she doing here?"

Squirrelflight didn't take her gaze from Tigerstar. "Bramblestar has sent me away. He accused me of being a traitor."

"He's got bees in his brain!" Outrage sparked in Tigerstar's gaze. "You're Firestar's daughter. You've been loyal to ThunderClan your whole life. When I was young, I heard many tales of your courage during the Great Battle. What is Bramblestar thinking?"

"He's right," Squirrelflight mewed simply. "I told my Clan

I was leaving to atone, but instead I went to SkyClan to tell them that he's not the cat I've known all my life. The real Bramblestar would never act this way. This *fox-heart* is punishing his Clanmates as though they're his enemies. They're *scared* of him." She shook her head. "No, this isn't Bramblestar."

Tigerstar's ears flattened. "I don't understand."

She glanced meaningfully at Rootpaw as though they shared a secret. "The real Bramblestar has been driven out, and something else has taken over." Her gaze darkened. "Something evil."

Tree padded forward. "She's right. That's what we came to tell you."

Tigerstar's gaze swung toward the yellow tom. "I thought I told you to leave!"

Rootpaw moved closer to his father. "You have to listen to us."

Shadowsight nodded. "Hear them out."

Tigerstar lashed his tail. "Do you expect me to listen to them spouting Bramblestar's nonsense about codebreakers when his deputy stands in front of me asking for sanctuary?"

"We haven't come to spout Bramblestar's nonsense," Rootpaw mewed desperately.

As Tigerstar's hackles lifted, Shadowsight stepped in front of Rootpaw. "They know why Bramblestar's acting like this." He glanced at Squirrelflight. "It's exactly like Squirrelflight just said. You have to listen to them."

Tigerstar padded closer, his gaze flitting from Squirrelflight to Tree. "Go ahead, then. Say what you have to say. I'm listening." He stopped in front of Tree.

"She's right about Bramblestar," Tree told him. "He's not really Bramblestar. He's an impostor who has stolen Bramblestar's body." Shocked whispers rippled around the Clan, but Tree pressed on. "I've seen Bramblestar's ghost. It's trapped in the forest. It can't return to its body, and it can't find StarClan."

Tigerstar blinked. "How can that be?"

Shadowsight lifted his muzzle. "When Bramblestar lost a life, the impostor took his place."

"How?" Tigerstar turned on his son.

Shadowsight's ears twitched. "I don't *know*." He sounded desperate. "The voice that told me that Bramblestar could only be cured on the moor wanted me to take him there. I think they *wanted* him to die so they could steal his body."

Rootpaw blinked at the ShadowClan medicine cat. *Of course.* Whichever cat had stolen Bramblestar's body had planned it from the start. Shadowsight's tail drooped. He looked defeated. Was he thinking this was all his fault?

Scorchfur padded forward, his pelt prickling. "I thought *StarClan* told you to take Bramblestar to the moor."

Shadowsight stared at the dark gray tom in exasperation. "I thought so too. But didn't you hear me at the Gathering? I told you! I told *every cat*. It was never StarClan talking to me at all."

Rootpaw's heart ached with sympathy as Shadowsight stared helplessly at his Clanmate. He knew what it was like to know something no other cat would believe.

Puddleshine padded into the clearing. "Shadowsight told me when he realized that the visions weren't from StarClan, but I asked him to keep it to himself. I was scared the other Clans would turn on us if they knew."

"I'm sorry," Shadowsight mewed. "I thought I was helping the Clans, but I was just being used by some cat who wants to hurt us."

Flowerstem's ears twitched nervously. "Then where *is* StarClan?"

Shadowsight shrugged. "They're not talking to us. That's all I know."

Whorlpelt whisked his tail. "But maybe Bramblestar—or whichever cat it is—is right. Won't punishing the codebreakers bring them back?"

"Don't you understand?" Tree snapped. "StarClan doesn't *care* about these codebreakers. The impostor is the only one who wants them punished."

A growl rumbled in Squirrelflight's throat. "I think he likes to watch cats suffer."

Scorchfur bristled as he stared at Shadowsight. "Why did you listen to this voice? You should have known better. You're supposed to be a medicine cat. We trusted you!"

Shadowsight seemed to shrink beneath his pelt.

Rootpaw stepped in front of him and curled his tail protectively over Shadowsight's spine. "He was doing his best."

Tigerstar lifted his muzzle. "What's done is done," he mewed firmly. "We can't change it now. ShadowClan warriors have always done their best to protect their Clanmates, and that won't ever change. Turning on one another is not the answer."

Flowerstem padded tentatively forward. "How do we know all this is true?" She glanced skeptically at Squirrelflight. "These cats might be trying to stir up trouble because they disagree with Bramblestar."

Tigerstar narrowed his eyes. "But we know Bramblestar isn't behaving like himself."

Scorchfur huffed. "ThunderClan has always been bossy."

Dovewing frowned. "Never *this* bossy."

"I can show you Bramblestar's ghost if you like." Tree gazed around the gathered cats.

Tawnypelt's eyes widened. "I forgot you could do that."

Rootpaw glanced nervously at his father. He was still tired after summoning the ghost for Shadowsight. He wasn't even sure how he'd managed it. Tree had told him to picture the ghost as hard as he could, and call out to him with his mind, focusing his thoughts onto a single patch of ground. Could he do it again so soon, especially knowing a whole Clan was watching? A whole Clan that would now know that Rootpaw was as strange as his father, if they realized who was actually summoning the spirit?

*I have to,* he told himself. *This is too important.*

He nudged Tree's shoulder with his nose. "What if I can't make it appear this time?" he whispered softly.

Tree nosed Rootpaw away and lowered his voice. "You'll be fine," he breathed. "Just do what I told you. . . ."

"What if I'm not strong enough?" Rootpaw glanced back at

the watching ShadowClan cats.

"You're stronger than you think," Tree told him. "And it'll be easier this time. He's your ghost, and he wants to come. You just have to open the way."

Rootpaw swallowed. "Okay. I'll try."

Tree slid in front of Rootpaw and faced the expectant warriors. Rootpaw closed his eyes. He pictured Bramblestar's ghost, imagining its watery outline, its tabby pelt, the wide forehead and muscled shoulders. He visualized it shimmering into view and felt himself shudder with the effort. His paws shook. Energy fizzed in his fur. This was how it had felt last time. It must be working. He half opened his eyes to look.

Tree was trembling slightly as he pretended to summon the apparition. But it was already there, standing in the clearing. Triumph pulsed beneath Rootpaw's pelt as the ShadowClan cats stared at the ghost, fur spiking with alarm. *I did it again!*

It stiffened as it seemed to realize every eye in the Shadow-Clan camp was on it. "Can you see me?"

Tigerstar nodded slowly as though wondering if he were dreaming.

"Some cat has stolen my body," the ghost mewed quickly.

Squirrelflight darted toward it, desperation in her gaze. "Bramblestar!" Her muzzle passed through the ghost's, which was no more solid than air, and she backed away, trembling.

The ghost glanced at her apologetically, then stared at the ShadowClan cats. "Don't listen to the impostor. It's not me!" It glanced at Shadowsight. "Don't blame Shadowsight—he was tricked. Whatever took my body will do anything to get what it wants."

Rootpaw's heart began to pound and his paws felt as heavy as stone. He staggered, every hair in his pelt suddenly drained of energy, but he fought to keep the ghost there.

"You're doing it!" Tree whispered beside Rootpaw.

His father's mew broke Rootpaw's concentration. The ghost flickered into thin air and the ShadowClan cats blinked with surprise, as though waking from a dream.

Rootpaw struggled to stay on his paws. He felt more tired than he'd ever felt in his life. But he didn't want the others to know he'd made the ghost appear. As he wobbled like a newborn kit, his father dropped beside him, pretending to be exhausted. Rootpaw felt a rush of relief as the gathered cats' attention flashed toward the yellow tom, their eyes glittering with shock.

"Was that really Bramblestar?" Flowerstem gasped.

"Yes!" Tawnypelt's ears twitched excitedly.

"It must be a trick," Scorchfur growled. "Bramblestar's still alive."

"We told you—the living Bramblestar isn't the *real* Bramble-star!" Squirrelflight snapped.

Rootpaw glanced past them. He could still see the ghost. It was standing in the clearing, watching the ShadowClan cats.

It padded to Rootpaw's side. "They know everything I know," it murmured. "They *have* to fight now."

Tigerstar's tail flicked ominously. "Who is this impostor?"

Tree struggled to his paws. "We don't know yet."

Puddleshine looked puzzled. "Is it a rogue?"

Squirrelflight frowned. "How could a rogue know about StarClan?" she murmured. "This cat must have been a warrior once."

Tigerstar snorted. "A *warrior* would never try to harm the Clans."

"Really?" Squirrelflight stared at him. "I suppose you're too young to remember the Great Battle."

"I know we lost Clanmates," he growled.

"They were killed by cats who used to be warriors," Squirrelflight mewed darkly.

"But the Great Battle threatened all the Clans." Tigerstar's pelt prickled. "This is ThunderClan's problem."

Rootpaw blinked. Did he really believe that? Alarm flashed in the ghost's eyes.

Shadowsight stepped in front of his father. "An impostor is leader of ThunderClan," he mewed. "Because of him, cats in every Clan want to punish their Clanmates. How can you say it's just a ThunderClan problem?"

The ghost leaned toward Rootpaw. "Remind Tigerstar that he and I are kin," he murmured. "And that I took him in when Darktail drove him from his Clan. He owes me. He owes ThunderClan."

Rootpaw stared at the ghost, still tired from making it appear. "How can I say that?" he murmured, as quietly as he could. Didn't the ghost realize that Tigerstar was the leader of another Clan?

The ghost stared at him sternly. "Say it however you like,"

he growled. "But say it. We need Tigerstar's help."

The ghost was right. Rootpaw squared his shoulders and faced the ShadowClan leader. "I thought Bramblestar was your kin."

"Clan is more important than kin," Tigerstar growled.

Rootpaw narrowed his eyes. "I heard he took you in when Darktail chased you out of ShadowClan."

"That's right!" Squirrelflight flicked her tail eagerly. "We gave you sanctuary."

Tigerstar looked at her warily as the ShadowClan cats exchanged glances.

Tawnypelt padded forward. "Darktail tore our Clan apart, and the other Clans stood up to him," she mewed.

Tigerstar frowned. "They did it to protect themselves, not us."

Dovewing gazed at the ShadowClan leader. "Do you really believe that this impostor doesn't mean to harm us all? We can't let him carry on as leader of ThunderClan. He's made it clear time and time again that he wants to tell every Clan what to do, not just ThunderClan."

Tawnypelt nodded. "He threatened to replace you with another leader, remember?"

Tigerstar met the tortoiseshell's clear, green gaze and held it for a moment. Then he dipped his head. "You're right." He looked around at his warriors. "This isn't something we can ignore. ThunderClan needs its rightful leader back for all our sakes."

As hope flashed in Rootpaw's chest, Dovewing lifted her

tail. "Can Squirrelflight stay here?" she mewed.

"Yes." Tigerstar met his mate's gaze. "She will be treated like a Clanmate for as long as she's with us. In the meantime, we need to come up with a plan to get rid of this impostor."

"Kill him!" Whorlpelt flexed his claws. "If he's not a leader, he won't have nine lives. It'll be easy."

The ghost bristled beside Rootpaw. "If you kill him," Rootpaw mewed, stepping forward quickly. "the real Bramblestar's ghost won't have a body to return to."

Tree tipped his head. "We have to bide our time," he mewed. "We need to get the support of every Clan. We can't let this turn into war."

Squirrelflight nodded. "The impostor mustn't realize that we know he's not Bramblestar." She looked at Tree. "You have to carry on with your atonement."

"Do I tell the other Clans what I've told you?" Tree blinked at her.

"Not until we're sure they're ready to hear," mewed Squirrelflight.

Puddleshine looked thoughtful. "I can share what we know with the other medicine cats," he suggested. "They might be able to influence their Clans without directly challenging the cats who support the impostor."

Tawnypelt frowned. "But surely no cat would support him if they knew he was an impostor?"

Squirrelflight shifted her paws. "It's not an easy story to believe," she mewed. "I wasn't ready to believe it at first, and I shared a den with him." She shuddered. "Puddleshine's right.

We should try to persuade the other Clans through their medicine cats."

"I'll tell the others at the next half-moon meeting," Puddleshine mewed.

Dovewing blinked at Tigerstar. "I'll have to go back into exile," she told him. "So that the impostor thinks we agree with him."

Tigerstar looked alarmed. "It's too dangerous."

"I won't go far," Dovewing promised him. "If I'm free to roam where I like, I might be able to keep an eye on Thunder-Clan."

"Be careful." Tigerstar's pelt lifted along his spine.

Dovewing met his gaze. "I'll be very careful," she promised.

Rootpaw glanced at the ghost. Hope was glistening in its eyes. He'd done what it had asked. And he'd made it visible to the others. He couldn't help feeling a glimmer of pride. Perhaps being like Tree wasn't so bad after all—as long as no cat found out. He looked around at the ShadowClan cats. They were willing to stand up to the impostor. Despite the fear swirling beneath his pelt, Rootpaw felt hopeful. And yet ShadowClan was only one Clan. What if they failed? What if the other Clans continued to support the impostor? Would following the warrior code lead them to their own destruction?

# CHAPTER 23
❧

Bristlefrost *half closed her eyes and* relished the warmth of the newleaf sun that washed the clearing. She was pretending to doze in a pool of sunshine beside the nursery, but she was really watching Finleap and Twigbranch struggle to uproot a thornbush at the edge of the camp. Bramblestar claimed that it would smother the warriors' den if it was left to grow, but the whole Clan knew it had been there for moons and barely grew at all. This was a punishment. The ThunderClan leader had accused Finleap and Twigbranch of codebreaking after they'd forgotten to thank StarClan for their catch earlier in the day. Berrynose, ThunderClan's new deputy, had been on patrol with them. He hadn't warned them at the time, but he'd told Bramblestar about their misdemeanor as soon as they returned to camp.

Bristlefrost's pelt prickled uncomfortably. *Was I that eager to please when I was trying to help Bramblestar?* She shuddered. *I won't ever tell on my Clanmates again.*

In the days since he'd driven Squirrelflight from the camp, Bramblestar had been insisting his warriors pay closer and closer attention to the code, but he was continually announcing new interpretations of rules, to the point where no cat knew what was codebreaking and what wasn't.

The ThunderClan leader was watching Finleap and Twig-branch from the Highledge. He lay there alone, his chin hanging over the edge of the stone while Finleap and Twig-branch dug deeper between the roots of the thorn tree. Their pelts were ruffled and specked with soil, and their paws were filthy as they tried once more to dislodge the stubborn bush.

Berrynose padded toward the exhausted warriors. "Get a move on," he growled. "Bramblestar wants it dug up by dusk. What's taking you so long?"

Bristlefrost saw the cream-colored tom glance up at Bramblestar. Was he hoping the ThunderClan leader would be impressed? Bramblestar stared straight through his new deputy, and Bristlefrost felt a shiver of satisfaction. The more Berrynose tried to please Bramblestar, the more Bramblestar seemed to despise him.

A fresh wave of dislike for the new ThunderClan deputy washed over Bristlefrost as Berrynose kicked loose earth back into the hole Finleap and Twigbranch had dug around the roots of the bush.

Finleap glared at him. "What did you do that for?"

"It was an accident," Berrynose sniffed.

"Yeah, right." Twigbranch narrowed her eyes at the ThunderClan deputy, clearly unconvinced.

Berrynose shrugged. "You shouldn't pile the earth so close to the hole."

Twigbranch bared her teeth, but Finleap nudged her back

to work. "Just keep digging," he murmured as Berrynose stalked away.

"Berrynose!" Bramblestar lifted his head.

Berrynose pricked his ears and scrambled eagerly up the rock tumble. He stopped in front of the ThunderClan leader. "Yes, Bramblestar? What can I do for you?"

Bramblestar eyed him coldly. "Why aren't the hunting patrols back?" He nodded toward the fresh-kill pile, which was still only half-full.

"They haven't been out for long," Berrynose told him.

Bramblestar flattened his ears. "You should have sent them out earlier."

"I'm a mouse-brain." Berrynose dipped his head apologetically at his leader. "I'll send them out earlier tomorrow."

Bristlefrost growled to herself. Didn't Berrynose have any pride?

Bristlefrost was relieved that Bramblestar had passed her duties to his new deputy. She didn't want to give orders on behalf of an impostor. But she couldn't help feeling that Berrynose didn't care who patrolled or hunted; he just enjoyed bossing his Clanmates around.

Bramblestar got to his paws. "Go away," he growled dismissively to Berrynose. He looked over the edge of the Highledge as his deputy slithered down the rock tumble. Bristlefrost tensed as the ThunderClan leader's gaze flitted toward her and stopped. Her heart lurched as his eyes flashed with interest.

Since Squirrelflight had left the camp, she'd expected to be accused of being a traitor at any moment. If Bramblestar had sent a spy after Squirrelflight, he could have sent spies after any cat. She wouldn't be surprised if he'd known about the secret meeting all along and was just leaving her dangling like prey while he decided how to punish her.

"Come and talk to me, Bristlefrost," he mewed silkily from the Highledge.

She got to her paws, trying hard not to look at Twig-branch and Finleap. They'd been at the secret meeting, too, and she knew they'd be watching her and worrying about why Bramblestar wanted to talk. Her paws itched nervously. Perhaps the two warriors' punishment had nothing to do with forgetting to thank StarClan. Perhaps Bramblestar knew about everything they'd been doing, and this was just the beginning of his reprisals. She swallowed back fear as she climbed the rock tumble, feeling queasy as Bramblestar pushed through the trailing stems that covered his den and beckoned her to follow with his tail.

She blinked, adjusting to the gloom as she followed him inside. She tried not to let her nose wrinkle. His den was stuffy and smelled of stale bedding.

Bramblestar sat down and stared at her from the shadows. "How do you like the new rules for the Clan?" He sounded cheery, and she tried to match his enthusiasm.

"They're great." She lifted her chin. "StarClan is *bound* to come back soon."

"Indeed." He leaned closer. "What do you think about making patrols walk in single file?"

"It's a good idea," she told him. "It'll stop Clanmates chattering when they should be hunting or checking borders."

Bramblestar looked pleased. "That's what I thought." He tipped his head thoughtfully to one side. "I wondered about making hunting patrols bring each piece of prey back to camp as soon as they catch it, instead of bringing back a whole day's hunting in one go."

"Wouldn't that make hunting harder?" Bristlefrost ventured.

Bramblestar narrowed his eyes. "But I worry that, when warriors are out in the forest too long, they forget that Clan rules apply to them."

Bristlefrost blinked at him eagerly. "In that case, it's a wonderful idea." Shame burrowed beneath her pelt. She was behaving like Berrynose. But what choice did she have? She didn't want to be exiled. She shifted her paws. *Exile might be better than groveling to this fox-heart.* She pushed the thought away. "The Clans have let the warrior code slip for so long," she mewed. "They need to be reminded of it at all times. It's the only way to bring StarClan back."

Bramblestar rested on his haunches. "I'm glad you see it that way," he mewed warmly. "In fact, you seem to understand me more than any cat in the Clan." His gaze lingered on her admiringly until she had to force back a shudder. He went on. "I appreciate your loyalty. You deserve more responsibility. I wish I could have made you deputy; it's a shame you're far too young. But I trust you, and I hope you realize that I rely on you to keep me informed about the Clan. You're so observant, and you take your warrior duties very seriously." He leaned closer. "Now that Squirrelflight has left, I value you as a confidante more than ever."

Bristlefrost dug her claws into the earth to stop herself from recoiling. "Th-thank you." She looked away, her pelt hot. "You're being too kind."

"Am I?" Bramblestar's eyes glittered suddenly. "Am I *really*?"

She saw him stiffen. Had she said something wrong?

"I appreciate it," she mewed quickly.

He seemed to relax again. "It's strange." As he paused, his gaze drifted past her. "I noticed you were out of camp a few nights before the Gathering. A night patrol, perhaps?" He didn't wait for her to answer. "I'm sure you had your Clan's best interests at heart. I don't doubt your loyalty, because you know what I do to cats who aren't loyal." He narrowed his eyes.

Her mouth went dry as his gaze flicked back to her. *That's a threat.* She stared at him wordlessly. *Is he telling me he knows about the meeting? Or is he just warning me to be careful?* "The warrior code is clear about loyalty," she mewed fervently. "A true warrior is loyal to their Clan above all." Her thoughts whirled. She had to warn Twigbranch and Finleap. *And Rootpaw!* Every cat who was at the meeting must know that Bramblestar suspected something. Her heart quickened. But how could she reach them when he was keeping such a close eye on her?

Bramblestar's tail flicked. "Would you do me a favor?"

"Of course." She pricked her ears.

"I want you to check on Squirrelflight," he told her. "I've

heard rumors that she's still somewhere around the lake, but I don't know where." His whiskers quivered. "Do you think you could find out?" Bramblestar hesitated. "I want you to make sure she's left Clan land."

He looked distracted, his eyes glittering anxiously for a moment, and Bristlefrost wondered if he was actually worried about Squirrelflight. "I could try," she mewed.

"*Try?*" His eyes widened.

"I'll do it," she promised. For the first time since the meeting, excitement fizzed in her paws. She might be able to speak to Rootpaw while she was tracking Squirrelflight. He'd spread the word. She tried to cover her enthusiasm. "When do you want me to leave?"

"How about now?" Bramblestar looked at her inquiringly, but she knew it was an order rather than a question.

She dipped her head. "I'll leave straight away." She hurried out of the den and scrambled down the rock tumble, sending stones clattering into the clearing.

Finleap looked up from his digging, and she met his gaze, hoping he saw the warning in it. He nudged Twigbranch, and they both watched her as she headed for the entrance. She quickened her pace as she ducked through it and broke into a run as soon as she was outside. Racing up the slope, she followed the route she'd escorted Squirrelflight along a few days earlier. The brambles they'd brushed past still smelled of their scent. Trees blurred around her as she charged through the forest, following the trail to the SkyClan border. That was where they'd left her. She'd told them she was heading toward the mountains, and they'd watched her pad sadly away before turning back to camp.

Bristlefrost pulled up as she reached the scent line and tasted the air. Did Bramblestar expect her to follow Squirrel-flight's scent onto another Clan's land? She frowned. *No.* That would be breaking the warrior code. She gazed across the border to where the land sloped upward and boulders jutted from the forest floor. Her heart quickened as she saw pelts moving through the undergrowth. Opening her mouth, she let their scents bathe her tongue, excited to taste Rootpaw's scent. She couldn't help feeling that StarClan—wherever it had gone—was still on her side.

She stared eagerly over the border, willing his patrol to head this way. She felt a surge of relief when she saw them padding toward her.

Dewspring and Harrybrook were with the SkyClan apprentice, and she caught their eye, beckoning the patrol closer with a nod.

Dewspring narrowed his eyes as he approached her. "Is something wrong?"

"I wanted to talk to Rootpaw," she told him.

Rootpaw stopped beside his mentor and frowned. "What about?"

"Something important." Bristlefrost stared at him urgently.

Harrybrook growled. "I thought we'd made it clear at the Gathering that you're from different Clans."

"I know." Bristlefrost blinked apologetically at the Sky-Clan warrior. "But I was so mean to him at the Gathering. I wanted to apologize."

"He'll live," Dewspring sniffed.

Rootpaw looked at his mentor and shrugged. "It would be *nice* to hear a ThunderClan cat apologize to a SkyClan cat."

Dewspring's eyes flashed with amusement. "I guess," he conceded. He exchanged glances with Harrybrook before looking back at Rootpaw. "Just make sure it's a good apology. She's embarrassed you a lot."

Rootpaw crossed the border and nudged Bristlefrost away. "Has something happened?" he whispered when they were out of earshot.

"I think Bramblestar suspects I'm up to something. He noticed I was away from camp on the night of the meeting."

Rootpaw's pelt prickled along his spine. "Does he know about the meeting?"

"I'm not sure," Bristlefrost told him. "He didn't say anything definite."

"We have to be careful." Rootpaw glanced past her into the ThunderClan forest. "Did any cat follow you?"

Bristlefrost stared at him, alarmed. "I don't think so." She followed his gaze, relieved as she saw the forest behind her was clear. "I ran all the way here. I would have heard if some cat was following."

"Why did Bramblestar let you out of camp by yourself if he suspects you?"

"He sent me to find Squirrelflight. He says he wants to

make sure she's left Clan territory, but I think he's worried about her." She paused, then wondered out loud. "It's weird. Why would the impostor be worried about Squirrelflight?"

"Who knows why he does anything." Rootpaw flicked his tail. "We don't have time to wonder about that now." He glanced back at his mentor. The gray tom was pacing impatiently. "Squirrelflight's with ShadowClan. She's safe there. ShadowClan knows everything. I think Shadowsight was right when he said his visions weren't from StarClan. He's going to meet with the other medicine cats and tell them about the impostor."

"I hope he does it soon," Bristlefrost told him. "It's awful back at camp. Every cat's scared and there are so many rules and punishments." She stared at him desperately. "We have to do something."

"We will." Rootpaw touched his muzzle to her cheek.

She pressed against it for a moment, relieved to have a friend she could trust. "I'm going to talk to Squirrelflight," she told him. "She needs to know what's happening in ThunderClan. But I won't tell Bramblestar where she is."

Rootpaw dipped his head and turned back toward his Clanmates. "Stay strong," he whispered. "It'll all be okay."

Bristlefrost blinked at him gratefully, hoping he was right, then hurried toward the ShadowClan border.

Her paws ached by the time she reached it. Afternoon sunshine filtered through the newly budding branches. She stared across the scent line eagerly.

"What are you doing here?" Yarrowleaf's sharp mew took

her by surprise. The ShadowClan she-cat slid from behind a bramble, Strikestone at her heels. The brown tabby tom turned his good ear towards her.

"I need to talk to Squirrelflight," she mewed.

Strikestone's eyes sparked with suspicion. "Go back to your Clan," he growled.

Bristlefrost met his gaze. Of course ShadowClan wouldn't admit to hiding Squirrelflight. *Why* would *they trust me? They think I'm one of Bramblestar's most loyal warriors.* But this might be the only chance she had to get away from camp alone. Frustration welled in her chest. She had to speak to Squirrelflight. Perhaps another ShadowClan warrior would listen. She looked past the patrol, scanning the pine forest hopefully. Her heart leaped as she recognized Shadowsight's gray tabby pelt moving across a slope in the distance. StarClan was definitely on her side. "Ask Shadowsight. He'll vouch for me." She raised her voice. "Shadowsight!"

Strikestone's tail bushed angrily, but Shadowsight was already hurrying toward them.

"Bristlefrost?" The ShadowClan medicine cat looked surprised. "What are you doing here?"

"I came to speak to Squirrelflight."

Shadowsight's eyes widened. "How did you know she was here?"

"Rootpaw told me," she mewed. "I know about Bramblestar's ghost too, *and* I believe what you said about your visions."

Shadowsight exchanged glances with his Clanmates, then

beckoned Bristlefrost across the border with a flick of his tail. "Come with me."

She hurried after him as he headed toward camp. Strike-stone and Yarrowleaf trailed behind, their pelts rippling uneasily.

"I think Bramblestar knows that cats have been meeting in secret," Bristlefrost whispered as she caught up to Shadow-sight.

"Has he said anything?"

"Not yet. But he's been using some of our Clanmates as spies."

"Be careful," Shadowsight warned.

"I will." Bristlefrost forced her fur flat as Shadowsight led her to the ShadowClan camp.

As they hurried through the entrance tunnel, Squirrel-flight leaped to her paws. The former deputy looked thin and anxious. She hurried toward Bristlefrost, her eyes glittering with worry. "What are you doing here? Has something hap-pened to ThunderClan?"

"The Clan's all right for now, but Bramblestar is getting worse," Bristlefrost told her.

"He's *not* Bramblestar," Squirrelflight snapped. "He's an impostor."

"I know." She held Squirrelflight's gaze. "But there's noth-ing we can do. Every cat is so scared that they hardly dare speak to one another."

Squirrelflight's gaze darkened. "ShadowClan is going to

support us," she told Bristlefrost. "And once Shadowsight has told the other medicine cats what's going on, the other Clans *must* support us. We can't let this impostor turn the Clans against one another."

Bristlefrost blinked at her. "Hasn't he already done that?"

"It's not too late," Squirrelflight told her. "We can stop this before it becomes a war. But Bramblestar *can't* know where I am. If he finds out that ShadowClan has been sheltering me, he'll declare war, and we're not ready to fight."

Bristlefrost nodded. "I won't tell him," she promised. Her pads felt hot. What *would* she tell him? He wouldn't be pleased to hear she'd failed to find out where Squirrelflight had gone, but she couldn't tell him the truth. Perhaps a half-truth would convince him.

Squirrelflight held her gaze, her eyes as dark as the night sky. "Make sure he doesn't find out."

"Did you find her?" Bramblestar hurried across the clearing to meet Bristlefrost as she padded into camp.

"Yes." She'd rolled in comfrey on the way back from the ShadowClan camp to disguise any scents he might detect on her pelt. "I found her in the Twolegplace."

"Did you speak to her?" Bramblestar's eyes were bright with interest.

"Yes." At least that was true.

"What did she say?"

"She doesn't know where she's going next, but she says she's never coming back here. She's angry. She's washed the Clans from her pelt for good."

"She was always hotheaded." Bramblestar's tail twitched. "But I didn't think she'd go to the Twolegplace."

Bristlefrost shrugged, trying to look casual. "She said she was just passing through."

Bramblestar's gaze narrowed. "I hope you're telling me the truth." A growl rumbled in his throat.

Bristlefrost's heart raced. "I wouldn't lie to you," she mewed quickly.

"You shouldn't." There was menace in his mew. "Because I'm sure you can imagine what I'd do to you if you did."

Bristlefrost's breath caught in her throat. Bramblestar stared at her, his gaze unwavering until a chill crept beneath her pelt. *Does he know I'm working against him?* She felt sick. Perhaps some cat had followed her after all. She wanted to scan the camp to see if Berrynose or Bumblestripe was there. But she didn't dare take her eyes from Bramblestar. It was like watching a snake preparing to strike.

At last he turned away and padded to the shade beneath the Highledge.

Bristlefrost tried to stop herself from trembling. *Am I safe in ThunderClan anymore?*

# CHAPTER 24

*Shadowsight gazed into the black night* sky. The half-moon dazzled him, shining brightly between the jagged pine tops. As soon as Rootpaw and Tree arrived, they'd leave for the Moonpool. He fluffed out his fur against the cold and glanced eagerly at the camp entrance. Paw steps were scuffing the earth beyond.

Puddleshine padded from the medicine den. "Are they here yet?"

"They're coming." As Shadowsight nodded toward the entrance, Rootpaw ducked into the camp, his gaze glittering nervously.

Tree padded after him. The yellow tom scanned the clearing. Most of the Clan had gone to their nests after a long day's patrolling. But Scorchfur and Whorlpelt lingered outside the warriors' den, watching Shadowsight and Puddleshine. Squirrelflight stood beside them, her pelt ruffled. They knew what this meeting could mean. If the medicine cats agreed that Bramblestar was an impostor, and that he meant to harm the Clans, it could lead to war. How else could the Clans drive him out?

Tree waited beside the entrance while Rootpaw hurried to meet Shadowsight.

"Are you ready?" Rootpaw mewed.

Shadowsight nodded. "I hope the other medicine cats will believe me."

"It'll be okay," Puddleshine reassured him. The medicine cat padded toward the entrance. Shadowsight followed, wishing this were another cat's problem.

"Be careful," Scorchfur called.

Shadowsight glanced back at the dark gray warrior. "We'll be back by dawn."

"Wait!" Tigerstar burst from his den, Dovewing at his heels. Tigerstar's gaze was dark.

Shadowsight halted, alarmed. "What's wrong?"

"You mustn't go," Tigerstar told him.

Dovewing's eyes shimmered with worry. "We've been talking. It's too dangerous. You have to stay here." She wove around Shadowsight protectively.

He ducked away from her. "But we have to tell the other Clans about Bramblestar."

"Let Puddleshine tell them," Tigerstar growled.

Tree frowned. "What are you worried about? Do you think the medicine cats will harm him?"

"Not the medicine cats." Tigerstar fixed Shadowsight with his gaze. "But you said you felt a presence in the hollow the last time you were at the Moonpool, right?"

"Yes," Shadowsight told him. "But it was just a feeling. I don't think it can hurt me."

Dovewing's ears twitched. "We don't know what we're dealing with, but we know it's powerful enough to silence

StarClan and to steal Bramblestar's body."

Tigerstar nodded. "You should stay with your Clan, where you're safe."

Squirrelflight hurried toward them. "He must go," she insisted. "Whoever's been interfering with the Clans has been doing it through Shadowsight."

Puddleshine nodded. "The medicine cats must be able to question him. They might see something he's missed."

Shadowsight lifted his tail. He didn't need any cat to speak for him. He met Tigerstar's gaze. "I'm going to do this," he mewed firmly.

His father bristled. "But it's dangerous!"

"I'm not a kit anymore." Shadowsight lifted his muzzle. His father had to trust him. "I'm a medicine cat, and the Clans need my help."

Tigerstar hesitated. Then he dipped his head. "You're right," he mewed. "We can't stop you."

Shadowsight blinked gratefully at his father. "Don't worry—I'll be careful. And I won't be alone."

Dovewing pressed her muzzle to Shadowsight's cheek. "Come back as soon as you can."

He rubbed his nose along her jaw. "I'll be home by dawn."

He turned before she could say any more and caught his father's eye. Tigerstar was watching him, fear shadowing his gaze.

It was nearly moonhigh. There was no time to waste. Quickly, Shadowsight padded from the camp. Outside, the forest was swathed in shadow, and he strained to see ahead.

He felt relieved as Rootpaw fell in beside him. The SkyClan apprentice's face was grim. Behind them, Tree and Puddleshine followed in silence.

Rootpaw glanced at him. "What do you think the medicine cats will do once they know?"

"I hope they'll tell their leaders." Shadowsight hopped over a trailing vine.

"If the Clans unite, it will be easy to drive out the impostor," Tree mewed.

Puddleshine quickened his pace. "But how will the ghost get back into his body then?"

Shadowsight glanced at the medicine cat. "Let's deal with one problem at a time."

They pushed on in silence, following the track to where it rose toward the ThunderClan border.

"Let's travel through the greenleaf Twolegplace," Puddleshine suggested as they skirted a large bramble. "So we avoid crossing ThunderClan territory."

"It'll take longer to get there." Shadowsight glanced at his Clanmate.

"It's better to be cautious," Puddleshine insisted. "ThunderClan can't be trusted."

Tree frowned. "Do you think Bramblestar might try to stop us?"

"He would if he knew what we were planning," Puddleshine mewed.

Shadowsight stifled a shiver. The forest seemed suddenly darker. A shadow flitted high in the branches ahead.

Rootpaw's gaze flashed toward it. "It's just an owl." The SkyClan apprentice sounded relieved. Was he spooked too?

The forest floor was cold beneath Shadowsight's paws. He could hear prey scurrying through the undergrowth. A warbler was chattering in the distance. He padded closer to Rootpaw, reassured by the warmth pulsing from the tom's pelt.

The warbler fell silent, and Shadowsight pricked his ears. Had something startled it? He glanced nervously ahead. *Don't be mouse-brained.* He'd made this trip plenty of times without feeling scared. As he shook out his pelt, his heart lurched. A screech of pain sliced through the air.

Shadowsight stopped. Tree spun around, scanning the forest, while Rootpaw tasted the air.

"Do you smell anything?" Tree blinked at his son.

Rootpaw frowned. "I can only smell mint."

Puddleshine looked puzzled. "Mint doesn't grow in this part of the forest."

Shadowsight was straining to see through the darkness. "Some cat's in trouble," he mewed.

"It sounded like the yowl came from over there." Tree began to head along a rise.

The screech sounded again. Shadowsight's pelt bushed. "We have to help them!"

"This way!" Tree broke into a run.

Puddleshine hurried after him. "I can smell blood." Alarm sharpened the medicine cat's mew.

Shadowsight paused as the others charged away. How could they help an injured cat? They had no herbs with them.

He glanced around. *Cobwebs!* If the cat was bleeding, cobwebs would staunch the flow until they could get them to safety.

"Shadowsight!" Puddleshine called from the darkness. "Are you coming?"

"I'm looking for cobwebs!" He hurried toward a gnarled oak. There would be cobwebs in the knotted bark. He ran his paw along a crevice, relieved as thick spider's web clung to his paw. He hauled it out. "Have you found him?" His mew rang through the trees. No cat answered. He hurried between the trees, limping on three legs as he tried to keep the cobwebs off the ground. Peering through the shadows, he strained to see the others. "I'm coming!" he called. The forest answered with silence.

He frowned. Was he heading the right way? As he opened his mouth to taste for scents, something hard slammed into his flank. It knocked him over, and as he rolled onto his side, the stench of mint hit the back of his throat. A shadow reared beside him, and his heart seemed to burst as the silhouette of a tom rose against the starlit sky. It fell on him like a hawk. Claws raked his cheek. A paw lashed at his muzzle.

Struggling to escape, Shadowsight rolled onto his belly. Blood roared in his ears, as he felt the sharp sting of strong claws hooking into his pelt. They hauled him backward as he scrabbled against the earth. Desperately, he tried to remember a battle move. Pouncestep had taught him some. He bunched the muscles in his hind legs and tried to push up and unbalance his attacker, but a leg swept beneath his belly, knocking his paws from under him.

He rolled onto his back and tried to kick out with his hind legs, but his attacker crushed him against the earth with large, heavy paws. Eyes flashed in front of Shadowsight's muzzle, glittering with hate. Shadowsight froze, helpless as he felt claws at his throat. He shrieked as he felt them dig into his flesh. His thoughts spun until he was dizzy with terror. The claws dug harder. His mind reeled as he fought for breath, pleading with StarClan for help.

But there was no answer, and darkness closed around him.

# WARRIORS

## How many have you read?

**Dawn of the Clans**
- ⭘ #1: The Sun Trail
- ⭘ #2: Thunder Rising
- ⭘ #3: The First Battle
- ⭘ #4: The Blazing Star
- ⭘ #5: A Forest Divided
- ⭘ #6: Path of Stars

**Power of Three**
- ⭘ #1: The Sight
- ⭘ #2: Dark River
- ⭘ #3: Outcast
- ⭘ #4: Eclipse
- ⭘ #5: Long Shadows
- ⭘ #6: Sunrise

**The Prophecies Begin**
- ⭘ #1: Into the Wild
- ⭘ #2: Fire and Ice
- ⭘ #3: Forest of Secrets
- ⭘ #4: Rising Storm
- ⭘ #5: A Dangerous Path
- ⭘ #6: The Darkest Hour

**Omen of the Stars**
- ⭘ #1: The Fourth Apprentice
- ⭘ #2: Fading Echoes
- ⭘ #3: Night Whispers
- ⭘ #4: Sign of the Moon
- ⭘ #5: The Forgotten Warrior
- ⭘ #6: The Last Hope

**The New Prophecy**
- ⭘ #1: Midnight
- ⭘ #2: Moonrise
- ⭘ #3: Dawn
- ⭘ #4: Starlight
- ⭘ #5: Twilight
- ⭘ #6: Sunset

**A Vision of Shadows**
- ⭘ #1: The Apprentice's Quest
- ⭘ #2: Thunder and Shadow
- ⭘ #3: Shattered Sky
- ⭘ #4: Darkest Night
- ⭘ #5: River of Fire
- ⭘ #6: The Raging Storm

## Select titles also available as audiobooks!

**HARPER**
*An Imprint of HarperCollinsPublishers*

www.warriorcats.com • www.shelfstuff.com